Darwin and Faulkner's Novels

Evolution and Southern Fiction

Michael Wainwright

DARWIN AND FAULKNER'S NOVELS
Copyright © Michael Wainwright, 2008.
All rights reserved. No part of this book may be used or reproduced in any manner whatsoever without written permission except in the case of brief quotations embodied in critical articles or reviews.

First published in 2008 by
PALGRAVE MACMILLAN™
175 Fifth Avenue, New York, N.Y. 10010 and
Houndmills, Basingstoke, Hampshire, England RG21 6XS.
Companies and representatives throughout the world.

PALGRAVE MACMILLAN is the global academic imprint of the Palgrave Macmillan division of St. Martin's Press, LLC and of Palgrave Macmillan Ltd. Macmillan® is a registered trademark in the United States, United Kingdom and other countries. Palgrave is a registered trademark in the European Union and other countries.

ISBN-13: 978-0-230-60462-9
ISBN-10: 0-230-60462-5

Library of Congress Cataloging-in-Publication Data

Wainwright, Michael.
  Darwin and Faulkner's novels: evolution and southern fiction / Michael Wainwright.
    p. cm.
  Includes bibliographical references.
  ISBN 0-230-60462-5
  1. American fiction—Southern States—History and criticism. 2. Darwin, Charles, 1809–1882—Influence. 3. Faulkner, William, 1897–1962—Criticism and interpretation. 4. Evolution (Biology) in literature. 5. Social Darwinism in literature. 6. Literature and science—Southern States. 7. Southern States—Intellectual life. I. Title.

PS261.W25 2008
813'.509—dc22   2007032120

A catalogue record of the book is available from the British Library.

Design by Scribe Inc.

First edition: April 2008

10 9 8 7 6 5 4 3 2 1

Printed in the United States of America.

In memory of two very different Englishmen

Shura Cherkassky

and

Keinosuke Enoeda

Contents

Preface		ix
1	Looking across the Atlantic	1
2	Hand in Hand with the Old Gentleman	21
3	The Complex Temple of Sexual Politics	45
4	Pangenesis and Southern Thought	77
5	From Race to Ecology	103
6	Philosophical Frontiers	131
7	The Enemy Within	159
8	Self-interest, Cooperation, and Beyond	185
Notes		211
Works Cited		223
Index		237

Preface

> I will here give a brief sketch of the progress of opinion on the Origin of Species.
>
> Charles Darwin, *The Origin of* Species (1859 i)

This volume studies the artistic and philosophical maturation of the author William Faulkner (1897–1962) from the perspective of an evolutionary hermeneutic. The context in which he lived and the fiction that he produced recommend this approach. For, spending the majority of his life in Mississippi, Faulkner's accustomed environment situated him in a region of ecological turmoil. Population expansion and fears about interracial familiarity fueled this condition as part of a countrywide struggle between centripetal orthodoxy and centrifugal modernity. Proponents from each side of this ideological divide drew on evolutionary ideas to further their cause. However, as scientific arguments concerning evolution became more rigorous, personal and communal introversion had to concede ground to an emerging global outlook. Faulkner's intellectual development benefited from and bore witness to this dynamic, his evolutionarily inflected fiction becoming a guide to the aggrandizement of America.

The present study employs an evolutionary hermeneutic along a number of trajectories to chart this literary maturation. One course contextualizes the epistemological progress of evolutionary ideas as they would have impinged on Faulkner; another route identifies the evolutionarily imbued sources, both archived and newly available, used by him; the third trajectory then tracks the evolutionary forms, figurations, and philosophical implications latent in the Faulknerian oeuvre. In recent years, scholars such as Gillian Beer and Joseph Carroll have begun to address these interconnections but without worthwhile reference to Faulkner. Only a few Faulknerians, Peter G. Beidler, Carol Colatrella, and Gail Mortimer being the most notable, have shown that direct relays between the writings of Charles Darwin (1809–1882) and Faulkner, on the one hand, and Faulkner's indirect routes to evolutionary philosophy, on the other hand, do have pertinence to his literary creations. Gary Lee Stonum is the singular exception in purporting to chart Faulkner's evolution in detail. Stonum's starting point is the bifurcated approach to literature proposed by Geoffrey H. Hartman. Hartman studies not only the relationship between his chosen author and the literary tradition (or *Genius*) available to that subject, but also the interaction between the author and his native environment (or *genius loci*). In the same manner, Stonum wishes "to establish a new sort of literary history" for Faulkner, one that tells "the story of Faulkner's career in an internal history of how his works come into being" (24). Acknowledging that predecessors certainly influence novelists, Stonum nevertheless implicitly reorients Hartman's initial criterion. The Genius of other writers does have a substantial initial effect on an author, Stonum reasons, but that pressure diminishes as his existing body of work grows. Therefore, an internal tension builds between that corpus and the latest work of the author, canonical tendencies resulting from "the peculiar freedom of the writer and the particularity of his text" (24–25). This means that old novels provide the base for new works so that the career of an author "does not proceed as a linear development or a gradual evolution of its own latent tendencies. Rather it develops by expressly questioning the assumptions on which the earlier work depends" (25). While agreeing that Faulkner's philosophical and aesthetic evolution is intimately connected to revisiting previous suppositions, Stonum's failure to draw on the Darwinian legacy attests to his hermeneutic providing an internal literary history. Unlike the method used herein, Stonum does not analyze the evolutionary paradigm left by Darwin nor chart the rise of attendant theories. He more readily attributes the Faulknerian oeuvre to an initial impulse from the literary past twinned to the effect of local surroundings, an environmental influence that recedes in the face of self-reverence. That Faulkner's novels from the late 1940s onward fail to impress Stonum should therefore come as no surprise. He reads these works as stalled repeats of the past, offerings that do not have a capacity for aesthetic or philosophical furtherance. This critical reckoning is the inevitable consequence of his hermeneutic. In contrast to Stonum, the present volume attributes personal, communal, literary, epistemological, and ecological factors as environmental impulses that Faulkner appears to have used to stimulate the evolutionary strand in his broadening worldview and to propel his overriding literary endeavor. Stonum's approach precludes this consideration of a global sense, his self-contained hermeneutic failing to appreciate Faulkner's desire to reach for and to express a cosmological vision. The following eight chapters seek to be the first such appreciation. Chapter 1 considers Charles Darwin's effect on religious and academic thinking in the southern states of America, subsequent restrictions to the teaching of evolution, and the culmination of these prohibitions in the Scopes Trial of 1925. This section thereby establishes the historical provenance and context of Faulkner's formative years. Chapter 2 then researches textual sources of evolutionary thought used by the young Faulkner, including those of the French critical historian Hippolyte Taine (1828–1893) and the American art critic Willard Huntington Wright (1887–1939); evidence cited for these Darwinian influences in Faulknerian practice includes *Mosquitoes* (1927), *Flags in the Dust* (1929, 1973), and the short story "Red Leaves" (1930). Chapter 3 turns to the social conditioning of sexual selection as Faulkner charts the emergence of an impersonal strain on twentieth-century living. The character of Temple Drake from *Sanctuary* (1931) and *Requiem for a Nun* (1951) as delineated within rural Yoknapatawpha and urban Memphis provides the mainstay for this analysis. Darwin's hereditary mechanism of pangenesis (or blood blending) provides the topic for Chapter 4, with further reference to *Flags in the Dust*, realigning the importance of this novel alongside the more familiar *The Sound and the Fury* (1929). Chapter 5 continues the pangenetic theme by showing how Faulkner extends his analysis to matters of heredity, pollution, and textuality in *Light in August* (1932) before developing his academic knowledge of miscegenation from Franz Boas (1858–1942), Earnest Albert Hooton (1887–1954), and Henri Louis Bergson (1859–1941) into a formal realization in *Go Down, Moses* (1942). Chapter 6 continues with a detailed textual analysis of this novel, instead of the overly quoted *Absalom, Absalom!* (1936), as Faulkner pushes at the frontiers of Western racial philosophy. Hereafter, as urged by Faulkner's aesthetic, the critical focus shifts to human relationships as mediated by emergent environmental factors. Chapter 7 demonstrates how the Snopes Trilogy, comprising *The Hamlet* (1940), *The Town* (1957), and *The Mansion* (1959), portrays hierarchical, communal, and socioeconomic patterns of behavior within a context of growing urbanization. Faulkner's anticipation of late-twentieth-century sociobiology in *A Fable* (1954) and his nascent Reductionism, a philosophical advance that came from a lifetime in which he had witnessed the inexorable expansion of America, provide the focus for Chapter 8. Postbellum vestiges of civil war introversion had evolved into the excesses of a nuclear-charged superpower. Accompanying this change from sectional to international interests should have been a rigorous attention to individual and collective accountability. Faulkner's body of work exhorts its readers to practice this scrutiny—applying an evolutionary hermeneutic to this oeuvre being an initial step toward fulfilling such a responsibility.

Michael Wainwright, Shepperton, 2007.

CHAPTER 1

LOOKING ACROSS THE ATLANTIC

There is something here for an anthropologist's notebook.
William Faulkner, *Selected Letters* ("To Malcolm A. Franklin" 165)

VESTIGES OF THE NATURAL HISTORY OF CREATION (1844), WRITES ITS Scottish author Robert Chambers (1802–1871), "is the first attempt to connect the natural sciences into a history of creation" (388). In unfolding this connection, Chambers posits a self-developing force acting in accordance with natural laws, the universe being a consequence of transmutation. This argument, as Chambers anticipated with his anonymous authorship, immediately provoked religious objections. Moreover, by concertedly addressing itself to the working class, his volume irritated academics. *Vestiges* may have entertained a few of this élite, but most were scathing. A letter from the naturalist Charles Darwin (1809–1882) to the botanist Joseph Dalton Hooker (1817–1911) characterizes this divide. "I have also read the 'Vestiges,'" writes Darwin, "but have been somewhat less amused at it than you appear to have been: the writing and arrangement are certainly admirable, but his geology strikes me as bad, and his zoology far worse" (179). Controversy, nevertheless, sold well, as nine editions in eight years testified. Then, just as the debate over *Vestiges* appeared to be abating, the tenth impression (1853) reignited the issue when reviewed by biologist Thomas Henry Huxley (1825–1895). "In the mind of any one at all practically acquainted with science," fumes Huxley, "the appearance of a new edition of the 'Vestiges' at the present day, has much the effect that the inconvenient pertinacity of *Banquo* had upon *Macbeth*. 'Time was, that when the brains were out, the man would die'" ("Vestiges" 1). The ironic postscript to this criticism came after Darwin published *The Origin of Species by Means of Natural Selection, or the Preservation of Favoured Races in the Struggle for Life* (1859). Darwin's volume, though championed by Huxley, would fail to outsell *Vestiges* during the remainder of the Victorian era.

Across the Atlantic, there was little suspicion toward natural science during the first half of the nineteenth century. Even in the American South, a predominantly Protestant culture overseen by gentlemen theologians, the subject had seldom evoked antipathy. However, after an American edition of *Vestiges* appeared in 1857, latent southern fears emerged when the Tombeckbee Presbytery of Mississippi unanimously agreed to inaugurate a chair in science and religion. Southern Presbyterians were worried that inexperienced ministers might have their faith unintentionally tested and found wanting by the work of backwoods physicians. Secular medicine could heal the sick without patients having recourse to restoratives of a metaphysical nature. To address this concern, and thereby to burke any involved discussion of scientific matters, the Tombeckbee institute decreed that it would produce seminarians "with such enlarged views of science, and its relationship to revealed religion, as will prevent them from acting with indiscreet zeal in defending the Bible against the supposed assaults of true science." Their new professor was, as notes historian Ronald L. Numbers, "to forearm and equip the young theologian to meet promptly the attacks of infidelity made through the medium of the natural sciences" (61). With similar intent, the Presbytery of South Carolina established the Perkins Professorship of Natural Science in Connection with Revealed Religion. The position required an interdisciplinary approach. James Woodrow (1828–1907) seemed ideal for the role. An English-born cleric who had studied at Harvard under Swiss-born naturalist Louis Agassiz (1807–1873), Woodrow had gained a doctorate in chemistry from the University of Heidelberg and, on his return from Germany, had taught at the Presbyterian Oglethorpe College in Atlanta, Georgia, where he had espoused a skeptical view of natural science and had professed a belief in biblical inerrancy. He accepted the South Carolina appointment, and his plenary address of 1861, a speech in which he rejected human plurality, augured well for the Presbytery.

Transmutation remained an esoteric notion in America while the contesting possibilities offered by *The Origin of Species*, which went on sale in the States in the year of Woodrow's inaugural lecture, were overrun by the preoccupations of civil war.[1] That the unity of nature in plan and purpose proves its numinous credentials was the generally held belief. The high school *A Text-Book of Geology* (1863) by James Dwight Dana (1813–1895) espouses this view. Not until the latter half of the 1870s, when Darwinian theories became common conjecture, did natural science generate further American concern. Geologist Alexander Winchell (1824–1891), a part-time lecturer at the Methodist Vanderbilt University in Nashville, Tennessee, was one of the first people to draw conservative attention. His *Adamites and Pre-Adamites* (1878), a treatise positing Africans as sole human antecedents, invited the displeasure of the church. The Vanderbilt trustees deemed the publication in violation of religious principles, and they dismissed Winchell without hesitation. Nonetheless, this case, speculations about Darwinian tenets, *Vestiges*, and numerous paleontological discoveries forced religiously inclined scientists like Dana to concede ground. Just as "modern geology has almost banished such views as the excavation of a great valley by a single diluvial wave," predicted Darwin in his sixth, final, and definitive edition of *The Origin of Species* (1872), "so will natural selection banish the belief of the continued creation of new organic beings, or of any great and sudden modification in their structure" (35).[2] Differential survival and reproduction, the evolutionary enabling process Darwin named natural (or primary) selection, did not convince ecclesiastics. For many, his theories were false; for others, even if Darwin were correct, his hypotheses did not contradict the scriptures. To harmonize the Mosaic version of the creation with Darwinism, this latter minority resorted to the exegesis of Princeton geographer Arnold Guyot (1807–1884). Interpreting the days of Genesis as geological ages, Guyot reasoned that divinely guided natural selection had proceeded throughout vast epochs until God had deemed the corporeality of His chosen subject to be ready for the soul of man. This hybrid account had interdisciplinary and theological appeal. From a scientific perspective, natural selection remained the species-splitting mechanism behind the process of evolution, proving Darwin's basic opinion that all animal and plant species are related by common ancestry; from a religious standpoint, God was responsible for the predetermination, ex nihilo, of evolution and the infusion of the human soul. "God still lies behind nature," explains southern historian Edward J. Larson, "but the secondary cause of evolution replaced His creative hand as the immediate instrument of speciation" (*Trial* 10).

For one theologian in particular, one who maintained acquaintance with the corporeal evidence of primitive humanity found by contemporary American archaeologists, this combined stance of *theistic evolution* was a persuasive reconciliation. James Woodrow presented his enlightenment to the assembled alumni at the Presbytery of South Carolina on 7 May 1884:

> We cannot go back to the beginning, but we can go a long way. The outline thus obtained shows us that all the earlier organic beings in existence, through an immense period, as proved by an immense thickness of layers resting on each other, were of lower forms, with not one as high or of as complex an organization as the fish. Then the fish appeared, and remained for a long time the highest being on the earth. Then followed at long intervals the amphibian, or frog-like animal, the reptile, the lowest mammalian, then gradually the higher and higher, until at length appeared man, the head and crown of creation. (17–18)

Woodrow's address brought his position as Perkins Professor under scrutiny. The pressure increased when he printed his speech in the *Southern Presbyterian Review* and then in pamphlet form. One of the foremost backers of the Presbytery threatened to withdraw financial support because his donations were for the church, not for the teachings of Darwin. For South Carolina theologian John Lafayette Girardeau (1825–1898), such a response was serious condemnation. Would his institute become infamous as the "Evolution Seminary" with an accompanying decline in student numbers? The trustees met in September 1884 to consider Woodrow's future. Unexpectedly, they agreed to retain him, accepting that although the scriptures assert the fact of creation, they are silent as to its modus operandi. Unsatisfied with this decision, Woodrow's opponents reconvened the board and obtained a call for his resignation. Buoyed by the previous decision and heartened by support from several of his colleagues, with two leaving the faculty in solidarity, Woodrow refused to stand down. On this occasion, he lost his position. Even so, the evolutionary question continued to trouble Presbyterian leaders in the South—as their continued harassment of Woodrow attests. Two years after his dismissal, the Presbytery of Augusta tried him for heresy. Woodrow won his acquittal by fourteen votes to nine, but the overriding tone of the proceedings was clear: Adam's body was fashioned by God, without any natural animal parentage, and any variance from this doctrine was a dangerous error. Pleased with this trenchancy, displeased with the sense of exoneration, the General Assembly of the Synod of Georgia contested the judgment. The members of this superior ecclesiastical court achieved their objective, overturning the Augusta verdict in 1888.

The Woodrow affair confirms the divided attitude of southern Presbyterianism toward evolutionary concepts at this time. At a formal level, as Don Harrison Doyle notes, "Church records reveal remarkably few cases of discipline or exclusion citing doctrinal heresy or theological disagreements about the true teachings of the faith" (115). At a personal level, prominent theologian George D. Armstrong (1813–1899) personified the complex compromise made by many Presbyterians. Armstrong claimed to reject all aspects of evolution on purely scientific grounds, but his pronouncements reveal that he considered the hypothesis neither atheistic nor biblically irreconcilable. Darwin's doctrine became controversial for Armstrong only when applied to humans. He avoided this issue by ignoring the evolutionary transition from inorganic to organic matter and by distinguishing between the evolution of animals and the numinous creation of man. Armstrong so undermined the reactionary grip of Presbyterian leaders in the South that some elders worried that their governing complement in the North would condemn their lack of Christian solidarity. This was not the case. Two leading theologians from the Princeton Presbytery, Archibald Alexander Hodge (1823–1886) and Francis Patton (1843–1932), allowed the notion of animal evolution by arguing that nonhuman species were beyond theological interest.

Catholics exhibited a similarly divided stance. Although Spanish explorers became the first Catholics in the Americas, settling in what is now Florida at the beginning of the sixteenth century, their main influx started after the Civil War. The greater number of these European immigrants would remain in the northern states of America. They are, therefore, of less immediate importance to Faulkner studies than their Protestant counterparts are, but one should be aware of the parallel. For, as Numbers and John Stenhouse demonstrate, Catholics also "split between the conservatives and the progressives" (175). The former group feared that uncritical evolutionists would inspire political anarchy. The latter faction, as personified by Harvard Medical School anatomist Thomas Dwight (1843–1911), openly disavowed the contradiction between divine design and evolution. Whatever the scientific outcome over Darwinian tenets, reasoned Dwight, God had provided the soul that made the species *Homo sapiens* human.

Theistic evolution had a foothold in America, and Woodrow, continuing to lecture at the University of South Carolina, would remain the preeminent champion of this principle until his retirement in 1897. By this time, as Numbers concludes, Darwinism had penetrated the American mind to a remarkable extent (74–75). Woodrow's retirement, however, left the South with an intellectual vacuum, one that expanded after his death ten years later. Publications of a religious character rapidly filled the void. Between 1905 and 1915, three million free copies of the *Fundamentals*, twelve booklets exhorting the essential doctrines of Christianity, were distributed across America. Their evangelical influence in the South was significant, and for the majority of practicing Christians—whichever way one categorizes them in terms of sex, race, or wealth—Darwinism gained little credence. One conservative contributor to the *Fundamentals*, James Orr (1844–1913), was an exception. He wished to reconcile evolutionary science with the Bible. Accepting that the Creative Power works on organisms from within rather than from without, Orr reached a compromise, but gained notoriety for doing so. The bulk of the southern populace would continue to reject Darwinism. This rejection became part of the overriding ethos in the region. Only some individuals, few in number but sometimes high in profile, would espouse an evolutionary theism.

Neither was the church the sole forum for such opposing opinions since concepts of evolution often caused tension at institutes of higher education. The University of Mississippi, chartered on 24 February 1844 at Oxford, provides a good example.[3] Opening four years later, the college soon gained a reputation for progressiveness by offering a degree course, the first in America, in engineering. Mathematician and natural philosopher Frederick Augustus Porter Barnard (1809–1889) arrived to teach the new discipline in 1854. His qualifications, bolstered by his status as an ordained minister, ensured an inexorable rise. Within two years, he had gained the chancellorship and pledged to transform his university into the greatest scientific institution in the country. In pursuit of this aim, Barnard obtained sufficient funds from the Mississippi legislature to construct an observatory on the campus for the largest telescope in the world. As a result of the Civil War, the instrument never reached Oxford; nevertheless, Barnard made enough progress during his six years as chancellor to leave his successor, the Presbyterian minister John Newton Waddel (1812–1895), a significant challenge.

Waddel came to the university in 1848 as one of its original trustees. Elected chancellor in 1865, he drew inspiration from Barnard's legacy, vowed to maintain the scientific reputation of the university, and redesigned the curriculum along progressive northern lines. He proved less tractable, however, on biological issues. Disillusioned by the teaching of theistic evolution on campus, Waddel resigned his position in 1874 to become secretary of education for the Presbyterian Church of America. Waddle's resignation did not deter his successor, Alexander Peter Stewart (1821–1908), from educational innovation. Nor did being the last ordained minister to hold the chancellorship prevent Stewart from becoming its most dynamic nineteenth-century incumbent. During his tenure from 1874 to 1887, the college awarded its first Ph.D. (1877), adopted coeducational status (1882), and appointed the first female member of a faculty in America (1885). Stewart also confirmed the teaching of evolutionary tenets by appointing the geologist George Little (1838–1924) in 1881. Little's personal library contained "the works of Darwin, Huxley, Tindall [sic] and Spencer."[4] One war veteran was so appalled on visiting the campus at this time that he sent Little a newspaper article deriding Darwinism. The inveterate, quotes Numbers, "prayed that God would save the students at the University" from the falsities of science. In reply, Little asserted that evolution was "a workable hypothesis, like Newton's law of gravitation and Dalton's Atomic Theory" (Numbers 69).[5] By now, as the Southern Presbyterian Reverend J. William Flinn (1847–1907) admitted, it was "doubtful whether any college deserving the name in the United States, North or South, used a textbook on geology or biological science whose author was not an evolutionist, and in which evolution was not taught" (545–46). The geology department at the University of Georgia went so far as to commission an evolutionary fresco and, by the turn of the century, university science faculties throughout the South were teaching theistic evolution. Progress toward a wider dissemination of Darwinian ideas had taken place, but, as Hollis Daniel Walker notes in his history of the University of South Carolina, academia rarely made the subject prominent (1: 165).[6] The University of Mississippi was no exception and disputes such as that engendered by Little had little effect on the education offered on campus.

The major review of university staff authorized by Chancellor Edward Mayes (1846–1917) on his appointment in 1887 did have repercussions though. After resignations and dismissals, only three of the resident professors remained. Mayes intended their replacements to be a new movement in American academia, individuals with cosmopolitan interests who would pursue sustained and original research. Mayes's initiative failed, his team reversing the academic orientation of Oxford with the renovation of southern traditionalism. Polymath and writer Stark Young (1881–1963), who received his degree from the university in 1901, recalls this conservatism: "At that time the education at the University of Mississippi followed the tradition of the Old South; it must in fact have presented some of the last vestiges of that tradition. The tradition was out of England, suited essentially to a ruling class" (125). Tuition was an inculcation of predominant virtues through exemplification. The works of Plutarch (c. 46–126), soliloquies by William Shakespeare (1564–1616), and the history of General Robert E. Lee (1807–1870) were standard material. Most of the professors were old-school aristocrats "with the kind of education which that term might imply." Undergraduates, longing to assimilate these indelible qualities, revered their tutors. Such academics, "men who had come off penniless from the Civil War," also suited the Oxford ruling class (126). Their presence confirmed southern values of rectitude, while their poverty substantiated plutocratic ascendancy. With further expansion, however, the potential of the university to undermine such verities regained momentum. Already a major presence in Mississippi, the opening of the geology and mining faculty in 1902 and the subsequent amalgamation of horticulture, chemistry, and biology into the school of agriculture confirmed this possibility. When biological science came under the auspices of two new departments in 1908—one covering botany and forestry, the other teaching zoology and entomology—epistemological enlightenment was a definite prospect. Evolutionists on the Oxford campus benefited from this bifurcated structure, the prominence of Darwinism enjoying a hitherto unexpected sense of freedom.

Nonetheless, secular impediments to the dissemination of evolutionary science persisted because Darwin's theories simply outpaced complementary disciplines. Certain aspects of his work, a pertinent instance is his refutation of biblical chronology in conformity with the *Principles of Geology* (1830–1833) by Charles Lyell (1797–1875), had been rapidly assimilated into geology and vulcanology. Agassiz's death in 1873 had then dampened the professional hostility of American biologists and paleontologists to Darwinian notions. Yet, no other scientific proposition, argues biologist Ernst Mayr, "had to wait as long to be accepted by the holders of its discipline" as did evolution ("Ideological Resistance" 124). The continuous variation implicit in natural selection, a radical departure from the dogma established by the ancient school of essentialism, remained a particular obstacle.

Derived from the geometry of Pythagoras (c. 570–500 BC) and extended by Plato (427–347 BC), essentialism posits the presence of an invariant divine Form for every natural phenomenon. Any divergence from this archetype is an aberration. Essentialists, who dominated the intellectual landscape of continental Europe in Darwin's time, denied variation any role in nature. They defined species according to constant characteristics and the discontinuities separating these classes were unbridgeable. Rejecting natural selection, such thinkers found sudden large-scale mutations, or *saltations*, evolutionarily expedient. Darwin, conversely, asserted that individual organisms were vehicles of independent selection, species changing gradually and not by saltations. "New characteristics do not appear preferentially in a single direction," explains historian-philosopher Peter J. Bowler, "*least of all* [in] a direction that will be useful to the species" (57). A stochastic essence underlying natural selection produces this lack of orientation (or dysteleology), and Darwin himself admitted to a profound ignorance concerning such variations. Essentialists cited this admittance in rejecting his scientific abstractions. They also proposed a deterministic attitude to knowledge with mathematical formulae the bases of universal scientific laws. Isaac Newton (1643–1727) had typified this form of reasoning with his contributions to mathematics, especially with his methods of *fluxions* (calculus) and *quadrature* (integration). Philosophers from Francis Bacon (1561–1626) and Galileo Galilei (1564–1642) to René Descartes (1596–1650) and Immanuel Kant (1724–1804) had followed the same practice. Mathematical proof and the ability to make accurate predictions were the benchmarks by which to measure a scientific law. Historical extrapolation and *biometry*, the application of statistics to biological investigation, as championed by his cousin Francis Galton (1822–1911), held an alternative appeal for Darwin. These procedures enabled him to simulate the small and continuous variations by which evolution proceeds. Orthodox thinkers expressed bemusement. The renowned British astronomer John Herschel (1792–1871), wishing to deny a dysteleological paradigm, ridiculed Darwin's techniques as anticipatory, inadequate, and "higgledy-piggledy." Darwin sought solace in an appeal to the inheritance of acquired characteristics. Jean Baptiste Lamarck (1744–1829) had argued that organisms could transmit characteristics acquired during their lifetime to their offspring. Darwin unenthusiastically resurrected Lamarckism but diverged from his predecessor on a number of issues. "Lamarck denied that species became extinct," explains Ludmilla Jordanova, "since their plasticity enabled them to adapt to changing external conditions. Darwin, more conscious of the limits of organic variation, found extinction to be a common feature of history" (105–6). Nor did Darwin agree that random variation promoted infinite complexity.

Using the work of a scientist with whom he so often differed did not aid Darwin's cause, but choosing in 1868 to recognize the terminology proposed by his coeval Herbert Spencer (1820–1903) only aggravated the situation: "This preservation, during the battle for life, of varieties which possess any advantage in structure, constitution, or instinct, I have called Natural Selection; Mr. Herbert Spencer has well expressed the same idea by the Survival of the Fittest. The term 'natural selection' is in some respects a bad one, as it seems to imply conscious choice" (*Variation* 1: 6). Four years later, Darwin lavished further praise on his contemporary's formulation: "I have called this principle, by which each slight variation, if useful, is preserved, by the term Natural Selection, in order to mark its relation to man's power of selection. But the expression often used by Mr. Herbert Spencer of the Survival of the Fittest is more accurate, and is sometimes equally convenient" (*Origin* 49).

Darwin, then, was partially to blame for the popularity of Spencer's expression. The substitution of "the survival of the fittest" for "the struggle for existence" would lead to significant ramifications because Spencerians did not interpret the word fittest in the Darwinian sense. The concept of fitness in Darwinism denotes supreme suitability to the environment, but in Spencerism, the term implies the strongest and most physically endowed. Interested parties soon exploited this difference. By the 1890s, as Numbers and Stenhouse chronicle, "American Catholic conservatives were writing about the ineradicable connections between Darwinism and Spencerian survival of the fittest, on the one hand, and Marxist atheism, on the other" (194).

Obfuscating the evolutionary effects of natural disasters did not help the Darwinist cause in America either. Sudden changes to the environment may have direct and definite consequences, concedes *The Origin of Species*, but these effects produce a "mere fluctuating variability" (131). American geologists, however, claimed that catastrophic events were the crucial factor in evolution. Clarence Rivers King (1842–1901) produced geological records from the West to evince this belief, and the suggestion by Dutch botanist Hugo de Vries (1848–1935) of evolution via drastic mutation provided such catastrophists with greater authority (Bowler 116). Three members of the National Academy of Sciences gained prominence on the back of de Vries's popularity; one of them, Charles Abiathar White (1826–1910), maintaining that Darwin's theory of natural selection was inconsistent with "the fossil evidence for both plants and animals" (Numbers 157). Some colleagues were not so convinced. Charles Otis Whitman (1842–1910), effecting a degree of reconciliation with primary selection, was one such pioneer. Whitman had gained a doctorate from the University of Leipzig and had worked at the Imperial University of Japan before accepting an appointment at the Harvard Museum of Comparative Zoology (1882–1886). After two years at the Allis Lake Laboratory in Milwaukee, Wisconsin (1886–1889), he worked for the Massachusetts Laboratory of Marine Biology in Woods Hole (1888–1908).[7] Elected to the board of the National Academy of Sciences in 1895, Whitman became the Head of Zoology at the University of Chicago, developing his theory of *orthogenesis* in which an internal mechanism propels evolution toward perfection.

The constitution of the National Academy of Sciences Board, examined in detail by Numbers, provides further evidence of the American reaction to Darwinism (137–59). Of the thirty-eight members who served in both the nineteenth and twentieth centuries, just one, J. Peter Lesley (1819–1903), rejected evolution completely, while only three, Eugene Woldemar Hilgard (1833–1916), Samuel Hubbard Scudder (1837–1911), and Charles Doolittle Walcott (1850–1927), retained a belief in theistic evolution. More than a dozen favored Darwin's own Lamarckian tendencies and the English naturalist's appeal to other appropriate factors in explaining the emergence of new species. The biologist William Keith Brooks (1848–1908) personified this approach. Of the remaining Academy Fellows, information on six provides no evidence as to their views, with the remaining five, John Shaw Billings (1838–1913), William Gilson Farlow (1844–1919), Grove Karl Gilbert (1843–1918), Edward Sylvester Morse (1838–1925), and Sidney Irving Smith (1843–1926), forming a Darwinian vanguard. Exceptional, these men readily appreciated and espoused the theory of primary selection. Their example ensured that Darwinism gained greater recognition in America and in the American South than would otherwise have been the case. Nonetheless, the pre-Darwinian model in which man is the center of the God-given universe was so ingrained in the Western ethos as to be intuitive, and the profundity of Darwinian thought remained largely unacknowledged by the philosophical *episteme* to which it belonged. "Today," writes Mayr, "we realize that Darwin through his many entirely new ideas had become the founder of a totally new philosophy. It was a philosophy which differed so fundamentally from the existing philosophies that the philosophers of the nineteenth century did not even notice that Darwin's teachings represented a philosophy" ("Ideological Resistance" 125). Prevailing ideologies remained dominant, and American institutes of higher education could not evade this dominance. The silent grave in which Western philosophy buried Darwinism, in the opinion of Louis Althusser, was "worth more than any open indictment" (28).

The European Armistice of 1918 signaled a change to the American social climate that would attempt to seal that silence. On entering the postwar era, writes George Brown Tindall, the South "surged into a strange new world of urban booms and farm distress, it entered an unfamiliar terrain of diversity and change in which there lurked a thousand threats to older orthodoxies" (184). Political and religious leaders acted to restrain freedom of speech in matters relating to their domains. Academia was a target. Prominent theologians from across America, deploring the spirit of rebellion among the postbellum masses, founded the World Christian Fundamentals Association (WCFA). At their inaugural conference of 1919, associate leader William Bell Riley (1861–1947) warned that America was "coming under the leadership of the new infidelity, known as 'modernism,'" and that "basic to the many forms of modern infidelity was [is] the philosophy of evolution" (Larson, *Summer* 36, 37). Once an on-going struggle between Northern Baptist denominations had been settled—a conflict for control that had prompted the conservative leader Curtis Lee Laws (1868–1946) to coin the term fundamentalism—the sectarian fight focused on the perceived depravity of contemporary developments within American politics and education. The fundamentalist movement, characterizing the Roaring Twenties as a period of moral dissolution, had its target; the twentieth-century crusade against evolutionary thought was under way.

Within five years, fundamentalists were prosecuting a concerted strategy against evolutionary science in southern colleges, with Union University in Tennessee and Furman University in South Carolina subject to sustained attempts to oust "offending" faculty members. Thanks to Joseph Neely Powers (1869–1939), a chancellor who vouchsafed academic autonomy at Oxford, fundamentalism did not impinge upon the University of Mississippi during his initial period in office (1914–1924). With the mathematician, astronomer, and Presbyterian elder Alfred Hume (1866–1950), then elected to replace Powers, matters changed. Decrying the campus as a retreat for recreation, rather than a place for study, Hume suspended college dances, prohibited the use of automobiles, and punished student absenteeism. Although amenable to fundamentalist restrictions concerning personal laxity, when a Mississippian version of the Butler Act came into force, Hume was less acquiescent.

John Washington Butler (1875–1952), having "read in the papers that boys and girls were coming home from school and telling their fathers and mothers that the Bible was all nonsense" (Allen 1), and having heard in sermons that "the teaching of evolution in the schools ought to be stopped, because it was attacking religion," was determined to act (Allen 1–2). A representative of Macon, Trousdale, and Sumner Counties in the Tennessee legislature, Butler introduced a bill banning the teaching of evolution in institutes funded by the state. It came into effect on 21 March 1925.

This is not the place for a minute analysis of the Butler Act, but a few points concerning the case brought by Rhea County prosecutors to enforce the law in Tennessee are relevant. The defendant, a general science teacher named John T. Scopes (1900–1970), had volunteered his services to the lawyer George W. Rappelyea (1894–n.d.) after the abandonment of a Chattanooga test case against Butler's statute. Rappelyea arranged to meet Scopes at the drugstore in the county town of Dayton. During their discussion, as furnished by historian Ray Ginger, Scopes remarked, "nobody could teach biology without using the theory of evolution" (123). Indeed, the widely used tuition manual, *The Teaching of Biology in the Secondary School* (1904), advised that "the modern doctrine of evolution, which was arrived at first by the study of animals and plants, is a far too important generalization from the point of view of education as well as science to be neglected in the high school" (138).

Avoiding detailed discussion because the subject was too complicated was the only caveat. This tutorial approach, broad conceptualization without dwelling on intricacies, as Larson adds, "was recommended by the American Society of Zoologists in 1906" (*Trial* 23). To emphasize this institutional lead to Rappelyea, Scopes took down *A Civic Biology* (1909) by George William Hunter (1873–1948) from a shelf in the pharmacy. "This," he explained, "is the official text." In this volume, Hunter, the departmental head at De Witt Clinton High School in New York City, elucidates the importance of organismic and environmental interaction, using the Darwinian paradigm of a genealogical tree of species. Tennessee schools had been using his publication since its first edition, the Tennessee Commission had adopted Hunter's text ten years later, and when the contract for the book had expired on 31 August 1924, the state board had not demanded a replacement. Nevertheless, in using this volume, goaded Rappelyea, "you have been violating the Law." "Then," replied Scopes, "so has every other teacher" (Ginger 123). Agreeing to collaborate, the pair sought a lawyer willing to accept contentious cases.

Clarence Darrow (1857–1938), who had come to prominence the previous year defending two university students in the case of *Illinois v. Leopold and Loeb*, was the obvious candidate. Nathan Leopold (1904–1971) and Richard Loeb (1905–1936) had kidnapped and subsequently murdered fourteen-year-old Robert Franks (1909–1924). Darrow's defense rested on psychiatric reports suggesting that his clients had inherited a predisposition to violence. The judge accepted these mitigating circumstances and commuted the death penalty to life imprisonment. "This decision," Darrow told the *Chicago Daily News*, "at once caps my career as a criminal lawyer and starts my path in another direction" (1).[8] Within months, this reorientation would lead him to Dayton. Here, where popular understanding of Darwinism had attached the *Scopes Monkey Trial* as a sobriquet to the forthcoming proceedings, Darrow would cement his place in American history—both with his defense of Darwin's theory and with his opposition to the evangelism of prosecutor William Jennings Bryan (1860–1925).

One strand of the ideology to which Bryan adhered came from Populist roots. This political movement had emerged during the 1870s as a southern counterbalance to the unreconstructed aristocracy. Populism, stresses Kevin Railey, "not only fought the ideology of social hierarchies, it also threatened the belief in individual effort and reward as well as the belief in white supremacy" (20). Owners of large plantations, land speculators, and railroad proprietors were common targets, but the racial stance of the Populist Party (which formed in 1892) ensured the movement limited appeal. Progressivism soon assimilated Populism by co-opting liberal ideas while championing an intense racism. "In reductive though accurate terms," insists Railey, "this combination summarizes the position of the Progressive Party in Mississippi" (22). From this paradoxical mixture came a gamut of policies: preventing the economic exploitation of children, women, farmers, and workers; rationalizing business competition through antitrust and labor law restrictions; combating political corruption; exerting popular control over government. Elected as Democratic presidential candidate in 1896, Bryan was "perhaps America's premier progressive" by the time of his next nomination in 1900 (Larson, *Trial* 31). One element of Bryan's Progressive credentials was his concern for adolescent development whereby he opposed the spiritual and moral harm inflicted on student development by the teaching of Darwinism. He publicly expressed his disdain for evolutionary notions in a 1904 sermon entitled "The Prince of Peace." Left idle four years later, after his third failure to secure the presidency, Bryan traveled throughout the United States and Canada delivering his antievolutionary address before disseminating his opinions as widely as Mexico, Cairo, Jerusalem, Manila, and Tokyo.[9] Prohibition and race were his other obsessions; and so, following the hiatus of World War I, Bryan combined his intolerance for Darwinism, alcohol, and immigration in a determination to control the physiological and moral inheritance of America. First generation German Americans, correlatives of the kaiser and often associated with the ownership of urban saloons, suffered most from his stance. The enforcement of prohibition and the establishment of immigration quotas became common political themes. Dubiousness of provenance even extended to foreign ideas, with the work of German biologist August Weismann (1834–1914), Moravian abbot Gregor Mendel (1822–1884), and German-born American anthropologist Franz Boas (1858–1942) failing to command an extensive audience. "Bryan's progressive activism never let up during his life," maintains Larson, "and it continued while he fought evolution during the twenties" (*Trial* 31). Committed to fundamentalism, and assured of the growing opposition to scientific innovation, Bryan expressed his solidified opposition to evolution in another three devoutly religious speeches: "The Bible and its Enemies" (1921), "The Menace of Darwinism" (1922), and "The Origin of Man" (1924). Reverence for Bryan was such that the Great Commoner, as he was now widely known, could volunteer his services to the prosecutors at Dayton confidant of their acceptance.

History has accounted for Scopes, Darrow, and Bryan, but what of William Faulkner (1897–1962) in July 1925. Having resigned as postmaster of the University of Mississippi in the previous autumn, Faulkner had taken the opportunity to travel. He spent some time in the Vieux Carré of New Orleans, but, more ambitiously, he wished to broaden his mind in Europe. Willing to work his fare, and after a number of attempts, he eventually secured a passage for Italy on 10 July. An accurate tableau of southern history on this day could therefore show Faulkner boarding a freighter, the *West Ivis*, at New Orleans bound for Genoa, while Bryan alights from the Royal Palm Limited at Dayton, as that small Tennessee town prepares for the prosecution of Scopes against a defense mounted by Darrow. While media organizations set up their coverage of the case, Faulkner settled into the unexpected comfort of a stateroom and began work on some short stories for the Louisiana *Times-Picayune*. On the following day, the *West Ivis* docked for three nights at Savannah, Georgia. Joseph Blotner's biography indicates that Faulkner spent part of this interval copying epitaphs in the Colonial Cemetery and the remaining hours on his fiction (1: 444). From 14 July to 18 July, the last four days of the global phenomenon that the Scopes Trial had become, Faulkner was on the Atlantic looking forward to what Louis Daniel Brodsky calls "his youth's grand gesture, his 1925 walking tour through Europe" (30). Accompanied by his friend, the silversmith Bill Spratling (1900–1967), Faulkner carried letters of introduction written by another acquaintance, the Mississippi lawyer Phil Stone (1893–1967). Arnold Bennett (1867–1931), Ezra Pound (1885–1972), T. S. Eliot (1888–1965), and James Joyce (1882–1941) were among the intended recipients. The possible reception of these missives worried Faulkner; this was his uppermost concern. Physically and mentally an ocean apart, the aspiring novelist was as isolated from the *Scopes Monkey Trial* as any literate man could be.

Is there a link between Faulkner and Dayton?

Journalism, through the vociferous reporter Henry Louis Mencken (1880–1956) suggests one connection. In his youth, Mencken had been an associate of the American Civil Liberties Union (ACLU) activist Arthur Garfield Hays (1881–1954). The two men had once sold books, titles banned under censorship law, on Boston Common. Hays was on Scopes's original defense team, and Mencken's loyalty to his libertarian friend is evident from his reports for the *Times-Picayune* and the Baltimore *Sun*. "In his dispatches," Ginger explains, "Mencken daily referred to the people of Rhea County as morons and hillbillies and peasants." Another of his targets was the "degraded nonsense which country preachers are hammering into yokel skulls" (129). Mencken concluded that the Civil War had crushed southern intellectualism; a reactionary wasteland was the result. His articles were so inflammatory that the commissioner of police had to disperse a group of local men determined to ride the journalist out of town. Mencken was unfazed and his rhetoric remained blistering. By the time the *West Ivis* reached Genoa on 2 August, the trial was old news, but later that month Faulkner would anonymously contact

Mencken asking for the publication of a poem entitled "Ode to the Louver." There is no evidence that he received a reply to this practical joke or any communication from Mencken concerning Scopes. The implied journalistic thread between Faulkner and Dayton breaks at this point.

Murry Falkner (1870–1932)—William had added the 'u' that distinguishes his surname from that of his father in 1919—provides another possible connection. For, explains William's younger brother John (1901–1963), Murry had never been a regular churchgoer until "the Darwin-Bryan 'Monkey Trial' in Tennessee scared him into it." This shaking of Murry's ontological confidence became something of a family joke, especially since his behavior "did not last long" (59). Faulkner's European letters provide no evidence that he heard contemporaneously of this paternal panic, but, coming from a clan of inveterate storytellers, someone surely acquainted him with the matter when he returned to America in December. Furthermore, the Dayton affair must have been palpable to Faulkner a few months later when Mississippi legislators followed in the wake of their Tennessean counterparts.

Thomas Theodore Martin (1862–1939) played an important part in this sequel. An Evangelist, whom Larson describes as "a fervent tent revivalist with a national ministry," Martin had been disclaiming evolution throughout Mississippi since the 1910s, subsequently using wartime propaganda to liken "evolutionary teachers to German soldiers who were said to have poisoned French children." His reaction to Bryan's death was to form the Bible Crusaders of America. Under this banner, he conducted a series of mass meetings in the state capital during February 1926. Martin's agitation in Jackson provoked a political debate to which he already knew the outcome, the Mississippi legislature being "entirely composed of rural Democrat lawmakers typically loyal to the ideals of their former standard bearer, William Jennings Bryan" (*Trial* 76). Fundamentalist Democratic governor Henry Lewis Whitfield (1868–1927) signed the statute on 11 March. At the University of Mississippi, Chancellor Hume was vehemently critical, but he had to abide by the law. Hume's opposition was not so much adherence to scientific rigor as a belief in free thought and a reluctance to see his staff compelled to evade the law. He oversaw a minor liberalization to his recently introduced campus rules, repealing antifraternity legislation for example, but could do no more.[10] Even the overturning of Scopes's conviction on technical grounds by the Tennessee Supreme Court on 17 January 1927 offered no hope. The decision merely served to stoke fundamentalist ardor—Arkansas becoming the third state to enact a prohibition on the teaching of Darwinism. The year was 1928. Faulkner's South was locked in an educational bind.

No wonder, then, that many influential historians present the region as a homeland for postbellum reactionary thought. W. J. Cash is a case in point. The overwhelming body of southern schools either so disapproved of Darwinism, or their governors and senior staff were so afraid of popular opinion, asserts *The Mind of the South* (1941), that evolutionary thinkers "could not get into their faculties at all or were intimidated into keeping silent by the odds against them" (140). Monroe Lee Billington concurs. Darwinism as an intellectual movement," laments *The American South: A Brief History* (1971), "bypassed Southerners" (301–2). Lester D. Stephens compounds this assertion. Half a century elapsed following the Civil War "before the South as a whole began to enter the mainstream of scientific research and," continues *Science, Race and Religion in the American South* (2000), "another half passed before it began to become an equal in such research" (267). The excruciatingly slow return of open-mindedness to southern universities helps to perpetuate this opinion. When African American student James Meredith insisted on entering law school at the University of Mississippi in September 1962, anxieties attendant on various forms of liberalism came to a head. He required more than three hundred federal marshals to exercise his rights. Another five years would elapse before a Supreme Court judgment on *Epperson v. Arkansas* (or "Scopes II") repealed the antievolution statutes of the 1920s. This finding affected only federal legislation, the Mississippi legislature not removing the final state-level ordinance until 21 December 1970.

Some contemporary historians are now questioning such an absolute conclusion about Darwinism and the South. In particular, the investigations of Numbers and Larson, as endorsed by the rare discernment of Fred C. Hobson and Bert Loewenberg, propose a more complex history. The argument over witnesses allowed to testify during the Scopes Trial has proven fruitful in this regard. On the one hand, Bryan staunchly persuaded the judge to preclude evidence from scientific experts. On the other hand, Butler, wishing to understand the evolutionary argument, displayed surprising equanimity in his disappointment at not hearing these specialists. The consequences of the trial for the chief protagonists are also of historical importance. Scopes was found guilty and was fined $100 in accordance with standard practice for a misdemeanor. True, he felt uncomfortable in Dayton after the trial, but thanks to a scholarship fund organized by defense witnesses, he soon moved to Illinois. Earning a degree in geology from the University of Chicago, he spent the remainder of his vocational years as a chemical engineer. Darrow profited from the case as well. That winter he accepted an invitation from the National Association for the Advancement of Colored People (NAACP) to act for Dr. Ossian Sweet and his codefendants. Darrow's seven-hour closing address helped to secure their acquittal—and his eminence as a lawyer. However, if the losers did well from Dayton, then the winner did poorly. Bryan, relaxing after his exertions, suffered a fatal heart attack within five days of his triumph. The statute he strove to protect may have remained in force for over forty years, but, noting the recommendation of the Supreme Court that Scopes should not be indicted, even Tennessean lawyers were hesitant to prosecute similar infringements. Victory for Bryan was of the Pyrrhic kind.[11]

Modern historians should note, therefore, that where science and religion were concerned, the South was not a region smothered by inane fundamentalism, but a milieu of charged, ambiguous, and irreconcilable contestation. This was the environment of William Faulkner's birth and maturation. His absence from America during the Scopes Trial may signify that he missed the crux of the evolutionary debate—search where one may, there appear to be no explicit citations to the proceedings at Dayton by Faulkner—but his environmental background implies otherwise. For, as Hobson asserts, "virtually every thoughtful Southerner had some response to the occurrences at Dayton" (148). Faulkner, despite living in an intellectually challenged region, and despite his European travels, was one such contemplative Mississippian. Moreover, as British biologist Richard Dawkins argues, an acceptance of Darwinism does not mean that everyone "has, graven in his brain, an identical copy of the exact words of Charles Darwin" (*Selfish* 195). Individuals have particular ways of interpreting ideas, and learning is often a circuitous process. Darwinian theories need not be learned from Darwin's own writings.

The present study will demonstrate this epistemological sense with reference to William Faulkner, a man who acquired the substantial portion of his evolutionary principles in an indirect manner over several decades, an author whose fiction bears witness to his ideational development and whose oeuvre attests to the emergence of modern America. Loewenberg encourages one to search for this critical route. For while Darwinism confronted antiquated ways of thinking: "the transformed physical environment challenged older ways of living and doing. The conflict mirrored a larger struggle of orientation to the facts of urban-industrial change. In retrospect, both reflected the perennial clash between an old and a new order, but while the physical revolutions jarred attitudes and institutions, Darwinism attacked the whole American *Weltanschauung"* (339).

Faulkner championed the power of reasoning, his work indicting impediments to knowledge, his art offering significant insight into the undeniable effect of Darwinian hypotheses upon the introversion of the United States. The following chapters chart this individual and communal maturation, and reveal that beyond American thought, Faulkner's prescience offers universal significance in line with the tenets of evolution.

CHAPTER 2

HAND IN HAND WITH THE OLD GENTLEMAN

> He saw all this and knew that he had pursued a phantom into a far land; that destiny had taken him across seas so that he might see with a clear eye that thing which his heedless youth had obscured from him.
>
> William Faulkner, *New Orleans Sketches* (33)

HAND IN HAND, MURRY FALKNER MARRIED MAUD BUTLER (1871–1960) on 8 November 1896 at the Methodist parsonage in New Albany, Mississippi. The newlyweds set up home in the town where their momentous biological bequest to literature, their first child, William Cuthbert, was born on 25 September 1897. For professional reasons, the Falkners soon moved to nearby Ripley, where Maud gave birth to sons Jack, christened Murry C. (1899–1975), and John. The family then relocated the short distance to Oxford, the county town of Lafayette, where their fourth and final child Dean (1907–1935) was born, and where William would officially reside until his death.

Protestant religion was the mainstay of Northern Mississippi, with Lafayette comprising Baptists, Methodists, Presbyterians, and Episcopalians.[1] The Butlers, a staunch and pioneering Baptist family, wished to oversee the spiritual guidance of their grandsons. Aegis such as this did not augur favorably for artistic inclinations. Lelia Dean Swift Butler (1849–1907), recollects John Faulkner of his maternal grandmother, "was a Baptist and her father was evidently of the hard-shell variety, for he thought that any creation which came out of thin air, like a painting, was the work of the Devil" (123). Possibly in reaction to such sternness, Murry and Maud christened each son as a Methodist and sent each to the affiliated Sunday school. The Falkners did not embrace religion fervently;

nonetheless, they upheld the common codes of Protestant practice, which, according to Don Harrison Doyle, "placed high value on self-restraint against the temptations of lust, anger, and greed" (115). When the family moved to South Street in 1904, the religious atmosphere was more palpable—a succession of neighbors being Presbyterian ministers. Evidence of local adherence to Protestantism arose publicly with the visit of William Jennings Bryan in 1909. A large Oxford crowd, which included the twelve-year-old William, warmly received a rendition of "The Prince of Peace." Despite this sectarian environment, however, the extent of the boy's religious indoctrination remains difficult to ascertain. Historian Joel Williamson, for example, asserts that Falkner "gained an intimate knowledge of the Bible" (*William Faulkner* 145), whereas literary critic Cleanth Brooks contends that William's "theological education was shaky" (123). A familial citation offers a more perceptive evaluation. "Though none of us ever became confirmed churchgoers in later life," writes Jack Falkner, "we all considered the existence of a Supreme Being as unquestioned" (23). Religion, as an ideological state apparatus, effectively conditioned the lives of Mississippians.

Nonetheless, the traditional agrarian environment—an era without stock market intervention, a time when children could play in the streets and visit homes uninvited, the Lafayette before billboards and neon signs—was in decline. Intrusions into the rural landscape dispelled dreams of permanent aristocratic splendor. Cotton, introduced from Mexico in the early nineteenth century, had become the most lucrative of southern commodities. By 1910 Mississippi farmers reserved approximately three million acres to the crop. Forest clearance provided much of this land while simultaneously feeding an unassuageable demand for timber. The small communities outlying Oxford were disappearing; the sense of Mississippi as a human-blighted Arcadia was prevalent. Protoenvironmentalists recognized this tension and George William Hunter's *A Civic Biology* testified to their concern. "Compare the unfavorable artificial environment of a crowded city," urges Hunter, "with the more favorable environment of the country" (2). Man is responsible for the destruction of this valuable asset, continues Hunter, an unnecessary encroachment "primarily due to wrong and wasteful lumbering" (112). One needed merely to live in Oxford to witness this agronomial evolution. Furthermore, the conventional schooling of which Falkner partook as a child would have apprised him of the matter too: Hunter's volume not only airing environmental anxieties, but also issuing a Darwinian challenge to religious orthodoxy. True, the young William lost interest in formal education by 1915, but these boyhood impressions left their mark. Once outside the school system, Falkner immediately turned to Phil Stone to guide his pursuit of knowledge. For the next two years, Stone would load his car with books and give his young friend the keys. "Bill would go out on some country road, a side road where it was quiet," recalls John Faulkner, "and park the car and spend the day reading" (130). This was a salubrious period for body and mind. However, Falkner's literary ambitions seemingly withered when his heartfelt intentions toward (Lida) Estelle Oldham (1896–1972) failed. Within three months of her marriage to Cornell Franklin (c. 1890–n.d.) on 18 April 1918, Falkner had joined the Canadian Royal Air Force as a cadet. To the relief of his mother, the Armistice prevented William from going to war. What is more, with the imminent return of her second son from the marines, and being the day on which her husband was appointed assistant secretary to the University of Mississippi, 11 November 1918, was especially momentous for the Falkners.

Murry, seemingly the first Falknerian epigone, had suffered a series of disappointments. His bid for the family railroad company auctioned by his grandfather had been too late, while his successive business interests in an oil mill, an ice plant, a livery business, and a hardware store had realized no profit. This post at Ole Miss, as the university at Oxford was now affectionately known, offered the patriarch a chance of social reinstatement in addition to a comfortable family home. The following autumn, William took advantage of these new surroundings by enrolling as a special student at the university. "Though neither Bill nor Jack had finished high school," explains their brother John, "they both qualified and signed up at the University in the fall of 1919" through the vocational training program for war veterans (141). William chose a first-year curriculum of French, Spanish, and English Literature, but surprisingly lacked confidence in his linguistic abilities (Collins, "Faulkner" 6). He wondered whether the discipline of mathematics would help. A family friend, Professor Calvin S. Brown (1866–1945) encouraged him in this regard. "He seemed quite interested the first few weeks," records Robert Coughlan, "but then he began cutting classes more and more and finally just drifted away. He seemed to be the same way in most of the subjects he took" (52–53). Faulkner certainly lacked conscientiousness as an undergraduate, so no one was surprised when, on 5 November 1920, he withdrew from his degree. Continuing to be based on campus for the next ten years, Faulkner partially satisfied his educational needs in the university library. The collection included seventeen of Darwin's publications by this date. Phil Stone's extensive repository also remained available.[2] Stone would even buy items from the Brick Row Bookshop in New Haven, Connecticut, specifically for his protégé—although circumspection is required concerning Stone's purchases, because his receipts give "no indication of which books Faulkner read or of what other books Stone may have ordered during the early and middle 1920's" (Blotner, *Faulkner's Library* 6). Nevertheless, believes John Faulkner, "What Phil picked for Bill to read was pretty much what she [our mother] would have chosen." This reading matter would have included "Plato, Socrates, the Greek poets, all the good Romans and Shakespeare. . . . other good English writers and the French and German classics" (130). Faulkner offset this cultural inheritance from the Old World with a restricted concern for contemporary southern authors. For although the Fugitive-Agrarians of Nashville, Tennessee—writers that included John Crowe Ransom (1888–1974), Donald Davidson (1893–1968), Allen Tate (1899–1979), and Robert Penn Warren (1905–1989)—were relatively close in geographical terms, their work remained of marginal interest to him. As a poet, Faulkner was an admirer of Algernon Charles Swinburne (1837–1909), as *The Marble Faun* (1924) attests, while the Fugitive-Agrarians not only rebelled against the poetry of late-Victorian England, but also eschewed contemporary values they deemed to be out of keeping with the economy of the South.[3]

Over the next few years, preferring to cultivate his relationships with Stark Young and Sherwood Anderson (1876–1941), Faulkner made the Vieux Carré his favorite haunt. Three hundred and fifty miles from Oxford, New Orleans was a vibrant contrast to the parochial standards of Lafayette. Savoring this difference, Faulkner began to express a desire for the elucidation offered by a foreign environment. Anderson counseled otherwise: "you're a country boy; all you know is that little patch up there in Mississippi you started from" (Faulkner, *Essays* 8). If men grow from native soil, wrote Faulkner thereafter in the *Morning News* (26 April 1925), then Anderson must be "a lusty cornfield in his native Ohio" (*New Orleans* 132–33). Publicly appreciative, but privately holding reservations about Anderson, the artist, Faulkner perceived strengths and weaknesses in geographical stolidity. He determined to avoid the disadvantages by traveling to Europe for enlightenment. It is paradoxical that in fulfilling this determination, Faulkner should miss the epistemological debate surrounding the Scopes Trial. It is a counterbalancing irony, then, that beyond his flirtation with Impressionism and Modernism at the Paris Exposition of 1925, Faulkner would encounter Darwinism nonetheless when concertedly engaging with other prominent aesthetic and critical arguments alive in France at this time.[4]

The definitive legacy from European culture, the approach to literature that would initiate Faulkner's artistic delineation of a Southern Republic, came from the *History of English Literature* (1863–1867) by the French critic and historian Hippolyte Taine (1828–1893). This account comprises one of the first evolutionary hermeneutics. The cultural geography of Carl O. Sauer (1889–1975) may have been, as British academic Neil Campbell believes, ideologically dominant in the United States during the 1920s, but Taine's interpretative approach offers a broader sense of art as a consequence of environment (5). His method explicitly affiliates literary theory with *The Origin of Species*, locating the dominant causal terms of literature in evolutionary biology. Cultural constructions, explains Taine, emerge from the interaction between "the *race*, the *surroundings*, and the *epoch*" (1: 10). "Race" implies innate and hereditary dispositions, physiological and psychological tendencies that vary across different peoples; "surroundings" are the physical and social circumstances of each people; "epoch" being a period and its prevalent ethos. These immanent and external forces necessarily condition human actions. Based on this deterministic doctrine, a critique of a particular writer must start with an analysis of his authorial powers of selection. "Imaginations differ not only in their nature," writes Taine, "but also in their object; after having gauged their energy, we must define their domain; in the broad world the artist makes a world for himself; involuntarily he chooses a class of objects which he prefers; others do not warm his genius, and he does not perceive them" (2: 240).

From this elementary relation between the mind and its object of contemplation, Taine develops detailed topologies of personality and ratiocinative character. These attributes, he maintains, regulate cognitive selection and the manner in which these choices are conceived. Topographical categories, as enumerated by the leading proponent of Taine's hermeneutic today, American academic Joseph Carroll, include emotional elements, conceptual components from the imaginative faculty, and cultural constructs that shape the individual disposition. The Tainian method posits that the internal dynamics of a culture operate only through the psyche of individuals. "The system of reference as a whole," Carroll explains, "is a cognitive map of the total world order, an order that includes the capacity, among human beings, to construct such maps" (99). Taine goes on to formulate a general principle concerning the evolution of this self-contained ability and, although he fails to fashion an adequate causal network between his Darwinian paradigm and his thematic cultural system, he does define an important principle by which literary critics can use the biological relationship between the individual and his surroundings. This theoretical intuition, insists Carroll, "is just and profound" (20).

William Dean Howells (1837–1920) had reviewed Taine's history for the *Atlantic* in 1872. A brilliantly effective method, Howells conceded, but a one-sided approach that is prone to inflexibility. Leslie Stephen (1832–1904) was more appreciative. Though unconvinced by certain opinions about particular artists, Stephen judges that the fundamental Tainian "doctrine is substantially true." Hence, "We ought to study the organism in connection with the medium. Botany becomes more fruitful as we investigate the relations between a given flora and the various conditions of its growth. In the same way a Dante, a Shakespeare, or a Goethe is a flower of literature in no merely fanciful metaphor. We first understand the full significance of their writing when we have made ourselves familiar with the intellectual soil from which they sprang" (82).

The non-Darwinian Henry James (1843–1916) praises Taine's accomplishment too. "He is the author of a really valuable history of English literature," believes James, "Add to this that he is one of the most powerful writers of the day—to our own taste, indeed, the most powerful; the writer of all others who throws over the reader's faculties, for the time, the most irresistible spell, and against whose influence, consequently, the mental reaction is most violent and salutary—and you have an idea of his just claim on your attention" (826). Despite such commendations, the Tainian critique would not command a significant American audience until *A Modern Book of Criticism* by Ludwig Lewisohn (1882–1955) appeared in 1919.

Intended to counter the humanism of Paul Elmer More (1864–1937) and Irving Babbitt (1865–1933) with the radical aesthetics of writers such as the recently deceased Randolph Bourne (1886–1918), *A Modern Book of Criticism* offers several perspectives on Taine. Arnold Bennett, for example, praises contemporary French critics: "When I think of Pierre Bayle, Sainte-Beuve and Taine, and of the keen pleasure I derive from the

Faulkner's vital engagement with evolutionary tenets in spite of his absence from America during the Scopes Trial.

The collection by Carvel Collins of Faulkner's *Early Prose and Poetry* helps to substantiate this Darwinian provenance while illustrating its literary manifestation. In an essay entitled "American Drama: Inhibitions" (1925), Faulkner considers the artistic importance of native subject matter. He cites the river Mississippi and local railroad construction as personal inspiration. Another topographical piece, his criticism of Eugene O'Neill (1888–1953), emphasizes the detrimental effect of shunning the parochial. "Someone has said—a Frenchman probably," writes Faulkner undoubtedly recalling Taine, "that art is preeminently provincial; i.e., it comes directly from a certain age and a certain locality. This is a very profound statement; for Lear and Hamlet . . . could never have been written anywhere save in England during Elizabeth's reign . . . nor could Madame Bovary have been written in any place other than the Rhone Valley in the nineteenth century; and just as Balzac is nineteenth-century Paris" (*Early* 86).

Faulkner also betrays a concern with language in this piece. "Nowhere today," he writes, "saving in parts of Ireland, is the English language spoken with the same earthy strength as it is the United States" (*Early* 89). American English is the "one rainbow we have on our dramatic horizon" (*Early* 95). Faulkner was already bringing the earth (as radix of the human environment), the spectrum (with intimations beyond binary logic), and the language toward a form of Tainian convergence.

The evolutionary critic may have problems substantiating this claim with Faulkner's first novel, *Soldiers' Pay* (1926), but his second, *Mosquitoes* (1927), is more availing.[7] While at the Vieux Carré, Faulkner and Anderson took a number of cruises together on Lake Ponchartrain. Much of *Mosquitoes* concerns such an excursion with Mrs. Maurier overseeing a group of artists on her yacht, the *Nausikaa*. One of them, Dawson Fairchild, is a caricature of Anderson. This depiction plays with various biographical details, including Anderson's year of further education at a small Lutheran college in Wittenberg, Ohio.[8] Fairchild recounts to Theodore Robyn, the nephew of his hostess, aspects of this sectarian education. His anecdote includes the only direct reference to the Old Gentleman of English science in Faulkner's canon. Briefly, but overtly, Darwin and Faulkner go hand in hand: "I learned in spite of the instructors we had. They were a bunch of broken down preachers: head full of dogma and intolerance and a belly full of big meaningless words. English literature course whittled down Shakespeare because he wrote about whores without pointing a moral and one instructor always insisted that the head devil in *Paradise Lost* was an inspired prophetic portrait of Darwin" (348).⁹

At one level, auguring Charles Darwin from a Miltonic character is a naïve comparison that provokes humor. At another level, Faulkner consciously upbraids those who want to rule unquestioned, those who dogmatize, and those who tell inquiring minds to be dilatory and discreet.

Obstinate disregard for Darwinism soon reemerges in a debate concerning education and art between Fairchild and two other guests, Eva Wiseman and her brother Julius Kauffman. This Tainian discussion is, in effect, an aesthetic rendition of factions diametrically opposed. Fairchild may be a published novelist, yet he lacks self-confidence. "Having been born an American of a provincial middle western lower middle class family," states Eva Wiseman, "he has inherited all the lower middle class's awe of Education with a capital E" (453). For Julius and Eva, this inheritance solidifies Fairchild's circumscribed views about art. They insist that "literature is art and biology isn't" (404), while alleging that their interlocutor clings "to one little spot of the earth's surface" with his "belief that the function of creating art depends on geography." The environment in which the artist works, counters Fairchild, is everything. "You can't grow corn without something to plant it in." Kauffman attributes this attitude to artistic lassitude, amassing trivialities to affect originality; Eva does not. "You don't plant corn in geography," she explains, "you plant it in soil. It not only does not matter where that soil is, you can even move the soil from one place to another—around the world, if you like—and it will still grow corn." Environmental concerns, she concludes, lead to aesthetic bewilderment. "You'd have a different kind of corn, though," retorts Fairchild, "Russian corn, or Latin or Anglo-Saxon corn." Kauffman closes the argument epigrammatically. "All corn," he concludes, "is the same to the belly" (406). The tension between topological determination and complex ontology is bearable for Eva and Julius, but difficult for Fairchild to stomach. Faulkner's analogy in *Mosquitoes* was premonitory. On the one hand, his awareness of Tainian ideas fed by concepts beyond Taine's ambit would establish him as a revolutionary writer with a developing aesthetic. On the other hand, Anderson would fail to develop as an artist. The inference was clear; Anderson and Faulkner fell out, never restoring their friendship.

Mosquitoes offers another split, one that helps to chart Faulkner's artistic debt to Darwin, in the apparent disparity between civilization and nature. Faulkner sets his excursion against the prelapsarian background of the Louisiana delta. Human power over nature, however, comes to a jarring halt when the *Nausikaa* grounds in shallows. Ennui sets in among the guests, and the conversation degenerates into uneasy social prattle. Patricia Robyn escapes the tedium early the next morning aided by the steward David West. They secretly disembark, hoping that a change of surroundings will cure their fatigue. Once on dry land, though, they discover an environment relinquished to the dawn of human time, a world inhabited by lizards and snakes, an ecology to which humans are no longer suited. The swamp is not deep, the two explorers are on their way, but they are soon out of their depth. Nature, as characterized by the indigenous mosquitoes, holds sway over humanity. The biting insects literally bring Patricia and David to their knees. Stranded on the margins between civilization and wilderness, they flounder in appalling straits. On board, meanwhile, Patricia and David's disappearance intensifies the unease engendered by the uninhabited surroundings. To provide relief, Fairchild begins to ridicule one source of the tension, the specter of evolutionary regression—his tale telling revitalizing the anecdotes that Faulkner had concocted with Anderson during the spring of 1925. One of their characters, recalls Faulkner, "was supposed to be a descendant of Andrew Jackson, left in that Louisiana swamp after the Battle of Chalmette, no longer half-horse half-alligator but by now half-man half-sheep and presently half-shark, who—it, the whole fable—at last got so unwieldy and (so we thought) so funny, that we decided to get it onto paper by writing letters to one another such as two temporarily separated members of an exploring-zoological expedition might" (*Essays* 7).[10]

Mosquitoes recapitulates these evolutionary vignettes in a slightly more considered fashion. Major Ayers, the retired English army officer, full of irksome hot air, is often the subject of this ribbing. Fairchild first tells of the animal breeding antics of Maj. Gen. Andrew Jackson (1767–1845). He had crossed horses with alligators to provide suitable mounts for his cavalry when confronting the British in the marshes outside New Orleans in 1812 (308–9). Ayers replies to Fairchild's story with a yarn of his own concerning the death of an Eton schoolboy from a surfeit of apple tarts. Parliament immediately passed a bill, Ayers assures his listeners, prohibiting children from buying the desert within the British Empire. "The former generation died off, and now the present generation never heard of apple tarts" (310). Inheritance is a fountainhead of mirth—biological in the case of the artist, cultural for the major. Even so, the party remains anxious concerning the immanent prospect of human atavism. These tendencies arise, Fairchild concedes, when there is a "submerging of civilized strictures before the grand implacability of nature and the physical body" (447). Civilization, a product of "that species all of whose actions are controlled by words," has a natural foundation (360). The grounded yacht symbolizes this spasmodically emerging and ineluctable essence. Aware of vestigial unease, Fairchild reprises Andrew Jackson and his "idea of taking up some of this Louisiana swamp land and raising sheep on it" (482). However, when accustomed to the water, and much to Jackson's chagrin, his stock becomes refractory. His farmers must now herd them using a boat. On landing their first catch, they discover that "only the top of its back had any wool on it. The rest of its body was scaled like a fish. And when they finally caught one of the spring lambs on an alligator hook, they found that its tail had broadened out and flattened like a beaver's, and it had no legs at all" (483).

Al's son Claude dives into the swamp to catch the remaining sheep, but he too suffers a form of evolutionary regression. Disappearing for a fortnight, he surfaces in local waters. Is it Claude? His "eyes had kind of shifted around to the side of his head and his mouth had spread back a good way, and his teeth had got longer." Though Claude was never seen again, adds Fairchild, "there was a shark scare at the bathing beaches along the Gulf coast." Women were particularly at risk. Therefore, insists Fairchild, the shark *was* Claude Jackson, because he "was always hell after blondes" (485). With the tale of Claude's degeneration, Fairchild has helped to deflate further the Darwinian fears among his companions. Meantime, a swamp-dwelling local, the only type of human fitted to that harsh environment, has rescued Patricia and David. With their return to the *Nausikaa*, and the refloating of the boat, the civilized domain restores its superiority over the natural world. When she "transforms nature into a decadent stage set," maintains Thomas L. McHaney, Mrs. Maurier immediately resumes her role as hostess while Fairchild, suitably cheered, makes claims for the superiority of fiction over reality (25). The Modernist precept that nature is not a natural construct and that "the many appearances in the world are less 'true' than the abstract design produced by their juxtaposition" are therefore, as McHaney argues, brought to the fore; Faulkner's formative point of view being one in which the artist "may do whatever is necessary with the natural world to render the world according to art" (29). *Mosquitoes* is a rendition in this vein, but one that implies, supplementary to McHaney's summation, that humankind ignores the revelations of Darwin at a potential cost.

Accepting that Faulkner's multifarious interest in Darwinism is apparent in this novel, how does *Mosquitoes* fit into his evolving body of work? Writing about the Faulknerian hero, James B. Carothers concludes that there is "a movement from situations of paralysis and despair for his early protagonists [*Soldiers' Pay* (1926) to *Sanctuary* (1931)], through situations of heroic gesture in the middle period [*Light in August* (1932) through to *Go Down, Moses* (1942)], to situations of cooperative action in the novels of the last phase [*Intruder in the Dust* (1948) to *The Reivers* (1962)]" (279).

Carothers's index offers a useful set of chronological phases with *Mosquitoes* a constituent of Faulkner's first creative period. However, the present study wishes to stress the continuous ideological and aesthetic advance of the Faulknerian oeuvre. The poststructuralist Karl F. Zender, unconsciously rejecting a series of synchronic stages in showing "how Faulkner's use of motif changes over time," therefore validates the diachronic approach followed herein (*Crossing* xiv). Thus, in considering the paradigm of Darwinian evolution as a literary hermeneutic, one acknowledges Carothers's broader assertion that: "There is certainly a design or a combination of designs within an individual Faulkner text, there are designs formed by the relations among successive texts, and there may even be a design or a combination of designs within the entire canon, but it is best to approach the latter design as a dynamic one" (258). Darwinian notions are crucial to Faulknerian dynamism, and they remain pressing issues as his art evolves.

Flags in the Dust (1929; 1973) evinces this development thanks in part to the editorial rejection of the original manuscript. Faulkner changed publishers. Nonetheless, Harcourt & Brace would accept this work only if he made alterations and extensive cuts. To complete his task, and in a pattern that would recur in later life, Faulkner decided to change his environment. He moved, temporarily, to New York, purposefully shifting the cultural constructs that shaped, limited, and directed his disposition. Robert Walton, Leon Scales, and James Devine shared his rented apartment (Blotner, *Biography* 1: 592). Scales, a postgraduate in philosophy, and Devine, a masters student in journalism, were both attending Columbia University seminars chaired by John Dewey (1859–1952) (Blotner, *Biography* 1: 588).

Dewey, a pragmatic educational and philosophical reformer, scrupulously conflated idealism with evolutionary science to advance a common faith. He eschewed a God of individual or Trinitarian form in favor of a divine presence. The numinous offers ideal possibilities to humankind, argued Dewey, with evolution promoting the desire toward such ends. Dewey believed that societal development could unify this struggle for actualization. One of his personal aims was therefore to compare ideal aims with actual conditions. In this manner, he wished to orient human actions along divinely inspired directions. Dewey's theistic evolution was controversial. Chapter 1 documents religious objections to this form of theism, but secular contentions also emerged, because Dewey's theory reasserted a challenge, an objection previously prosecuted along different lines by Arthur Schopenhauer (1788–1860), to the established doctrine of secular teleology.

Developed in Germany from the work of Gottfried Wilhelm von Leibniz (1646–1716), Immanuel Kant, Gotthold Ephraim Lessing (1729–1781), and Johann Gottfried von Herder (1744–1803), this school of thought dispenses with the notion of divine intervention while attributing an immanent drive toward the predetermined goal of perfection to all natural processes. Ernst Heinrich Haeckel (1834–1919) extended this German teleological provenance throughout the second half of the nineteenth century by developing a monistic interpretation of Darwin's theories. This *Darwinismus*, as explicated in his *Generelle Morphologie der Organismen* (1866) and *Natürliche Schöpfungsgeschichte* (1868), recognized evolution as the unifying principle directing life on Earth.[11] Haeckel's tenet helped the philosopher Friedrich Nietzsche (1844–1900), also a member of the Darwinismus movement, to evaluate whether particular patterns of human behavior were either evolutionary or degenerate. Thomas Henry Huxley objected. While Darwinism leaves the divine open to question, argues *Man's Place in Nature* (1863), teleology plays no part in evolution. Darwin appreciated the prescience of his "Bulldog" and *The Descent of Man and Selection in Relation to Sex* (1871) would assimilate some of Huxley's rhetoric and imagery. Nonetheless, this formidable collaboration failed to disillusion adherents to the old school, as the publication of Haeckel's *Anthropogenie oder Entwickelungsgeschichte des Menschen* (1874) averred.[12] A cultural history formulated from the same basis was also proposed by Matthew Arnold (1822–1888), teleological evolution retaining credence until Dewey published *The Influence of Darwin on Philosophy* in 1910. Dewey's text argues that the logic behind teleology results from an evolutionary predisposition toward attaining the ideal. "In all living forms," reasons Dewey, "a specific type is present directing the earlier stages of growth to the realization of its own perfection. Since this purposive regulative principle is not visible to the senses, it follows that it must be an ideal or rational force. Since, however, the perfect form is gradually approximated through the sensible changes, it also follows that in and through a sensible realm a rational ideal force is working out its own ultimate manifestation" (10). Extending these inferences to nature: "(a) She does nothing in vain; but all for an ulterior purpose. (b) Within natural sensible events there is therefore contained a spiritual causal force, which as spiritual escapes perception, but is apprehended by an enlightened reason. (c) The manifestation of this principle brings about a subordination of matter and sense to its own realization, and this ultimate fulfillment is the goal of nature and of man" (10).

Arnold's rationale, summarizes Dewey, was natural.[13] The pre-Darwinian model of humans at the center of a divine universe was intuitive to Western reasoning. Innate, concludes Dewey, but erroneous. The fallacious aspects of teleological beliefs could now be unmasked by sorting all seemingly end-directed phenomena into four classes. The first two categories, the *Zweckmässig* and the *cosmic*, are false. Zweckmässig phenomena, Kant's understanding of intricate organic structures like the brain or heart, are actually organismic adaptations that have evolved for specific and complex purposes. Cosmic teleology, the immanent purpose of the world as an unrelenting impulse toward perfection, lacks scientific proof. The second two categories, the *teleomatic* and the *teleonomic*, do exist. Teleomatic phenomena are natural processes with an automatic termination strictly determined by the laws of physics. A hot object cooling is a common example. Teleonomic processes are those controlled by genetic codes. Organismic development from conception to maturation is a notable instance. Modern reasoning thereby establishes natural selection as the self-concealing yet liberating teleology within evolution. Being an end in itself, this autotelic process offers innumerable dysteleological futures. One particularly pessimistic outcome was extinction. Humans must remember, advises the first edition of *The Origin of Species*, "that every single organic being around us may be said to be striving to the utmost to increase in numbers; that each lives by a struggle at some period of its life; that heavy destruction inevitably falls either on the young or old, during each generation or at recurrent intervals" (23).

If circumstances work to mitigate the struggle for members of a species, then the size of their colonies can soar. The consequences for other organisms might be grave. "The face of Nature," continues Darwin, "may be compared to a yielding surface, with ten thousand sharp wedges packed close together and driven inwards by incessant blows, sometimes one wedge being struck, and then another with greater force" (23). The benign appearance of nature was a culturally constructed facade. Dewey appreciated the starkness of this conclusion. Furthermore, in recognizing Darwinism as a philosophy, the American reformer was a rarity.

Faulkner gained from Dewey's prescient ambit, and his New York experience tempers the contention of Ransom and Brooks that he lacked any form of intellectual society as a result of his Mississippian residence (Brooks 10). On the one hand, Faulkner would benefit from a Deweyan influence on his religious beliefs. Rejecting God as a human persona in favor of a divine presence, Faulkner would come to abjure the Christian Church (in whatever denomination) as a form of dogmatic establishment, the theistic strand of his evolutionary philosophy developing toward a divinely imbued stoicism. This designation confirms the long-accepted stoic Christianity with which John Hunt labeled Faulkner in *Art in Theology Tension* (1965), but contends further that the self-associated verities of "courage, honor, pride, compassion, pity" would remain of a numinously inspired importance to him (*University* 133).[14] On the other hand, Dewey's philosophical course would enable Faulkner to resist the predisposed trap into which Arnold had fallen. Faulkner would preserve the divine within an evolutionary paradigm full of dysteleological possibilities.

Only with the publication of the original *Flags in the Dust* in 1973 did scholars have the chance to appreciate Faulkner's next attempt to illustrate this conception, because the shortened novel (named *Sartoris*) crucially attenuates his evolutionary imperative. This study therefore cites the unexpurgated version. The novel opens in the wake of the Armistice to World War I. Three local men, survivors of that exceptionally hostile environment, are coming home to Yoknapatawpha from France. The county town of Faulkner's Southern Republic, Jefferson, offers them the prospect of a benign future. Such hope, Faulkner will emphasize, is naïve. Horace Benbow, Bayard Sartoris, and one of the Sartoris servants, Caspey, have survived, but Bayard's twin brother, John, remains lost in action. Until Bayard's reappearance at the family home, his grandfather

Old Bayard (1849–1919) has refused to acknowledge John's death. Now, with these homecomings, he must accept a sense of closure. Committing the name of his lost grandson to paper symbolizes this conclusion. Old Bayard retrieves the family Bible for this act and adds John's name to the family tree.[15] His patriarchal actions adumbrate an understanding of aristocratic heredity. Aristocracy, Gail Mortimer insists, "can justify itself only by an appeal to a divine and static order, which it strives to emulate" (195). The ordered fluidity of a scientific world as proposed by Darwin—or a godless world such as that propounded by Nietzsche—has no place in Old Bayard's philosophical outlook. Hoping to safeguard the social status of his family, Old Bayard continues the process of *paleonymy*. On the one hand, he suppresses new names, meanings, and concepts; on the other hand, he sustains the revenants of living memory. Elderly diviner Will Falls, one of a diminishing number of Civil War veterans whose gift for nostalgia maintains aristocratic pretensions, thereby remains a welcome guest.[16] However, in recalling an exchange between Col. John Sartoris and a captured Northern officer during the American Civil War, Will unintentionally discloses the fate of the South. "No gentleman has any business in this war," the Unionist had asserted. "There is no place for him here. He is an anachronism" (*Flags* 21). The imminent threat of carpetbaggers endorsed this contention. Southerners applied this term to Northerners seeking private gain in the postbellum South, concurrently assuming them proponents of African American political enfranchisement.[17]

Col. John Sartoris's response to Northern encroachment was severe. During his railroad building days of the 1870s, Falls recalls, the colonel shot such men dead (6). Repeating himself later, Falls reassures his listeners that the "two cyarpet-baggers [who] brung them niggers in to vote that day in '72" (263) were "two nawthuners" (264). If one construes these murders as part of an ecological struggle for existence, then the colonel's violent death is a fitting riposte. The epitaph on his gravestone may describe him as a "Soldier, Statesman, Citizen of the World," but it also reads, "Fell at the hand of——Redlaw, Aug. 4, 1876" (428). The red law of tooth and claw is ascendant.[18] The effigy of the colonel on the pedestal to his gravestone, a figure with head "lifted a little in that gesture of haughty arrogance which repeated itself generation after generation with a fateful fidelity, his back to the world," does not dispel the allusion (427).[19] The statue not only embodies the introspective component of the southern states of America, but it also symbolizes extinction as the ultimate fate for loyalty to such an ethos. This verity, suggests *Flags in the Dust*, is set in stone.

By 1918 the youngest generation in the Sartoris lineage is composed of a single member. The family line is heading toward a dead end. New families coming to Yoknapatawpha, empowering a dynamic between systematic stasis and social evolution, threaten to hasten rather than to avert this conclusion. A parasitic presence, the family Snopes, has already settled from this flux. Blotner notes that the Oxford *Eagle* for 23 April 1925 "recorded in the society notices the visit of a Mrs. Otis Snipes of Tyro" (*Biography* 2: 1798n). This news may have inspired Faulkner in naming the Snopes clan but, as Harry Modean Campbell and Ruel E. Foster suppose, he may have chosen a surname beginning with "Sn" because the English language contains so many unpleasant and crude words starting with this root (104). Sneer, snide, and snotty immediately come to mind. One must also take into account the onomatopoeic sense of the name. The 1933 edition of the *Oxford English Dictionary* (OED) states that "snop" is a dialect verb, one imitative of the noise made by a smart blow. To snop can also mean to break an object in such a manner. Quoting from the posthumous *Field and Hedgerow* (1889) by Richard Jefferies (1848–1887), the OED explains that threshing was a job much enjoyed by agricultural hands, "but only a few of them could get barns to snop away in." This action nicely describes the Snopeses breaking into and settling down in Jefferson. Joseph R. Urgo surmises that the name Snopes also articulates a constant denial of authority, the family's "nopes." All these proposals, especially Urgo's are cogent, but further significance remains. In "A Note on the Origin of Flem Snopes," Gerald J. Smith makes a proposal that anticipates my own. Faulkner did not concoct the surname Snopes "from the reaches of his immense imagination," argues Smith, but figured this family as "the shrewd, calculating modernistic order that takes over in the South" (56). The proceedings at Dayton, he continues, epitomized this spirit of modern rapacity: "Scopes came to be synonymous with the scientific method of proving everything, admitting of no sentiment or warmth. Whether he wished it or not, he became allied with what the South called the atheistic, tradition-hating forces of Progress. He became the figurehead of all that Flem Snopes represented later, in Faulkner's fiction" (56–57).

Smith's supposition is a bold one. Making the false assumption that Faulkner was working in New Orleans throughout the trial does not favor his argument. Faulkner may have intended a parallel between John

T. Scopes, as an agent who exposed southern tensions with respect to modernity, and these outlandish agents of self-interest, but a one-to-one relationship between the Tennessean teacher and a particular Snopes cannot be defended. Phil Stone's testimony validates this conclusion. According to Stone, he and Faulkner first invented a rapacious clan during the early twenties. However, "it is the seminal distinction between the two friends," writes Susan Snell, "that Faulkner and not Stone gave those creatures the name Snopes. Stone could not remember at what stage that occurred, only that the 'name had no connection with the Stopes [*sic*] trial'" (198). "All Bill ever said about" the Snopes surname, Faulkner's brother John would later write, "was that it was the luckiest thing that ever happened in his writing" (269). The most one can claim, then, is that the Scopes Trial pulled Faulkner's Snopesish sense of the struggle for existence into sharper focus.

Thus, remnants of the Old South in Yoknapatawpha attempt to stay, or at least ignore, the advance of modernity personified by the Snopes. Grandfather Bayard is one such inveterate. Wealth, servants, and leisure, all bear witness to a habitual disposition that owes more to genealogy than to class or race. The family retainer, Simon, exemplifies this form of thinking with his faithfulness to the patriciate cause. Williamson explains: "The concern of many late masters for their ex-slaves was matched by the interest of individual Negroes in the welfare of their recent owners. A freedman seeking relief for a white family from a Bureau officer explained his motivation: 'I used to belong to one branch of that family, and so I takes an interest in 'em'" (*After Slavery* 295).

Old Bayard and Simon, children from the antebellum racial divide, retain modes of behavior established long before secession. Their lives, circumscribed by demarcation, follow strict routine. The end of each working day at the Sartoris Bank conforms to this pattern. Old Bayard, as president, retains a hitching post outside his office "with a testy disregard of industrial progress" (*Flags* 7). Simon collects him every afternoon in a surrey drawn by a team of matched horses. "De ottomobile," Simon muses, "is all right for pleasure and excitement, but fer de genu-wine gen'lmun tone, dey aint but one thing: dat's hosses" (259). Implicit in this conflict between the Old South and modernity is the contrast between the power of horses and horsepower. On another errand, Simon goes to pick up great-aunt Jenny, but another woman's car obstructs his accustomed parking bay. "Block off de commonality, ef you wants," chides Simon, "but dont intervoke no equipage waitin' on Cunnel er

Miss Jenny. Dey wont stand for it" (26). Simon practices a steadfast allegiance.

Social evolution, however, undermines deference. World War I was responsible for a denuding of the younger generation, but the repatriation of survivors also signaled the gradual extinction of previous generations and their mores. With the conflict in Europe settled, Aunt Jenny trusts that the Sartoris household will revert to the forms of etiquette established before 1917. The return of Simon's grandson, Caspey, disillusions her. "Who was the fool anyway," complains Jenny, "who thought of putting niggers into the same uniform with white men? Mr. Vardaman knew better," she continues, citing the Mississippi senator who objected to the conscription of African Americans: "He told those fools at Washington at the time that it wouldn't do" (68). The war opened Caspey's eyes to the possibilities of freedom beyond manumission. Men in uniform appear homogeneous and the uniformity of men at war adumbrates the possibility of a social system without segregation. The shared danger of conflict has implied equality in peace. Caspey's interpretation of this promise sustains unease because beyond his Saturday night exploits and newly acquired ambivalence toward work, his assertion that "I got my white in France, and I'm gwine git it here, too" invokes the specter of interracial sex (67). Although a braggadocio, Caspey is now identified, to appropriate Walter Benn Michaels, "with the failure of the white reproductive ability and the increased prominence of nonwhites in America" (94). Even *The Rising Tide of Color against White World-Supremacy* (1920) by Lothrop Stoddard (1883–1950), a Spencerian tract that dismisses blacks as recklessly procreative, would offer the ruling race little comfort in these circumstances. *Flags in the Dust* certainly exposes these fears, but it does so to dispel them. By the close of the novel, and much to Jenny's relief, Caspey "had more or less returned to normalcy"—white normalcy that is (224).

Caspey's attitude toward the Sartorises, though, is as nothing when compared to the danger Young Bayard now presents. The only surviving male heir of the House of Sartoris, Young Bayard is torn between the cultural expectations implicit in his recorded genealogy, and the possibilities promised by a modern world where such standards are no longer of overriding importance. Emerging technologies, especially cars and airplanes, manifest this enticement. Henry Ford (1863–1947) had established his Detroit-based automobile company in 1903. Within ten years, he had developed assembly line techniques.[20] Tradition was moribund; modernity was mechanization. Aeronautical exploits had made Dayton, Ohio, and Kitty Hawk, North Carolina, other prominent places in the national consciousness. The first location was the birthplace of Wilbur (1867–1912) and Orville Wright (1871–1948), later being the site of many of their experimental flights. The second locality was the setting for their first powered flight, also in 1903. The Schneider Trophy then helped to establish the reputation of American aeronautics worldwide.

This form of modernity is unfortunate for the genealogical prospects of the Sartorises. This "roaring" environment appeals to their prominent male characteristic of recklessness. Young Bayard, as Faulkner intends, embodies the tension that plays out between these antithetical demands. Symbolic of his postwar disaffection is the horse-riding accident that leaves him with concussion. Even traditional means of southern conveyance have become unreliable. Concurrently, vestiges of tradition taint his ability to control mechanical means of transport. Driving about Yoknapatawpha at high speed, Young Bayard has two serious crashes. The first incident requires his incarceration for several months in a plaster cast; the second accident leaves his grandfather, a senior citizen not adaptable to emerging forces, dead.

Confronted with his actions, Young Bayard absconds to the backwoods. He leaves Yoknapatawpha for a fraught existence, one of dissipation that comes to a violent end over an airfield in Ohio. Flying a prototype, the symbolic apogee of modernity, he is killed at Dayton in 1920. Localizing Bayard's death at a spot that combines intimations of the Scopes trial with the history of aeronautics, Faulkner ingeniously spells out the reason why the long-established order is tending toward extinction.

Flags in the Dust reiterates the cultural aspect of this closure through the character of Simon. Blinded by patrician inculcation, he predicts a phoenix from the dust of the old system. He pins his reactionary anticipation on Bayard's pregnant wife Narcissa (née Benbow). She eventually gives birth to a boy on the day of her husband's death. "And soon as I get that fool boy home"—says Simon, as yet unaware of Bayard's fatal accident—"it'll be like old times again" (421). Narcissa's labor forebodes otherwise. The family doctor, Loosh Peabody, does not attend the birth. "This is the first Sartoris you've been a day late on in how many years, Loosh?" jibes Simon, who then asks Loosh when will he visit the newborn. "Soon, Simon" is the noncommittal reply (422). Loosh's tardiness and his reticence hint that the baby will not fulfill Simon's expectations.

His diagnosis proves to be correct. News of Bayard's accident reaches Jefferson, and Simon is dead shortly thereafter—his murder by an African American signifying the violent repudiation by the subjugated of subjects who remain unreconstructed. Only Bayard's son, Benbow, remains to sustain the European American old guard. He will have to struggle for existence, *Flags in the Dust* concludes, in an inescapably deterministic environment.

The short story "Red Leaves" (1930) further illustrates Faulkner's interest during this period in the ineluctable force of evolution.[21] Darwin's *A Naturalist's Voyage* (1839) is, Peter G. Beidler asserts, the main source for this tale (421). That Darwin's publication was influential on Sherwood Anderson mitigates any surprise at this prominence. "When I read stories of the lives of genuine great men," admits Anderson, "how they have struggled and suffered, from Abelard to Thomas Mann, Keats and Anton Chekhov in their loving and fight against disease, de Maupassant and van Gogh struggling against insanity, Herbert Spencer against poverty, Charles Darwin on his trip to the tropics in the ship *Beagle* to his long months of horrible suffering, his determination and perseverance . . . and then look back on my own small efforts as an American storyteller, I have to sum up the story of my own life as a most fortunate one" (*Memoirs* 11).

Specific to "Red Leaves" is chapter 10 of *A Naturalist's Voyage* in which Darwin documents his experiences in Tierra del Fuego. Faulkner's Native Americans are correlatives for Darwin's Fuegians. The Chickasaw name "Three Basket" is a Faulknerian appropriation from the common South American appellation of "Basket" referred to numerously in the naturalist's diaries. More significantly, Faulkner appears to have modeled Moketubbe on Darwin's description of the "short, thick, and fat" Jemmy Button. "Vain of his personal appearance," comments Darwin, "fond of admiring himself in a looking-glass," Button "used always to wear gloves, his hair was neatly cut, and he was distressed if his well-polished shoes were dirtied" (207). From a Faulknerian perspective, these quotes recall Moketubbe's physical appearance in addition to his insistence on fashionable dress. Furthermore, the similarity between Faulkner's figures of Ikkemotubbe (or Doom) and Issetibbeha, and two Fuegians, York Minster and Fuegia Basket, is undeniable. Darwin's Fuegians were returning home after their abduction by Captain Robert Fitzroy (1805–1865) three years earlier, Faulkner's Ikkemotubbe experiencing a return to his people after a lengthy spell mixing with the white Americans of Mississippi.

Though not discussed by Beidler, Faulkner also draws his representation of onerous dependency from Darwin. African slaves in "Red Leaves" are coterminous with Fuegian dependants in *A Naturalist's Voyage*. The ultimate doom of Doom's slave resonates with the Darwinian account of utility and rankness in Fuegian culture. When starvation threatens, notes Darwin, the young men "kill and devour their old women before they kill their dogs." Dogs can catch wildlife; old women cannot hunt. If potential victims escape, then "they are pursued by the men and brought back to the slaughter-house at their own firesides" (207). The flight of Ikkemotubbe's African slave after his master's death is an analogue to these desperate and futile efforts to evade capture. "When the chief went back to the earth," according to Faulkner's understanding of Chickasaw custom, "his body servant and his dogs and his horse went with him" (*University* 63). In the Faulknerian natural economy, apparent in the protracted recapture of the African slave, irremediable inactivity denotes death, while serviceable dynamism asserts the power and potentiality of evolution. "The red leaves referred to the Indian," Faulkner explained. They were "the deciduation of Nature which no one could stop that had suffocated, smothered, destroyed the Negro. That the red leaves had nothing against him when they suffocated him and destroyed him. They had nothing against him, they probably liked him, but it was normal deciduation which the red leaves, whether they regretted it or not, had nothing more to say in" (*University* 39).

This extirpation of the individual is part of an inescapable process that, as the term deciduation indicates in stripping a tree, can decree the fate of an entire people. The Chickasaw may have accounted for the occasional African, but in Faulkner's paradigm, extinction was the natural fate of autochthonous Americans. History confirmed this belief. "The last days of the Chickasaws in Mississippi were," laments Doyle, "a sad spectacle" (51). Wandering primitives capable of relocation without hardship had been the picture "effectively promoted to justify their dispossession" by land hungry commissioners. Reality, as Doyle asserts, proved somewhat different: "Suspended between the world they had been dispossessed of and the strange new one they were headed for, many of them simply refused to accept their fate. Some fell into a demoralized pattern of drunkenness and violence, while others played ball and frolicked, spending their land proceeds liberally" (51).

Those who remained in their accustomed environment could extend their legacy, but their genealogy was no longer unique. "The Indians in my part of Mississippi," believed Faulkner, "have vanished into the races—either the white race or the Negro race. You see traces of the features in the Negroes and a few of the old names in among white families, old white families" (*University* 9). These originals, the Algonquian, Chickasaw, Choctaw, Natchez, and Pascagoula, were "the obsolescent, dispossessed tomorrow by the already obsolete": demographic fluxion brought about by the "alien nations" of England, France, Portugal, and Spain (*Essays* 13). Similarly, when the red leaves fell in Tierra del Fuego, the Oens, according to Darwin, would cross the mountains to attack their neighbors in an attempt to wipe them out (*Naturalist's Voyage* 220). Faulkner's youthful determinism, the analogy insists, goes hand in hand with pessimistic Darwinism.

CHAPTER 3

THE COMPLEX TEMPLE OF SEXUAL POLITICS

"What's Talliaferro's trouble?" asked the semitic man.
"The illusion that you can seduce women. Which you can't: they just elect you."

William Faulkner, *Mosquitoes* (359)

ALTHOUGH *THE ORIGIN OF SPECIES* POSITED SEXUAL SELECTION AS A counterpart to natural selection, Charles Darwin's rigorous explanation of his secondary theory did not appear until the publication of *The Descent of Man* twelve years later. Darwin had based his primary mechanism on dispassionate observations of nature with his mold-breaking arguments influenced above all by the ecology of the English North Downs. Unexceptional in comparison with the exotic locations encountered during his youthful expeditions overseas, the county of Kent nevertheless provided a landscape of rich diversity, which filled Darwin with enthusiasm. Surrounded by untrammeled countryside, in an environment conducive to contemplation, he spent much of the 1860s reevaluating his thoughts concerning evolutionary selection. The limitations to his principal theory proliferated with physiological overstatement and sexual dimorphism the most pressing of ambiguities. His supplementary hypothesis thereby gained importance as an additional evolutionary process and demanded further development.

Darwin took a basic asymmetry in gamete size to be the first principle of sexual differentiation in the *Mammalia* class of vertebrates. Females produce large eggs, while males form far smaller spermatozoa. As a corollary, female production of gametes is scarce in comparison to the superabundance of sex cells carried by males. This relative rarity makes females the more valuable members of mammalian species, males the more expendable. Sexual difference therefore affords females a choice of partners. In primal populations, reasoned Darwin, male desirability depends on physiological indicators of evolutionary fitness. Males must compete among themselves in the presence of potential mates to demonstrate their sexual potential. Demure females choose sexual partners depending on the impression made by combative males. The Darwinian term for this demonstrative competition and subsequent choice is courtship. This interactive process holds significance for the forthcoming generation because progeny tend to inherit paternal traits—male offspring appertaining to attractive fathers will themselves embody physical attractiveness. These male descendants will dominate copulation during the next generation. Natural selection continues to favor descendants of such individuals because sexual attractiveness becomes the most desirable quality an individual can possess. Retaining the term sexual selection from *The Origin of Species* to designate this reproductive advantage as realized over numerous generations, *The Descent of Man* then partitions this subdivision of selectivity into intrasexual and intersexual classes. In the former category, males compete among each other for access to females; in the latter class, females discriminate among males in search of partners. Intrasexual selection, according to Darwin, has promoted the physiological enhancement and the fighting ability of males, while intersexual selection has fostered elaborate male displays under the authority of female choice. Hence, courtship contains features evolved through selectivity with respect to sex, sexual selection that in turn relies on mating behavior to aid the furtherance of the species through procreation. Secondary selectivity acts in a less thorough manner than natural selection does, *The Descent of Man* concludes, yet the "exertion of some choice on the part of the female seems a law almost as general as the eagerness of the male" (132). Procreation, as Darwin realized, is not the limiting sphere of influence for sexual selection, because the kindred interactions involved in this process contribute to societal progress. Evolution, powered by natural and sexual selection over innumerable generations, is therefore a biological base capable of spawning a social superstructure. Humans, Darwin concluded, have begun to fulfill this potential.

What Darwin did not appreciate to a profound degree, however, was the manner in which this superstructure has conditioned humans to think themselves divorced from the animal kingdom and the natural order as a whole. Darwin's own formulation of sexual selection suffered from this conditioning on two fronts. Firstly, as American academic Rosemary Jann argues, isolation at Down forced Darwin to rely on social anthropology as his major research material, *Primitive Marriage* (1865) by John Ferguson McLennan (1827–1881) and *The Origin of Civilisation and the Primitive Condition of Man* (1870) from Sir John Lubbock (1834–1913) being important texts (296). It is monogamous marriage, these works insist, that confirms the ascendance of *Homo sapiens* over lower forms of life. In consequence, human sexuality is not rooted in animal behavior; rather, the projection onto other species of attitudes and qualities attributable to humans offers an appropriate tool for dealing with the primal form of sexual selection evident in animals. To British scholar John R. Durant, this anthropomorphic technique was Darwin's second misjudgment, an error whereby he cast animal courtship in terms of a reserved Victorian woman selecting her desired mate for a life of spousal fidelity (291–92). Moreover, having constructed animal sexuality in accordance with Victorian mores, Darwin then reversed his direction of interpolation, projecting his construction onto the selection techniques of humans. Nineteenth-century sexual politics—defined as sexuality, secondary selection, and sex within a sociobiological context—had merely validated nineteenth-century conventions. Darwinian sexual selection begged the question.

Thomas Henry Huxley, while agreeing with Darwin about the insufficiency of natural selection as the sole mechanism behind evolution, remained reticent about secondary selectivity until after his mentor's death. This eventual engagement concentrated on the overriding importance of direct selection as controlled by humans. "I remain of the opinion," Huxley concludes in *Darwiniana* (1893), "that until selective breeding is definitely proved to give rise to varieties infertile with one another, the logical foundation of the theory of natural selection is incomplete" (Preface II). Although not refuting Darwinian sexual selectivity as a theory, Huxley's lack of comment on the subject speaks volumes: secondary selection is too arbitrary and overly subject to female caprice. The direct alternative, which enables the assessment of procreative results for their utility, is more assured in Huxley's view. This approach should lead to more rapid and exploitable progress in plant and animal breeding than natural processes can attain. His "Prolegomena" (1894) drives home this point. Nature, on the one hand, "uses unrestricted multiplication as the means whereby hundreds compete for the place and nourishment adequate for one; it employs frost and drought to cut off the weak and unfortunate; to survive, there is need not only of strength, but of flexibility and of good fortune" (*Collected Essays* 13–14). The gardener, on the other hand, "restricts multiplication; provides that each plant shall have sufficient space and nourishment; protects from frost and drought; and, in every other way, attempts to modify the conditions, in such a manner as to bring about the survival of those forms which most nearly approach the standard of the useful, or the beautiful, which he has in his mind" (14).

For the horticulturist, therefore, nature is "only one of the means by which selection may be effected" (15). With the ideal of utility and beauty concerning vegetables, fruit, and flowers in mind, and despite the manner of sexual selection in plants being very different to that in animals, Huxley nevertheless extends his metaphor to global politics. The administrative authority charged to deal with the "human elements" in a colonial province "would proceed in the same fashion as that in which the gardener dealt with his garden" (17). Following this method, believes Huxley, imperial powers could produce ideal colonies "not by gradually adjusting the men to the conditions around them, but by creating artificial conditions for them; not by allowing the free play of the struggle for existence, but by excluding that struggle; and by substituting selection directed towards the administrator's ideal for the selection it exercises" (20).

Directed selectivity becomes an ethical necessity contingent on colonization, because, Huxley concludes, individuals beyond "the State of Art of an organized polity" (45) will never "possess enough intelligence to select the fittest" (34).

Huxley's argument must have heartened colonialists, but one eminent descendent of imperialist conquest, that early Faulknerian influence, John Dewey, was appalled. "Evolution and Ethics" (1898), which takes particular exception to his predecessor's Spencerism, articulates Dewey's reaction: "That which was fit among animals is not fit among human beings, not merely because the animals were non-moral and man is moral; but because the conditions of life have changed, and because there is no way to define the term 'fit' excepting through these conditions. The environment is now a distinctly social one, and the content of the term 'fit' has to be made with reference to social adaptation." Humankind can work with nature, reasoned Dewey, so there was "no reason here to oppose the ethical process to the natural process" (41).

When Huxley's grandson Aldous (1894–1963) came to write his first novel, *Crome Yellow* (1921), such biological and philosophical arguments provided an abundant source of ideas. Sexual selection is one of the major themes in this work, and, as experienced by Ivor and Mary, a comforting dynamic. The young lovers attempt to pluck a feather from a strutting peacock. Huxley's choice of avian species is particularly acicular. One of the most renowned exhibitors of sexual dimorphism, the peacock had provided Darwin with early intimations toward his supplementary theory (*Origin* 70). Ivor gains his "feather, a long-lashed eye of purple and green, of blue and gold," and hands it to his companion in an act of courtship. "It's extraordinary to think of sexual selection," reflects Mary. "Extraordinary!" replies Ivor, "I select you, you select me. What luck!" (146). Although an aleatory process, secondary selection appears to be efficacious. Recalling the thoughts of his grandfather concerning selection and subjugation, however, Huxley coterminously undercuts this semblance through Scogan's unflinching perspective. Future authoritarian states, working with the consequences of natural selection, Scogan insists, will separate people "into distinct species, not according to the colour of their eyes or the shape of their skulls, but according to the qualities of their mind and temperament." Individual *Homo sapiens* will belong to either the "Directing Intelligences," the "Men of Faith," or the "Herd" (164). The first two categories will scientifically direct the "almost boundless suggestibility" of the third (166). Ideologically manufactured consent will blind the herd to ruling-class intentions concerning sexual selection. Personable Ivor and Mary, insinuates Scogan, are pertinent examples of this deception. Impersonal sexual politics is set to expunge the "deplorable associations" between Eros and Lucina: "I look forward to it optimistically. Where the great Erasmus Darwin and Miss Anna Seward, Swan of Lichfield, experimented—and, for all their scientific ardour, failed—our descendants will experiment and succeed. An impersonal generation will take the place of Nature's hideous system" (31).[1] Scogan's cynically reductive hope is in keeping with his character. For he was "like one of those extinct bird-lizards of the Tertiary. His nose was beaked, his dark eye had the shining quickness of a robin's. But there was nothing soft or gracious or feathery about him. The skin of his wrinkled brown face had a dry and scaly look; his hands were the hands of a crocodile. His movements were marked by the lizard's disconcertingly abrupt clockwork speed" (14).

The rapid manner in which Scogan stretches out "a small saurian hand with pointed nails" to catch the attention of fellow guests at Crome House, further testifies to his physical peculiarity (160). He is a species in his own right, a pterodactyl from prehistory. Without a mate, the last of his kind, he is an individual attuned to the impersonal relationships required by the twentieth century. This fracture between love and reproduction, implies Huxley, is a future his grandfather had not envisaged.

Faulkner read *Crome Yellow* in April 1922 (Blotner, *Faulkner's Library* 125). Huxley's sociobiological treatment of sexual selection must have seemed revolutionary, because visions of southern womanhood remained shackled to the provenance of writers such as John Pendleton Kennedy (1795–1870). The plantation belles of *Swallow Barn* (1832) and associated works haunted American literature. Labor pressures in the 1850s had helped to promote this specter in southern minds when domestics moving north had necessitated the angel in the house to clean and cook. A household necessity had tarnished a male ideal. The southern patriarchy had reacted to this unpalatable fact by reifying their dream. Their archetypal woman, historian David Goldfield confirms, "became a marble statue, beautiful and silent, eternally inspiring and eternally still" (104). With fewer homegrown men to uphold this standard after the Civil War, and with the prospect of outsiders encroaching on their domain, the increasing intensity of this projection effectively closed Darwinian intersexual secondary selection. A woman no longer selected her partner. Demure female behavior in deference to male proprieties of race (European American), class (patrician), and upbringing (exclusive) fulfilled a postbellum phallocentric standard. This intersexual closure was altogether different from a female perspective. Their male-constructed pedestal concealed a tension between the constraints of public behavior and the longings of personal desire. Women had to "mask the imperfections of the world" at the expense of submerged lives (104). The paradox identified at the end of the eighteenth century by Mary Wollstonecraft concerning English womanhood had now materialized in the American South. "Riches and hereditary honours have made ciphers of women to give consequence to the numerical figure," laments Wollstonecraft, "and idleness has produced a mixture of gallantry and despotism in society, which leads the very men who are slaves of their mistresses to tyrannize over their sisters, wives, and daughters" (28). A southern gentlewoman of the late nineteenth century had to conform, rebel, or go crazy (Goldfield 106). Those willing to risk a fourth option were rare.

Nonetheless, the distaff side of Faulkner's genealogy provides two such exceptions. Maternal grandmother Lelia Dean Swift Butler ("Damuddy") had been a modest young woman. She had married for love and a future of spousal fidelity, but when her husband broke the expected codes of marriage and deserted her, social limbo beckoned. Precedent dictated that she resort immediately to another courtship or capitulate to a physical or mental breakdown. Lelia eschewed the tradition. She determined to continue without male support and, with the help of her daughter, Maud, succeeded. "Mother had had to quit school at Mississippi State College for Women, where she was studying art," John Faulkner recalls, "and take a quick business course to learn stenography in order to support Damuddy" (124). Employment opportunities for patriciate women were "few and far between," corroborates Jack Falkner, "and Mother became a stenographer when few women entered the world of business in any capacity. She went on to graduate from the women's college at Columbus" (9). Lelia and Maud had become American New Women in a region particularly indisposed to dispositional change. The political rallies that James Kimble Vardaman (1861–1930) held in 1903 verify the reactionary characteristics of this environment. "His typical campaign speech went a full two hours and began with gracious flattery of the virtue of southern women," notes Don Harrison Doyle, but few of his honorees dared attend these gatherings, "for Vardaman also delighted his male audience with coarse, vulgar humor" (320).

The reified belle, then, was still the male fabrication upon which Mississippian women should model themselves when Faulkner came to address the issue of sexual politics in *Soldiers' Pay*. His grandmother and mother provided worthy alternatives to this archetype. Thus, the strong-willed Margaret Powers, a woman actively negotiating a dramatic shift in intersexual relations during the aftermath of World War I, is a compound echo of Faulkner's distaff-side lineage. Margaret's decision on the death of husband to be more than a man's other half indicates her resolve. Furthermore, by caring for war veteran Donald Mahon—whose surname, as critic David Rogers recognizes, one pronounces "Man" (173)—she arrogates the powers of man. Mahon's family had believed Donald to be dead, as had his fiancée Cecily Saunders, but his reappearance under the supervision of Margaret and ex-serviceman Joe Gilligan unsettles the complacent courtship environment. Cecily has already selected another husband-to-be and is loath to fulfill her earlier promise to Mahon, whose disfigurement she finds unpalatable. Instead, Margaret marries Donald, ratifying with this commitment her embodiment of male powers ("Powers"). A woman who has achieved equality according to the criteria of sexual politics, Margaret must make a final decision to cement her achievement. Following Donald's death, Joe asks for her hand in marriage. "I couldn't marry a man named Gilligan," she replies (245). Prescient with respect to human courtship, Margaret knows that she must never become a girl again ("Gilligan").

Faulkner followed his able rendition of sexual politics in *Soldiers' Pay* with a more concerted engagement with Darwinian sexual selection in *Mosquitoes*. Major Ayers, accepting a challenge to dive into the water while the *Nausikaa* is still at full speed, initiates an important incident in this dynamic. Only when safely at anchor do the rest of the men and a few of the women join him. Fairchild, keen to maintain the sexual prerogative demonstrated by Ayers, pinches and splashes the women. With the major's help, he drives all but one of them permanently from the water (319). The exception is Patricia Robyn. She deals masculine pride a serious blow by pulling Fairchild below the surface before standing erect on the shoulders of the major. Ayers can only plunge "about in a kind of active resignation." For good measure, Patricia puts "her foot on the top of his head and thrust[s] him deeper yet" (320). Both men, their sexual egos sufficiently choked, are left gasping for breath. This is not sexual selection as postulated by Darwin. The incident, a blow to Ayers's masculinity and the extinguishment of Fairchild's vestiges of mastery, thereby illustrates a facet of social evolution. To Fairchild, this ongoing correction of Darwinian theory is not to be applauded, merely confirming a lesson he wishes to teach the sexually incompetent (but ardent) Ernest Talliaferro. Courtship for men is more an illusion than a matter of tactics. Southern women were loosening their male-constructed restrictions and reopening intersexual relationships. Many men found this disquieting. Physical violence was one means of punishing this rupture of silence and inanimation. The sculptor Gordon—whose feminine ideal, the marble figure of "a virgin with no legs to leave me, no arms to hold me, no head to talk to me," stands in mute contrast to animate flesh—personifies this response when he eventually spanks Patricia for talking too much (275). Fairchild's response to female selection during courtship is at least as brutal. Shattering counters breaking with his understanding of the contemporary belle, "merely articulated genital organs with a kind of aptitude for spending whatever money you have," as a synecdochic animation of valued parts that costs men dear (453). Impersonal economics simply replaces the male component of intersexual courtship. The shocking unpleasantness of Fairchild's remark has unfortunately obscured the complex authorial debt *Mosquitoes* owes to Darwin and the Huxleys. Critics have projected their disgust of Fairchild onto Faulkner. On this account, Mortimer rebukes the author for his "oblivion . . . to any possible evolutionary role for women" except as gestational carriers (197) while Frederick C. Crews concludes that Faulkner retained a "saturnine resentment of women" (xxi). Maintaining this critical attitude when reading *Sanctuary* (1931) would appear to compound these accusations, but the scientific dispassion of an evolutionary hermeneutic, while producing a more somber interpretation than is usual, demonstrates that Faulkner's sixth novel is neither misogynistic nor indifferent toward the sexual status of women. An evolutionary approach rises above the critical hysteria that continues to submerge this text without relegating the seriousness of rape. Faulkner may have claimed he wrote *Sanctuary* for money, exploiting the subject of sex for increased sales, but whatever his utterances in public, his text is far from perfunctory. His amendments to *Sanctuary* testify to this conclusion. Faulkner, notes Joel Williamson, "made furious and costly attempts to improve it just before it was printed" (*William Faulkner* 231). Even so, the published novel divided local reaction. Faulkner's stepson, Malcolm Franklin (1923–1977), records: "Those that read *Sanctuary*, in Oxford, probably did not know how to read it, nor did they know what Billy was writing about to begin with. When they finally waded through it they just thought it was a dirty book and seemed shocked. That is, the large majority did. But in Columbus it was different. Actually, more people in Columbus had read the book than had those in Oxford; they were a more traveled and sophisticated group of people than Oxonians were" (67). This indeterminate reception helps to substantiate a textual complexity that remains contentious, a provocation that concerns how sexual selection mediates between the conditioning factors associated with both the biological base to human nature and the cultural superstructure of society.

Sanctuary violently dislocates the Faulknerian aesthetic from nineteenth-century patterns of literary and scientific influence. The figures of Temple Drake and Popeye, in particular, expedite this trauma. At the opening of the narrative, Temple is a mere seventeen, but her tender years do little to palliate family expectations. Temple's immediate relations—her mother being dead—are a traditional southern patriarch and four brothers in their father's mold. Each of these men wishes Jefferson to reverence their demure Temple as an exemplar of southern womanhood. The male Drakes, like Anatidaen protectors of their female charge, carefully guard Temple's reputation while circumscribing her freedom. As a circuit judge, her father is socially empowered to oversee this vigil, and courtship becomes his especial focus. In one incident, the shotgun-brandishing judge confronts a suitor he deems unworthy. Youngest brother Buddy is also an officious sentinel in this regard, Temple affirming "that if he ever caught me with a drunk man, he'd beat hell out of me" (216). The male standards of the House of Drake are stiflingly rigid in both principle and practice.[2] If Scarlett O'Hara in *Gone with the Wind* (1936) by Margaret Mitchell (1900–1949) "had lived too long among people who dissembled politely" while projecting their codes of propriety onto her, then so has Temple (239). Reacting against conformation, Temple turns for the first time to the second behavioral option for women as identified by Goldfield above: rebelliousness. This tactic secures her some leeway. Judge Drake allows his daughter to attend the University of Mississippi, satisfied that the relevant authorities carefully supervise coeducational status. The dormitory for women is known as "the Coop"—freedom for female undergraduates appears ostensible rather than actual (*Sanctuary* 198). For Temple, though, Ole Miss nonetheless offers a tangibly looser domain, Faulkner carefully designating the distance between Jefferson and Oxford as a two-stage railway journey. Now Temple can enjoy the sexual economy from a biological basis far less restrained by familial strictures.

Oxford offers two fields of play for young women interested in heterosexual courtship. Locals constitute the first sort, the second type comprising undergraduates. Since Faulkner portrays the early years under the Butler Act during which Chancellor Hume had relaxed some nonacademic restrictions, each division offers certain advantages. On one side, town males can exploit their automobile ownership because "students in the University were not permitted to keep cars." On the other side, university males can enjoy exclusive Ole Miss events specifically arranged for the purposes of intersexual politics such as "the Letter Club dances" held "on alternate Saturday evenings" and "the three formal yearly balls" (198). The automobile as a detached modern appendage, or impersonal twentieth-century display tool, is thereby countered by the intimacy of the courtship dance. Faced with these competing fields, Temple chooses to sample both kinds coextensively. "I am on probation" (216), she admits, "for slipping out at night. Because only town boys can have cars" (217). Yet, she remains "cool, predatory and discreet" while participating in life on campus (198). Does this split mentality propound a "cruelly selfish lust which makes her completely disregard the well-being of any other person," as critic Sally R. Page insists (81)? No, her teenage response to the Oxford environment is Faulkner's rendition of a de facto case of biologically fostered and culturally conditioned behavior.[3] Late-twentieth-century amendments to sociobiology, especially those forwarded by Richard Dawkins in *The Selfish Gene* (1976) and British biologist John Maynard Smith, enable the literary critic to appreciate Faulkner's subtlety in this portrayal.[4]

The relevant refinements concern the basic asymmetry in gamete size that Darwin analyzed in mammals. In honing this first principle, contemporary theorists understand the politics of mammalian breeding to be a conflict between male and female interests. Hence, the fundamental sexual difference in gamete production results in the predominance of male promiscuity. All courting males aspire to the *strategy of selfish exploitation* to which females respond with their *he-man strategy*. Female sexual selection in this instance is a matter of recognizing prospective mates whose hereditary characteristics augur well for breeding. Those males that suffer intrasexual disadvantage in terms of manifest robustness are left to employ the *strategy of fidelity*. The female *strategy of domestic bliss* has evolved to assess these signs of faithfulness with the prospect of securing a trustworthy suitor. By extracting a prenuptial investment from each potential partner, females can attempt to foster qualities of domesticity in advance. The demand for a long period of celibacy will induce casual males to give up in frustration with perseverance certifying devotion.[5]

These two courtship domains, selfish exploitation relaying with the he-man strategy and fidelity interacting with that of domestic bliss, are unlikely to exist in isolation from one another. Females will tend to employ the he-man strategy when faced with a preponderance of male *philanderers*, using the strategy of domestic bliss when dependable males predominate. Females resorting to the he-man strategy in an environment of male philanderers are *fast*, and those employing domestic bliss in response to *faithful* males are *coy*. Over numerous generations, an environment develops in which x percent of females are fast and $(100-x)$ percent remain coy while a respective y percent of males philander as $(100-y)$ percent stay faithful. When any population implementing such a mélange of fixed individual behaviors becomes resistant to invasion from mutant strategies, then an evolutionarily stable state has developed. However, cautions Smith, an entire intrasexual community is unlikely to consistently practice a single strategy; concomitantly, two different types of individual within each sex are improbable. The courtship behavior of a particular female is more liable to switch between her two available modes depending on the frequency with which she encounters the corresponding male strategies. A mixed *evolutionarily stable strategy* (or ESS) would then be achieved if each female spends x percent of her time being fast and the remaining (100-x) percent being coy, with each male a philanderer for y percent of his time, spending the remaining period in faithful mode. Inconstant mating behavior can be consistent with an established set of mating strategies.

Having asserted this, however, one must sound another cautionary note. Such modeling makes no presumption that philandering is more likely than faithfulness in male practice. Genetic causation must work in an environment, and, as Dawkins plainly states in *The Extended Phenotype* (1982), "there is no general reason for expecting genetic influences to be any more irreversible than environmental ones." Although genes are significant factors in behavior, the effects of genetic variation "may be overridden, modified, enhanced or reversed by other causes" (13).

With this caveat in mind, not the whims of lust, but the long-established mixed ESS at Oxford underlies Temple's switches in courtship behavior. The he-man strategy recommends itself when courting the philandering complement of Oxonian youths and the strategy of domestic bliss when probing the dependability of undergraduates. Only when Gowan Stevens enters the courtship scene does her bifurcated fast-coy response appear to near resolution. Here is a man who combines a robust biological basis for sexual selection with an aristocratic command over the cultural superstructure. Furthermore, as a graduate of the University of Virginia, Gowan is allowed to attend social events at Ole Miss while simultaneously enjoying the freedom of car ownership. Temple enjoys this seemingly all-encompassing combination of attractions but fails to investigate his provenance. Gowan's history in the sexual economy is less innocent than Temple assumes. Narcissa Benbow, "with that serene and stupid impregnability of heroic statuary," is, in fact, Gowan's archetype of southern womanhood (*Sanctuary* 253). He only turns to Temple for solace when rejected by this reification of his dreams. What is more, resentment toward his previous setback abounds.

An intrasexual component to male behavior during sexual selection, the *assessor strategy*, draws this emotion from Gowan. Smith defines this exclusively male behavior as a capacity to rank rivals in natural and sexual selection according to a perceived level of threat. When an individual believes he holds primacy over an antagonist, the assessor strategy suggests the employment of aggressive tactics, but if an individual deems himself inferior, then assessment advises passivity. One tactic of intrasexual evaluation often conducted during courtship is the *parallel walk* in which rivals concurrently display a particular ability. This reciprocal test soon unmasks any difference between the contestants. If no distinction is apparent, then the ensuing contest is usually protracted. To signal a high value for a contested ability tends to be an expensive exercise. "Otherwise," as Smith explains, "assessment strategies would be vulnerable to cheating" (110). Under normal conditions, then, assessed ability and fighting success correlate (the paradoxical inferior victory is the rarest of exceptions). Although the gradations of behavior are more refined than implied by this précis, a courtship evaluation of resource-holding power takes place between males in most mammalian species, including *Homo sapiens*.

Sanctuary presciently tracks these ramifications in the case of Gowan and his rivals for Temple following a formal dance at the University of Mississippi. After taking Temple home, Gowan must drive past the Oxonians excluded from the event. One of them breaks an empty liquor bottle, "propping the jagged shards upright in the road" (*Sanctuary* 199). The desire to burst the tires on Gowan's car—or deflate his ego—is aggressively apparent. Gowan, aware of the intrasexual politics at play, thwarts the scheme by pulling to their side of the road before reaching the debris. He invites his competitors to join him for a drink in town. Defeated at this initial stage of assessment, one of Gowan's competitors acknowledges the fact by warning him that "somebody broke a bottle there" (200). Having bought some illicit whiskey from a local "confectionery-lunchroom," the antagonists embark on a second phase of intrasexual evaluation: a drinking contest as a parallel walk. Bragging that the liquor "hasn't got much kick," Gowan seals victory by significantly outdrinking his opponents (201). Nevertheless, the contest has been squalid, as his overnight convalescence in the toilet at Oxford Station confirms.

On her way to Starkville by rail the next morning, Temple is to join Gowan on the platform at Taylor for a secret assignation. They plan to spend some hours together before Gowan drives her to Starkville to coincide with the arrival of the train. Because of his hangover, however, Gowan only reaches Taylor as the service pulls away. To fulfill their plan, Temple must jump from the moving vestibule, springing down and running beside the car while an official shakes his fist at her. But the ire of this male "conductor" is the least of Temple's worries, because Gowan, taking over the directorial role, and recalling her scrawled name on the lavatory wall at Oxford, subjects her to a verbal attack. That women can employ a double courtship strategy has been an unpalatable discovery. "Think you can play around all week with any badger-trimmed hick that owns a ford, and fool me on Saturday, don't you?" Gowan fumes. Temple's sexual politics appears to be a massive obstacle to their future together. The prospect of alcoholic oblivion proffers Gowan an immediate remedy. Touring the backwoods for liquor, though "apparently looking straight ahead," he drives "into the tree at twenty miles an hour" (205). The collision damage suffered by his car and the hazard entertained by the occupants not only echo the impact imparted on his consciousness by the revelation of Temple's nature, but also foretell the trauma to be inflicted on her when their search for help leads to the perverse sanctuary of the "Old Frenchman place" (184). This refuge "for crimps and spungs and feebs" accommodates the mentally arrested Tommy, the decrepit old Pap, and various hoodlums (185). Moreover, Temple will discover a courtship trajectory here, as advanced by the gangster Popeye, to which her rebelliousness makes her perceptive, but for which she has no biologically engendered response.

A peculiar aura invests Popeye as an exception to the regular type of male circulating in the sexual economy. Faulkner was determined to locate the initiation of this difference in terms of biological inheritance and some of his late alterations to *Sanctuary*, as Philip Cohen affirms, concerned the "addition of Popeye's childhood biography" ("Faulkner by the Light" 176). These emendations posit a twofold betrayal at conception. Popeye's mentally deranged maternal grandmother points to an infirmity on the distaff side of his lineage, while his father taints the spear side with syphilis. His mother, pregnant with Popeye before her marriage, begins to ail within three weeks of her wedding. The prognosis for her fetus is not hopeful. Even being born on "Christmas day" offers little prospect of a miracle, because, as Faulkner must have known, syphilis during pregnancy can cause physical deformity, mental illness, and infant mortality. "At first," the doctors attending Popeye's birth, "thought he was blind. Then they found that he was not blind, though he did not learn to walk and talk until he was about four years old" (*Sanctuary* 389). Having "no hair at all until he was five," his physical development remains excruciatingly slow. "With care," specialists advise his mother, "he will live some time longer. But he will never be any older than he is now." Struggling more than most to survive childhood, Popeye proves his doubters wrong. Only the fact that "he will never be a man, properly speaking" is incurable (392). Hence, a cruel irony undermines the Freudian conjunction between eye and penis that associates the nickname Popeye with machismo. Indeed, when Horace Benbow first meets Popeye, he notes that his guide to the Old Frenchman place "smells like that black stuff that ran out of Bovary's mouth and down upon her bridal veil when they raised her head" (184). Popeye's very breath seems laced with a syphilitic legacy that leaves the masculinity of his mien and build diminished. His sobriquet therefore holds a second irony—the gangster displaying a severe diminution of the physical prowess secreted in the comic strip hero.[6] Horace concurrently notices that Popeye's "face had a queer, bloodless color, as though seen by electric light" (181). Even the "feeb" Tommy comments on "them gal's hands of hisn" (210). Certainly, one can interpret Popeye in effeminate terms, but his face "like a mask carved into two simultaneous expressions" suggests otherwise (182). Another aspect of this alterity surfaces when Popeye visits his mother. "Prosperous, quiet, thin, black, and uncommunicative in his narrow black suits," he is recognized by his mother immediately (393). Successful in capitalist terms, despite his challenged biological inheritance, Popeye's demeanor and dress nonetheless imply that he remains reticent according to the criteria of courtship communication. Blackness does not proclaim the vivid colors so readily associated with a mastery of the sexual economy. Even so, this supposedly undistinguished specimen, aware that he is outside the patriarchal norm, has developed a culturally dominated approach to the politics of sex, a trajectory that bespeaks alterity.

With her rebellious inclination, Temple will find this difference tempting. Coming face to face with the gangster for the first time, she cannot help but flash that "grimace of taut, toothed coquetry." Intriguingly for Temple, as Popeye walks by, he offers no relay to her signal—"the finicking swagger of his narrow back did not falter" (211). Temple next cajoles Popeye to take her and Gowan back to Jefferson. The gangster's "soft, cold voice" issues a sharp reply. "Make your whore lay off of me, Jack" (212). Temple's response is to goad Popeye further. This reaction establishes a reciprocal temptation that predicates Temple as a possible inductee into

Popeye's particular sexual economy. Gowan breaks this hiatus, intervening in the developing interplay by forcing Temple into the Frenchman house. Gowan's maneuver initiates the last courtship dance between the graduate and his belle: "Their feet scraped on the bare floor as though they were performing a clumsy dance, and clinging together they lurched into the wall" (213). Disorienting conditions have broken down the formalities of a university ball into a leaden-footed shambles. This dance, more an abysmal performance than an intimacy, anticipates a macabre dénouement.

Gowan starts drinking again, this time embarking on a parallel walk with the owner of the Old Frenchman place, Goodwin, and the mysterious Van. Forsaken by her desultory protector cum suitor, Temple continues to focus her attention on the seemingly disadvantaged Popeye. Women, *Sanctuary* implies, can learn to expose any pretence of sexual vitality. As a corollary, men with palpable honesty tend to win their favor. Through her Oxford experiences, Temple appears to have developed this ability. Popeye, who has survived and prospered despite his obvious deficiencies, must embody a singular kind of evolutionary fitness. Withheld from Temple for the present, the perverseness of this successful adjustment and correspondence to some niche in modern living allures her via mystery, singularity, and enforced ignorance.

Popeye's particular response to biological inferiority has been to exploit the detached and impersonal twentieth-century possibilities for secondary selection to create the mutant courtship *strategy of impersonal gratification*. The automobile and the gun become his phallic signaling tools of choice: his yellow car stands out against the black background of Model T Fords (which one assumes the "hicks" of Oxford drive), while his reputation with a pistol is second to none. Excluded from the standard biological and patriarchal constructions of courtship, Popeye situates himself at the forefront of a culturally directed sexual selection. Being at the vanguard of this revolution, Popeye exerts a sexual fascination over Temple, drawing her into his unfamiliar territory. Only Ruby Lamar, Goodwin's lover and mother of his child, appreciates the teenager's growing sense of disorientation. Ruby has known Popeye since her whorehouse days in Memphis. An escapee from that particular sexual economy, one in which men use money to subvert the biological determinant of female choice, she impresses on Temple that her goading of Popeye is a case of "riding" too far (217). Furthermore, "playing at it" in sexual terms with the gangster is a dangerous game (220). This, however, is the extent of the older woman's warning. For, as Diane Roberts makes plain, "Even though she speaks to Temple in the traditionally female space of the kitchen, her child at her feet, Ruby's voice oscillates between feminine and masculine situations" (*Faulkner* 132). There is a sense of female accommodation to male impositions, intimated in Ruby's "naked ankles" above "a worn pair of man's brogans" (*Sanctuary* 184) that are constantly "unlaced" (219), which Temple would do well to escape. Unsurprisingly, the youngster's first night in the backwoods augurs ill. Sitting in bed, with her "hat tilted rakishly upon the back of her head," she presumably awaits Gowan (227). Beset with three domains rampantly contesting for her choice of sexual dominion—selfish exploitation interacting with the he-man strategy, fidelity relaying with that of domestic bliss, and impersonal gratification expecting a correspondingly detached response—Temple's inconsistent behavior intensifies. "A raincoat and a khaki-covered canteen" hanging on the wall symbolize this confused state of mind (226). Although she contemplates the canteen as a metaphorical chastity belt, she also puts on the raincoat as a form of rubber protection. This latter act answers for her decision to have sex. That Temple then produces "a compact from somewhere," arranges her hair, and powders her face, compounds this implication (227). When the comatose body of Gowan accompanies Van's declaration of resource-holding power, "we're bringing you a customer," her preparations have been to no avail (229). Despite and in contrast to Gowan's state, however, the sexual atmosphere does not dissipate.

By the following morning, the presence of Temple's fear-induced instability has started to destabilize Ruby's relationship with Goodwin. "Motionless, facing one another like the first position of a dance," the couple confront one another "in a mounting terrific muscular hiatus" (245). When the impasse breaks, Goodwin strikes, and Ruby suffers. Having acted heroically in offering her "own body as sacrifice," Ruby can do nothing more to protect Temple (Roberts, *Faulkner* 132). The teenager, abandoned by Gowan, who has admitted intrasexual defeat in walking alone toward town, must face her coming ordeal with only Tommy for a guard. Faulkner's text now becomes rampant with intimations of danger. For, in her attempt to hide that evening, Temple chooses to enter through the "trap" (*Sanctuary* 243) into the "crib" (237) of the "broken-backed" barn (207). Here, caught in the ironic embrace of the crib, Popeye will succeed in breaking Temple. Awaiting her fate, Temple's inability to control her usually amicable body, testifies to the self-alienation to come. She thinks of her legs, all that "I'd done for them," all the "dances I had taken them to," but they do not repay her in staying Popeye's intent (329). The gangster murders the gallant Tommy. Then, realizing his strategy of impersonal gratification, he penetrates Temple's reserve in a manner detached from common expectations by raping her with a corncob. The "loose hulls," or empty husks, of the maize seeds on the crib floor have foretold this device (243). The impersonal dildo has replaced the personal flesh. Both impotent and infertile—the woody cylindrical stem substituting for an erect penis, the maize seeds for semen—Popeye's tool of choice nevertheless confirms his position in the vanguard of a revolution, a traumatic transformation of sexual politics from which Temple will never recover.

Popeye, immune to the personal suffering of his object, intends to continue enjoying this peculiar prowess. Thus, his relocation of Temple following her rape is less concerned with murder and more determined by his need for a salubrious sexual environment. The Old Frenchman place, some "twelve miles from town," is unsuitable for Popeye's predilection (262). "Set in the middle of a tract of land," Goodwin's house is the most substantial remains "of cotton fields and gardens and lawns long since gone back to jungle" (184). There is no "sign of husbandry—plow or tool; in no direction was a planted field in sight—only a gaunt weather-stained ruin in a somber grove through which the breeze drew with a sad, murmurous sound" (206). This is nature in the raw where even "what had once been a kitchen garden" is today choked "with cedar and blackjack saplings" (210). *Natura naturans*, or the Arcadian Great Mother, is on the verge of regaining her dominion through sheer fecundity. *Naturam expellas furca, tamen usque recurret.* While conveying the state of the former plantation, this apt proverb concurrently emphasizes the alienation of those without biological sympathy. Horace had glimpsed this lack in Popeye during their inadvertent backwoods trek. Led by the gangster along a peripatetic track, Horace asked why they could not take a short cut. "Through all them trees?" is Popeye's rejoinder. Sticking to the path, Popeye maintains the lead, "his tight suit and stiff hat all angles," startlingly out of place "like a modernist lampstand" (183). Only in the city, manmade and impersonal, does he feel at home. Memphis, specifically the brothel owned by Miss Reba Rivers on Manuel Street, is his destination with Temple.

Popeye feels immediately at home on entering the whorehouse with its "weary quality. A spent quality; defunctive, exhausted—a protracted weariness like a vitiated backwater beyond sunlight and the vivid noises of sunlight and day" (278–79). This is an environment where man has perverted the biological. Darwinian sexual selection does not come into play in Reba's place. "We dont stand on no ceremony here," she explains (280). A detached setting, "full of sounds" that are "indistinguishable, remote" (287), the bordello vibrates to the discordant jangle of "a mechanical piano" rather than to the intimate music of love (288). The naïve experience of Virgil Snopes confirms the impersonality of the house. Staying in the brothel without initially cognizant of its function, Virgil goes to sleep hearing "the whispers of silk that came through the walls and the floor, that seemed as much a part of both as the planks and the plaster" (314). The reification of women, not as marble statuary but as sex objects, appears complete. Reba's prostitutes are not so much *on the game*, as in the English expression, but *integers of impersonal gratification*. Here Temple remains, submerged by the violent repercussions of violation, in an impersonal state of unconscious submission; Popeye, though, feels safe. Instead of backwoods flora, Manuel Street merely offers "a forlorn and hardy tree of some shabby species—gaunt, lop-branched magnolias, a stunted elm or a locust in grayish, cadaverous bloom—interspersed by rear ends of garages" (277). When flowers do appear, as Reba's hat attests, they are "rigidly moribund" (279). Popeye has secured a perfect location for his impersonal needs.

Temple's boudoir, a room in which "the mantel supported a wax lily beneath a glass bell," may conform to Popeye's weird standard, but modern dissembling, shallow pretences, and gestures to the natural economy cannot satisfy her (325). She finds this side of urban America a remote and godless prison; for, as soon as Temple relates critically to her surroundings, she feels "in as complete an isolation as though she were bound to a church steeple" (289). Popeye's power over Temple starts to evaporate hereupon. The sense of procreative sex still applies to Temple, the biological imperative perversely helping to break the stranglehold of bordello politics, while Popeye must translate that reproductive standard into the impersonal. Realizing that the gangster can never consummate their relationship helps to bring Temple back from her forced translocation as she begins to consciously relate to her initial rape and her continuing ordeal. In focusing on the gangster's impotency, the personal undermining the impersonal, her second rebellion gets under way. Reba, who has known Popeye far longer, articulates this feeling. "A young man spending his money like water on girls and not never going to bed with one," she declares. "It's against nature" (356). Even to the jaded eyes of a madam, Popeye's proclivities appear exceptional. The Manuel Street prostitute Minnie soon notes of the Popeye-Temple relationship, "How he wasn't here hardly at all, gone about every other night, and that when he was here, there wasn't no signs at all the next morning." One of Reba's friends later advances a reason for his absences and the lack of sexual detritus. "Maybe he went off and got fixed up with one of these glands, these monkey glands," Myrtle opines, "and it quit on him" (357).[7] Ribald humor, yes, but Faulkner also intimates that Popeye, signaling himself as a nascent subspecies of *Homo sapiens*, is especially suited to testicular material transplanted from another species.

Popeye employs two tactics to compensate Temple for their lack of sexual congress. He derives the first from normal male standards. Mirrors, brushes, perfumes, and powders start to clutter Temple's dressing table. Beginning to resist her abuser, she throws these accoutrements aside. His approach fails because directing capital largesse along patriarchal lines cannot mask Popeye's alienation from the biological economy. From his perspective, therefore, a secondary tactic needs be, and is, more innovative. He employs a fellow hoodlum, named Red, to replace the dildo as his detached sexual tool; the surrogate male becomes the whole simulacrum that precedes the less-than-complete sinews of Popeyean flesh. In this manner, Popeye aims to assuage the incarnate rebellion of Temple and better satisfy his own impersonal needs (since there no longer exists a substantial connection between his body and that of his victim). Red enables Popeye to become a voyeur in the sex act, to remain apart from other flesh, and to enjoy a singular sense of consummation. Popeye's perspective, characterized by his grotesque "whinnying sound," is now that of another species (358).

The performances of others empower Popeye's climaxes, but they also seed a fatal tension. *Naturam expellas furca, tamen usque recurret.* On the one hand, Temple understands that she and Popeye will never stimulate each other personally. On the other hand, she now satisfies her need for personal human contact through her dubious interaction with Red. A relationship seemingly bordering on love springs up between the two active players in Popeye's sexual economy. Full of vitality, as his name implies, Red is in stark contrast to Popeye. Not only is he "almost a head taller than anybody else," but he is also a man who enjoys flaunting the sartorial plumage of "his gray suit and [a] spotted bow tie" (342, 341). He may not be a multicolored specimen, yet his grayness stands out against the white and black background associated with Gowan and Popeye, and his outstanding "Red" head adds to this impression by symbolizing an engorged phallic glans. In addition, as a town dweller who nonetheless "looked like a college boy," Red embodies the two courtship fields that Temple coextensively enjoyed at Oxford (341). No wonder, then, that her means of escape from the trauma of the impersonal involves the rejection of the master in favor of the master's erstwhile tool.[8]

The tension so engendered between Popeye, Temple, and Red comes to a head at the Grotto nightclub. Again, the courtship ritual of the dance comes to the fore, Popeye employing an assessor strategy overwhelmingly weighted in his favor by the presence of numerous henchmen. Red ought to back down in these circumstances, but he does not. Popeye initiates the proceedings by leading Temple to the dance floor. Fondling for the gun that lies "rigid" at his armpit, her partner's prosthetic manhood attracts Temple's impersonally tainted impulses. "Give it to me," she whispers as her hand begins "to steal down his body in a swift, covert movement." Suddenly, as consciousness synchronizes with natural sense, Temple withdraws her fingers "in a movement of revulsion" (342). Red, trying to seize the initiative, chooses this juncture to ask Temple for a dance. The presumption of his intervention is fatal. Popeye allows the pair to meet briefly in a private room. With his suspicions confirmed, Popeye has Temple returned to Reba's whorehouse, shooting Red dead outside the nightclub. Temple's enforced third rebellion, paradoxically a cultural one, but belonging to the well-established order, has achieved its aim. The opportunity repeatedly afforded her by Popeye—"'I'm giving him his chance,' he said. 'Will you go back in that house, or will you get in this car?' . . . 'I'm giving him his chance'" (338)—but left untaken is evidence to this effect. This refusal asserts Temple's rebellion against Red as another of her abusers (just as her contempt of court will later signal Goodwin's punishment too). The irony of Red's failure to secure a farewell dance with his sexual victim soon becomes apparent after his death. At his wake, supposedly a teetotal event in keeping with the Volstead Act, there is a stash of whisky in the backroom liberally used to pep up the fruit punch. Drunkenness ensues, a scuffle breaks out, and the resultant jostling tips the coffin over. Red's final appearance is a dance macabre with his mourners as they maneuver him toward the empty casket.

Popeye's murderous actions at the Grotto repeat two ghastly incidents from his childhood. At a party, Popeye had locked himself inside the bathroom for some minutes before absconding. The adults only discovered what had happened in the interim on breaking down the door. They found "a wicker cage in which two lovebirds lived; beside it lay the birds themselves, and the bloody scissors with which he had cut them up alive" (392–93). The young Popeye later repeated this vendetta on another typical object of human affection, cutting up "a half-grown kitten" (393). These episodes evince a victimized child, an individual damned by reckless procreation, becoming a victimizer. In their turn, Temple and Red had become Popeye's tormenting lovebirds.

"He will never be any older than he is now," the doctors had said of Popeye, but his immaturity is of a different order than that exhibited by Dawson Fairchild in *Mosquitoes* (392). This difference signals Faulkner's complex and swift maturation as an artist. At one level, as Dawson's surname paradoxically implies, Fairchild remains a juvenile concerning sexual politics, but a blatantly unfair one. The female body confronts him as "merely articulated" parts rather than as an animated whole (*Mosquitoes* 453). At another level, Popeye becomes far more unbalanced at a similar stage of sexual development, the established relations that predominantly govern society continue to constitute a greater anguish, and his effect on Temple is physically and psychologically shattering in a manner to which Fairchild's synecdochic projection significantly palls. Temple and Red's closeness, the socially determined difference that enabled their ambiguous relationship, reiterated Popeye's exclusion not only from relations both sexual and social with women, but also from social relations with men (the Irigarayan hom[m]o-sexual). This was a realization that Popeye did not wish to face. He therefore killed Red. Yet, because she continued to manifest his enigmatic ideal, he spared Temple. Worshipping her as an impersonal physical space has supplied him with proof of metaphysical perfection. Extending this critical inference helps to suggest Popeye's reasoning hereafter: he can only forsake the material and reach this spiritual goal via his own death. His calmness before execution would seem to concur with such a conclusion, his evasion of justice through passive suicide adding another disagreeable layer to his legacy.

A trap had closed to snare Temple in the barn loft; the opening of another such door signals Popeye's demise. One may be inclined to imagine his spasmodic last moments on the hangman's noose solely as an impersonal dance of death, but his kicking legs also signal the possibility of an inverted parallel of continuing distress. The prospect of embodying Red's child leads Temple into another trap rather than offering any hope of salvation from the wounds of a perverse society. Trying to convalesce, surrounded by Old World culture as she sits in the Luxembourg Gardens of Paris, attended by the stalwart Southern patriarch that is her father, but reminded of a new order from within, Temple remains "sullen and discontented and sad" (*Sanctuary* 398). A future, which she conceived in a perverted escape route masquerading as love, but one that the impersonal still hauntingly commands, beckons. Interwar Europe during "the season of rain and death," insists Faulkner, is fitting temporally and spatially for this singularly lost member of an American generation (398). A nascent form of twentieth-century sexual politics has generated incurable trauma, four deaths, and the probability of troubled lives to come. Cold impersonality has undone the solidarity offered by warm personal relations.

How could sociobiological evolution have produced this state of affairs? The answer, as Faulkner figures in Temple's posttraumatic expression, is complex. He writes, "Her face was quite pale, the two spots of rouge like paper discs pasted on her cheek bones, her mouth painted into a savage and perfect bow, also like something both symbolical and cryptic cut carefully from purple paper and pasted there." (376)

Although Faulkner evinces his maturation from *Mosquitoes* to *Sanctuary*, he was neither willing nor ready to address this unsettling ambiguity. Preferring to develop other aspects of his evolutionary aesthetic, he left the issue suspended. Yes, he would return to sexual politics in his fiction, as subsequent chapters in the present study will show,[9] but the cryptogram left hanging at the end of *Sanctuary* needed extensive contemplation. Indeed, twenty years would pass before Faulkner returned to the matter. In doing so, his evolving aesthetic would call upon his remarkable ability for long-term recall in revitalizing the provenance left to him by *Crome Yellow*. Urbanization imposes an impersonal strain on ontology, but if one is unable to deal with the schism between personal and impersonal relations so engendered, figures Huxley, then the results can be devastating. Faulkner's continuation of Temple Drake's story in *Requiem for a Nun* (1951) delineates the sociobiological background to this split and illustrates its ramifications in an emergent species of text, a nascent form of fiction and drama, which exhibits the characteristic bifurcation of evolution. Despite a sense of experimentation, this work attains to the artistic level reached by the most eminent of Faulkner's contemporaries. The relationship of *Requiem for a Nun* to ideas is, as Lionel Trilling writes of Faulkner at his best, "in competition with philosophy, theology, and science, [in] that it seeks to match them in comprehensiveness and power and seriousness" (293).

Of the three narrative sections, "THE COURTHOUSE (A Name for the City)," "THE GOLDEN DOME (Beginning Was the Word)," and "THE JAIL (Nor Even Yet Quite Relinquish—)," the second not only illustrates most concisely an authorial knowledge of Darwin's evolutionary theory and attendant hypotheses, but also demonstrates to the greatest extent Faulkner's appreciation of subsequent amendments to scientific epistemology. In 1948, for example, George Gamov (1904–1968), Ralph Alpher (1921–), and Hans Bethe (1906–2005) had proposed the Big Bang theory as the origin of the universe. The event that determined the topographical position of Jackson in the firmament—"one seethe one spawn one mother-womb, one furious tumescence, father-mother-one, one vast incubant ejaculation already fissionating in one boiling moil of litter from the celestial experimental Work Bench" (540)—is a Faulknerian synthesis of this latest cosmological tenet, the language of nuclear physics, and divine anteriority. Faulkner's text also benefits from his summary rendition of the organismic outcome imputed to the Ice Age. "The gigantic quadrupeds, the Mastodons, Elephants, Tigers, Lions, Hyenas, Bears, whose remains are found in Europe from its Southern promotories to the northernmost limits of Siberia and Scandinavia," writes Agassiz in *Structure of Animal Life* (1866), "may indeed be said to have possessed the earth." However, their reign ended when a "sudden intense winter, that was also to last for ages, fell upon our globe" (208). Darwin understood Agassiz's concept of the Ice Age but found the views of Scottish geologist Charles Lyell (1797–1875) more agreeable: extinction as a result of subtle changes in climate, invasion by competing species, and excessive predation by man. Gradual elimination was the key. "If we see, without the smallest surprise, though unable to assign the precise reason, one species abundant and another closely allied species rare in the same district," argues *A Naturalist's Voyage*, "why should we feel such great astonishment at the rarity being carried one step further to extinction?" (176). Although Darwin would later concede that climatic changes "must have rendered discontinuous the formerly continuous range of many species," he continued to preference natural selection as the primary, and almost exclusive, mechanism behind extinction (*Origin* 321): "It is most difficult always to remember that the increase of every living creature is constantly being checked by unperceived hostile agencies; and that these same unperceived agencies are amply sufficient to cause rarity, and finally extinction. So little is this subject understood, that I have heard surprise repeatedly expressed at such great monsters as the Mastodon and the more ancient Dinosaurians having become extinct; as if mere bodily strength gave victory in the battle of life" (*Origin* 295).

Faulkner possibly uses *The Origin of the Species* to substantiate his own paradigm in this regard, or he may draw upon the multifarious "Song of Myself" (1855) in which Walt Whitman (1819–1892) enthuses:

> My embryo has never been torpid, nothing could overlay it.
> For it the nebula cohered to an orb,
> The long slow strata piled to rest it on.
> Vast vegetables gave it sustenance,
> Monstrous sauroids transported it in their mouths and deposited it with care. (1161–1164)[10]

In Faulkner's conception, the topography of the Earth, having endured "longer than the miasma and the gigantic ephemeral saurians" (*Requiem* 547), finally emerged from the Ice Age as a series of "recessional contour lines like the concentric whorls within the sawn stump [of a tree]" (541). Hereon, the numinous "laboratory-factory" had spawned the "unalien shapes" which inhabit the world today, modern man being the most familiar of all (541).

"The most closely-allied forms," according to the Darwinian model, "generally come into the severest competition with each other; consequently, each new variety or species, during the progress of its formation, will generally press hardest on its nearest kindred, and tend to exterminate them" (*Origin* 86). Societal development and the outbreak of interethnic conflict thereby accompanied the emergence of *Homo sapiens*. Those more skilled as artisans prevailed in this struggle for existence:

> We can see, that in the rudest state of society, the individuals who were the most sagacious, who invented and used the best weapons or traps, and who were best able to defend themselves, would rear the greatest number of offspring. The tribes, which included the largest number of men thus endowed, would increase in number and supplant other tribes. Numbers depend primarily on the means of subsistence, and this depends partly on the physical nature of the country, but in a much higher degree on the arts which are there practised. As a tribe increases and is victorious, it is often still further increased by the absorption of other tribes. (*Descent* 128)

Iron Age practitioners replaced the vestiges of the Bronze Age people who had superseded the remainder of Stone Age tribes. Even at the time of writing, concludes Darwin, "civilized nations are everywhere supplanting barbarous nations, excepting where the climate opposes a deadly barrier" (*Descent* 128).

Requiem for a Nun follows the Darwinian model with the evolution of society operating via displacement and conquest. Europeans bent on establishing colonial America are the prime example. Their advance across the continent erases not only indigenes, but also the stratigraphic traces of autochthonous existence:

> not because of the grooved barrel but because they could enter the red man's milieu and make the same footprints that he made; the husbandman printing deep the hard heels of his brogans because of the weight he bore on his shoulders: axe and saw and plow-stock, who dispossessed the forest man for the obverse reason: because with his saw and axe he simply removed, obliterated, the milieu in which alone the forest man could exist; then the land speculators and the traders in slaves and whiskey who followed the husbandmen, and the politicians who followed the land speculators, printing deeper and deeper the dust of that dusty widening, until at last there was no mark of Chickasaw left in it any more. (619–20)

Even so, biological inheritance does not spare genealogies found wanting, whatever their supposed credentials. The estate of Louis Grenier, the original founder of Frenchman's Bend, evinces this reality: "his manor, his kitchens and stables and kennels and slave quarters and gardens and promenades and fields which a hundred years later will have vanished, his name and his blood too, leaving nothing but the name of his plantation and his own fading corrupted legend like a thin layer of the native ephemeral yet inevitable dust on a section of country surrounding a little lost paintless crossroads store" (495).

The continued arrival of settlers even extinguishes memories of the patriarchal pioneer: "new names and faces too in the settlement now— faces so new as to have (to the older residents) no discernible antecedents other than mammalinity, nor past other than the simple years which had scored them; and names so new as to have no discernible (nor discoverable either) antecedents or past at all" (482). Men of the frontier, whatever their race, have become an "anachronism out of an old dead time and a dead age" (499).

From here, as "THE COURTHOUSE (A Name for the City)" recounts, social evolution begins in earnest. This section describes the creation of the town as a moment of the book that is given significance when the importance of communal records detailing local land grants and liens is acknowledged with the need for their safe storage. Before this realization, the community had existed as a European settlement and then a hamlet, pioneering people with a frontier mentality in which "personal liberty and freedom were almost a physical condition like fire or flood, and no community was going to interfere with anyone's morals as long as the amoralist practised somewhere else" (477). Eventually, however, the members of an outlandish gang exercise their amorality within the local environs. There is no alternative but to imprison them in the makeshift jail. Old Alec Holston's padlock is commandeered from the federal mail pouch to secure a cell door that until now has never required fastening. The residents of the hamlet have been accustomed to relying on miscreants to serve their time. The outlaws are not so obliging; they escape, taking the padlock with them.

Not effective for protecting the mail, since one could easily cut the leather pouch, the lock nevertheless carries a symbolism that its disappearance makes apparent. The hamlet is no longer a satellite of the United States but is tied to the federation. Maintaining this relationship is a responsibility that ensures freedom. The theft of the lock, then, is a matter for concern. The community "had already realised its seriousness from the very fact that Peabody had tried to make a joke about it which everyone knew that even Peabody did not think humorous" (486). Ratcliffe appears to solve the dilemma. Why not, he asks, put the cost of a replacement lock on the Indian settlement ledger and let America pay? Written down in this way, they can write off the debt: "they could have charged the United States with seventeen thousand five hundred dollars worth," in Ratcliffe's scheme, "and none would ever read the entry" (487).

Thomas Jefferson Pettigrew, the federal mailman whose job transcends state boundaries, will not allow such an evasion of responsibility. Following the theft, as Noel Polk notes, "Pettigrew sets himself up as arbiter of right and wrong in the settlement" (34) and thereby personifies "the whole vast incalculable weight of federality, not just representing the government nor even himself just the government; for that moment at least, he was the United States" (*Requiem* 488). To write off the padlock is an infringement of the mutual trust that guarantees the federation.

This is an issue of finite freedom, autonomy as its own prisoner—another solution is required. Who better to cure the problem than the local physician? Peabody settles the dilemma with his pronouncement that "we're going to have a town" and that "her name's Jefferson" (492, 493). Cartographic significance on the American map beckons. This process satisfies Pettigrew, who, being kinless, senses that his presence, and by analogy the federal constitution, will last in perpetuity. This nomenclature is especially fitting, because Faulkner depicts Mississippi evolving from prehistoric ages and the mailman exuding an evolutionary essence that owes much to Huxley's Scogan. Pettigrew is "a pterodactyl chick arrested just out of the egg ten glaciers ago," a person "so old in simple infancy as to be worn and weary ancestor of all subsequent life" (485). Nevertheless, the concept of the town remains scarcely tenable to its residents until they begin construction of a courthouse. Then "somewhere between the dark of that first day and the dawn of the next, something had happened to them" (493). This symbolic hub realizes Jefferson but coterminously effects a shift toward the human detachment conditioned by a modern urban environment. Consequently, the men working on the project immediately become "a little unfamiliar even to one another" (494).

This impersonality remains predominantly under the auspices of human relationships in relatively small county municipalities like Jefferson up to the Faulknerian present of 1951, but in larger urban spaces such control becomes increasingly unassured from the outset of the twentieth century. Temple Drake, molded in the former environment, cannot avoid sufferance within the sexual dynamic of the latter, as practiced by Popeye. Evolution has spawned not only personal but also impersonal sexual selection. Faulkner's first narrative section hereby comes to a shocking halt, formal disjunction registering this conclusion, and the translation of characters into dramatis personae affording a means of assessing the effect on individuals of this evolutionary endowment.

Act 1 immediately addresses the issue by undermining the patriarchal intimations of perfection invested in certain events from the interstice between *Sanctuary* and *Requiem for a Nun*. Temple had married Gowan, and although he had continued to envisage his wife as tainted goods, their return from honeymoon had boded well. Haunted by the specter of Red, doubting the paternity of their son, the arrival of their daughter soothed his concerns. The reanimation of Temple's bordello experience dispels this transitory calm. Her letters from this period to Red reappear in the hands of Red's brother Pete. The exhumation of these poisonous epistles revitalizes Temple's hostility to social mores and male impositions. Memories of the biological imperative seem to clash with her fulfillment of the patriarchal demand to marry. Her affair with Pete and their decision to elope evince Temple's psychosexual desires. She follows this disturbing post-Popeyean mixture of biologically fostered and culturally conditioned responses at the expense of familial responsibilities. Not only does Temple break female codes of propriety, but she also repeats the doubly secret essence to this betrayal. She may deny the figuration of chaste womanhood, but she does so unwittingly. Temple Stevens does not seem able to understand the hegemonic relays that enforce her continued predicament as a twentieth-century woman in the South any better than Temple Drake did. Indeed, she may be worse placed in answering this dilemma, because she is still traumatized from the events to which she was subjected at the Old Frenchman place and at the brothel in Memphis. To Temple's deranged reasoning, the maintenance of any sense of fidelity requires her to retain a token of purity. Her daughter manifests this symbol, but to one exceptional source of judgment, Temple's determination to take the child on eloping is misguided. This insight comes from the most unexpected of quarters: the nursery-nurse, Nancy Mannigoe, determining to frustrate her mistress's scheme.

Act 2 elucidates the relationship between the two women. Temple employs Nancy, a one-time prostitute and drug addict, as an ostensible sign of charity. On the surface, Temple is purity per se, while Nancy personifies degradation, but genealogical details belie the views of the communal majority. Temple's lineage does not rank alongside Nancy's descent. "I really sprang from gentlefolks," says Temple, "not Norman knights like Nancy did" (556). With reciprocal awareness, Nancy recognizes that Temple is no purer than anyone else is. The nurse understands, however, that as an object of veneration, Temple is imprisoned in the sacrary of southern womanhood. Although implicitly acknowledging Nancy as a kindred spirit, and despite Nancy's vocation as a nurse, Temple fails to appreciate the healing powers of her employee. Ultimately, then, Nancy has no alternative but to dispel the concept of purity. The baby girl under her charge embodies that fallacy, and Nancy must sacrifice this child as well as herself to press home this lesson. When she is arrested for infanticide, Gavin Stevens (Gowan's uncle), that ubiquitous Faulknerian figure and most learned Yoknapatawphian, acts in her defense. He is a master of letters, a Harvard graduate, a Phi Beta Kappa, and a Heidelberg postgraduate capable of discussing relativity theory with university professors. Despite his efforts, found guilty of infanticide and with the death sentenced passed, Nancy becomes nothing (or "none") in official terms. Only the interval between sentencing and death enables the validation of her actions. Her determination to enlighten Temple, and thereby partially alleviate her former mistress's continuing mental pain, will make Nancy the eponymous "Nun."

Temple almost evades this tutelage by taking a vacation with Gowan in California. The trip is an attempt to put distance between herself and her instructor. In Temple's understanding, this space corroborates the difference between them. Her son exposes the obvious weakness of this technique when asking where they will go once Nancy is dead. Childish innocence forces Temple to face up to her personal history. Unless she completes some sense of closure, a specter will continue to haunt her. Returning to Yoknapatawpha before Nancy's execution, Temple talks through her past as if in a psychiatrist's chair. Her interlocutors are Gavin Stevens and the state governor in whose office the interview takes place; her husband is also (secretly) present. She admits that getting off the train at Taylor makes her to some extent complicit in the events that followed; she confesses that the biological imperative of her rebellion meant staying in Reba's brothel by forced choice; she avows that identifying Goodwin as Tommy's murderer was contempt of court. Unconscious biological inherence, as Temple assures her listeners (though in less evolutionary terms), may have motivated all these actions, but in the final analysis, her Memphis confinement rested on her need to escape. Yoknapatawphians had judged Temple's marriage to Gowan as her resurrection into the southern aristocracy. Temple deluded herself in a similar fashion. Rather than realize her complex sociobiological essence, Temple had merely reformed her old self, marrying and procreating for reformation through evasion. Still haunted and hunted by the impersonal space, she cannot be an exemplar of modern motherhood. Her ordeal at the hands of Popeye and Red has alienated her from this role.

Faulkner personifies the worthy matriarch in Cecilia Farmer, whose story unfolds in the narrative section entitled "THE JAIL (Nor Even Yet Quite Relinquish—)." Cecilia is the exceptional role model who echoes Lelia and Maud Butler. As with so many of Faulkner's characters, the Civil War is a turning point for Cecilia: she scratches her name on the jailhouse window on the day the conflict starts, she meets her future husband during the war, marries him upon the cessation of hostilities, and bears him twelve sons despite anemia allied to the possibilities of posttraumatic stress. Cecilia's inscription on the windowpane marks a change in the sexual economy. "Women," Goldfield contends, "became the keepers of history, archangels of the dead, ministers to the maimed, until living and dead merged into one solemn, glorious, and holy story." This was a switch "from family chroniclers to community memorialists" (111). Nevertheless, one cannot avoid heredity. Thus, when Karl Zender suggests that Yoknapatawpha is an escape from "the ravages of modern America," he fails to estimate the larger Faulknerian scheme in which previous generations of evolution account for the present state of living phenomena (*Politics* 124).

Act 3 confirms Nancy as a contentious modern issue from this model with her emergence from beneath Cecilia Farmer's historical shadow. Temple, no longer defining her employee as a "dope-fiend nigger whore," must awaken to Nancy's unfamiliar talents (520). For instance, confined to jail, Nancy nevertheless knows the details of Temple's revelations at the governor's office. "You cant know that yet," Temple protests, "no matter how clairvoyant you are" (654). Now a counselor not only for her former mistress, but also for her own defense counsel, Nancy fleetingly overthrows the hierarchy of power associated with the Stevenses. Hoping for someone else to fulfill your own responsibilities, she insists, is "the hardest thing of all to break" (655). Her Delphic advice—that one must believe but never hope—demands a future in which the false objectification of nature is banished. Nancy, mere hours from execution, is a heroine who obstinately continues to proclaim this message, a heroine who turns a morality play into the most genuine and earnest of medicine shows. Her acceptance of death counsels Yoknapatawphians that in future, a horizon under the influence of divinely inspired evolution, they should dispel the fallacies of race. Nancy—a passive suicide exhibiting an inverse relation with Popeye's execution—holds the possibility of de-alienating Temple; Nancy too has suffered terrible assaults; Nancy too should have been a matriarch, but a prostitute at the time of her only pregnancy, an assault by one of her clients induced a miscarriage (660). The actions of this white man, unnamed and thereby the impersonal figuration of his race, starkly emphasize the irony of sexual idealism. Nancy embodies the sexual desires of these men more than their objectified ideal does. Biological desire betrays the perverse ideology of race; one sees how the exaggerations and misunderstandings of cultural inheritance imbue sexual politics with another strand of questionable authenticity. The medium for Cecilia's trace evinces this caution, the glass that bears her name becoming nacreous over time with "a faint quiet cast of apocrypha" (640). Dubiousness frames every text. Mythology lasts longer than history. Mythology can overwhelm the trace. Evolution creates this uncertainty because the evolutionary essence, by its very nature, moves on. Social progress, the narrative passages from *Requiem for a Nun* imply, evolves the ability to evolve. Biology appears less absolute to modern *Homo sapiens* than heretofore—Jeffersonians witnessing humankind's usurpation of nature with the defoliation of their town. "The last forest tree was gone from the courthouse yard," and in its place, "formal synthetic shrubs contrived and schooled in Wisconsin greenhouses" (636). Moreover, there is a change to the medium of the circumambient ethos. National Radio means "no more Yoknapatawpha's air nor even Mason and Dixon's air, but America's . . . one air, one nation" (637). No longer of the South but of the United States of America, as Polk concurs, "Jefferson becomes indistinguishable from all other cities its size" (172). No wonder "the last old sapless indomitable unvanquished widow or maiden aunt had died" (*Requiem* 638). The habitual American disposition, once of regional introversion, now extends beyond mondialization to a vision as capacious as can be humanly envisaged. With radio telescopes emitting electromagnetic waves that bounce back to the earth from distant constellations, there is "one universe, one cosmos" (639). Hence, according to Louis Daniel Brodsky, Faulkner's mature art expresses "the *Weltanschauung* that he must have been perceiving during the twilight of his life" (117). Presaging this end, widening a singular demise to global proportions, Faulkner represents the doom of humankind as an express train "grooved ineluctably to the spidery rails of its destiny and destination" (*Requiem* 640). These two rails, like the two chromosomal rods of biological inheritance, direct mankind along a "steadfast and durable and unhurryable continuity against or across which the vain and glittering ephemerae of progress and alteration" wash (641).

    This course, Faulkner wished to make clear, is alterable. Culture, as *Requiem for a Nun* adduces from the basis of *Sanctuary*, can enable advancement. The twentieth-century hegemony of sexual politics, power structures once predisposed to male dominance through intrasexual competition, must be increasingly reoriented by the intersexually fostered intelligence of modern women.

CHAPTER 4

PANGENESIS AND SOUTHERN THOUGHT

natura abhorret vacuum

IN 1842, SWISS BOTANIST KARL WILHELM VON NÄGELI (1817–1891) AND Belgian cytologist Edouard van Beneden (1846–1910) made intriguing separate discoveries. Nägeli noted some peculiarly large filaments within plant cells, while Beneden identified threadlike structures in the cells of worms. Although the similarity of these fibers suggested a common biological role, the apparent simplicity of their construction seemed to preclude them performing a hereditary function. Without any major improvements to the scientific equipment and methodologies available to analyze these filaments, the field of heredity remained open to conjecture for the next forty years, with Charles Darwin's *The Variation of Animals and Plants under Domestication* (1868) a particularly significant intervention. In this volume, Darwin reasons that the procreative transmission of mammalian characteristics from generation to generation is a matter of *pangenesis* (2: 369–70). Corporeal cells throw off undeveloped atoms, or *gemmules*, which are passed to the reproductive organs via the blood stream; conception then blends these components in various combinations, the resultant elements multiplying by self-division during fetal development. A year after Darwin's treatise, Swiss physician Johann Miescher (1844–1895), continuing in the direction laid down by Nägeli and Beneden, discovered nucleic acids. Again, however, these compounds appeared to be too simple to be involved in heredity.

The persistent void in the epistemology of biological inheritance left Darwin free to expatiate on his pangenetic theory. Pangenesis, according to a twenty-first-century interpretation of *The Descent of Man* (1871), complies with a convoluted form of hematological taxonomy. Strain, species, genus, and family constitute this system of classification. Each individual embodies a strain of blood according to speciation. A species is a group of individuals associated in a continuous reproductive sequence; related species belong to a genus; affiliated genera constitute a family. The degree of separation on this taxonomic tree is vital to procreative success. Reproduction between genera from the same family is one end of the pangenetic spectrum. Constituent bloods are antagonistic, fecundity is rare, and only infertile progeny may result. The other end of the spectrum, incest matching strains too closely, is sanguinely reductive to a similar extent. Darwin insisted that between these limits is a sliding scale of blends with differing degrees of compatibility. Wide strain divergence occurs between distinct species in a genus, moderate difference between subspecies, and narrow variance between members of the same species. While leaving unanswered the question as to whether races are equivalent to human subspecies (*polygeny*) or minor variations from a common origin (*monogeny*), *The Descent of Man* nevertheless attributes hybridity, ancestral reversion, and the physiological and psychical constitution of twins in *Homo sapiens* to pangenetic differences.

Darwin, of course, was wrong. Francis Galton indeed disproved pangenesis experimentally in the same year that *The Descent of Man* appeared, when a transfusion of blood between black and white rabbits produced no effect on their offspring. However, as a rarified restatement of *soft inheritance*, which has a history in Western epistemology stretching back beyond Pythagoras, pangenetic theory remained extremely specious.[1] Finally admitting in 1875 that he had been somewhat in error over the hereditary mechanism, Darwin nevertheless maintained that pangenesis was the best hypothesis to date and had "not as yet received its death-blow" (*Life* 3: 195).

Research promised to hasten this demise in the year of Darwin's own death when German anatomist Walther Flemming (1843–1905) overcame the problems of unsophisticated equipment that had prevented Nägeli, Beneden, and Miescher from furthering their discoveries. Flemming's use of aniline dyes revealed the hitherto unrealized complexity of somatic threads and nucleic acids. Staining techniques also enabled him to follow the process of cellular division in detail. Cell filaments, Flemming observed, split along their lengths into two identical halves. He named this fundamental action *mitosis*. The hereditary picture was taking shape, and another piece of the jigsaw turned up within twelve months, when August Weismann propounded the *continuity of the germ plasm*. According to this proposal, there is a generational transfer of the sexual matrix, or germ plasm, during procreation. Furthermore, although giving rise to somatic cells, the germ plasm is not a product of them. Heinrich von Waldeyer (1836–1921) then consolidated the concept of cellular rod-like filaments in 1888 with the term *chromosome*. The next major advance came twelve years later. Erich von Tschermak-Seysenegg (1871–1962) in Austria, Hugo de Vries in Holland, and Carl Erich Correns (1864–1933) in Germany simultaneously rediscovered the work of Gregor Mendel. Obscure during his lifetime, Mendel had nonetheless formulated three important principles. *Uniformity of the first generation, gametic purity,* and *independent assortment* combined to signify that mammalian reproduction paired, rather than blended, hereditary units. The concept of *hard inheritance* now vied with pangenetic theory for the seal of scientific validity.

This was a surprisingly long-fought battle. While Darwin's publications appeared to fill many of the spaces left empty by natural science, his overenthusiastic plenitude actually created new omissions, widened existing cracks, and prevented the work of others closing notable fissures. Moreover, although Mendelian research did flourish in Britain during the first decade of the twentieth century, as Ernst Mayr makes plain, the resistance to pairwise inheritance remained intense (*Growth* 732). On the one hand, Galton still believed in small and continuous variations between organismal generations in accordance with blending. His *Biometrika*—a "Journal for the Statistical Study of Biological Problems," founded in 1901 with W. F. R. Weldon (1860–1906), professor of zoology at University College London, and the mathematician Karl Pearson (1857–1936), therefore continued to disseminate pangenetic theory. On the other hand, the English zoologist William Bateson (1861–1926) claimed a universal validity for *Mendel's Principles of Heredity* (1902). Bateson thereafter founded the discipline of genetics (1905) and within four years, Danish biologist Wilhelm Johannsen (1857–1927) christened the term *gene* for the hereditary unit of hard inheritance. Chromosomes and genes started to become familiar topics of scientific discussion. Yet, internal discord beset academic biology. The death of Galton in 1911 offered to settle this schism, but when Pearson assumed his mantle, the biometrician-Mendelian divide remained.

Two Americans then emerged in a successful challenge to the British dominance of hereditary research. William E. Castle (1867–1962) was a professor of zoology at Harvard, who believed hybridization to be a form of degeneracy (Mayr, *Growth* 785); Thomas Hunt Morgan (1866–1945) was also an outspoken zoologist, whose early work at Columbia University accepted continuous variation in accordance with blending.[2] Crossbreeding pedigree albino and mongrel guinea pigs, Castle classified their offspring as physiologically indeterminate. Blood of a low strain, he concluded, had contaminated that of a superior caliber. Morgan, meanwhile, began to embrace chromosomal theory, and his conversion led him to question the hypothesis of contamination. Castle agreed to run a series of retrials in deference to his eminent colleague's convictions. These tests discredited the last blending hypothesis proposed by a respected biologist. Science rejected pangenesis. The year was 1919. Morgan subsequently exposed another common misconception through his work on the fruit fly *Drosophila melanogaster*. The monofactoring surmise drawn from Mendelism that each gene affects no more than a single characteristic was incorrect. A multiple-factor theory in which several genes modify a particular trait was a better contention. Extrapolating from the fruit fly, human genetics had to be extremely intricate. Pangenetic theory survived in the wake of this problematization.

The contrast between the intuitiveness of pangenesis and the esotericism of hard inheritance was tangible; hence, epistemological dissemination of genetics suffered. George William Hunter's *A Civic Biology* demonstrates this conundrum from an American perspective. Chromosomes, states Hunter, "are believed to be the structures which contain the determiners of the qualities which may be passed from parent plant to offspring or from animal to animal" (261). Despite displaying this up-to-date knowledge, however, a section on eugenics, chillingly subtitled *Blood Tells*, expresses Hunter's opinion that the disabled, the poor, and those of non-European descent are hematological inferiors. Henry Fairfield Osborn (1857–1935), in the estimation of Harvard academic Stephen J. Gould, "the dominant paleontologist of his era," personifies the paradoxical practice engendered by the contending heredity theories of the period (314). Prompted to engage publicly in an assertion of evolution by reports of William Jennings Bryan's fundamentalist speeches in the *New York Times*, "this leading man of scientific freedom and reason," writes Lawrence W. Levine, "was the same man who wrote the preface to Madison Grant's racist tract in 1916 and warned the Second International Congress of Eugenics of the peril of race crossing in 1921" (287).[3] Eugenicists exploited Mendelian monofactoring, as David Kadlec explains, by elaborating "from this miscast framework a similar correspondence between genetic units and particular character traits, such as laziness and wanderlust" (178). Confused and confusing education had paved the way for the enactment of laws compelling, in Edward J. Larson's words, "the sexual segregation and sterilization of certain persons viewed as eugenically unfit" (*Summer* 27). Political interventionism vouchsafed such academic retardation.

The engagement of Vardaman with evolutionary philosophy is a Mississippian instance relevant to Faulkner studies. While Democratic governor (1904–1908) and still editor of *The Big Issue*, Vardaman had approved the celebration "of Huxley and of Hamilton, of Isaac Newton and Adam Smith, of Darwin and of Tyndall, of Spencer and Maury and Humboldt and Edison" by A. H. Ellett (1863–1911) in an article entitled "Our Heritage" (1908) (Coody 216).[4] From the forefront of scientific thinking, Ellett nonetheless reverts to pangenesis: "Beyond it all I am grateful to God that I belong to the race that through the stress of all its history has fixed its heart upon the individual home. That through it all, and with it all, and by it all the Anglo-Saxon blood has sought to build a home with the snow-white wreath of Chastity crowning the threshold, with the altar of God by the fireside, with the crown of a queen on the Mother's head as she rocks her child to sleep." (Coody 217).

A vacuum had swallowed the modern theory of biological inheritance and Vardaman "shortly led his state into a phase of racial extremism that has, perhaps, never been equaled in the American experience" (Williamson, *William Faulkner* 156). Vardaman would continue to exploit this void throughout his political career, which climaxed in his election to the Senate (1913–1919), maintaining that since both the Bible and Darwinian theory teach that creation proceeded from simplicity to complexity, then the African American must be a retarded form of humanity. Any progress attained by them can only be the result of the guidance of the superior race (to which Vardaman belonged). Professor William Benjamin Smith (1850–1934) from Tulane University compounds, although not intentionally, the charge of racism against the "Darwinian" Vardaman. "What does the South stand for in this contention—stand alone, friendless, despised, with the head and heart, the brain and brawn, the wealth and culture of the civilized world arrayed almost solidly against her?" asks Smith. "The answer is simple: She stands for blood, for the 'continuous germ-plasm' of the Caucasian Race." This proclamation, boasts Smith, enjoys Senator Vardaman's wholehearted support (Coody 197–98). Vardaman was a polygenistic interpreter of Darwinian pangenesis who regarded the University of Mississippi as a repository of paternalistic gentlemen dedicated to the vestiges of aristocracy rather than to the aspirations of middle-income families, that is, demarcation appealed to his interracial, but not to his intraracial, sensibilities. Although his attempts from the Senate to restrict curricular activities on campus were unsuccessful, because his governorship coincided with the chancellorship of Joseph Neely Powers, his precedent was widely recognized, and an interventionist legacy transpired. One threat propitious to this bequest, as Don Harrison Doyle records, involved relocating the university to the state capital. First imputed by Democratic governor Lee M. Russell (1875–1943) in 1920 as "retaliation against enemies in Oxford," the idea gained credence among Progressives because it promised firmer control of state education. Theodore G. Bilbo (1877–1947), who would contribute to establishing a state tubercular sanatorium and a state charity hospital during his first term as Mississippi governor from 1916 to 1920, would also attempt to fulfill the interventionist vision of Progressivism. Faced with Governor Bilbo's 1927 advocacy of Russell's proposal, Chancellor Hume had to appeal to the sentiments of local alumni to keep his institution in Oxford. "His speech," Doyle avers, "was widely credited with swaying the legislature to desist in attacking Oxford" (342). Estimating the university as a waywardly inclined satellite, however, Bilbo maintained his pressure and, in the wake of the Scopes Trial, succeeded in exerting pressure from Jackson during his second tenure as Mississippi governor between 1928 and 1932. Bilbo's control reached a peak in 1930 when he fired dozens of faculty members and administrators at the university, becoming the patron who vetted all appointments. The casualties included Hume. Bilbo's reign must have been extreme in Faulkner's eyes. For although, as Kevin Railey states, the Young Colonel (John Wesley Thompson Falkner [1848–1922]) "supported Vardaman and helped his campaign, he would not support Bilbo" (35). Only when Bilbo's governorship ended, did Hume resume his duties as chancellor, serving in the role until 1935. If Faulkner was to evolve an ideology at the vanguard of evolutionary thought, then he must contend with a milieu in which the politically exploitable fallacy of pangenesis reigned, and genetics languished beyond the epistemological horizon. Why was pangenesis so important to southern thought? The deep shadow cast by the Civil War helps to answers this question. With a soil soaked incarnadine, blood remained a vital issue.

The work of Mississippian sociologist Henry Hughes (1829–1862) anticipated this prorogation. Although Hughes, as his biographer Douglas Ambrose explains, "did not represent a dominant tendency in antebellum southern thought," his conclusions found a new audience following the war (7). Hughes echoed the inclination among southern intellectuals and other cultural leaders to preserve their regional aristocracy. His proleptic vision about blood blending, manumission, and peonage would come to express postbellum fears in this domain. Hughes's writings constantly reiterate a cult that dates back to the founding of the British colonies: Anglo-Saxonism. His most noted work, *Treatise on Sociology: Theoretical and Practical* (1854), sustains this mythology. In Hughes's paradigm, southerners—a purity of rare and refined homogenous breeds benefiting from a unique blending of bloods—are racial quintessence. Embodying French, Norman, Spanish, Welsh, Teutonic, and Scottish blood, the South boasts a patrilineal hierarchy dedicated to the maintenance of its lineage. The American aristocracy now descends, avers Hughes, from one of only two genealogies. This distinction leaves Germanic heredity prevailing in the North and Celtic inheritance in the South. Nonetheless, as Hughes would later confirm, consanguinity is not fail-safe; one must also consider blood strain. "As to the pureblooded Indians," states his "Reopening of the Slave Trade: A Series by 'St. Henry'" (1857–1858), "they will not be civilized, and therefore must, directly or indirectly, be benignly slaughtered" (99). Both predominant descents hold similar convictions as to the tainted blood of the disabled, the poor, and the African American. The enslavement of African peoples, Hughes argues, provides particular evidence of white supremacy. Even so, Northern pressure concerning manumission and attendant worries about hematological amalgamation, dilution, and infection threatens to upset the status quo. *Warranteeism*, a recasting of race prejudice in an economic form that superimposes a class order over the existing racial hierarchy, is Hughes's suggested defense. European Americans would remain superordinate *warrantors*, with African Americans as subordinate *warrantees*. Hughes deems the small percentage of superordinate men with no slaves *nonwarrantors*; they are a limbo caste worthy of little attention.[5] Segregation is fundamental to this system, because "sexual intercourse follows social intercourse" and warranteeism forbids "two races within the same class." Exceptions to this rule would invite "the evil of amalgamation and the violation of natural law." Taboo, Hughes insists, must prohibit this risk. "It is the duty of caste to prevent amalgamation." The South must abide by "caste for the purity of the races" (*Treatise* 243).

The southern ethnologist Dr. Josiah Clark Nott (1820–1873) played a major role in this aspect of the debate. Nott, who began his research in 1842, wished to categorize hybridity in *Homo sapiens*. His definition of species is "a type, or organic form, that is permanent; or which has remained unchanged under opposite climatic influences for ages." Classifying species as "remote," "allied," or "proximate" according to their "disparity" or "affinity," four degrees of hybridism emerge. Firstly, that "in which hybrids never reproduce; in other words, where the mixed progeny begins and ends with the first cross." Secondly, that "in which the hybrids are incapable of reproducing *inter se*, but multiply by union with the parent stock." Thirdly, intercrossing "in which animals of unquestionably distinct species produce a progeny which is prolific *inter se*." Fourthly, hybridism "which takes place between closely proximate species, among mankind for example, and among those domestic animals most essential to human wants and happiness: here the prolificacy is unlimited" (375–76). From this taxonomy and his own observations, Nott concludes that the human amalgam, or *mulatto*, is an intermediate form. Mulattos are the shortest lived of any race, less capable of undergoing fatigue than either of the parent races, their women are unhealthy and poor breeders, their men effeminate with low fertility, their hybrid offspring partaking of the African American type more than of the European kind, and their intermarriages less progenitive than pairings with parent stock. Lack of vital sanguinity, he continues, produces mental conditions such as schizophrenia, paranoia, and psychosis. Although Nott posits no final law, he confidently states that mulattos exhibit a hybrid nature resulting from the biological repulsion between the parental bloods they embody. Environmental fitness depends upon the degree of affinity during amalgamation and no intermixture is perfect nor embodies the power of perpetuation. Reassuringly for the inveterate South, either a few generations would subsume hybrid offspring into one or other of their original types, or defective intermixture would result in extinction. That decay and extinction are both present in the first departure from each primitive type were Nott's solace: mixed bloods would eventually prove unable to reproduce. Nott's thoughts found widespread approval among southern ethnologists who could now gauge the advisability of amalgamation in accordance with race.

One member of the Charleston Circle, clergyman-naturalist John Bachman (1790–1874), begged to differ. Bachman's eminence stemmed from his zoological studies and the analogies he drew between the kingdom of nature and the domain of man. Since the laws of hybridism apply equally to all species, and man is a single species, the evidence that "all the races of mankind produce with each other a fertile progeny, by which means new varieties have been produced in every country," reasons Bachman, "constitutes one of the most powerful and undeniable arguments in favor of the unity of the races" (119). Hybridism is a test of specific zoonomical character, he contends, because no two species of animals ever produce a prolific hybrid. Bachman's confidence in this potential for generational reproduction evoked widespread opposition and he stood virtually alone as a southern monogenist.

Samuel George Morton (1799–1851) headed the polygenist (sometimes called the racial pluralist) movement. He believed, as David C. Lindberg and Ronald L. Numbers note, "that, with the exception of the Eskimos, all Native Americans belonged to the same race or type, distinct from all other types" (168–69). Morton backed up his claim in 1844 by conducting a study on ancient Egyptian skulls and mummified heads, which established to his satisfaction "that racial distinctions were as old as recorded history" (169).

Polygenists were not wrong—animal hybrids are not necessarily sterile—but in their eagerness to disprove this preconception, "they readily accepted fanciful crossings" (Stephens 176). Bachman, conversely, believed too readily in the extreme rarity of hybrid fecundity across species. When Morton died in 1851, Bachman hoped that the polygenist movement had died with him. He was wrong. Nott and George R. Gliddon (1809–1857) continued to argue for the "types of mankind." Nott's volume with this title, published in 1854, was an unexpected success. "The subscription list numbered almost one thousand," note Lindberg and Numbers, "and the book quickly went through at least nine editions, a major achievement for an expensive book on science" (173). The subscribers included "such northern naturalists as Timothy Conrad, John Eatton LeConte and Joseph Leidy, and such Southern naturalists as Robert Gibbes, Holmes, Holbrook, Ravenel and Tuomey" (Stephens 196).[6] Nott remained convinced that the African race had developed from one hundred original pairs. Distinct but proximate, admixture had been on going between these pairs for at least ten thousand years. To support this conclusion, *Types of Mankind* cites various opinions, including those of French zoologist Honoré Jacquinot (1815–1887) and American physician Charles Caldwell (1772–1853). For Nott, blood blending meant that the inferior types of mankind would inevitably fulfill their destiny and pass into extinction, leaving their superiors to "overspread the world" (405).

Polygenism did not die alongside Morton, but prevailed as an important tenet of racial difference. The southern ethnologist and white supremacist Dr. John H. Van Evrie (1814–1896) gauged this importance as "an *eternal truth*," stating that: "amalgamation with separate races of men, as ourselves and the Negro, is followed by a mongrel brood, however superior mentally to the Negro, yet vastly inferior to the white, and as certain to perish as the mule, or any other hybrid generation" (8).

With southern ethnology affirming common belief, the case against amalgamation was clear. Violation of this axiom would reduce European America to racial inferiority. God had never intended sexual congress between the races, and even Bachman "sanctioned slavery as a biblically ordained institution" (Stephens 165).

Warranteeism could uphold this divine decree, the *Treatise on Sociology* avows, but only if patricians fulfill the prerequisites of venerating women and taking staunch political action. Southern men should reify their women as silent, beautiful statues; their presence should be one of eternal inspiration, rather than as a possible source of labor. For the North, to appropriate Faulkner's Charles Bon in Hughesean mode, "would have made them slaves too, laborers, cooks, maybe even field hands" (*Absalom* 95). Ambrose notes that Hughes, discerning an inclination among "southern intellectuals and other cultural leaders, especially among the clergy, toward what might best be termed the modern authoritarian state," responded by conflating sociology with politics (188).

Northern domination of governmental power since the Missouri Compromise (1820–1821) had stimulated a basic Southern intolerance toward heteronomy, and, Hughes argues, state authoritarianism in defiance of central authority is still vital.[7] Otherwise, the aristocratic South will be reduced to a dependency and southerners will become mere provincials. Warranteeism, as Ambrose concludes, therefore promotes the political, religious, and intellectual reorientation of Southern society "from a defense of slavery as a necessary evil to the defense of slavery as a positive good" (1). Adherence to slavery impels secessionism. An ordered sovereignty in the South, sharing interests among the white populace of the region, would excel over the free society demanded by the North. In warranteeism, as Ronald Takaki explains, "what is owned is the labor-obligation, not the obligee." Workers depend on their employers for subsistence (135). In comparison, the Northern system suffers from direct antagonism between the interests of capitalists and the desires of their workers. Riotous assemblies and the threat of strikes under the aegis of the labor movement beleaguer Northern businessmen. Union protectionism, laments Hughes, is another manifestation of Northern laxity.

The Civil War "killed Hughes, slavery, and the Old South," writes Ambrose, "but it did not kill the principles that united them: order, hierarchy, human interdependence, and hostility toward free labor and its ideology of freedom and the marketplace version of individualism" (181–82). Moreover, when Darwin's notions became common conjecture, postbellum southern exegetes could scientifically corroborate their beliefs about hybridity. For, in his final edition of *The Origin of Species*, Darwin writes with a hitherto unprecedented certainty about hybrid impotency:

> The subject is in many ways important for us, more especially as the sterility of species when first crossed, and that of their hybrid offspring, cannot have been acquired, as I shall show, by the preservation of successive profitable degrees of sterility. It is an incidental result of differences in the reproductive systems of the parent-species. In treating this subject, two classes of facts, to a large extent fundamentally different, have generally been confounded; namely, the sterility of species when first crossed, and the sterility of the hybrids produced from them.
>
> Pure species have of course their organs of reproduction in a perfect condition, yet when intercrossed they produce either few or no offspring. Hybrids, on the other hand, have their reproductive organs functionally impotent, as may be clearly seen in the state of the male element in both plants and animals; though the formative organs themselves are perfect in structure, as far as the microscope reveals. (235)

Lessened fertility and robust vitality is not a contradiction as the mule, "so notorious for long life and vigour, and yet so sterile," demonstrates. "Other analogous cases," adds Darwin, "could be cited" (*Descent* 171). To Southerners following the provenance left by Hughes and Nott, interracial procreation was one such analogy.

Some sought to engender this rationale in Northern minds too. The Democratic attempt to discredit the reelection campaign of Abraham

Lincoln (1809–1865) in 1864 is the foremost example. David Goodman Croly (1829–1889), managing editor of the *New York World*, and George Wakeman (1837–1923), one of his reporters, anonymously published a pamphlet, supposedly funded by the Republican Party, entitled *Miscegenation: The Theory of the Blending of the Races Applied to the American White Man and Negro*. Their booklet advocates human hybridity and promotes a new designation for interracial sexual congress. They argue that amalgamation is an inexact term, whereas *miscegenation* is more precise. Croly and Wakeman's neologism combines the Latin words *miscere* (mix) and *genus* (race). Miscegenation also echoes the Greek word *melaleukation*, which derives from *melas* (black) and *leukos* (white). The pamphlet implied that Republicans sanctioned an act that Lincoln's presidency would not staunch. Whites must vote Democrat. Ironically, the animism of racist language, terms such as mulatto and mongrel, remained predominant. Croly and Wakeman's racism failed, Lincoln regained the White House, and miscegenation has accreted acceptability as an academic term for the interbreeding of human beings supposed to have originated from different races.

Although manumission, migration, and immigration made miscegenation an important issue in the South during Reconstruction, this interest did not provoke a taboo. Quantitatively, sexual congress between those solely of African ancestry and Africans of partial European descent was most common during the last generation of slavery. Offspring from these encounters were tacitly recognized as having a stabilizing infusion of white blood. This *internal miscegenation*, concludes Joel Williamson, did not carry a palpable threat to the patriarchal system (*Crucible* 39–40). The qualitative danger came from the alternative miscegenate experience as realized in two subcategories. *Complete external miscegenation* denotes sexual congress between white and colored hematological strains both deemed to be pure; *partial external miscegenation* indicates admixture between presumably unalloyed European American blood and that of internal human hybrids.

Miscegenes were held to be a threat to white supremacy, and some of them were even capable of *passing* (or indiscernible mimicry of their masters). External miscegenation therefore most potently conceptualized superordinate fears, worries that deepened for warrantors after manumission. Fewer southern families retained black servants, two races under a single roof became less prevalent, and with miscegenate children sworn to their white fathers at three hundred dollars each, sociological and economic effects further suppressed interracial contact. Miscegenation of the external variety, as Williamson concurs, was "markedly less common after emancipation than before" (*After Slavery* 295). Paradoxically, this scarcity, this very lack of integration, magnified paranoia among superordinate Americans. Williamson agrees: "In the minds of the native whites, children of mixed blood personified the adulteration of the superior race and embodied in living form the failure of Southern civilization. Many whites, turned to soul-searching by their defeat, fixed upon miscegenation as their great sin" (*After Slavery* 296).

Supremacists could blame miscegenation for the North overrunning and destroying the South. Nonintraracial sex provoked such an uneasy state of mind that the southern patriarchy created a new, postbellum enemy. This "black male," explains David Goldfield, "enabled white men to fulfill their roles as protector of white women, a role they had forfeited during the war and now could redeem. Elevating women also elevated white men to the noble cause of guardian and protector while simultaneously establishing the necessity for control over blacks" (101).

African Americans had won their legal right to equality, but a pattern of separation had become fixed in a significant percentage of ruling-class minds. By the end of Reconstruction, Williamson concludes, "the physical color line had, for the most part, already crystallized." Physical separation confirmed mental separation through symbolism. Thereon, a "duo-chromatic order prevailed on streetcars and trains, or in restaurants, saloons and cemeteries" (*After Slavery* 298). The boundary to racial sex was set; crossing that line was abhorrent. The hybrid form, a debilitative species of a species, embodied this abhorrence. Subspecies were perversions of nature. This burgeoning ideology ensured that human hybridity remained a crucial issue when conservatives returned to dominate southern politics in the late 1870s. Often termed Redemption, this political regression actually eroded advances made in domestic, civilian, and political life. The explicit manifestation of Redemption was lynching. Throughout this period and into the early years of the twentieth century, southern whites determined to disfranchise African Americans by legal and constitutional means. Literature provided prominent adherents to this cause in William Z. Ripley (1867–1941), author of *The Races of Europe* (1899), and the lawyer, conservationist, amateur zoologist, and eugenicist Madison Grant (1865–1937). Not only did Grant argue from a Spencerian perspective that unfit infants and adults should be eliminated, but his *Passing of the Great Race* (1916) re-presents antebellum anxieties in persuasively Lamarckian terms. Darwin had been loath to accept Lamarck's ideas on acquired characteristics, notions that Weismann's continuity of the germ plasm had then explicitly refuted, but as with pangenesis, the concept retained an intuitive sense. Exploiting this appeal enabled Ripley and Grant to disseminate polygenist demarcations of racial difference.

Fears of manumission weakening the southern bloodline also found a prominent acolyte in Charles Davenport (1866–1944). At the turn of the century, Davenport was conducting studies into epilepsy and neurofibromatosis, but when the government formed the American Breeder's Association in 1906, he set up a Committee on Eugenics under its auspices. Davenport worked on inheritance and criminology with Harvard coevals Prescott Hall (1868–1921) and Robert De C. Ward (1867–1931) and, with a ten thousand-dollar endowment from a wealthy widow, soon established the Eugenics Record Office (1910–1944). Davenport's team amassed hundreds of thousands of family pedigrees, classifying immigrants in polygenist terms and hastily adapting Mendelian-based research to augment Darwinian proposals concerning hybrid reversion. In 1911, the Eugenics Record Office reported on practical means for "Cutting off the Defective Germ-Plasm in the Human Population." One of their measures was euthanasia—past the age of reproduction even members of the supposedly purist race could lose their social value. The "growing nativist fear of American 'race suicide,'" concludes Kadlec, resulted in the 1924 Johnson-Reed National Origins Act to maintain the white identity of America by increasing the admission of North European immigrants in proportion to the number entering from the Mediterranean (157). Alongside federal action, thirty-five states enacted statutes to improve the hereditary qualities of people within their boundaries. Granted political significance with such legislation, immigration and the effects of miscegenation retained national importance. Hughesean ideas had mutated into a bulwark for a self-perpetuating oligarchy. The absurdity of this deplorable situation was, as Richard Gray writes, "symptomatic of the pressures that inspired it: only desperate states require desperate remedies" (32).

Before the genealogies of Yoknapatawpha could explore this desperation, Faulkner would have to banish his own youthful ignorance toward race and blood. The interchange of criticism about his poem "Une Ballade des Femmes Perdues" hints at his southern indoctrination. Published on 28 January 1920 in *The Mississippian*, a fellow University of

Mississippi student parodied the piece, a witticism to which Faulkner retorted in the 3 March edition: "The most deplorable thing was his meaningless and unnecessary parading of his doubtless extensive knowledge of the Latin language. To my mind there is nothing as vulgar as a conscious mingling of two languages—unless, of course, the mingling gives shades and tones that the work would not otherwise possess" (Collins, "Faulkner" 9).

The twenty-two-year-old Faulkner was, despite the caveat, tense with respect to amalgamation and the "vulgarly stupid agglomeration of words" used by his critic (Collins, "Faulkner" 9). "Peter," a 1925 Faulknerian experiment unpublished in his lifetime, expresses similar tensions. Peter's mother is a miscegene, a woman in whose eyes "was all the despair of a subject race and a thinned blood become sterile except in the knowledge of the ancient sorrows of white and black" (*Uncollected Stories* 493). Her son is "an incidental coin minted between the severed yet similar despairs of two races" (490). The theme of sorrowful admixture appears again in Faulkner's stories for the *Double Dealer* and the *Times-Picayune* during this period. For instance, hematology bespeaks strength or weakness to the Semitic protagonist in "New Orleans: The Wealthy Jew." "Heirs to my pleasures and pains will rise phoenix-like," asserts the Semite, "for the blood is old, but strong. O ye mixed races, with your blood mingled and thin and lost; with your dream grown tarnished and pointless, knowing not what ye desire!" (*New Orleans* 4).

Beyond Faulkner's writing, friends also noted his attitude. Sherwood Anderson testifies that the New Orleans Faulkner of 1925 thought mulattos to be infertile beyond a third generation ("A Meeting South" 269–79). Anderson would expand on this testimony seventeen years later in his memoirs. Race to the young Faulkner appeared to bespeak subspecies: "I remember when I first met him, when he had first come from his own little Southern town, sitting with him one evening before the cathedral in New Orleans while he contended with entire seriousness that the cross between the white man and the Negro woman always resulted after the first crossing, in sterility. He spoke of the cross between the jack and the mare that produced the mule and said that, as between the white man and the Negro woman, it was just the same" (474).

Joseph Blotner is reluctant to concede Anderson's point: "It is not impossible that Faulkner, at twenty-seven, may have believed this, but it seems highly unlikely" (*Biography* 1: 498). That "tall tale-telling" (1: 498–99) was characteristic of him and that "evidence to the contrary had been around him all his life" (1: 498) are further citations exonerating Faulkner from pernicious racial attitudes. But if, as Williamson emphasizes, effeteness resulting from mixed blood remained "a strangely vital myth in southern white thinking" (*William Faulkner* 199), then Blotner's sense of telling tales can be dismissed, *gradu mutato*, as a chant or spell—repeat the rubric often enough and the lie appears to manifest truth. Mississippians of Faulkner's generation had grown up and continued to live within this environment of ideological inculcation, and although this context does not excuse the immature thoughts of the emerging author, this historical placement does help to explain their prominence. His family history enhances this explanation.

The familial spotlight thrown on the drunken incompetence of Faulkner's father had prompted the boy to suspect a weakness in his own bloodline. Both of William's grandmothers, as Railey underscores, "were active members of the Women's Christian Temperance Union" (35). Murry Falkner simply failed to live up to their expectations and to the illustrious pedigree that their membership of another organization, the United Daughters of the Confederacy, wished to perpetuate. Landowner, Confederate officer, lawyer, railroad constructor, politician, and author William Clark Falkner (1825–1889) was a more fitting role model. Familial and local tales depicted the Old Colonel to his great-grandson as an exemplar of southern manhood. Yet, though Faulkner may not have wished to admit it, pangenetic reasoning blames William Clark for the reductiveness that was supposedly to blight his descendants. His questionable marriage to Holland Pearce in the 1840s had produced that inconsequential imitation of Confederate manhood, the Young Colonel, whose own son was the troubled specimen Murry. As a pale throwback to William Clark, the eldest incumbent of the fourth generation, William Cuthbert, seemingly completed the reductive genealogical descent: vestigial antebellum gemmules fighting back in vain against successive generational infusions of incompatible distaff-side blood. Being born into such a history, the cultural importance attributed by the South to reversion was bound to influence the young William. "Tradition" for an American, he admitted later in life, "is not much older than his grandfather" (*Lion* 99). Spiritually associating with his revered antecedent gave William a sense of European heritage, confidence in his aristocratic pretensions, and a masculine aura that a profession in writing would fail to provide. Imagining himself as his father's grandfather also doubly enabled him to dismiss the paternal epigone. Not only was William anterior to the previous generation, but he also indicted Murry as a genealogical interloper. Never quite surmounting this personal anguish, though, the sense of lineal betrayal seems to have impelled Faulkner's artistic vision, hematological strain in *Flags in the Dust* providing an ample resource by which to explore pangenetic questions. Eschewing obtuse humor in favor of a more considered treatment of pangenesis, Faulkner prosecutes this strategy in his first Yoknapatawpha novel through a substantial and seemingly abstruse shift in focus. Blood strain, rather than internal or external miscegenation, is his paramount concern. Two families, each with pretensions to aristocracy, but each simultaneously undermined from within, are his hematological vehicles.

On the one hand, Sartoris blood not only provides characteristics readily associated with the status of southern patricians, nineteenth-century verities of courage, honor, and pride, but also endows its bearers with recklessness. An outward manifestation of this internal schism is the lack of protection Old Bayard Sartoris affords to the blood he otherwise values so highly. His perfunctory attitude comes to a head when an irritating wheal appears on his face. The old man is willing to ignore the pustule, but his sister, Jenny, is not. She demands he seek medical advice. The environment of Jefferson offers three choices in this regard. Each of these doctors personifies a period in the history of medicine from the shaman, Will Falls, via the bonesetter, Loosh Peabody, to the physician, Dr. Alford. Locals tend to put their faith in Peabody, but Old Bayard subscribes to the shamanic, while Jenny believes in Alford's general practice. Old Bayard, under pressure from his sister, consults Alford, but does not undergo the recommended invasive procedure, preferring to apply a homemade salve from Falls. "You've got to let that old quack of a Will Falls give you blood poisoning?" frets Jenny. "After what Dr. Alford told you, when even Loosh Peabody, who thinks a course of quinine or calomel will cure anything from a broken neck to chilblains, agreed with him?" (257). Even so, after a course of treatment, the papule falls off. Falls seems to have worked his magic without substantiating Jenny's hematological fears. The doctor of old may have eclipsed the present-day physician, but Loosh Peabody, the country doctor of practical experience, displays the profoundest insight. He also examines Old Bayard before Falls's success. The wean worries Peabody, not so much as a cancerous growth, but rather as a psychosomatic symbol intimately concerned with Sartoris recklessness. On examining his patient, he diagnoses tachycardia. Unexpected excitement could prove fatal; Old Bayard must no longer be careless toward his health. Events, as *Flags in the Dust* relates, will confirm Peabody's prognosis, but hereditary traits are hard to disown.[8] For, "Sartoris men, from the Carolina Bayard and Colonel John Sartoris to the twin grandsons Bayard and John," comments James B. Carothers, "are capable of action and are drawn instinctively to it" (267). The sense of hematological condemnation encompassing the Sartorises, unsuspected by the characters in the novel, but upon which Faulkner insists, comes from the status of Bayard and John as twins.

At one level, Faulkner draws on the Old World myths of Castor and Pollux, Baldur and Hodur, and Romulus and Remus in pursuing an interest in necessary supplementarity. "Faulkner," as Dexter Westrum confirms, "sees twins as complementary parts that need each other in order to exist as a whole" (370). Iroquois and associated autochthonous tales provide a second provenance. These creation stories attribute the physical phenomena of the Earth and the divided human psyche to the twins of the sky woman. One of these sons is a peacemaker; his counterpart is an evil warmonger. At a third level, Darwin's thoughts on heredity in mammals elucidate the pangenetic aspect to Faulkner's figuration of twins. Gemmules, *The Variation of Animals* explains, are "capable of transmission in a dormant state to future generations and may then be developed. Their development depends on their union with other partially developed or nascent cells which precede them in the regular course of growth" (370). Darwin illustrates this theory by describing a set of identical twins under his observation. He writes, "They even had their little fingers on both hands crooked; and in both children the second bicuspid tooth of the second dentition, on the right side in the upper jaw was misplaced; for, instead of standing in a line with the others, it grew from the roof of the mouth behind the first bicuspid" (240).

Neither the parents nor any members of their families exhibited the same peculiarity. "Now, as both the girls were affected in exactly the same manner," reasons Darwin, "the idea of accident is at once excluded." If the latency of some gemmules lasts over generations, then pangenesis would explain the matter as "reversion to some long-forgotten progenitor" (240). Furthermore, the familial side to which the throwback corresponds has partially overridden the influence of its hematological complement.[9] Although throwbacks may be triggered by environmental flux, "under conditions which favour the multiplication and development of certain dormant gemmules, as when animals become feral and revert to their pristine character" (396), the plainest cause of reversion is "by crossing" (394–95). Inadvisable hybridity is the extreme manifestation of this antithesis. Nonetheless, relying on an article in the "British and Foreign Medico-Chirurgical Review" of July 1863, Darwin later notes that "it is at least known that with mankind a tendency to produce twins runs in families" (*Descent* 45).[10] Multiple births, as had suggested his case history in *The Variation of Animals*, tend to be throwbacks to a previous generation and, as a corollary, they evince corrupted procreative blood. Bayard and John Sartoris embody, therefore, a previous lineal betrayal. By making them identical twins, Faulkner heightens the impression of a tainted descent.

Conversely, Benbow blood bestows "a golden Arcadian drowse" while undermining that bequest with the dubious qualities of dilettantism and incestuousness (*Flags* 177). That Horace Benbow embodies these traits is especially noticeable with his reverence for his sister Narcissa. Separated from her by service in World War I, Horace takes up the art of glass blowing in France. The vases he creates are representative of southern womanhood. His initial attempt, "a small chaste shape in clear glass not four inches high, fragile as a silver lily and incomplete," he names Narcissa (179). This gynecological-like product of *blowing* his sister reveals an incestuous desire. By summer 1919, Horace has made four more examples; each is named and, one suspects, modeled in remembrance of different southern women whom he idolizes (228). On demobilization, he brings his glassware back to Yoknapatawpha, protecting its transit in an almost hysterical fashion. As soon as his freight is unloaded from the train at Oxford, Horace asks the porter, "She's all right on de inside, aint she?" (172). His subliminal question concerns the chastity of southern womanhood and is prompted by the ever-present specter of incestuousness among a postbellum populace shorn of male vitality. A post-Darwinian for whom "lying is a struggle for survival," Horace cannot openly acknowledge this fascination (222).

Philip Cohen is therefore correct in stating that *Sartoris* suffers in comparison to *Flags in the Dust* from the excision of much of this intimate Benbow material ("Last Sartoris" 30–39). Both versions do retain, however, Faulkner's botanical imagery. Each family is associated with a particular plant. The wisteria, redolent of nostalgia and wistfulness, represents the Sartorises; the rose, beautiful but barbed, symbolizes the Benbows. In a tangled Sartoris flowerbed, a rose is slowly overgrowing and steadily killing a trellis-trained wisteria. This horticultural depiction is a

Faulknerian allusion to the closing allegory in *The Origin of Species*. "It is interesting to contemplate a tangled bank, clothed with many plants of many kinds, with birds singing on the bushes, with various insects flitting about, and with worms crawling through the damp earth," writes Darwin,

> and to reflect that these elaborately constructed forms, so different from each other, and dependent upon each other in so complex a manner, have all been produced by laws acting around us. These laws, taken in the largest sense, being Growth with reproduction; Inheritance which is almost implied by reproduction; Variability from the indirect and direct action of the conditions of life, and from use and disuse: a Ratio of Increase so high as to lead to a Struggle for Life, and as a consequence to Natural Selection, entailing Divergence of Character and the Extinction of less improved forms. (429)

Thus, Darwin concludes, "from the war of nature, from famine and death, the most exalted object that we are capable of conceiving, namely, the production of the higher animals, directly follows" (429). This Darwinian tangled bank, notes Carol Colatrella, unearths the paradox "that for there to be life, there must be death" (20). The wisteria and the rose in *Flags in the Dust*, as Colatrella corroborates, are similarly revelatory. The Benbows are agents of destruction for the Sartorises, and Narcissa is particularly in the frame. Her name echoes the horticultural theme and, initially enamoured of Bayard's dead brother, John, she need only marry Bayard to effect a drastic generational change on the Sartoris lineage. Narcissa, "odorless and unpickable," a strangling rose of self-absorption, is a secret agent of extinction (*Flags* 11).

The consummation of Bayard and Narcissa's relationship compounds the problems of soft inheritance evinced by both families. Incompatible Sartoris and Benbow gemmules soon combine to leave Narcissa pregnant. Bayard is fretful; yet, he is unaware as to the cause of his anxiety. Only when his Sartoris impulsiveness comes to a head in another way, does Bayard experience a shattering enlightenment. Driving his car at high speed with his grandfather in the passenger seat, Bayard has an accident. At one level, the significance of irritants, wheals, and wheels has been realized. The anxiety-ridden and stress-provoking Young Bayard has exercised Old Bayard to the point of a fatal heart attack. At another level, not only has the inherent recklessness in Sartoris blood accounted for another of its bearers, but the blighted conception of Bayard and Narcissa's expected child has also exhausted the Sartoris genealogy. Wishing to avoid the backlash over his grandfather's death, Bayard stays with family friends, the MacCallums, in the backwoods. A patriarchy, with Virginius MacCallum at its head and "his sons around him" (362), the men's "aquiline faces" attest to the perpetuation of old values, their names (including Lee, Stuart, and Jackson) to Confederate standards (365). Virginius remains obsessed with the Civil War. He refuses to respect the decorated World War I service of his son, Buddy, because "it's a Yankee medal," and he "and Stonewall Jackson aint never surrendered" (368). Rafe perpetuates this feeling into the next generation with his contention that "that was the biggest mistake the world ever made, when Lee surrendered. The country aint never got over it" (383). In this type of southern formulation, an ethos without outlook, the world and the country are equivalent.

Keeping quiet about the accident, Bayard believes he can escape the consequences of his behavior. This is a forlorn hope, because the ramifications of poor hematology soon find him out. "Good Lord, boy," Rafe exclaims early one morning, "you look like a hant" (372). Agitated by his grandfather's death and the MacCallums' reminiscences about his brother, to whom their farmstead was special, Bayard is gaunt and pale. He finds little respite during his stay, begins to fear that his blood is already "spent," and cannot help but subconsciously summon the specter he dreads (371).

A litter of puppies manifests this fear. Their father is the patriarch of the MacCallums' dog pack, the "General," a "blue-ticked hound with an expression of majestic gravity"; their mother is the fox called Ethel (358). These two animals, supposed progenitors of a new breed "with a hound's wind and bottom, and a fox's smartness and speed" (372), had been put together as "a experiment" (373). Since the hound and the fox are species from different genera of the exceptionally varied *Canidae* family, Faulkner's figuration correctly actualizes the possibility of positive fertility while nevertheless clearly illustrating pangenetic antagonism in the physiological disabilities of their progeny.[11] "No two of them looked alike," notes the narrator, "and none of them looked like anything else. Neither fox nor hound; partaking of both, yet neither; and despite their soft infancy, there was about them something monstrous and contradictory and obscene" (374). As a "patient, voiceless confusion," they cannot see, smell, or bark (375). The hematological incompatibility of their parental bloods has doomed them to an early death. The fox-hound figuration in *Flags in the Dust* thereby counsels on at least three fronts. Firstly, sexual congress between different species, animals that are close enough in physiological terms for positive fertility, but distinct enough to be a poor match, is an ill-advised union. Secondly, artificial selection may be proactive, but can be so unnatural as to create insurmountable difficulties. Thirdly, natural selection is benign, yet more powerful than direct selection. The puppies provide a formal as well as a figurative triumph for Faulkner: blighted hybridity anticipating the closure to a text that had opened with the augury of a strangled wisteria. Unsuited procreative species in Faulkner's analogy of flora and fauna correspond to reproductively strained human partnerships. The differentiated species of the male hound and female fox echo the unworkable pangenetic relationship between the strains of Sartoris and Benbow blood. To repeat the earlier quote, the puppies are a "patient, voiceless confusion." Patients, invalids, they are not valid. Bayard should have avoided Narcissa, but she had subdued him into "a smoldering hiatus that might have been called contentment" (228). She was *natura naturans* who had temporarily tamed but concurrently deceived. Pangenesis had never worried her. The more natural of the two lovers, she had remained benign but powerful. Thus, "neatly tricked by earth, that ancient Delilah," Bayard had succumbed to marrying and impregnating her (230).

Face to face with his offspring, the General is fascinated, baffled, and horrified. Having inspected his puppies in Bayard's presence, the hound departs with "his tail between his legs" (375). Virginius voices the human analogy. "Well, I dont blame the old feller," he ponders. "Ef I had to look around on a passel of chaps like them and say to myself Them's my boys. . . . Yes, suh, I reckon I'd feel 'bout as proud as he does" (375–76). Bayard must leave the backwoods. On departure, he looks back at the farmstead. He notes the farewells of Henry and Buddy, but he is preoccupied with the presence of Ethel. She apparently knows the contribution Bayard has made to the death of the aristocratic South. The vixen is "looking at him covertly; near her the half-grown puppies moved about in the sun" (385). Reaching the road, Bayard turns, not toward home, but in the opposite direction. The father-to-be cannot face the Benbow-tinted future of Yoknapatawpha.

Spending Christmas Day with an African America sharecropping family, Bayard experiences humanity forgetting "its lust and cowardice and greed," humankind "touching for a moment and fused." The white man and the black man, "two opposed concepts antipathetic by race, blood, nature and environment" are recognized as the "illusion of a contradiction." Nevertheless, with the holy day over, the "moment" does not last (393). Over the following months, Bayard begins to squander his financial inheritance on drink. His desperation unsatiated, pushed to new heights by alcohol, he takes a job as a test pilot and soon dies in an accident at Dayton, Ohio. The prominence of this place in American aeronautical history coincides with the significance of this time for the Sartorises. The demise of Bayard heralds the birth of his son. Just as the bloodhound, the General, had left the narrative with his tail between his legs, so Bayard's plane breaks up, its rear section shearing away beneath him. Bayard now rejoins the brother whom he lost in French airspace during the war. The Sartoris family is all but spent, Faulkner's narrative connotes, their paleonymy all but a petrified history.

Jenny, despite her protestations, is now the last of the pedigreed Sartorises. As such, writes Mortimer, she attempts to preserve "a world sustained by a belief in aristocracy and the ethically superior nature of man" (194). Noticeably, she continually calls Narcissa's baby John instead of Benbow (*Flags* 432). In doing so, Jenny not only demotes Bayard in comparison to his twin, but also nullifies the sense of neonatal hybridization in the concatenation of parental surnames. The baby's spear-side blood, Jenny subconsciously maintains, will overthrow his maternal hematology.

Tantalizingly, the novel ends with Narcissa and Jenny contemplating Benbow's future. "Beyond Miss Jenny's trim fading head the window curtains hung motionless without any wind," and "beyond the window evening was a windless lilac dream, foster-dam of quietude and peace" (433). Benbow's natural background, the Arcadian inheritance of "quietude and peace" from his mother, appears in stark contrast to the recklessness bequeathed him by his father. Yet, this is Narcissa's point of view, and Benbow blood is tainted too. An unnaturally odorless eglantine, a singular southern rose, she observes the scene "a little dreamily" as Jenny fades into the background (and the past). Narcissa's vision is a rose-tinted deception. That unmatched procreative bloods produce a benign mixture is, as Faulkner's analogy intimates, illusory too. The mingling shades and tones, the positive value of hybridity that Faulkner appends as a caveat to his retort in *The Mississippian* of 3 March 1920, has not managed to filter through to this work. Whether supposedly derived from the same racial category or not, *Flags in the Dust* contends, the strain of blood constituents is paramount. Explicit as this demonstration of Darwinian attitudes to blood is, Faulkner's novel also contains indications as to his widening scientific perspective. The MacCallums testify to this growing authorial knowledge in one respect. The members of this family are an early Faulknerian figuration of hard inheritance. Their countenances are "stamped all clearly from the same die" (363). With no female presence and no trace of miscegenation, Faulkner merely avoids genetic complexities, presenting a genealogy dominated by the male line and retaining the characteristics of a stolid descent. Loosh Peabody and his son afford the second perspective on biological inheritance in *Flags in the Dust* that reveals a deepening of authorial knowledge. On the one hand, Loosh is a practitioner with some medical knowledge, common sense, and years of practice. This combination posits him as the personification of medicine at its best. He is a compromise between the magician of old and the scientist to come. On the other hand, as a New York intern associated with a renowned surgeon, his son represents the future of medical research. When he comes to visit his father in Jefferson, the old man cannot help but dispense some advice. The classroom is the Sartoris burial plot in the local cemetery. This family's blood, suggests Loosh, sealed their fate. Furthermore, baby Benbow's hematology will be vital to his struggle for existence. "Maybe that Benbow blood will sort of hold him down," the young man muses. "They're quiet folks, that girl; and Horace sort of . . . and just women to raise him." Loosh retorts that the baby has "got Sartoris blood in him, too" (431). This conversation betrays the pangenetic reasoning of both father and son. That Old Peabody conceives of the Sartorises in terms of blood is not a surprise, but that Young Peabody, a doctor from Thomas Hunt Morgan's city of hard inheritance, is prone to similar speculation is less expected. Faulkner is aware of the conundrum. That the New Yorker performs cutting-edge procedures with the "celerity of a prestidigitator" is significant (429). Science, biology, and doctoring remain beset with the dubiousness of intuition. Apparently talking of blood in metaphors, the Peabodys fall foul of a predominant ethos that sedulously superimposes the metaphoric onto the literal. Figurative language weighs heavily upon the actual situation.

While revising what was to become *Sartoris*, Faulkner concurrently reengaged with the consequences of inappropriate pangenesis in his next work, *The Sound and the Fury* (1929). With a drunkard for a father and a mother who is constantly ill, the younger Compson generation appears tainted at conception. Uncle Maury, whose business failures reveal distaff-side fragility in another manner, confirms the sense of lineal infirmity. Faulkner compounds such beliefs with the figure of Benjamin, whose monologue introduces the novel in the Shakespearean idiom of the idiotic signifying nothing. Originally christened Maury, then renamed Benjamin, he is the pangenetic near inarticulation of body, mind, and language that results from incest. Moreover, the remotest of prospects for the Compson line through Benjamin hit a dead end when Jason has him castrated. Other Compsons from Benjamin's generation offer little more in terms of furthering their genealogy. This hopelessness results from the pangenetic apocalypse immanent in their blood: Maury's closeness to his sister finding a correlative in the relationship between Quentin and Candace in the next generation. Faulkner's insistence on incestuousness, however, condemns more than a single bloodline. Interbreeding plantation aristocracies in the South are doomed. For, intent on maintaining their patriarchal status, the rules by which they operate endanger their entire social class. Acknowledging only the spear side is a form of favoritism almost certainly ill-fated. "The number of noble names," writes geneticist Steve Jones, "is hence bound to decrease each generation: any sonless marriage kills the title" (*Blood* 90). Aristocracies are liable to extinction. This is their tragedy—they are exclusive, but they do not endure. Pangenesis bespeaks amalgamation; sex in pangenetic terms should mix and disperse parental bloods to successive generations. If the transmission of biological capital were thoroughly analogous to the bequest of economic assets, then this would preclude a lack of perpetuation. "Sex, not death," asserts Jones, "is the great leveller" (*Blood* 83). The one surviving member of the Compson family to succeed economically, the figure through which Faulkner again illustrates his growing sense of sexual democratization, is Candace. Conflating both biological and cultural mechanisms, Faulknerian inheritance in *The Sound and the Fury* promotes neither sex over the other. Candace, to the anger of her brother Jason, brings her body to intimate relationships while her suitors bring money. Hence, the father of her daughter, Quentin, is anyone but an aristocrat. Faulkner's revised thoughts about pangenesis play between uncle and niece. Blood ideology divides them as antithetical figures. Young Quentin is an enterprising, free spirit untroubled by thoughts of hematological blending; Jason is an inveterate shackled to his pangenetic maxim that "blood is blood and you cant get around it" (*Sound* 1064).

CHAPTER 5

FROM RACE TO ECOLOGY

> A state which in this age of racial poisoning dedicates itself to the care of its best racial elements must some day become lord of the earth.
>
> Adolf Hitler, *Mein Kampf* (629)[1]

A REACTIONARY DISCOURSE, OR TRANSPERSONAL LANGUAGE SYSTEM, THAT rigidly embodies the ideas, values, and terminology of a community of knowledge exhibits a marked evolutionary reluctance. The inveterate ontology to which William Faulkner shows Jason Compson subscribing befits this description. Pangenetic notions were vital components in this discursive buttressing of the Old South from both ideational and physical invasion. *Population viscosity*, the inclination to remain close to where one was born, had progressively diminished in the region after the Civil War. For generations, mutually resembling individuals had found themselves clustered together in local aggregations. Society had meant accumulated kinship, and mutual resemblance had signified biological closeness. Reconstruction had loosened lineal coherence to a moderate extent and the movement of men to Europe during World War I had confirmed this trend. Now the requirements of postwar industrial production effected a more radical change. Hereon, a shifting populace crossed the American scene and population fluidity predicated a negative correlation with mutual resemblance. Communal stalwarts in the South swore that miscegenation would not exacerbate the situation. In an environment where kinship resemblance no longer maintained racial segregation, extending the color bar helped to accomplish this task. "Blackness," explains Joel Williamson, "had become not a matter of visibility, not even, ironically, of the one-drop rule. It had passed on to become a matter of inner morality and outward behavior. People biologically black in any degree could not openly aspire to whiteness; but whites could easily descend into blackness if they failed in morality. Thus there was created in the white mind a new and curious kind of mulatto—a mulatto who was in fact genetically white but morally black. In sum, 'Negro' became an *idea*" (*New People* 108). Assumptions about blood blending then conflated this idea into a procreative mandate that trapped suspected miscegenes in the reproductive limbo of the *pangenetic chokepoint* (or *bottleneck*).

The maturing Faulkner would prove himself worthy to contest this injunction in *Light in August* (1932). By far his bloodiest, and, for African Americans, his most controversial work, Faulkner's novel graphically analyzes the inculcation into, the constriction within, and the ontological effects of the pangenetic chokepoint.[2] Three case histories—those of Gail Hightower, Joanna Burden, and Joe Christmas—are examined to this end. Childhood indoctrination is crucial to each and leads to a sense of genealogical sterility. The concept of marriage to Gail's parents, for example, is not "men and women in sanctified and living physical intimacy, but a dead state carried over into and existing still among the living like two shadows chained together with the shadow of a chain" (754). Gail's supposed susceptibility to Darwinian reversion, as implied by the derivation of his Christian name from his grandfather, serves to endorse this belief. Constant exposure to tales of his forebear's Civil War heroics conflates this feeling. "Some throwback to the austere and not dim times not so long passed," Gail is haunted by his paterfamilias (749). "So it's no wonder," he concludes, "that I skipped a generation." Rather than dedicated to the furtherance of his lineage, Gail is shackled to the past, determined to find salvation "where my life had already ceased before it began" (752). Jefferson, the haunt where his grandfather had died, becomes his aim. Posted there after seminary training, he achieves his paradoxical and self-negating goal: "As though the seed which his grandfather had transmitted to him had been on the horse too that night and had been killed too and time had stopped there and then for the seed and nothing had happened in time since, not even him" (445). Even marriage cannot prevent the feeling "that I had no father and that I had already died one night twenty years before I saw light" (752). His wife, intolerant of this situation and seeking sexual relief, dies mysteriously in Memphis. Her demise seals Gail's life as a living death within the pangenetic bottleneck.

Soon thereafter, circumstances call on Gail to assist at a birth. Not a professional medic, the intervention of such an indeterminate figure in the sexual economy of Jefferson enrages public opinion. Neighbors make violent attempts to expel him from the town. Gail steadfastly resists until a gradual relaxation of tension allows him to slip into the communal background. Treating him as one of the most marginalized men in Jefferson, the community barely passes comment on his subsequent relationship with Byron Bunch. If intimations of a homosexual relationship between the two men arise, Byron being the one person with whom Gail has regular "intercourse," then they emanate not from the community but from the narrator (433). Nonetheless, a second marriage for the "queershaped, not-quite-familiar figure" of Gail appears improbable (704). He is a genealogical dead end.

Joanna Burden is Gail's female counterpart in terms of marginalization. The constrictive effect of the pangenetic chokepoint dictates her situation too. Contesting bloods seem to betray her descent. The origins of her northern grandfather, Calvin, and his Huguenot wife impute a racial difference in Joanna's forebears. Their son Nathaniel's marriage to a Mexican of Spanish descent, Juana, who looks uncannily like the mother he never knew, implies incestuous as well as further racial imperilment to the bloodline. Procreation by this couple has already produced a son out of wedlock, whose name, Calvin, proffers a reversion to his spear-side grandfather. Following Juana's death, Nathaniel Burden marries a woman (unnamed in the novel) from New Hampshire. Joanna is the daughter of this union. Born of a supposedly hybrid father and christened in memory of that father's first wife, a miscegenate ambience surrounds baby Joanna. She then suffers, as did Gail, from the cultural inheritance immanent in nurture. The contradictory beliefs of her grandfather Calvin are at the root of this inculcation. At one level, Calvin appears to be a liberal who abjures slavery, so progressive a figure that Col. John Sartoris will murder him and Joanna's brother for "threatening white supremacy" (582). At a second level, though, Calvin's stance on race understands Africans as a divine load placed on warrantors in penance for their fall from grace. His combination of religious and pangenetic logic affirms that the Civil War was the apogee of this hardship but that following manumission white blood will "bleach out" the miscegenate heredity of the South. Within a hundred years, the descendants of hybrids "will be white folks again" (581). Nathaniel stresses this aspect of their ancestral rationale when he lectures the young Joanna by the graves of her grandfather and brother: "murdered not by one white man but by the curse which God put on a whole race before your grandfather or your brother or me or you were even thought of. A race doomed and cursed to be forever and ever a part of the white race's doom and curse for its sins. Remember that. His doom and his curse. Forever and ever. Mine. Your mother's. Yours, even though you are a child. The curse of every white child that ever was born and that ever will be born. None can escape it" (585).

Joanna, repeatedly admonished with this dubious lesson, will dedicate her adult life to the needs of African Americans. This charity, founded on the belief that she is raising a burden, may never reconcile principle with practice but is altruistic enough to aggravate racist diehards when she moves to Jefferson. Only mitigating circumstances save her from the violence meted out to Hightower. Firstly, she is a single woman. Secondly, her property, which lies in the hinterland between the European American center of Jefferson and its African American outer quarter of Freeman Town, maintains her on the communal margins. Maintains Joanna there, that is, until her murderous relationship with Joe Christmas relocates her to the center of public consciousness.

Joe is the third case history concerning the pangenetic bottleneck in *Light in August*. Blood lore nominates Joe as a genealogical dead end before he is born. For, although his spear-side grandparents are unknown, the distaff-side members of this generation, the Hineses, appear to be incompatible with *Homo sapiens*. On settling in Mottstown, Eupheus Hines and his wife are regarded as "a little touched—lonely, gray in color, a little smaller than most other men and women, as if they belonged to a different race, species" (651). Their daughter Milly falls pregnant to "a fellow with the circus" (676). Eupheus, because of his conviction that the man embodies black blood, shoots him dead—Mrs. Hines later recalling how "the circus owner come back and said how the man really was a part nigger instead of Mexican, like Eupheus said all the time he was" (678). Unattended during the baby's delivery, Milly dies of blood loss. Mrs. Hines wishes to care for the infant, but Eupheus abducts him. Anonymously leaving his grandson at the orphanage where he works, Eupheus maintains vigilance over this "devil's spawn" (730). The old man hopes to witness, through a black child uncertainly passing in an institute for whites, God's retribution for the unnatural act of miscegenation.

The process of naming immediately heightens intimations of hybridity. Abandoned at the end of December, the institute calls the child Christmas. Eupheus, regarded in the care-home as something of a mad prophet, proposes the Christian name Joseph. Joe Christmas is "born."

Each half of his name coming from a different source, the baby is both an ordinary Joe and an exception to the rule. This hybridity of nomenclature augurs badly for the child's future, as do his initials, which place him on the dominated side of the inveterate equation opposite his similarly initialed counterpart from earlier in the Faulknerian canon, Jason Compson. Rather than the community welcoming this newborn J. C. as a messianic opening, Joe Christmas's life will be one of martyrdom. Indictment as the "Nigger" by his fellow orphans is a step toward confirming this fate (492, 497). Eupheus contends that he never told the children to taunt Joe in this manner, but his denial is too strenuous. He has instigated a repeated act that serves to inculcate the child with paranoia concerning his own racial constitution.

Joe's exploration of the orphanage not only confirms this designation but also snares him in the pangenetic chokepoint. The room belonging to the female dietician becomes a favorite haunt. He has developed a taste for toothpaste as "something sweet and sticky to eat," and her washbasin supplies his habit (488). Swallowing the pharmaceutical, Joe enacts a ritual attempt at cleansing, an act impelled by the racial indictment instigated by Eupheus. On one occasion, swallowing an excess of paste, the unexpected return of the dietician traps Joe in the room. Her lover accompanies her. Watching the coitus from behind a curtain, Joe's choking emesis leads to his discovery. Believing her job to be in jeopardy, the dietician identifies Joe to the matron as a black child passing for white. His situation at the home has become untenable and, as a corollary, he will find the sex act permanently problematic. The pangenetic bottleneck has caught another victim. Evidence of this capture appears during Joe's time with the childless couple who adopts him from the orphanage. These new parents are far from ideal. Simon McEachern's reason for fostering Joe is an economic one. He can put the lad to work on his farm, where, as the surname of this Calvinistic guardian suggests, each person must earn his keep. Mrs. McEachern, abject in the presence of her husband, merely earns Joe's derision. In one incident, having gone without food for a day while refusing to learn his Bible, Joe nevertheless tips out his stepmother's carefully and surreptitiously prepared food onto the bedroom floor. Rejection of domestication as an attribute of family life becomes another of his characteristics, and, capping his adoption with his possible murder of McEachern as familial head, Joe signals his extended withdrawal from all but a minimum of social interaction by fading "phantomlike" from the narrative (515).

When Joe reemerges into communal consciousness, he is thirty-three years old. The same age as Jesus when he appeared from the wilderness, the messianic aura still clings to Joe, but his hematological status continues to cause him unease. He rents a deserted slave cabin on Joanna Burden's estate. Situated between the white and black districts, this shack suits his marginal status. The presence nearby of other hybrids, his landlady and the ex-minister Gail Hightower, offers further solace. The cabin is a sanctuary, Joe passing in the community for a "parchment-colored" Mediterranean—a categorization that estranges him from Jeffersonians without stigmatizing him as a child of miscegenation (487, 603). Joe recognizes this alienation when he walks through town of an evening. On the wide streets of the white district, he deems himself "a phantom, a spirit, strayed out of its own world, and lost" (483). Temporary relief comes when he loses his shadowy sense on entering Freeman Town. However, myriad voices, as if "his blood began again, talking and talking," soon become his anguish (484). On these occasions, Joe's delusions of hematological contestation threaten to engender a passionate frenzy. His consciousness, drowned out by his supposedly vociferous blood, fails to register his actions. In one incident, he narrowly avoids a violent confrontation with a group of African Americans only to discover an open razor in his hand. Returning to his lodgings, Joe feels lucky not to have betrayed his distress. An affair with Joanna Burden will prove less fortunate.

The indoctrinated belief that miscegenate sex is an injudicious pangenesis of black and white blood blights their relationship. The strain thereby induced comes to a crisis when Joanna tells of her pregnancy. "Almost before she ceased to speak," Joe wishing otherwise, "he believed that she was lying" (594). Nevertheless, that "autumn was almost upon her" in the form of the menopause tantalizingly fails to preclude this condition (592). A specter, a phantom gestation that accompanies his realization that she is in earnest, now pursues Joe within the confines of the pangenetic chokepoint. Joanna's attempts at domestication by cooking meals (recapitulating his experiences with Mrs. McEachern) and her Calvinistic endeavors to ratify their relationship before God (reviving his memories of Mr. McEachern) exacerbate the situation. Joe's temporary release from this burden, as when the situation with Simon McEachern became untenable, can only come through violence. The man who shares his cabin almost suffers the backlash: "He stood in the darkness above the prone body, with Brown's breath alternately hot and cold on his fingers, thinking quietly *Something is going to happen to me. I am going to do something* Without removing his left hand from Brown's face he could reach with his right across to his cot, to his pillow beneath which lay his razor with its five inch blade. But he did not do it. Perhaps thinking had already gone far enough and dark enough to tell him *This is not the right one* Anyway he did not reach for the razor" (475).

Italics, as for all characters in the novel, signify interiority of expression. The first such entry in the previous quotation testifies to Joe's fear for the future; the second snatch of consciousness, however, belies narratorial omniscience. Having "already gone far enough and dark enough" into the thoughts of Joe, the narrator can no longer follow, as his "Perhaps" at the beginning of the last sentence indicates. This second italicized portion is therefore an occasion when there is no narratorial power of entry into Joe's stream of consciousness. The man abused by the discursive practice of pangenesis can hereby escape this construction via an exclusively private monologue. Lacunae confirm Joe's continued resistance against a reactionary discourse: a final meeting with his lover offers another such significant absence. Joanna's lack of menstrual blood intimates a double sense of stalemate. On the one hand, the pangenetic bottleneck infers their unfruitful relationship. On the other hand, the participants are deadlocked in desperate straits. Joe must efface the haunting that pursues him, and Joanna must consecrate their congress. The situation comes to a head when she threatens Joe at gunpoint to kneel before God. He refuses the logos of the white patriarch as an intolerable imposition. The events that follow—those between the opening of Joe's razor and the discovery of Joanna's practically decapitated body in her burning house—remain uncertain. Unable to gain uninterrupted access to his consciousness, the narrator is inclined to charge Joe with the crime and to assume that the effects of pangenesis have structured his actions. The narratorial assumption is that Joe suffers a schizophrenic fit in which dangerous tendencies emerging from his dark side overpower worthy qualities emanating from his European American side. Joe's black self—concludes the narrator, revealing his own white status—predetermines the violent actions he commits. Blood lore reigns supreme.

This ethos receives no explicit condemnation in *Light in August*. Faulkner knew that his criticism of an inveterate discourse had to be subtle. Otherwise, reactionaries would reject his novel as a liberal tract. A narrator in keeping with the social and racial hierarchy of the South enables Faulkner to achieve his aim. Any terminal violence committed by or ascribed to Joe against his lover comes from without, from the superordinate community, a collective consciousness that has succeeded in terminating (or choking) Joanna's chances of successful pregnancy.

The pangenetic bottleneck around Joe tightens on his arrest. Eupheus, on hearing the name Christmas, but on keeping their kinship secret, urges the crowd to perform a lynching. "Kill the bastard!" he cries. "Kill him. Kill him" (654). Hines wants to superintend the strangling hold of the chokepoint; and, known to the community as "Uncle Doc," he wishes to do so in the quasi-medical role of eugenicist (652). The old man's intervention, although not meeting with immediate success, nonetheless establishes the tenor of mob rule. Within this atmosphere, Gavin Stevens offers Christmas his services as a defense lawyer. He counsels Christmas to admit murder and serve life imprisonment. If he refuses plea bargaining, then he will surely face the death penalty. Unwilling to accept a life sentence—consistent in his disavowal of the white logos—Christmas rejects Stevens's advice. Later, marshaled across town for transfer to another jail, Joe makes what appears to be an attempt at escape. This is, however, a predetermined act. Joe, cognizant of the growing communal pressure against him, desires sanctuary. Gail Hightower's property, the halfway house of a marginal man, is appropriate to fulfilling his purpose. Joe gains his sanctum but is cornered there by lynch leader Percy Grimm. After shooting Joe, Grimm castrates his victim. With this bloody amputation, Faulkner brings metaphor and reality, a conjunction initially and less forcefully expressed by the Peabodys in *Flags in the Dust*, together: "When the others reached the kitchen they saw the table flung aside now and Grimm stooping over the body. When they approached to see what he was about, they saw that the man was not dead yet, and when they saw what Grimm was doing one of the men gave a choked cry and stumbled back into the wall and began to vomit. Then Grimm too sprang back, flinging behind him the bloody butcher knife. 'Now you'll let white women alone, even in hell,' he said" (742).

The narrator, so conditioned to the fallacy of pangenesis, can only obfuscate the report of Joe's death. "For a long moment he looked up at them with peaceful and unfathomable and unbearable eyes. Then his face, body, all, seemed to collapse, to fall in upon itself, and from out the slashed garments about his hips and loins the pent black blood seemed to rush like a released breath. It seemed to rush out of his pale body like the rush of sparks from a rising rocket; upon that black blast the man seemed to rise soaring into their memories forever and ever" (742–43).

Live blood is red, not black, but the narrator recounts the latter. Even so, the "unbearable eyes" of the dying man puncture narratorial obscurity, the castration permanently scars the memories of those who witness it, and the rupture of Joe's body breaches the substitution of the actual by the metaphoric. Triumphant in death, his disgorging blood reveals the shocking power of metaphor to conceal reality. Joe's severed penis and Joanna's virtually severed head are results of the pangenetic chokepoint *in extremis*. The irony is stark. Pangenesis posits Christmas and Joanna as an infertile couple, but, as Williamson perceptively notes, the "totally sterile young man" in the novel, the man whose Christian name is slang for penis, is Percy Grimm (*Crucible* 309). The disposition toward hematology and hybridity championed by racists, asserts Faulkner, is fallacious.

Christmas had refused to plead guilty because this would have supported the semiotics of the white state. Christmas's passive suicide resists the clear-cut binary oppositions imposed by this means. That even his supportive defense counsel represents such a system becomes patent when Stevens explains his client's forswearing of clemency. Race approaches subspecies. Christmas's blood, reasons Stevens, was not sanguine: "It would not be either one or the other and let his body save itself. Because the black blood drove him first to the negro cabin. And then the white blood drove him out of there, as it was the black blood which snatched up the pistol and the white blood which would not let him fire it. And it was the white blood which sent him to the minister" (731).

Unwittingly extending the blood fallacy into parody, Stevens accounts for Joe's striking of Hightower: "Then I believe that the white blood deserted him for the moment. Just a second, a flicker, allowing the black to rise in its final moment and make him turn upon that on which he had postulated his hope of salvation. It was the black blood which swept him by his own desire beyond the aid of any man, swept him up into that ecstasy out of a black jungle where life has already ceased before the heart stops and death is desire and fulfillment. And then the black blood failed him again, as it must have in crises all his life" (731).

Joe had simply wished to protect Hightower from Grimm, the erstwhile minister's later demise confirming Faulkner's intent to expose the delusion that is pangenetic reasoning. Gail is the only Jeffersonian to appreciate the terminal weight of figurative language in these bloody events. Trying to rest after the lynching, he sees numerous faces in his reverie, recognizing all but one. Then, separating the countenances of Joe Christmas and Percy Grimm, he clarifies the exception. Gail alone perceives that Joe's behavior results from the imposition of reactionary politics onto an individual determined to resist this demand. Separating the discourse of pangenesis from reality, Gail's enlightenment is so ferocious that he suffers a bloody rupture of his own: "Then it seems to him that some ultimate dammed flood within him breaks and rushes away. He seems to watch it, feeling himself losing contact with earth, lighter and lighter, emptying, floating. 'I am dying,' he thinks. 'I should pray. I should try to pray'" (763).

A fatal heart attack rives Gail from the possibility of communion with God. Like Joe, he cannot supplicate to the ruling discourse that had accounted for Joanna, a predominant logos so untenable that he can no longer endure, as Louis Daniel Brodsky and Robert W. Hamblin concur, "the wrack / of worn theology" (75). Gail Hightower joins Joanna Burden and Joe Christmas in Faulkner's sagacious indictment of racist discourse.

Having castigated Faulkner for his youthful receptiveness to hematological mythology, as evinced in the *Double Dealer* and the *Times-Picayune*, and then acknowledged his more subtle consideration of the subject in *Flags in the Dust*, the rapidly maturing artist now deserves praise for his progressiveness in *Light in August*. Part of Faulkner's advance stemmed from his self-reliance. Contemporary writers, even the Fugitive-Agrarians who shared his passion for the South, continued to offer a paucity of ideas.[3] Creating new artistic works in line with epistemological advances became one of his underlying trademarks. Faulkner's acquaintance from boyhood with Whit Rowland, who later "made something of a name for himself in the medical world as a pediatrician" (John Faulkner 28), and Benjamin McDaniel, who "studied medicine at Ole Miss," was propitious in this regard (John Faulkner 128). There were other scientific authorities too: fellow Ole Miss sub-*rosa* fraternity members Spencer Wood and Charlie Townsend had been "medical students" (John Faulkner 144); family friend Felix Linder was Faulkner's doctor (Blotner, *Biography* 2: 1282); Harvard Medical School graduate Arthur Guyton was to become "an internationally-known cardio-vascular physiologist" (Blotner, *Biography* 2: 1008). A reciprocal intellectualism also stimulated Faulkner's relationship with his stepson. With their forages into the Lafayette countryside, as Franklin explains, "began a series of lessons in herpetology that Billy was to teach me during the coming months—the foundation and beginning of my scientific studies" (17). By the winter of 1937, they were reading "various anthropologists" and discussing "Darwin and variations in species" (Blotner, *Biography* 2: 979). Just as Phil Stone had counseled young William, Faulkner mentored Malcolm, but who were the influential anthropologists they discussed and in what terms did anthropology discuss miscegenation?

The work of Franz Boas is a possible thread in Faulkner's growing awareness of the social, scientific, and literary complexities concerning this issue. Although not one of his publications is on the shelves of Rowan Oak, his preeminence in the field of anthropology and citations to him in another household volume, *Apes, Men and Morons* (1937) by Earnest Albert Hooton (1887–1954), propose Boas as a Faulknerian source. Born in Germany, Boas gained a Ph.D. from the University of Kiel in 1881. He immigrated to America and by 1899 was Professor of Anthropology at Columbia University. Not a pure Darwinist—while on the National Academy of Sciences Board he attested to the truth of orthogenesis—Boas nevertheless brought an evolutionary perspective to bear on his subject. This approach disavowed the dominant anthropological paradigm of Louis Henry Morgan (1818–1881) and Edward Burnett Tylor (1832–1917). Their form of global culturalism posited numerous developmental stages in the attainment of civilization. Boas countered with his historical methodology of cultural relativism. Anthropology must acknowledge historical, social, and geographic conditions. Particular races had attained different types of civilization, not because of inherent faculties, but because of historical events. All cultures are unique, equally valid, and resist analysis by universal laws of social evolution.

Boas's initial thoughts about miscegenation coalesced in 1894 when collecting data for the Department of Ethnology of the World's Columbian Exposition. One of his conclusions, that "the fertility among the half-breed women is considerably larger than among the full-blood women," notes George W. Stocking, was rather unexpected (194). Boas, aware he was contradicting the accepted belief in hybrid infertility, continued his investigations along a different course. He turned to the work of Samuel George Morton. During the first half of the nineteenth century, Morton had used cephalic measurements—the ratio of the maximum breadth of a skull to its maximum length—not only to promote polygenism, but also to grade racial groups according to brain size. Morton had argued that the average of pureblooded ratios accurately represented hybrid specimens. Boas disagreed: this figure has no significance.[4] Modern science concurs. "There is no evidence at all," as Jones asserts, "that there are, or have ever been, populations whose members all share the same cephalic index." As for Morton's survey, when his specimens "were re-measured with modern instruments the differences disappeared." His erroneous results "were due to the omission of some groups which did not fit his ideas, confusion of males and females, and a failure to correct skull size for differences in body size." As a result of racism, as Jones plainly states, such "scientists were blinded to their own results" (*Language* 257).

Boas's subsequent work, which included *The Mind of Primitive Man* (1911), was a sustained attempt to promote the beneficence of miscegenation. The interaction of distinct peoples, interracial congress as the inevitable agency operating at the intersection of different cultures, fascinated him. "Races and sub-races were mixed and possessed no stability," writes Paul Radin of Boas's convictions, "no language was, in any meaningful sense, superior to another or better capable of expressing ideas than another, and . . . no connection existed between the physical type of a given population, its language and the culture it developed" (131). Boas became a committed Universalist. He sought fundamental psychological and sociological data in an attempt to develop more enlightened and more complex concepts of culture and race.

Despite his genuine endeavor, as Nancy Stepan makes clear, the impact Boas made "on physical anthropology, and therefore racial thinking in science, was delayed for a long time in the United States," because his pluralism unintentionally played into the polygenist legacy left by Morton (142). Boas hoped that cultural anthropology would dispel racism by extolling the virtues of social difference. Couching his ideas in esoteric terms, however, obscured their pertinence—other theorists could employ his methodology to the opposite effect. Aided by cultural anthropology, the gradual reentry of race into social pluralism disabused Boas of his dream. He had inadvertently helped to spawn nativism, defined by John Higham as an "intense opposition to an internal minority on the grounds of its foreign . . . connections." Race remained an element of individual identity within America and an essential component of American citizenship. Racial acceptance, as Higham concludes, continued to provide "the connecting, energizing force of modern nationalism" (2). Further to these difficulties, as a letter to a Cornell University colleague affirms, Boas did not deem blood blending a redundant hypothesis: "Broadly speaking, the question before us is that of whether it is better for us to keep an industrially and socially inferior black population, or whether we should fare better by encouraging the gradual process of lightening up this large body of people by the influx of white blood" (213). Boasean reasoning in which predominant blood subsumes that of other races undermined his sophisticated defiance of racial supremacy.

One coeval who also called for historical particularity in anthropology, but one who managed to avoid the contentions of pangenesis, was William Edward Burghardt Du Bois (1868–1963). The relays between the two men's work are fascinating. Indeed, Boas's anthropological paradigm, maintains Shamoon Zamir, "was identical to the one signalled by Du Bois's rejection of Spencer and Giddings and a metaphysical science in favour of a more localised social science and historical research" (91).[5] That Du Bois, drawing on similar sources for his research as Boas, also teetered on the edge of a pangenetic trap should come as little surprise. Du Bois's engagement with Darwinian and Huxleyan science in "The Conservation of Races" (1897) adds weight to this surmise. Wishing to promote human solidarity, Du Bois retains an economics of blood, decrying the tendency for African Americans "to deprecate and minimize race distinctions, to believe intensely that out of one blood God created all nations, and to speak of human brotherhood as though it were the possibility of an already dawning to-morrow" (*W. E. B. Du Bois Speaks* 73). Blood defines race and "it is certain that all human striving must recognize the hard limits of natural law, and that any striving, no matter how intense and earnest, which is against the constitution of the world, is vain" (74). To Du Bois's mind, biological science posits "at least two, perhaps three, great families of human beings—the whites and Negroes, possibly the yellow race," and "that other races have arisen from the intermingling of the blood of these two" (75). Appreciating the similarities rather than the differences attributed to race, however, Du Bois skillfully manages to elide soft inheritance: "This broad division of the world's races which men like Huxley and Raetzel [*sic*] have introduced as more nearly true than the old five-race scheme of Blumenbach, is nothing more than an acknowledgment that, so far as purely physical characteristics are concerned, the differences between men do not explain all the differences of their history. It declares, as Darwin himself said, that great as is the physical unlikeness of the various races of men, their likenesses are greater, and upon this rests the whole scientific doctrine of human brotherhood" (75).[6]

Du Bois's next major engagement with Darwinism came at the National Negro Conference of 1909. "The Evolution of the Race Problem," his speech to launch the NAACP, while retaining the concept of biologically distinguishable races, eschews pangenesis in underlining how "the splendid scientific work of Darwin, Weismann, Galton and others" has been generally misinterpreted (202). To pretend that "no philanthropy can or ought to eliminate" (202) the constructionist inequality among the races is "indefensible and monstrous" (204).

In April 1956, when challenged to a public debate concerning the practicalities of racial integration by Du Bois, Faulkner replied that he did "not believe there is a debatable point between us. We both agree in advance that the position you will take is right morally, legally, and ethically" (Peavy 78). Had valuable Boasean insights prompted this Faulknerian magnanimity? That Boas's followers may have gained less enlightened views on hematology, race, and nativism than he intended problematizes the answer yes. Earnest Albert Hooton, a diligent student under Boas at Lawrence University in Wisconsin, and a possible influence on Faulkner, demands particular scrutiny.

"The Pre-Hellenistic Stage of the Evolution of the Literary Art at Rome" (1911), his doctoral thesis from Lawrence, led to a career at Harvard. Here, Hooton's obsession with the topic of racial impurity soon became evident. Scientists had discovered the existence of blood group antigens in the first years of the twentieth century. Advances in serology were consolidated during World War I. In his first professorial monograph, *Up from the Ape* (1931), Hooton praises these achievements on racial grounds. However, "the fact that some of the most physically diverse types of mankind are well-nigh indistinguishable one from another in the proportions of the agglutinogens," he concedes, "is very discouraging." His hope "is that more refined methods of racial analysis, by the selection of physically homogeneous types, will yield important correlations with the blood groupings" (*Up* 490). These expectations seemed to be fulfilled later that year when the Scottish mathematical biologist J. B. S. Haldane (1892–1964) announced that blood groups were, as American scholar Jay Watson chronicles, the "basis for racial classification" (95). This approach, believed Hooton, had advantages. "For an objective classification of mankind what was needed," explains Stepan, "was traits whose genetic determination were known, which were found in all human groups, which were not easily altered by environmental factors, and which were nonadaptive and therefore unchanging in their frequencies" (178). Science deemed blood groups suitably stable.

Furthermore, since studies by William Bateson, William E. Castle, and Thomas Hunt Morgan considerably complicated the subject of biological inheritance, science retained a void into which theories of blood heredity flooded. Pangenesis continued to flow freely as a concept in academic circles, with innumerable scientists, as Stepan avers, continuing to categorize race hematologically (179). Physical anthropologists subsequently attempted, as Hooton described six years later in *Apes, Men and Morons*, to correlate antigen data with "metric and morphological observations." To determine "racial and ethnic differences in the blood groups is a major field of endeavor in physical anthropological research." Nonetheless, "if any significant and certain correlations with racial type have been established, I am unacquainted with them." Clear-cut blood grouping "seemed to have been secured in the case of the American Indian, who, when of pure blood, was thought to belong invariably to Group O," but, "the unique serological purity of the American group was spurious" (163). As with any other single test of race, concludes Hooton, "the blood group is totally inadequate" (162).

Unsurprisingly, then, human hybridity draws the most pronounced use of pangenetic terminology in *Apes, Men and Morons*. Moreover, the durable myth of erasure via dilution necessarily emerges from Hooton's conceptualization of soft inheritance. "Thus, there is little or no stabilization of hybrid types," he states, "but only a small seepage of blood from the socially exalted race to that which is socially abased" (142–43). Vacillations in science left Hooton free to claim that "many of the peoples who have a physical status midway between, for example, Whites and Negroes owe their position not to environmental modification but to hybridization" (151). Hooton does acknowledge a molecular mechanism for heredity. His glossary cites "WEISMANN," "CHROMOSOME," and "GENE," but simultaneously undercuts this inclusion by insisting, "science really knows, as yet, comparatively little about human genetics." The occasional endorsement of hard inheritance does not deflect from his overarching appeal to blood blending. "Genetics," he writes, "which once looked so simple and beautiful, turns out to be such an intricate business, involving such a multiplicity of factors, that its application to man is as yet confined, for the most part, to the inheritance of a few diseases, malformations, and anomalies. Even in these cases the data are usually not conclusive, and the positive affirmations of hopeful geneticists have to be bolstered up with a certain amount of faith. Of course, there is no real doubt of the validity of Mendelian inheritance, but we cannot work it out for ordinary human physical features, or at least, we have not yet done so" (62).

Hence, one of the obfuscating techniques of *Apes, Men and Morons* is to recast blending ideals in terms of hard inheritance. Amalgamation is the same whatever the science behind heredity. "Mixtures," writes Hooton, "have taken place whenever propinquity has permitted, but usually in a clandestine and surreptitious manner." Hereon, reasons Hooton, "hybrid offspring of such marriages are socially rejected by the dominant and usually paternal race and are relegated to the subordinate stock which absorbs them by back crossing" (142).

Apes, Men and Morons seeks additional solace in the concept of acquired characteristics. After World War I, Oskar Hertwig (1849–1922) had vigorously promoted Neo-Lamarckism and had supported the idea of "the metabolic influence of the atmosphere upon hereditary dispositions, [while] criticizing at the same time the theory of selection" (Freyre 291). In support of his theses, as expounded in *Das Werden der Organismen, eine Widerlegung der Darwinschen Zufallslehre* (1916), Hertwig cited the experiments of Paul Kammerer (1880–1926).[7] The disgrace of Kammerer's suicide in 1926, attributed to the professional denouncement of his perfunctory and unscrupulous experiments, was subsequently mollified by the work of Halsey Joseph Bagg (1889–1947), Ross Granville Harrison (1870–1959), and Clarence Cook Little (1888–1971) in England. The physical types of man, Hooton decided on such evidence, are susceptible to their physical and chemical environment. Coupled with the inheritance of acquired characteristics, which Haldane's serology supported, assimilation was the predicted fate of immigrants. Do not fear the outlandish, counseled Hooton, because their hereditary differences will considerably diminish over successive generations in a shared environment.[8] An established populace will subsume the majority of aliens and an inveterate race will remain unaltered. Any nonassimilable immigrants fitted Hooton's pathological class of criminals, the mentally handicapped, and those with physical disabilities. Moreover, as a Harvard professor, Hooton felt "wholly competent to suggest measures which would prevent the birth of the majority of our imbeciles and morons" (*Apes* 295). That offenders on parole should be restricted to a segregated area provided for them by repressive state apparatuses was one proposal; that those with substandard biological heredity required permanent incarceration was another safeguard; that the inferior should be restrained from procreation was a third contingency. To improve the biological status of humankind and to promote human relations that are "more honest, more unselfish, more decent and considerate" were Hooton's stated aims. His own decent consideration insisted "that a biological purge is the essential prerequisite for a social and a spiritual salvation. Let us temper mercy with justice and disperse charity with intelligence. We must stop trying to cure malignant biological growths with patent sociological nostrums. The emergency demands surgical operation" (*Apes* 295).

"We must either do some biological house-cleaning," stipulates *Apes, Men and Morons*, "or delude ourselves with the futile hope that a government of the unfit, for the unfit, and by the unfit, will not perish from the earth" (294).

Painstakingly documenting his research using anthropometric data, photographs, progress reports, lectures, manuscripts, and correspondence, Hooton became the leading racial anthropologist in late-1930s America. His discussions with colleagues concerned natural selection, theories of physical anthropology, relevant research methodologies, and the quandary posed by Karl Pearson's biometry. Thanks to Pearson, race was becoming, as Stepan explains, "a populational and statistical concept. It meant, therefore, the opposite to race in anthropology" (135). One anthropological solution to this challenge was to classify human behavior and racial characteristics according to type and then put biometrical methods to typological use. "That," continues Stepan, "is what American anthropologist Ernest Hooton did." This form of arbitrary data division, of course, merely echoed the racial assumptions of the anthropologist rather than essentialism.

The Harvard archive confirms Hooton's involvement in public health projects for the Sterilization League during his most influential period. Fortunately, these documents also show that the ideological superstructure of America was an impediment to Hooton's eugenic zeal. For "the majority of the professional leaders of Christianity and other established religions," writes Hooton, "evolution is not merely an unsubstantiated theory but an atheistic and antisocial philosophy, the promulgation of which is subversive to the welfare of man" (*Apes* 6). Perfusion of Darwinian tenets, Hooton believed, would greatly counteract religious and governmental indifference toward American genealogy; epistemological dissemination would prevent the imminent crisis guaranteed by "man's *laissez-faire* policy with respect to biological welfare" (*Apes* 7). Rationale such as this had a Hughesean appeal in the South, where, as historian Daniel Aaron explains, "individualism was a different sort from that preached by the legal casuists of laissez faire capitalism" (14). That Darwinism had "not permeated the medical profession—at any rate as a dynamic, scientific reality upon which it must necessarily base any technique of procedure" therefore remained a source of frustration for Hooton (*Apes* 6). The abiding paradox of this failure, the simultaneous empowerment of his pangenetic anthropology, appears to have passed Hooton by.

Progressive with its acknowledgement of genetics, Hooton's work is, in the final analysis, deplorable. Malcolm Franklin's signature in his personal copy of *Apes, Men and Morons* and the retention of this volume at Rowan Oak trace a provenance that implicate Hooton as a possible impingement on Faulknerian thinking (Blotner, *Faulkner's Library* 48). Lay reading in the contemporary sciences was fraught with contradictions. Scientific indecision maintained a tension between the theories of soft and hard inheritance. The youthful Faulkner of New Orleans would not have noticed this unease, the discerning artist of the late 1930s did. Yuletide gifts for 1938 emphasize his continued engagement in this domain. "Will you get me a good Darwin?" Faulkner asked a New York friend, "I want it for my fifteen year old boy who is messing with anthropology. *Origin of the Species* I mean, and what about Huxley?" (*Faulkner* 2: 1008). This scientific guidance would pay dividends on two fronts: Franklin would become a respected zoologist; Faulkner would reject pangenetic theory in favor of the revolutionary potential of genetic inheritance. That he wrestled with reactionary views concerning hematological heredity and eventually resisted them is to Faulkner's credit. Hematology would remain critically at stake, inveterates would continue to populate the South and, by extension, Yoknapatawpha, but the Faulknerian perspective would evolve. On turning forty, and facing the prospect of another global war, he started to construct a *conception du monde* (or Weltanschauung *in the making*). The liberative possibilities of miscegenation would be central to Faulkner's broadening philosophy. Interrogating an economics that equates hematological purity with purity of form, *Go Down, Moses* (1942) would express this paradigmatic integrity. With the exception of *A Fable*, Faulkner would spend more time on this novel than he would on any other. Therefore, contends Arthur F. Kinney, *Go Down, Moses* remains "powerful, indelible, important, and inescapable" (xi). The evolutionary philosophy of Henri Louis

Bergson (1859–1941), and specifically his conceptualization of chronicity and memory, underpins this ineluctability.

Educated in Paris, Bergson graduated from the École Normale in 1881. After spells as a professor of philosophy in Angers and Clermont-Ferrand, and the publication of his doctoral "Essay on the Immediate Data of Consciousness" (1889), he returned to his original university as a Maître de Conference. His next significant treatise, *Laughter*, appeared in 1900. Awarded a chair at the Collège de France, the Academy of Moral and Political Sciences then elected Bergson as a board member. *L'Évolution créatrice (Creative Evolution)*, inspired by *The Origin of Species*, was published in 1907. This volume secured Bergson's worldwide reputation, his lectures becoming weekly events attended by the Parisian élite. English, French, German, Polish, and Russian editions of all his principal works appeared over the next seven years. This period marked his influential peak. Although he continued to publish until shortly before his death, his attempt to be both existential and pantheistic led to his gradual marginalization by the academy. Nonetheless, strains of his philosophy retained a Modernist appeal.

Of general interest was Bergson's concept of the élan vital: a God-given life drive that promotes all manifestations of life. Having triggered evolution, this vital phenomenon, argues Bergson, continues to sustain the multitudinous bifurcations of that process and to provide the fecund momentum from which ideational generation and artistic creation appear. Generalities concerning artistic fecundity may have intrigued Faulkner—like many of his contemporaries, Faulkner rated Bergson's *L'Évolution créatrice* highly, recommending the volume to a friend with the commendation that "it helped me"—but his closer affinity with a specific Bergsonian notion, *durée*, is undoubted (Blotner, *Biography* 2: 1302).

Time, Bergson reasons, is real. This seemingly innocuous statement leads to important conclusions. On the one hand, chronicity, as an exclusive succession of homogenous segments in an infinite series, is an abstract notion. Hence, the physics of time cannot give access to time proper. On the other hand, real time, or *durée*, is possible only through an organic memory that accumulates the fullness of the past. Each conscious moment carries the entire flow of the past; nothing is lost and nothing is reversible. *Durée* is the tension of self-development that makes each conscious moment new yet unrepeatable. In an age of splits and ruptures, in a period such as World War I, when the meaning of life was often hard to discern, *durée* offered the individual a degree of control. Temporal flux could draw together fragmentary and disjunctive episodes. This sense of unity appealed to Faulkner: "I agree pretty much with Bergson's theory of the fluidity of time. There is only the present moment, in which I include both the past and the future, and that is eternity. In my opinion time can be shaped quite a bit by the artist; after all, man is never time's slave" (Blotner, *Biography* 2: 1441). Moreover, constructing time and delimiting the types of humankind, realized Faulkner, share the essence of liminal abstraction. Just as consciousness beclouds the structure of chronicity, miscegenation works to erase the boundaries of race. If *durée* could be a liberating tool, then so could interracial sex.

Go Down, Moses illustrates formally, stylistically, and thematically how time and ontopology contest this liberation.[9] Appearing to be a series of unconnected short stories rather than a sequential whole, both out of order and of the order of madness, Faulkner's formal miscegenation offers textual derangement. Syntax, as Faulkner's instructions to Random House in the winter of 1941 affirm, is the crucial stylistic counterpart to this overall construction. "DON'T CHANGE EITHER THE PUNCTUATION NOR THE CONSTRUCTION," he insisted (Blotner, *Biography* 2: 1090). Form and style must denote miscegenation. His intention, however, was not readily apparent to literary critics. Trilling, as John Earl Bassett records, bemoans the lyrical drone of *Go Down, Moses* and the loss of controlled syntax (296–97). Faulkner's desire, of course, goes beyond syntactical obfuscation. He understood, as Carvel Collins explains, "that aesthetic profit can come not only from subtlety of order but from skilful, imaginative ambiguity and understatement, which lead readers to become partners with the author and thereby, through the required exploration and the tapping of intuition, to enrich their perception and enjoyment of the work of art" ("Afterword" 201).

Enrichment in this instance includes the presentation of chronology under the auspices of *durée*. Thus, the past and the future catch the most significant character in the novel, Isaac McCaslin, that supposedly pure scion of the patriarch Lucius Quintus Carothers McCaslin, between two directions of absence. Faulkner figures this trap as a narrational enigma. Consequently, the narrator's syntax forsakes approved grammatical form; his somnambulism denotes the fatigue produced by the issue of miscegenation; his ventriloquism replaces omniscience too confused for direct expression. Syntagmatic miscegenation was a denial of Old World grammatology: dissent that Trilling could not appreciate, dissent that was

Faulkner's aim. Bergson's philosophy was broadening the Faulknerian conception du monde. "In the mature Faulkner," explained François Pitavy at the 2003 Faulkner and Yoknapatawpha Conference, "there is in the last analysis no possible man-nature relation: Isaac McCaslin will renege on the lessons of his brief epiphanies during his initiation into the wilderness by Sam Fathers. The wilderness in Faulkner remains an aporia—an ontological impossibility, a dead end."

Also severely compromised is the ecology between men, specifically the Isaac-man relation of the 1940s. The affair Carothers Edmonds ("Roth") conducts with a mulattress suggests that miscegenation may erase the contours of segregation. That Isaac's white kin could consummate such an erasure, that the future of the McCaslins is exclusively the right of miscegenes, however, is too violent a realization for the old man. His physiological and psychological seizure in this hybrid woman's presence echoes the fate of his metaphysical paterfamilias—and Sam Fathers's enlightenment proved fatal.

Isaac's imminent death would appear to be a suitable point at which to end the novel, but for Faulkner, this culminating event must remain forever imminent. The closure of his text must be consistent with his authorial challenge to purity. Some disruption, as Philip Cohen notes, "may have resulted, in part, from Faulkner's creation of the novel by combining new material with rewritten unpublished pieces and six previously published short stories" ("Faulkner by the Light" 178). Formal disturbance may also show, as Cohen contends, the "shifts in Faulkner's own racial identity as he repeatedly tried and failed to imagine a black consciousness" ("Faulkner by the Light" 179). Nevertheless, Faulkner's portrayal of African American rebellion is a defense against these charges. The disturbed textual purity of Isaac McCaslin's Bildungsroman is intentional. Fragmentary tales of insubordinate African Americans are the cause of this disturbance, and many of Faulkner's later revisions concerned Lucas Beauchamp as such a character. Isaac's mythology must contend for dominance with African American stories, including Lucas's "The Fire and the Hearth," tales that counteract the inflexible narrative inspired by the McCaslins. The final notable rebellion to this dominant and repressive narration is the episode that completes the novel, "Go Down, Moses."

The year is 1940 and Samuel Worsham Beauchamp ("Butch"), a grandson of Lucas and his wife Molly, has committed murder. According to southern blood lore, Samuel's conception was fated by "some seed not only violent but dangerous and bad" (*Go Down, Moses* 272). His mother died in childbirth and his father deserted him. As an orphaned hybrid, nothing could save him—even his anabatic journey across the Mason-Dixon Line failed; Butch's rebellious life ends in the North with his execution. Molly wants his body brought home to Mississippi. At one level, that identified by Thadious M. Davis, Butch is another one of the "southern-born, southern-bred young black men who lost their way in Chicago, but who can come home again to the South for burial" (232), a Faulknerian version of Bigger Thomas as created by Richard Wright (1908–1960) in *Native Son* (1940). At another level, though, Butch enables Faulkner to comment upon the patriarchal response to the miscegene. To raise the necessary money for Butch's burial, Molly appeals to the lawyer Gavin Stevens. After initial consternation, Stevens agrees to help. He raises sufficient local capital to effect Butch's return, the coffin passing through Jefferson on the way to interment. Molly is grateful to Stevens but unaware that he is concurrently fulfilling private motives. The county attorney may be the most academically qualified of Yoknapatawphians, but he is also at one with country folk, people whose upbringing he shared. "Faulkner must have fairly soon discovered," explains Cleanth Brooks of the immature artist, "that he needed a character who could express the sometimes inarticulate feelings of the community" (93). Stevens, the communal white voice in "Go Down, Moses," a figure with a questionable blood philosophy, as his provenance from *Light in August* contends, has brought the issue of miscegenation back to Jefferson. His antiquated lore, one that repudiates human hybridity, has brought home to his community the consequences of interracial sex. In Stevens's opinion, marginal figures must remain beyond the communal center, and Samuel Worsham Beauchamp's burial in Yoknapatawpha—but outside Jefferson—indicates their appropriate position.[10]

Butch, of course, was yet another descendant of Lucius Quintus Carothers McCaslin. Faulkner's final chapter therefore formally resists pure closure while narratively reestablishing a sense of archetypal delimitation. "The basic movement of *Go Down, Moses*," in Kinney's estimation, "is a continual wavering between acceptance and avoidance" of miscegenation (47). Kinney is correct because this hesitancy was Faulkner's aim. James B. Carothers concludes, however, that this indecision stems from Faulkner's personal need "to preserve the images of peace and harmony that are worthy of preservation" (282–83). Carothers thereby conflates the intention of inveterate Jeffersonians with the desires of William Faulkner. This conflation is flawed.

During the late thirties and early forties, as *Go Down, Moses* confirms, the ideological struggle over miscegenation was intense. Biological heredity, on the one hand, offers no choice; cultural inheritance, on the other hand, offers hereditary options. Biological determinism posits the benefits of variegated breeding, while hegemony denies these advantages. Many of the cultural choices pertaining to inheritance pit concern for others against concern for oneself. According to the élan vital, in an aleatory universe that pessimistically seals individual fate, selfishness is preferable to altruism.[11] Boundaries such as race and time are human constructs constantly in conflict with nature. Faulkner's Bergsonian expression of evolutionary philosophy scorns the antiquated economy that equates hematological purity with purity of form while simultaneously admitting the speciousness of that economy. Isaac's tragedy is that of segregation: his incapacity to accept a world without limits.

Go Down, Moses demonstrates that the middle-aged Faulkner did not share this inability. His perspective on blood, race, and miscegenation had shifted for good from the limited sphere characteristic of his youthful New Orleans days. Darwin's specious theory of pangenesis was no longer credible to the maturing artist. Personal enlightenment, however, did not mean that inveterates in the South had traversed a similar logic. Mississippi in the twentieth century was a chronotopic interstice where the human economy met the economy of nature. Pangenesis was vital to the first of these systems. An ideal economy had pure blood continuing pure race begetting pure blood. Miscegenation threatened to extinguish this utopia. Continuing to project the economy of man onto the economy of nature, the southern woodlands became repositories of purity and the natural world a revitalizing source by which tainted man could experience the numinous ideal. Faulkner's account of human encroachment into the Mississippi Delta in *Go Down, Moses* identifies this intrusion—one replete with mutative, selective, and dysteleological possibilities—as the death knell to southern blending theory.

Experiments had been undertaken since the 1920s to show that genetic mutation controlled natural selection, but only when Haldane and R. A. Fisher (1890–1962) in England and Sewall Wright (1889–1988) in America finally reconciled biometry with Mendelism during the next decade was dramatic progress made. These three biologists, as Stepan notes, "worked out the ways in which genes with particular, mathematically defined, selective advantages would spread through particular populations of organisms" (174). Fisher's *The Genetical Theory of Natural Selection* (1930), *The Causes of Evolution* (1932) by Haldane, and Wright's "Statistical Genetics in Relation to Evolution" (1939) were significant publications, and Julian Huxley's *Evolution: The Modern Synthesis* (1942) helped to bring the subject to a wider audience. An epistemological advance in evolutionary theory, modern synthesis soon penetrated all areas of geology, paleontology, embryology, genetics, and biology. Natural selection had met scientific and philosophical resistance for almost a century. Only now did science incontestably establish selectivity as the sole direction-giving factor in evolution.

This certainty led to broader questions concerning the ecological context of evolution. The ethical implications of human interference in the established environment of other organisms came to the fore. Ecological thinking began to take on philosophical and moral aspects. Hunting, a traditional rite through which individuals could confirm their social status, was one activity to come under scrutiny. In the American South, the class of the hunter dictated his appropriate game: squirrels, chipmunks, and raccoons sufficed for adolescents and African Americans, while deer, bear, and puma provided prize game for landowners. Some patricians may have insisted, as Lawrence Buell argues, that all species had "a right to exist as a matter of biotic right," but, when a significant number of aristocrats could not resist speculation in the lumber industry at the beginning of the twentieth century, they thoroughly impaired their ethical stance on ecology (13).

The destabilizing ecological effects of modernity on the South were significant. Cotton became king, with Mississippi producing more than one million bales by 1900. Output fluctuated—two million bales in 1910, only six hundred thousand at the end of World War I, recovering to nine hundred thousand in 1920 before a slump during the Depression—but 1937 witnessed a record yield of two million seven hundred thousand bales, with approximately four million acres of Mississippi farmland devoted to the crop. Forestry logging was necessary to provide this land. The first timber merchants had been small groups of stave cutters who sought special hardwoods for the manufacture of whiskey barrels (John Faulkner 91). Hand felling barely affected the environment of Lafayette, but with the introduction of planing mills to Mississippi, practically every species of tree had potential as timber. "By 1860," notes Don

Harrison Doyle, "there were eight sawmills in the county, located along the creeks where they could harness the waterpower" (90). Furthermore, "Mississippi still offered promise to those coming from the East" because land was relatively cheap and "the rewards of cotton planting in northern Mississippi continued to be more profitable than in the East" (90, 91). The ecological impact of forest clearance was evident and, as the prominence afforded to the topic in *A Civic Biology* attests, was of national concern. George William Hunter laments "the destruction of this nation's most valuable assets." He believes "this is primarily due to wrong and wasteful lumbering. Hundreds of thousands of dollars' worth of lumber is left to rot annually because the lumbermen do not cut the trees close enough to the ground." Waste is prevalent, asserts Hunter, "in every step from the forest to the finished product (112). Mississippi state geologist E. N. Lowe comes to a similar conclusion in *Plants of Mississippi: A List of Flowering Plants and Fern* (1921). Environmental degradation was now a permanent condition affecting the Mississippi floodplain. Strategies put forward by the agricultural colleges affiliated to the University of Mississippi for less invasive timber production made little impact. Their woodland management may have been progressive, but, as Buell explains, prospective ecologists lacked the power of land ownership (11–15). Furthermore, if virgin land was not lost for cotton, then deforestation resulted from the demands of urbanization. Between 1840 and 1900, the population of Mississippi had grown from 376,000 to 1,250,000. This figure rose to 1,790,000 within twenty years, and 1930 saw the two million mark surpassed. Ranked foremost among timber producers in 1936, Mississippi was simultaneously last in terms of reforestation.

The southern wilderness constituted a terrible paradox. Material use threatened the terminal decline of an American metaphysical resource. Established Old World settlers, especially second- and third-generation Puritans, had realigned their transatlantic vision of a New Canaan in a transcontinental direction. Protestantism in Europe, as Sacvan Bercovitch argues, "rejected the notion that places were invested with a special spiritual significance because it smelled suspiciously of Catholic superstition: in effect, the New England Puritans delivered sacred space back to Protestantism with a vengeance, in the form of America" (77–78). Ralph Waldo Emerson rejoiced in this deliverance. Our "continent," he declares, "is to be physic and food for our mind, as well as our body. The land, with its tranquilizing, sanative influences is to repair the errors of a scholastic and traditional education, and bring us into just relations with men and things" ("Young American" 214). Championing the experiential possibilities of the panoramic American landscape, Emerson espouses a Neo-Platonism, the myth of a new terrestrial continent, which, as David Howell Evans confirms, can be traced "through a series of eighteenth- and nineteenth-century transformations" ("Place of Nature" 186). This history of privilege extends from the speleology of the first human inhabitants to the Romantic secularization of nature as an antidote for the cultural inferiority that defined the relation of the New World to its forebear. "America," eulogizes Emerson, "is a poem in our eyes; its ample geography dazzles the imagination" ("Poet" 335).

The twentieth-century Mississippian environment, however, bespoke bedazzlement by capitalism. For, as Thomas L. McHaney explains, with the sale of their first cotton bales on the world market, planters in the South had "lost any claim to the term agrarian" (30). Prestigious city dwellers in their ruling cliques now began to dictate the economics, politics, and morals of rural communities. Patricians attempted to protect themselves through the maintenance of a regional socioeconomic system, but geographical seclusion and self-sufficiency were systematically undermined by economic necessity. Interdependent states (and nations) must serve the consumer-led revolution. Changes in the modes of production created a modern bourgeoisie to the detriment of the patrician land-rentier. Population agglomeration attested to the subjection of the countryside to the urban domain.

Lafayette underwent this modern challenge and the perspicacious Fa(u)lkner would discern the numerous facets of the effected change. His ecological training, brother John records, "started in those autumn walks with Dad" (90) and continued when he became "a scout" (147). The participatory distinctions and contesting rationales involved in field sports would have been apparent to him when he participated in local hunts; the evidence of large-scale clearance and exploitation of the Mississippi Delta for cotton and urbanization would have been unavoidable; the interchange, to appropriate Karl Marx (1818–1883), of labor market for slave trade would have been felt too (1: 254). The last of these aspects, a case of *mutato tempus de te fabula narratur*, was possibly the most disheartening for Faulkner as he grew into manhood. Capitalism had seized "the very root" of the people. For "even the country labourers," continues Marx in Darwinian mode, "in spite of fresh air and the principle of natural selection, that work so powerfully amongst them, and only permits the survival of the strongest, are already beginning to die off as they increasingly replace the human resources lost to capitalism's rapacious need" (1: 256).

The social trauma suffered by southerners as the distinction between agrarian and corporate America shrank was not only intense but also remarkably protracted. Part of Faulkner's intellectual progression comes from his ideological engagement with the economy of nature while sharing this pain. Faulkner, aligned with the Arcadian stance of the American transcendentalists, intimately relates his notion of declensionary progression to moral issues. Recognition of this link has long been constrained by a lack of academic interdisciplinarity. "As our concern with ecology grows," explains scholar Donald M. Kartiganer, "we begin to see how Faulkner's work, his Yoknapatawpha world, is about relationship: How his distinct communities, black and white, town and country, native and foreign, relate to each other" (1). To develop this approach further loosens the grip of Malcolm Cowley, whose taxonomy of three themes— the historic reasons that account for regional tradition, the tendency to pessimism incited by twentieth-century chaos, and the dependence on a return to humanism to secure the future of humankind—have dominated Faulkner studies. Yes, Cowley's *The Portable Faulkner* (1946) succeeded in redeeming his subject from literary obscurity, but his appraisal simultaneously ensured a narrowing of critical focus. Faulkner's post-laureate work and his continuing maturation have gleaned little attention in consequence. Expressing the preeminence of the South in American environmental mythology is a component of this philosophical development. "It's the only really authentic region in the United States," Faulkner asserted in 1955, "because a deep indestructible bond still exists between man and his environment" (*Lion* 72). Mississippi is a "country still in the seethe and turmoil of being opened and developed and in a sense civilized" (*Lion* 187). Faulkner, like the Fugitive-Agrarians, observed this process closely. Beyond this contemporary movement, however, he retained an awareness that civilization was an accomplishment of human animals; and the mature Faulkner understood that species better than most. The "pathology of contemporary literature," argues Scott Slovic, is "its tendency to ignore the fact that we are animals, two-legged sacks of meat and blood and bone dependent on the whole living planet for our survival." Faulkner embodies Slovic's ideal of that rare species, the environmental author: a novelist who "feel[s] the organic web passing through our guts, as it truly does," a writer ideally positioned to scrutinize the juncture between the economies of nature and of man ("Visceral Faulkner").

That an ur-environmentalist strain imbues *Go Down, Moses* should come as no surprise.[12]

CHAPTER 6

PHILOSOPHICAL FRONTIERS

> It is a central part of Faulkner's unflinching insight—and here his achievement through fiction—to show how every character in *Go Down, Moses* is to some degree victimized by his or her cultural heritage, by custom and tradition that have taken impervious root and fossilized over time.
> Arthur F. Kinney, *Go Down, Moses: The Miscegenation of Time* (122)

IN CHARTING THE DETERMINATION OF POSTBELLUM REACTIONARIES TO stabilize the economy of man with their idealized concept of the economy of nature, *Go Down, Moses* foregrounds environmental concerns to a greater extent than Faulkner's previous novels. The supposed preclusion of miscegenate practices by the second of these economies was crucial to conservative tenets. Southern womanhood must remain unsullied. Antebellum patriarchs had consoled themselves with the knowledge that internal miscegenation accounted for the greatest share of interracial sexual incidents, but Reconstruction fostered a change in attitude. Namely, the patriarchal South began to equate manumission with external miscegenation under the auspices of African American men. In Mississippi, the legislature acted to protect their women. Interracial marriages, state sanctioned since 1870, were outlawed. Other states followed suit with the United States Supreme Court upholding this form of prohibition in the 1883 case of *Pace v. Alabama*. Ironically, because the criteria demarcating hybrids from African Americans were so contestable, inveterates now wrestled with the notion of miscegenation like never before. A biased perspective on census figures was an additional factor. For, although registered hybrids in the South rose by a mere 1.9 percent of the entire southern population between 1860 and 1890, this rise constituted an increase from 37,200 to 85,166 in miscegenate numbers (Kinney 12). Even though secondary miscegenation accounted for more than 90 percent of them, this greater than twofold increase in the hybrid population was an effective propaganda tool.

Faulkner matured within this reactionary framework—at least sixteen states, including Mississippi, retaining a statutory prohibition of primary miscegenate marriage throughout his lifetime. Only with the aptly named case of *Loving v. Virginia* in 1967 would the Supreme Court overturn its original nineteenth-century ruling. *Go Down, Moses*, which records anxieties about external miscegenation and analyzes the consequences of these feelings over successive generations, is an ecological text especially relevant to southern racial thinking. Events begin with the birth of Lucius Quintus Carothers, or L. Q. C., McCaslin in 1772, and close in 1942 with the imminent birth of George and Nat Wilkins's first child. The novel opens, however, in 1859, with the story "Was." L. Q. C. McCaslin died twenty-two years ago and his twin sons, Amodeus ("Buddy") and Theophilus ("Buck"), are now in their early sixties. Unorthodox, they house their slaves in the family mansion while running their plantation from a cabin originally intended for African Americans. The narrative starts with the discovery that their pet fox has broken free of its cage. The fox is pursued around the cabin by the twins' dogs as confusion reigns: distraction heightened when they realize that one of their slaves, Tomey's Turl, has also broken loose. Turl, enamoured of a woman on the neighboring Beauchamp plantation, is constantly breaking out.[1] Faulkner constructs him, Thadious M. Davis ably contends, as a "player who uses games as a site of resistance to power and, importantly, as a means of deregulating claims of ownership." Turl, because he exists in the "dialectic" between his social condition and personal autonomy, remains an individual of ambiguous and contested identity (44). Since he is no mere slave, but possibly the McCaslins' half-brother too, Turl's disorderly behavior also conveys a sense of genealogical destabilization. At this critical juncture in the McCaslin lineage—neither twin is married, neither is a father, the family tree remains stunted—Turl is a genealogical loose canon of the miscegenate variety, whose actions in repeatedly breaking free also prefigure federal laws concerning the end of slavery. Manumission, as a term that stems etymologically from the Latin *manumittere* or *manu emittere*, is a concept that is getting out of hand. Faulkner invokes a parallel between the temporary freedom of the fox and the escape of Turl. At one level, the hunters assume superiority over the hunted. At another level, Faulkner undercuts the connotations of racial inferiority by depicting the torment of the supposedly dominant. Juxtaposing foxhunt with manhunt, "Was" implies that the blood sport of race is an unsettling race to recapture unnerving hematology. On this occasion, Turl manages to gain his immediate objective, which is the plantation owned by Hubert Beauchamp and his sister Sophonsiba, for a liaison with his sweetheart Tennie. Amodeus returns home, leaving Theophilus to complete the task of Turl's retrieval.

Another strand to the fox-human parallel now becomes clear. The fox's attempt to escape their dogs also parallels Theophilus's evasion of his romantically intentioned neighbor, Sophonsiba Beauchamp. Theophilus would certainly be a faithful male, but he is too steadfast. Over the years, he has maintained his bachelor status, Sophonsiba failing to secure his troth. However, his rare overnight stay with the Beauchamps demanded by Turl's escape, enables Sophonsiba to exploit her accustomed environment. Ensuring that she looks her best is Sophonsiba's first measure. She then plies her visitor with alcohol, before prosecuting her most effective tactic. Retiring late to bed, and a little the worse for alcoholic wear, Theophilus is unsure as to the location of the spare bedroom. Despite his stupor, he reasons carefully before entering a room inconceivable as Sophonsiba's boudoir. Theophilus's rationale is correct, but on getting into bed, he is startled to find a screaming Sophonsiba beside him. Having previously traversed the same logic, she has tricked the confirmed bachelor into the philanderer's role. "Well 'Filus," says Hubert in the morning, "She's got you at last" (19). Theophilus remonstrates, but Amodeus speculates on the affair in the hope of curing the constant irritation posed by Turl.

The McCaslins gamble at cards against Hubert for the rights of slave ownership and marriage. The outcome is a radical compromise. Hubert gives Tennie up to the twins, who in turn allow her to marry Turl, but Theophilus must (eventually) wed Sophonsiba in recompense. This plan both secures Sophonsiba a husband and appears to have restored the racial status quo. Faulkner's tale, however, immediately explodes any sense of stability. Breaking through the wooden slats of its cage, "Was" ends with the fox loose again within the McCaslins' cabin. By analogy, further African American rebellions are to be expected. In fact, as *Go Down, Moses* later confirms, even after the Confederate defeat, no release date will ever appear next to Turl's name in the McCaslin ledgers. Freed by the governmental law of Washington, many southerners will nevertheless attempt to stay manumission in a continued hunting down of the miscegenate. Racial tension remains.

Faulkner, being etymologically acute, understood the inextricable bond between hunting and haunting. On the one hand, the prospect of a close encounter with the hunter haunts the hunted. On the other hand, when pursuit becomes an obsession, the hunter can suffer visitations from his imagined quarry. "What does it mean to follow a ghost?" asks French philosopher Jacques Derrida. "And what if this came down to being followed by it, always, persecuted perhaps by the very chase we are leading?" (*Specters* 10). That Faulkner was aware of this autotelic essence is evident in *Go Down, Moses*, a work in which hunting not only conflates the issues of blood and environmental intrusion, but also symbolizes pursuit. Human hybrids may suffer the visitations of supposedly pure whites, Faulkner's novel concedes, but miscegenate offspring will eventually return to discredit the economics of blood purity.

Scrutiny by Richard Godden and Noel Polk concerning the antebellum manumission instigated by the McCaslins has enlightened this imminence. Despite giving up the family mansion for their workers, and although never buying more than a single slave (Brownlee)—Amodeus and Theophilus inherit their plantation workers from L. Q. C. McCaslin—textuality will implicate the twins as instigators and enforcers of a distasteful regime. Their ledgers, when read by Theophilus and Sophonsiba's son, Isaac, will indict them for interracial homosexuality. Faulkner renders this reading in textual parentheses. Isaac's forbears, suggests this syntax, wished to consign this episode to the margins of McCaslin history. The chronicle, compounding the charges against them with the sin of bestiality, reverberates down the generations nonetheless.

Brownlee's involvement in the mysterious injury to a mule attests to his penchant for vice. Having to put down the animal emphasizes the seriousness of the incident. Sexual practice between different species, the transgression of special evolutionary boundaries, as Darwin knew well, is particularly heinous. By structural analogy, maintain Godden and Polk, Isaac projects this infamy onto the previous generation of McCaslins. He superimposes his understanding of Amodeus, Theophilus, and Brownlee's behavior over L. Q. C. McCaslin and two of his female slaves (Eunice and Tomasina ["Tomey" or "Tomy"]). The McCaslin mansion, although returned to patriarchal occupancy when Theophilus and Sophonsiba married, remains forever haunted by generations of unnatural practice.

The affiliated Beauchamp estate suffers a similar degradation. Left to Hubert to manage when Sophonsiba weds, he betrays her trust. Hoping to endow her lineage with a sense of pre-American aristocracy—that she had named the plantation "Warwick" is not coincidental—her endowment is tainted by her brother's affair with his housekeeper. His plea, "They're free now," does nothing to palliate Sophonsiba's disgust, especially after she notices the cook's silken dress (*Go Down, Moses* 224). Formerly reserved for the genteel, all races now appear fit for such garments. On recognizing the frock as one of her own, Sophonsiba becomes distraught, insisting on the woman's dismissal. Hubert sacks the housekeeper, who is last seen leaving Warwick wearing a "man's overcoat" (225). Faulkner may intend this diminution of the obvious demarcations of sex to result from questionable heredity, because Sophonsiba's racial politics implicates the servant as a mulattress. Consequently, external miscegenation has irremediably stained the aura of Warwick. The estate has nothing left for the heir apparent. Hubert's actions concerning the inheritance of gold coins he had secured for his nephew confirm this conclusion: Isaac will discover on coming of age that his uncle squandered this bequest on a dissolute life. All that remains are IOUs and some copper coins. As if to confirm this deficiency, a fire raises the mansion to the ground a few years later. This conflagration posits an undeniable sense of genealogical burnout.

Isaac's conception augured this end. His father was one of twins, so, as with Bayard and John Sartoris in *Flags in the Dust*, a reading conditioned by pangenetic notions comes to the fore. Amodeus and Theophilus exhibit a relationship of necessary supplementarity. Mortality posits the starkness of this necessity. Amodeus and Theophilus are "dead inside the same twelve-months" (202). This disquieting interdependency could point to the inheritance of dubious blood. The twins' parents, Isaac's grandparents on his spear side, might have been unsuited procreants. With very few biographical details available concerning this generation, the attribution of a dubious match falls on L. Q. C. McCaslin. His supposed moral paucity, his predilection for miscegenation and incest, impute his biological sanguinity. By extension, Isaac suffers in this regard too.

Moreover, a lack of nurture also plays a significant role in the outcome of Isaac's maturation. His father dies when he is three and in the seven years before his mother's death, Sophonsiba exposes him to her putative stance concerning miscegenation. The censuring of Hubert over the mulattress is one of the boy's formative experiences so that hybridity will always evoke his confusion, excitement, and distress. When Sophonsiba dies, Isaac's first cousin adopts him. However, Carothers McCaslin Edmonds ("Cass") leaves the woodsman Sam Fathers to nurture the boy. Faulkner resuscitates in Fathers the autochthonous genealogy from "Red Leaves." The woodsman is the son of the Chickasaw chief, Ikkemotubbe, and an octoroon slave. Pregnant, but rejected by Ikkemotubbe on racial grounds, Sam's mother remarries. Now with a stepfather, Sam's surname mutates to "Had-Two-Fathers" before compression through usage changes it to "Fathers." With this figuration, Faulkner purposefully presents what to Yoknapatawphians is a confused and confusing identity. In terms of blood blending, Fathers is half Chickasaw, three-eighths European, and one-eighth African. He is a hematological amalgam, but "a vessel," as Godden explains in *Fictions of Labor*, "in which three ethnicities meet and flow in amity" (234). Fathers is exceptional. Despite his supposedly antagonistic blood, the community perceives him to retain a spiritual purity.

This metaphysical essence recommends Fathers to Jobaker. The last of the indigenous Delta people, Faulkner's blood figuration for Jobaker knowingly contests the type of anthropological data gathered by Franz Boas for the Department of Ethnology of the World's Columbian Exposition. At the end of the nineteenth century, the Iroquois, Cherokees, Chickasaws, and Choctaws contained very few individuals whose descent could be classified as pure. Being to Mississippians the final manifestation of the unsullied Chickasaw makes Jobaker an anachronism of blood. "Nobody," recounts *Go Down, Moses*, "knew his history at all" (127). He appears to be both self-progenitor and the end of his lineage. Jobaker, in his own mind both hematologically and spiritually pure, believes himself to be the wilderness manifest in man. His specific role is that of a hierophant: an ascetic shaman capable of revealing sacred ecological mysteries and dedicated to the maintenance of nature. That there has never been a time in human history when, as Evans avers, "the lay of the land was not shaped by human interests and intentions" is beyond hierophantic consideration. That "the concept of the natural landscape is incomprehensible apart from the culture that defines it as its own opposite, which constitutes it by designating particular pieces of geography as noteworthy, investing them with symbolic significance, and enabling their social use or appreciation" is also unimagined ("Taking the Place" 180). Practicing his singular philosophy, Jobaker determinedly avoids all forms of human contamination. "The sublime vision," to appropriate Ralph Waldo Emerson, "comes to the pure and simple soul in a clean and chaste body" ("Poet" 327). Hidden from the civic community, Jobaker lives as a hermit on the outermost margins of society. Joanna Burden and her like from *Light in August* reside in the hinterland between racially divided communities, but the last of the Chickasaw must survive in the declensionary wilds. A quintessential example of Emerson's philosophy that, "if thou fill thy brain with Boston and New York, with fashion and covetousness, and wilt stimulate thy jaded senses with wine and French coffee, [then] thou shalt find no radiance of wisdom in the lonely waste of the pinewoods" ("Poet" 328), Jobaker fulfils the Emersonian remit that a spiritual man's "habit of living should be set on a key so low and plain, that the common influences should delight him. His cheerfulness should be the gift of the sunlight; the air should suffice for his inspiration, and he should be tipsy with water" ("Poet" 328).

Only Sam Fathers is approximate to his type. The verbal communication between the two ascetics, one that pertains to a particular *parole*, should have indicated to them the manner of their philosophical failure. "Talking in a mixture of negroid English and flat hill dialect and now and then a phrase of that old tongue," their shared language, a particular intermixture that takes latent possession of Isaac, originates from three different social groups (*Go Down, Moses* 127–28). Language bespeaks miscegenation. Oblivious to this evidence, Sam is content to be the heir apparent. Hence, on Jobaker's death in 1877, Sam invigilates alone over the cremation rites. There is no grave. At one with the natural world in life, Jobaker has, believes Sam, returned to nature on death. Furthermore, as Jobaker's spiritual beneficiary, "it seemed perfectly natural" that Fathers should inherit a specific role (128). Remote from the people of Yoknapatawpha, biologically, spiritually, and topographically, Sam's ontopology secures him the position of hierophant. Coinciding as it does with the death of Isaac's mother, Jobaker's demise is particularly telling for the young McCaslin. Fathers chooses Isaac as his legatee. He must initiate the boy into the enigmatic wilderness. In doing so, Fathers instills in Isaac a metaphysical vision of nature, one that resonates to an essentialist evaluation. Plato's theory of Forms is the bedrock of this perspective, Faulkner purposefully acknowledging the longevity of this cultural legacy, while opening that inheritance to scrutiny from an evolutionary hermeneutic.

Platonism asserts, according to classical scholar Walter Hamilton, "that the manifold and ever-changing phenomena of the world of sense are imitations or copies of eternal and absolute Forms, which alone have true reality" (20). The sensible world exists as a partial reality originating from this perfect realm. For almost every material and abstract class, there exists a Form, or Idea, (an *eidos*) in eternity. This paradigm is a hierarchy in which the Form of Good has primacy. The Platonic philosopher's task is to pass from the shadowy representations of the sensible world to the contemplation of Forms. The ultimate object of the Platonic vision is absolute beauty as enjoyed by man before incarnation. Universal moral concepts manifest the governing impulse in this anabasis. However, man is generally a *daemon*, a creature that partakes of both the sensible and the eternal worlds. To become a philosopher necessitates the transcendence of the physically daemonic. Numerous steps compose this spiritual ascent. In the preliminary stage, the philosophical trainee must accept the procreative act solely as a physical impulse between men and women. Spiritual procreation attributed to the marriage of noble minds is far better. Such metaphysical parenthood, with extremely rare exceptions, is possible only for men. Philosophical advance, writes Hamilton, therefore requires a maturation from the "love of particular examples of physical beauty to physical beauty in general; thence to beauty of soul . . . and so to moral beauty in general; and finally to the beauty of knowledge" (23–24).

Two of Faulkner's epistemological guides were ill disposed toward this route. Yes, admits John Dewey in "Darwin's Influence upon Philosophy" (1909), "the conception of *eidos* was the central principle of knowledge as well as nature" to Plato, but this provenance does not guarantee philosophical validity (94). Conditioned by two millennia of education, twentieth-century intuition may be disposed to invoke hidden forms and real essences, but this immediate response to phenomena is a delusion; rather, the cerebral apprehension of experiences makes perception indeterminate. Dewey's response to Platonism, argues David Kadlec, "reflected the tenor of the decade by locating the future of philosophy in evolution and genetics" (169). The pragmatism of William James (1842–1910)—who asserts that "Darwinism has once and for all displaced design from the minds of the 'scientific'"—sounded a similar chord (111). James's reorientation of deterministic attitudes accounted for reality being constantly in the making. This Jamesian formation, explains Kadlec, "took place not in any given thing, but only in the junctures between moments in 'the stream of experience'" (26–27). James's approach, as David Howell Evans makes clear in his doctoral thesis, appealed to Faulkner (2651). Now the evolutionary and genetic assault on essentialism, as Kadlec concludes, "could be forcefully applied to language and genre by writers who were engaged with contemporary social issues" (4). The contingency that determines the generational transmission of life might serve as a constitutive force in language for skilled practitioners. Faulkner's reflection on and continued engagement with such debates resonated with these practical implications of evolution.

Go Down, Moses evinces this contemplation with Faulkner's critique of the hierophantic, a line of descent that he examines from Jobaker through Sam Fathers to Isaac McCaslin. Sam's relationship with the orphaned Isaac is paternal and Platonic. Their love, a search for truth and beauty inspired by mutual affection, sublimates physical desire into a philosophical ascent. At an individual level, the Mississippi Delta is the pure source from which to propel the soul toward the numinous essence of life. At a communal level, the southern wilderness forms the permanent standard against which civilization should measure social progress. Genealogy and societal past signify nothing without such a background. This void is Fathers's fear.

His inheritance from Jobaker becomes an increasingly troubled one. The wilderness is no longer isolated from the intrusiveness of man. That Fathers must scare intruders from Jobaker's cremation with warning shots is a telling intimation of encroachment. Although Fathers will not admit it, his own biological heredity signals the end of the unadulterated South as much as the death of his tutor does. During his stewardship of the Delta from 1877 to 1883, Fathers witnesses the increase in ecological pressure between man and nature. Committed to the cause, as his withdrawal to the Big Bottom of the Tallahatchie indicates, the wholesale demand for timber betrays his tenure.[2] The ecological stance of Fathers conflicts with the interests of the landowners over whose estates he roams. A change in status from hierophant to miscegene looms large. Willing to be a scapegoat, the "pure selflessness [and] holy indifference" of Fathers, Ihab Hassan believes, reveal his courage (16). He also retains insurance against decisive scapegoating in his heir apparent. Fathers must now accelerate Isaac McCaslin's ascent through the metaphysical mysteries of the Delta. Theosophic overtones mark Fathers as ideal for this role.

In the beginning, Fathers shows Isaac a glimpse of the numinous essence to nature by invoking the Buck as eidos. All deer, corporeal avatars of an eternal Form, supposedly emanate from this divine archetype; so it is that Fathers, using the magic of Jobaker's old, secret, and unsoiled Indian language, summons up this visionary form. For, in line with Emerson's belief, the heroic naturalist "knows that he speaks adequately, then, only when he speaks somewhat wildly, or, with 'the flower of the mind'; not with the intellect, used as an organ, but with the intellect released from all service, and suffered to take its direction from its celestial life; or, as the ancients were want to express themselves, not with intellect alone, but with the intellect inebriated by nectar" ("Poet" 326).

The conjuration effected by Fathers instills an ardent spiritual belief in Isaac. The boy now equates his mentor with the divine. Isaac appears to believe Sam Fathers's veins run the same numinous blood that circulates in the Buck. Later, Cass will admit that Fathers had shown him the Buck too, but the calmness with which he says this to Isaac—the repeated exhortation to remain "steady"—intimates an immanent lack of suggestibility (*Go Down, Moses* 139). This hierophantic unsuitability seems to have been apparent to Fathers; his search for a successor had then moved on.

Isaac soon undergoes the next stage of his indoctrination. He shoots his first buck and has his face smeared with its blood. Fathers's tutelage has unwittingly exposed a contradiction in the status of his protégé. The hierophant apparent is coterminously a future patrician. Isaac is not only Sam Fathers's heir, but he is also scion to General Compson and Maj. Manfred de Spain, two of the foremost aristocrats in Yoknapatawpha. This European side to his patrimony teaches Isaac about the lives a hunter spills. The association of the Buck with numinous purity and the vital essence of blood in the physical realm, now converge in Isaac's mind. Purity of blood correlates with purity per se. This is the hybrid philosophy passed down to Isaac as his cultural inheritance. However, as Derrida explains, there is "no inheritance without a call to responsibility" (*Specters* 91). Cultural heredity "is always the reaffirmation of a debt, but a critical, selective, and filtering reaffirmation" (*Specters* 91–92). Isaac, retaining an essentialist perspective throughout his life, lacks this necessary discrimination.

The prospective climax to his indoctrination is the hunt for the mythical Tallahatchie Bear. Isaac's dream of this confrontation necessarily conflates the corporeal with the metaphysical as his aspiration resonates with American ursine mythology. "The most powerful wizards," James George Frazer (1854–1941) states in *The Golden Bough* (1907–15), "are they whose external souls have the shape of stallions, elks, black bears, eagles, or boars" (895). Humans have been worshipping bears for more than fifteen thousand years, ever since caves have provided human habitation. Hence, the aura surrounding the bear in America dates back to the beginnings of speleology in the continent. Sacred significance invested in the foundations both topological and metaphysical of self-definition has much to do with the Americanization of such Occidental myths, suggests Faulkner. *Go Down, Moses* thereby admits to a legion of tales concerning "The Bear." With the asseverations of Fathers about this animal, which Isaac is in no position to refute, the presence of this animal "loomed and towered" in the boy's dreams long before any physical encounter (*Go Down, Moses* 141). A chimera "too big for the very country which was its constricting scope," an embodiment of "an old dead time, a phantom, epitome and apotheosis of the old wild life," the metaphysical presence of the Bear becomes familiar to Isaac (141, 142). The parallel Faulkner draws between this animal and the late Jobaker implies that pure blood runs in its veins. Like Jobaker, "so long unwifed and childless as to have become its own ungendered progenitor," the Bear is also the self-progenitive end of its type (154). Naming completes the sense of anthropomorphism: "Old Ben" is a correlative protector of this habitat.

Isaac's encounter with this animal promises to be the culmination of his initiation. Transcendental advancement must continue apace. When close to unity with the numinousness of nature, Isaac will be able to complete his ascent. The maturation of his orienteering skills testifies to this final attainment. That he can discard manmade navigational aids, his compass and watch, but retain complete topographical awareness, signals his spiritual maturity. No longer tainted by personal effects, Isaac comes upon the Bear for the first time. Harmony with nature is complete. Yet, his encounter in the Big Bottom reveals the startlingly small and ragged stature of Old Ben. As in the case of Joe Christmas and hybridity, there is a gap between theory and actuality. The physical reality fails to match the phantasm. The philosophy of divine eternal Forms should be manifest in the physical presence of this legendary creature. Isaac sees the discrepancy but fails to acknowledge its significance, and Fathers does his best to bolster the illusion by recalling to his protégé the old times peopled by pure-blooded Indians, a time before Europeans and their African slaves. Young Isaac is immersed in these tales and, with "Sam Fathers' voice the mouthpiece of the host," he ceases to regard them as bygone. Engendering anachronism, the past becomes "part of the boy's present" (127). The Bear, a moth-eaten and man-ravaged beast, remains to Isaac a *zōion* in purest form.

The gathering pace of land clearance, fueled by a growing need for cotton, timber, and living space, appears stark set against this metaphysical backdrop. From Isaac's perspective, however, something else is responsible for this ecological denudation. Two dogs intimate this other source. The first is Isaac's fyce; the second, "Lion," is the feral that Fathers catches, trains, and names. These animals exhibit the characteristics necessary for baying the Bear. The fyce may prove too small physically, but its courage avers the pertinence of a mongrel lineage. Lion, "part mastiff, something of Airedale and something of a dozen other strains probably," also exemplifies a courageous descent (160). Lion, as his name suggests, is a fearsome creature ideally fitted to the struggle for existence. The "almost impersonal malignance like some natural force" from its yellow eyes seems to confirm a mentality in tune with physical stature (160). Faulkner completely overhauls canine hybridity, as formerly expressed in the vitiated fox-hound puppies from *Flags in the Dust*, in this figuration. Not the product of human supervised breeding, Lion is naturally determined. This dog is a coalescence of evolutionary forces, an animal that infers "not only courage and all else that went to make up the will and desire to pursue and kill, but endurance, the will and desire to endure beyond all imaginable limits of flesh in order to overtake and slay" (175). When first seen by Isaac, Lion "was in motion" (159). The youngster, however, fails to comprehend the evolutionary significance of this dynamism. According to a pangenetic discourse, Lion is akin not only to his new owner Sam Fathers, but also to his custodian, Boon Hogganbeck, who is one-quarter Chickasaw and three-quarters European. Sleeping with the mastiff, Boon's physical closeness to Lion intimates their shared status.

News of this dog spawns a new legend with numerous strangers coming to witness its first hunt for the Bear. Close to trapping their quarry, more outlanders appear. The forces of man cannot wait to encroach on the wilderness once expunged of its protective presence. Marked out by their apparel, the "hunting-clothes and boots they wore had been on a store shelf yesterday," these outlanders get lost in the woods and Fathers has to rescue them. Come evening, these city men are "still terrified" (165). This untamed space, Faulkner intimates, continues to resist human intrusion. Two more years elapse before the decisive hunt. Isaac, now aged sixteen, participates in the conclusive attack on the Bear spearheaded by Boon and Lion. Old Ben is bayed by the dog pack, savagely bitten by Lion, and Boon's knife imparts the fatal wound. Old Ben, the final aristocrat of Delta, crashes to the ground, brought to heel by the proletariat.

As the Bear hits the earth, Sam Fathers suffers a seizure. The demands of civilization, so it seems, are now destroying the vestiges of unadulterated numinousness. Faulkner explained in 1955 that Old Ben is "symbolic of nature in an age when nature in a way is being destroyed. That is, the forests are going, being replaced by the machine, and that bear represented the old tradition of nature" (*Lion* 140). Lawrence Buell censures the author in this regard. *Go Down, Moses*, the critic asserts, sets up "an ironic distinction between the spiritual teleology (Old Ben's death means end of wilderness), and the propertarian teleology (Major de Spain's sale means death of wilderness) without resolving the issue" (16). This textual tension, to answer Buell, is intentional. Nature, Faulkner's indeterminacy stresses, is sublime. The chaos inherent in the natural world arouses not so much positive pleasure as admiration and respect.

By middle age, then, Faulkner was thinking for himself. He had successfully undermined the evolutionarily endowed propensity for passive reason. Heteronomy of thought, prejudice, and superstition were coming up against a mind far less liable to be deceived. Faulkner's maturity indicates a man overriding subjective judgments and reflecting on his own conception du monde, a man more at ease with indeterminacy, an author for whom nature would always escape the meaning of language since writing, that benchmark of civilization, was the disappearance of natural presence.

The actions of Sam Fathers emphasize this conclusion. His paralysis on the death of the Bear is permanent, and Boon, sanctioned by Fathers, euthanizes him. With this authorization, Fathers finally accepts that hybridity, not purity, is the unstoppable essence to ecology. Isaac reasons in a similar vein, but his conclusion is different: hybridity is suffocating purity. For Isaac, the fracture that prevents the realization of idealized Forms in nature, the rupture that has perverted purity, is enforced by the spectral space he associates with the agency of primary miscegenation. As hierophant of the Delta, Isaac will staunchly practice the spiritual philosophy passed down to him in an attempt to suture this gap.

His theosophic undertones distinguish Isaac for this role, but the irony of his hierophantic designation is harsh. Putatively a specially gifted man with an unusual control over nature, his abnormality does not extend to preventing that which he finds heinously abnormal. Miscegenation dooms his desired aegis over the Delta. In the early years of timber production, the wilderness remained unmarked—the rapacity of man was "never quite so fast as the Hand" (*Go Down, Moses* 238)—the train Isaac boarded for the woods resembling "a small dingy harmless snake" (236). Nevertheless, times have changed. The harmlessness of machinery was specious, the railway forthwith appearing "apparently from nowhere in one endless mathematical line overnight" (237). This infringement recalls the spoliation by loggers and railroad gangs of the New England forest around the ponds so loved by Henry David Thoreau (1817–1862) at Walden, Massachusetts. Such invasive agents often appear in Faulkner's novel ex nihilo. They are seldom stoppable. That the railway presages the increasing disrespect of humankind for nature is symbolized by a young bear, which, after its first encounter with a locomotive, remains cowering in a tree for hours.

Entering the Delta three years later for another hunting expedition, Isaac acknowledges that the region is "different now." He realizes that "not only the train but himself" constitute a pernicious threat; together they bring "the lingering effluvium of a sick-room or of death" (238). The camp cook, Ash, meets him on arrival. This presence reminds Isaac of happier days. Ash's failed attempt to shoot game comes to mind. Hunting a young bear, the cook had failed to hit his target from close range. Three bullets misfired and the fourth detonated by accident. The gun had rebelled against Ash as a soulless individual who burnt wood on his fire. The arboreal consumer had to defer to Isaac's marksmanship. In the present, though, Ash is effectively the camp commandant. He sets the time by which Isaac and Boon must return each evening. Has hunting become soulless too?

While searching for Boon in the Big Bottom on the first day, Isaac comes across the graves of Sam Fathers and the Bear. That this site lies within the boundary markers set out by a lumber company comes as a "shockingly alien" insurgence of the capitalist economy into the fecundity of God's earth (243). For Isaac, the graves of Sam and Old Ben reinforce the feeling that his predecessors were at one with the land. He can find little trace of their plots; they have already been "translated into myriad life" (244). Hierophantic Isaac appreciates the tumescence of nature, and he confirms his guardianship when, coming across a snake, he addresses this prelapsarian presence in the Indian language of Jobaker. The snake revitalizes Isaac's Edenic vision, pure words come from his lips, but his comfort is momentary. On finding Boon, Isaac discovers him to be in tears. Sat beneath a gum tree teeming with squirrels, his friend is hysterical. Wildlife is up a gum tree and Boon, whose gun jammed on firing, finds himself disjoined from nature in the manner of Ash. Boon has dismantled his rifle but cannot free the trapped cartridge. Just as the gun is out of joint, so is humankind dislocated from the natural order. The southern environment by this time is, as Kate Soper writes, "suffocating, traumatic, bloody, and generally dysfunctional" rather than "nurturing, happy, organically unified, and generally functioning" (47). Boon's hysteria acknowledges not only his inability to return the wilderness to an orderly state, but also his partial awareness that, as a hybrid, he has been an agent in its destruction. That he and Isaac will be unable to sustain the southern tradition of man in harmony with nature is dawning on the pair of them.

The physical manifestation of hybridity is the phantom that now haunts Isaac. The resulting suppressions thus incited will be personal and familial. Within months of Sam's death, Isaac decides to investigate the genealogical state of his own family. How pure, Isaac wonders, is the McCaslin genealogy? He has long known of the written record of his lineage, but now in receipt of his cultural inheritance, he examines the tomes. Procrastination in this instance equates to predestination. For despite the ledgers being, as Godden and Polk avow, "virtually unmoored from conventional linearity and periodicity" (301), Isaac "knew what he was going to find before he found it" (*Go Down, Moses* 198). Blood meets writing in the McCaslin ledgers. Ostensibly to refresh his memory, Isaac spreads the volumes "upon some apocryphal Bench" (193). In one respect, they are a testimony in which the older entries appear as a faded, almost indecipherable code. The ledgers bespeak confusion. They are the amalgamation of many hands; they are a portentous miscegenation of writing. In another respect, the ledgers are a microcosm of southern history, a record starting with the birth of L. Q. C. McCaslin.

One side of this genealogy particularly troubles Isaac, as the "rank" nighttime atmosphere of the commissary adumbrates (198, 200). Isaac confirms his culturally provoked suspicions concerning a history of blood blending within his clan. A predilection for miscegenation, according to Isaac's interpretation, haunted L. Q. C. through his relationship with the slave Eunice. In this regard, L. Q. C. neatly fits into the category of the *interracial bigamist.* Joel Williamson describes this type as the "man who reared a mulatto family in the servant's quarters at the very same time that he maintained a white family in the main house, in effect, having two wives simultaneously" (*William Faulkner* 25). Sometimes a mulatto facsimile of the white family, the label of *shadow family* applied to these other kin.[3] Isaac believes that his patriarch later compounded miscegenation through incest with Tomasina, the hybrid daughter from his first liaison. On learning of her daughter's defilement, reasons Isaac, Eunice committed suicide. In coming to this conclusion, the dialogue in the ledgers between his father and uncle concerning Eunice's death is crucial. To Theophilus's "*Drownd in Crick Christmas Day 1832,*" Amodeus added "*Drownd herself*" (*Go Down, Moses* 197). There is no reason for a slave to commit suicide, responded Theophilus, only for Amodeus to repeat "*Drownd herself*" (198). A two-handed, or hybrid, entry is the result. Ambiguity, fostered by the predominant southern ethos about race, runs amok. Still confused twelve months later, Isaac determines to solve the riddle and inspects the ledgers again. Under the gaze of the hierophant, as if by magic, the pages turn automatically. "The connection between the events in the forest and the events in the commissary, between the scene of hunting and the scene of reading," as Evans argues, becomes "crucial" ("Taking the Place" 182). The form of the novel propounds this importance. Four sections located in the Delta surround section 4 of "The Bear," which is set in the commissary.

Isaac has learned to construe untamed spaces as purity per se. Nature is the fountainhead of purification for the ills of society, a civilization tainted by the incestuous and miscegenate behavior encountered in the McCaslin ledgers. He reads both extremes of sexual congress into his lineage. Darwin may have held abhorrence toward incestuousness as "universal" (*Descent* 90) while appreciating "the good effects of intercrossing," but Isaac rejects both activities (*Origin* 55). Interfamilial sex has soiled human interaction, believes Isaac, and interracial sexual congress has been particularly vitiating. Furthermore, metaphysical impurity is manifest in physical impurity. Hybrid blood evinces this manifestation. Sullied at conception because of the heinous behavior of the family patriarch, generations of McCaslins have suffered the consequences. Isaac's rendition of family heritage is a synecdoche for his (Hughesean) version of American history. Anxieties about the repercussions of blood blending, as Evans suggests, correspond "to patterns of historical interpretation with a long history in American thought" ("Taking the Place" 189). In turn, this chronicle is a synecdoche for a human history in which a fascination with hybridity emanates from the tension between cultural dictates against miscegenation and the evolutionary truism that interracial sex is biologically acceptable. Faulkner's middle-aged awareness of this opposition evinces the maturation of his own introversion toward a mondial view of the human condition. The issue of land-ownership looms large in this vision.

From Isaac's perspective, the erstwhile aristocratic status of the McCaslins paradoxically confirms their impurity. His philosophy posits the natural world as a divine source of regeneration. Land-ownership betrays this numinous bequest. From this misunderstanding comes Isaac's resolve to atone for the McCaslin past. One step on his road to redemption is his attempt to pay off familial hybrids, the descendants of Tomasina, with the legacy established for them by L. Q. C. and augmented by his sons.[4] Lucius ("Lucas") Beauchamp is the youngest, Sophonsiba ("Fonsiba") and James ("Tennie's Jim") being the other two members of this family branch. At the age of twenty-one, each is entitled to one thousand dollars from the McCaslin estate. The eldest, James, cannot regard antecedent miscegenation with equanimity. Intimacy with the white patriarchy besmirches his African lineage. James feels impelled to change the topology of his ontopology. He moves from Jefferson and crosses the River Ohio so that running water separates him from "the land of his grandmother's betrayal." By this act, he interposes "latitude and geography too, shaking from his feet forever the very dust of the land" of his white ancestor (*Go Down, Moses* 81). Isaac follows the émigré with the purpose of presenting him with his thousand dollars, but the trail goes cold.

Fonsiba Beauchamp marries a northerner and sets up a homestead with him in Arkansas. To the weary southern eyes of Isaac, this man, with his belief in African American self-sufficiency, sustains a "tiny image" (204). Nevertheless, Isaac determines that Fonsiba receive her inheritance when she is twenty-one. Eventually tracking her down, Isaac, inculcated with hybrid lore as he is, likens himself to "an experienced bloodhound" (204–5). Coming upon the couple's farm, a crooked house in the barren Arkansas landscape, Isaac perceives a crazy desire for social freedom. Even their domesticated animals wander unchecked. He believes that Fonsiba accepts this perverse idealism in deference to her husband, presumed obedience that forces Isaac to deposit her McCaslin bequest at an Arkansas bank. Faulkner's explicit citation from Eliot's "The Journey of the Magi" (1927) encompasses this section of the text: nascent African American autonomy is *hard and bitter agony* for Isaac to bear (205). Unlike for the magi, however, this pain fails to enlighten.

The third African American McCaslin is Lucas Beauchamp. In the estimation of Carothers Edmonds ("Roth"), Lucas is an archetype who preempts pangenesis. This figuration compounds the importance of Lucas's descent from L. Q. C. McCaslin: *"He is both heir and prototype simultaneously of all the geography and climate and biology which sired Old Carothers and all the rest of us and our kind, myriad, countless, faceless, even nameless now except himself who fathered himself, intact and complete, contemptuous, as Old Carothers must have been, of all blood black white yellow or red, including his own"* (91).

A practitioner of an evolutionary hermeneutic cannot help but note the Tainian overtones of "race," "surroundings," and "epoch" in this description. Even so, Faulkner's figuration moves beyond Taine, because by changing his first name from Lucius—he was named after his white great-grandfather—Lucas was "by himself composed, himself selfprogenetive and nominate, by himself ancestored" (208). His resistance to standard authorship, authoritarian writing concerning the subjugated, is impressive. Self-progeneration and autobiography, the Faulknerian aesthetic implies, makes Lucas the symbolic head of the McCaslin clan. As if to affirm this, Lucas often wears "the hand-made beaver hat which Edmonds' grandfather had given him fifty years ago" (92). When coming of age, Lucas additionally determines to control his personal finances. Depositing his endowment at a bank in Jefferson, he makes sure he gets a receipt.[5] This act of defiance is less extravagant than that effected by James or Fonsiba in emigrating from Yoknapatawpha, but shrewder. Forced back into his consciousness in rebuffing the dictates of the social environment, Lucas withdraws into himself and becomes an independent thinker. Seemingly tied to Yoknapatawpha—in an echo of Turl's behavior in "Was"— Lucas rebels by means of tricks, lies, and procrastination.

Lucas's rebelliousness, however, fails to protect him from the obloquy of miscegenation, Faulkner presenting an African American perspective on enforced sexual subservience in "The Fire and the Hearth." A portion of this tale, his perceived cuckolding by Cass's son, Zachary Edmonds ("Zack"), aggravates the apparent blight of miscegenation manifest in the suicides of Lucas's antecedents. This mindfulness will bear no repetition. He can no more than suspect his wife, Molly, of infidelity (following the death of Zack's wife in childbirth), but the McCaslin genealogical burden produces paranoia. The *interracial widower*, whom Williamson describes as "a man who lost his wife by death and then took in her stead one of his slaves, sometimes his wife's maid and thus a woman uniquely well prepared for the position," was not uncommon in the Old South (*William Faulkner* 25). Faulkner's figuration further implicates Molly. She returns from her vigil at the newborn's bedside wearing a pair of shoes owned by Zack's late wife. Symbolically, Molly has stepped into the shoes of the dead woman. Lucas's anger at the possible intimacy boils over into violence. Striking Molly, drawing blood, he taunts, "It aint none of your blood that's trying to break out and run" (*Go Down, Moses* 39). Zack's white seminal blood, implies Lucas, is desperate to escape from Molly's black body.

In many cases, antebellum plantation owners did force sexual demands on their slaves—there would have been no reparation. Reconstruction promised otherwise. Yet, as Davis is aware, Lucas's response "reveals an anxiety and shame about cuckoldry which as a racial inferior he is powerless to prevent" despite manumission (131). Expecting expiation, Lucas turns his anger on Zack, but his gun misfires. The need for violence satiated, Lucas returns home to Molly. Significantly, she no longer "wear[s] the white woman's shoes" (45).

Does Lucas ever forgive his wife for her supposed unfaithfulness? The answer is no. For Lucas, cuckolded or not, Molly has demonstrated a spiritual infidelity. In a reaction to this episode, as "The Fire and the Hearth" reveals, his endeavors to divine his own authenticity become obsessive. The pursuit of Civil War gold attests to Lucas's preoccupation. An antesecession coin—found in attempting to hide his distillery apparatus in an Indian burial mound—is the trigger for this hunt. Rebellion, blood, and southern soil come together in this discovery when the tomb collapses over Lucas and with it "the old earth, perhaps the old ancestors themselves" (30). Lucas now "walks a fine line, his tightrope, between being an entrepreneur with capital and being expendable capital" (Davis 131). To Molly, his obsession is sacrilegious. To resurrect gold from the land is the task of God and God alone. "What's rendered to My earth," she quotes, "it belong to Me unto I resurrect it" (*Go Down, Moses* 79). For Molly, the earth holds a numinous essence that Lucas has reduced to an alchemical depository. The curse of the Lord, she prophesies, will "destroy him or her that touches what's done been rendered back to Him" (94). Lucas continues in his quest for buried treasure, for the discovery that will set him truly free, either extreme wealth or divine inspiration, but Molly is vindicated at last. Lucas has to admit defeat; he does so with little grace. Despite banking his McCaslin legacy, despite Molly's moral superiority, and despite the fact that his grandchild, expected by Nat Wilkins in the winter of 1942, will sustain the McCaslin genealogy, Lucas remains a hard man.

Stubbornness is possibly a McCaslin trait. Isaac exhibits this characteristic in his desire to elicit appreciation from the intended benefactors of L. Q. C.'s endowment. The specters of inheritance are not paid off so easily and Isaac's obstinacy concerning austere frontier philosophy will provoke the return of further revenants. Isaac extols personal liberty and freedom as a physical condition, a tripartite philosophy of the frontier that combines his Platonic abhorrence of miscegenation with his contempt for land-ownership and his reliance on nature as the only harbinger of divine inspiration. Ideologically buttressed from reality, Isaac continues in his misinterpretation of the interaction of humankind with their natural environment. He views the American wilds as a remedy for cultural falsities. With this belief, he takes his place in a tradition that runs from the Puritans through the transcendentalists and beyond. Like Jobaker and Sam Fathers before him, Isaac therefore attempts to flee society by immersion in the wilderness. Nonetheless, as is inevitably the case, contradictions suffuse such ventures. Nature must contrast human culture but, as Evans indicates, "at the same time it is invested with cultural forms and values that must appear to grow, as it were, directly out of the soil" ("Taking the Place" 186–87).

Isaac's tenure as hierophant is thereby fraught regarding both strands of ecological interaction. Having turned twenty-one, he officially comes of age and enters the propertied class. The year is 1888, a turning point for the young man, occasioned by his discussion of the McCaslin ledgers with his cousin. Cass attempts to dispel Isaac's austere philosophy as an anachronism, but hematological politics dooms his argument. He has a low estimation of Sam Fathers's heredity, the mixed blood of the woodsman being "the scene of his own vanquishment and the mausoleum of his defeat" (*Go Down, Moses* 125). Isaac resents this suggestion from a man who is only a McCaslin via the distaff side; rather, Fathers was a hierophant judged a failure by society because that community was unworthy of his heroic commitment. Within this tension ensues a protracted dialogue concerning the ledgers. Cass attacks Isaac's ideology with the complementary philosophical method of *elenchus*. His series of (Socratic) questions intends to expose ideological errancy.[6] The cousins agree that the commissary books record their plantation as "a whole land in miniature, which multiplied and compounded was the entire South" (217). Nevertheless, the younger man retains his labored philosophy, reading American history with a morbid fatalism that Cass cannot share. Isaac's interpretation testifies to a forfeit. Nature is no longer a source of inward happiness. The indigenous peoples are as guilty of this loss as settlers from the Old World are. Native Indians were arrogant to believe that they had land to sell, while émigrés from Europe brought with them the curse of land-ownership. Only the African race, concedes Isaac, is pure enough to inherit the New World.

To back this claim, Isaac again relies on dubious testimony. This time he turns to the apocryphal Book of Ham. Léon Poliakov provides a summary of the Christian Apocrypha and racial politics relevant to this argument. Poliakov contends that although early Christianity taught "that all men descended from a common ancestor, Adam, through the patriarch Noah and his sons," the founders of the Christian Church revitalized these genealogies by combining them with regional and local traditions. Descendance passed through Noah via his sons Japheth, Shem, Ham, and, in some readings, a fourth brother named Jenithon (or Manithon). The paternity of Europeans came from the children of Japheth, Asian descent from those of Shem, and African lineage from Ham. "It should be noted," writes Poliakov, "that the latter were the objects, according to the Bible, of a mysterious curse, for they were condemned to serve their cousins as slaves" (7). Three main medieval social orders developed from this designation with nobles descending from Japheth, clerks from Shem, and serfs from Ham. Hence, reasons Poliakov, "the Hamites or Blacks were placed on the bottom rung of the human hierarchy" from the earliest of times (7–8). Isaac's exegesis of the Book of Ham provides a resounding "no" to miscegenation concomitant with his admission that African Americans constitute the purest presence in the South—his admittance echoing that made by Earnest Albert Hooton in 1938. "A 'pure' race," states Hooton, "is little more than an anthropological abstraction; no pure race can be found in any civilized country. Racial purity is restricted, at best, to remnants of savage groups in isolated wildernesses. The present races of man have intermingled and interbreed for many thousands of years so that their genealogical lines have become inextricably confused" (*Apes* 153).

Pureblooded Africans should endure reasons Isaac. He then conflates his reading of the Book of Ham with his fears concerning the Jeremiad (or "Book of Lamentations"). Puritan emigration to the New World fulfilled God's plan for the Elect. They were to inherit the Promised Land. However, no sooner had these Europeans "set out on their mission than they began to fail in it" (Evans, "Taking the Place" 191). This deficiency was caused, in large measure, by the sin of ownership. African Americans, denied the land through enslavement, were therefore the most victimized. Nevertheless, Puritans believed that divine prescience had foreseen European American failure, the Lord sending punishments such as the Civil War as restoratives. "Some devoutly religious women," writes David Goldfield, "looked upon their crumbling nation and concluded that God, not the Yankees, had rendered judgment on them" (96). These divine corrections confirmed the Jeremianic fate of the South. Africans, being pure of blood, were the inheritors to whom the Lord had bequeathed New Canaan. Isaac hates to admit this understanding, because, despite its hematological purity, African blood remains to him of low rank. His own unadulterated and prestigious constitution, so Isaac believes, posits him as the embodiment of the Jeremiad and the end of southern white history. His failure to procreate will confirm this delusion.

Cass's catechism has failed. Twenty-one years of age, inheritor of the McCaslin plantation, Isaac determines to practice his idealism in the face of prophecy. He too rejects his McCaslin inheritance, not deigning to own the land of his predecessors.[7] As an "apostate to his name and lineage" (*Go Down, Moses* 31), Isaac becomes a hierophant who empathizes only with the wilderness, ignoring "the tamed land which was to have been his heritage" (187–88). Moreover, by abnegating his responsibility, he merely passes on this burden. Roth will eventually have to bear this weight. Isaac's tortured philosophy, as Evans concurs, merely repeats "the essential American gesture." His denunciation "is ultimately a reinforcement of the essential providential assumptions of epistemological privilege and special election that have subtended the history of America [that history] from the beginning" ("Taking the Place" 194).

Isaac rents a "cubicle in a back-street stock-traders' boarding-house" and becomes a carpenter (*Go Down, Moses* 259). His Christlike renunciation is, however, an empty gesture. Not only do McCaslin funds continue to subsidize him, but his carpentry, in a minor way, also aggravates the deforestation of Mississippi. Isaac weds. The uncertainty in the McCaslin genealogy as to the year of his marriage, either 1889 or 1890, adumbrates through denial the part his wife plays in the future of that lineage. She remains unnamed, a marginal figure, but her role is definitive. On learning that Isaac has disclaimed the McCaslin plantation, she reacts not with consanguinity but with hysteria. Finding Isaac intransigent, she refuses him sexual relations. In practice, the idealism supposed to protect the McCaslins from contaminated blood effaces their spear-side genealogy from the Yoknapatawphian landscape. Isaac's narrative, as if in sympathy, will not reappear until 1940 when the next generation on the McCaslin distaff side has emerged into adulthood.

"Delta Autumn," which is the penultimate episode in the novel, chronicles the hunting trip of that year. The widowed Isaac, his wife died circa 1937, is neither a biological nor a spiritual father; many of the locals simply call him "Uncle." The autumnal setting matches the twilight of Isaac's life and simultaneously presages the fall of the wilderness. Rapid modernity has taken over the Delta of which he remains the nominal hierophant. When Isaac was a boy, he need only travel thirty miles from Jefferson to reach the woodlands, now a journey of two hundred miles is required; once there had been the scream of panthers, now just the hooting of locomotives is heard. Isaac's sacred space has become an anachronism. Out of step with evolutionary time, the "inverted-apex, this —shaped section" has been outdated rather than conquered or destroyed by man (253).

Major de Spain and General Compson had appreciated this twilight. They gave up hunting and sold their land in the Big Bottom after the death of the Bear. Isaac, though, needs the revitalization provided by the camp despite the experience being a shadow of former times. Licenses are required to shoot. What was once a responsible freedom has suffered from practice without accountability—as Boon's hysteria augured fifty-four years earlier, there is a paucity of game. Ruminating on these changes, Isaac tells the assembled hunters that God "created the kind of world He would have wanted to live in if He had been a man," but, he cautions, the Lord also foresaw that the environment man "devastates will be the consequence and signature of his crime and guilt, and his punishment" (257). To Isaac's mind, there is a generational growth of insensibility toward the natural and toward miscegenation as the basest transgression of nature. His obsession with this topic presages an imminent confrontation.

Revenants, augured by Isaac's austere frontier philosophy, now make their return. There has already been a premonition during the journey from Jefferson to the Delta. After hours on the road, Isaac glimpses the woodlands. He begins to salute the emerging scene when Roth's violent braking interrupts him. Although having fleetingly seen someone by the roadside in an ex nihilo apparition, Roth manages to conceal his consternation. Even so, around the campfire that night, their other traveling companion jibes him about doe hunting. A coded reference to Roth's illicit lover, and his violation of old standards that held female deer to be sacrosanct, the campfire embarrassment Roth endures is lost on Isaac.

No longer at one with the hunters, Isaac's remoteness is reiterated when they leave him to lie-in the next morning. Half asleep, he is taking comfort from the remains of "his land" when a portentous shadow looming over the tent disturbs his meditation (260). Roth enters, however, dispelling any apprehensions. His grandnephew having departed, Isaac's ease is soon intruded upon for a second time. He notes the alarming bulge in the canvas above him because of the rain. Someone then "jarred sharply against the end of the cot" (262). It is Roth again, but pregnant with symbolism the "globe" of Isaac's tent continues to prefigure the frontiers of a global philosophy impinging on the inveterate (261). Soon after Roth's second departure comes the "mounting snarl" of an outboard motor (263). This ominous sound heralds a third visitation: the revenant, the coming of the other as "the absolute and unpredictable singularity of the *arrivant as justice*" (Derrida, *Specters* 28).

Manifest as a woman, this specter exhibits the unpredictable nature of the other, Faulkner again using the semiotics of fashion to deconstruct gender. She wears "a man's hat and a man's slicker and rubber boots." This cross-dresser brings with her into Isaac's tent "an effluvium which he knew he would recognise." She has a "face indistinct and . . . queerly colorless" (*Go Down, Moses* 263). The mulattress associated with Hubert Beauchamp must be playing somewhere in Isaac's id, a valid supposition, because this woman is not only Roth's paramour, the roadside figure as they drove to the Delta, but also James Beauchamp's granddaughter. The mother of Roth's child, whom she carries in her arms, has come for an answer concerning their marriage. She already knows the outcome, conceding that her lover's code of conduct forbids their union before God, but wishes to extract some familial response. In an echo of his granduncle's pecuniary gifts, still culture-bound by patriarchal codes of conduct, Roth has decided to pay her off. He fits nicely into the category of the *interracial bachelor* who was, in Williamson's words, "a male of the slaveholding class . . . who never married but rather took as his de facto wife a mulatto slave and by her conceived a sequence of children" (*William Faulkner* 25). Roth, without identifying his expected visitor, has left money with Isaac to close this relationship.

Isaac recoils at the encounter. The signs of the woman's troubling essence, which he detected on her arrival, slowly become more apparent.

Reading her "face's dead and toneless pallor" as signs of deficient biological inheritance, reality nevertheless forces Isaac to conclude that she and the baby are "incredibly and even ineradicably alive" (*Go Down, Moses* 265). After all these years, incest and the haunting issue of miscegenation have come back to Isaac. "You're a nigger," he cries in terror (266). He finds these hybrid manifestations unbearable. Isaac's frontier philosophy requires dialectics rather than the spectral neither-nor that confronts him. Isaac refuses to acknowledge the woman and denies her son the slightest McCaslin legitimacy. Go back to the North, he tells her, and marry your own kind. In his rational of blood, she is irrevocably black.

Isaac expects that Roth's money will make the woman vanish, but she does not, because her overriding mission is to teach a final lesson. In repudiating the McCaslin estate, she explains to Isaac, you have merely transferred the curse of land-ownership onto Roth. In attempting to seal the monetary transaction, Isaac touches her hand, "the smooth young flesh where the strong old blood ran after its long lost journey," but "he didn't grasp it" (267). The old man cannot catch hold of the new idea that miscegenation is not evil. Seemingly unable to learn from this visitation, his eyes "apparently pupilless," Isaac henceforth resigns himself to self-righteousness (265). Confined to his "cot," he is so old as to be infantile (267). If Isaac suffers a seizure at this moment, as did his paterfamilias Sam Fathers under similar circumstances, then he too may receive enlightenment. For both men, purity dispelled before their eyes is an insight with which they cannot live. Alternatively, one may conclude that Isaac's reaction matches his wife's on learning that he had forsaken the McCaslin plantation, or his mother's at Hubert's sexual congress with a miscegene, or Boon's at the end of "The Bear." In effect, Isaac freaks out in the face of this hybrid, the hierophant put out of joint by the reality of miscegenation, a form of life that he deems to be monstrous. As Godden and Polk argue, Isaac's teleology means "he is a bad reader of the commissary documents in genre terms because he develops them in a form that begs no questions." This philosophical base does not allow Isaac to face the "radical potential" of sexual and racial politics that his father may well have practiced (305). His hierophantic effort has been the pusillanimity of a feverish brain seeking to enforce conformity to his ideal system, the lapse of an orderly prophet who cannot see that orderliness betrays his natural oracle. An attempt to enfold nature within the metaphysical template of eternal forms fails because the elusive and ungraspable essence of the cosmos bears witness to divinity. All Isaac has left is the rhetoric of blood lore. He wishes to banish a common acceptance of miscegenation into the far future. "*Maybe in a thousand or two thousand years in America,*" he silently implores. "*But not now! Not now!*" (*Go Down, Moses* 266). The irony of Isaac's belief that "Sam Fathers set me free" is now clear (222). Their philosophy bestows an ideal priority on the ego. Isaac turns to Sam Fathers, as Godden makes plain, "for insight into how black passes into white and white passes into black." This is a crucial mistake, because in Fathers "the mixture is less social than myths, because it involves 'blood' rather than economics, and includes in the sum of those 'bloods' the Chickasaw 'red'" (233–34). Isaac, supposedly the most soulful of men, fails in spirituality because he abdicates yet retains the sovereignty of ipseity. America can "cope with one Austrian paper-hanger," Isaac had asserted by the campfire on the previous evening when the prospect of war against Germany had been discussed (*Go Down, Moses* 249–50). His language of turmoil when faced with Roth's lover indicates, nevertheless, how confusing the concept of patriotism has become in the twentieth century. Isaac's failure to learn from her evinces the difficulty in resolving this confusion.

James Beauchamp's granddaughter is a modern agent from that spectral gap between the theory and actuality of human hybridity. Her demeanor revives memories of the compassionate tenor of Franz Boas's philosophy. She is vital literary evidence that commonly accepted oppositions, European versus African or pure blood versus hematological taint, are often deceptive. Synthesis between traditionally antagonistic concepts, formulations that compose one with the other are possible. Her baby, never referred to by name, is the symbol of a future beneficent society, a form of anonymous communal solidarity to come. Have you forgotten, the young mother asks Isaac, everything "you ever knew or felt or even heard about love?" (268). Her tuition having failed, she leaves with her child. This spectral agent of miscegenation departs as she arrived— with a flap of the tent, she disappears into that ambivalent time and space in which night meets day. Embittered, Isaac can only restate his fear that miscegenation will accomplish God's revenge for the debasement of the divine through blood blending: "*Chinese and African and Aryan and Jew, all breed and spawn together until no man has time to say which one is which nor cares. . . .* No wonder the ruined woods I used to know dont cry for retribution! he thought: The people who have destroyed it will accomplish its revenge" (269).

In positing nature as the ultimate prosecutor of this revenge, Isaac remains unconcerned with the circularity of his frontier philosophy. Nature, of which man is a part, *is* a moiling mass. To repeat: Darwinian evolution accounts for this turmoil as a tangled bank of unavoidable variation, inexhaustible dissimilarity in which individuals are never identical, never equally suited to their environment, and always subject to natural selection. *Go Down, Moses* appreciates the profundity of this principle with modernity (miscegenation offers a beneficent future) meeting the Old South (pure blood secures the endurance of an inveterate dispensation) in a tension prescient of continued racial intolerance. Faulkner's *Homo sapiens*, as personified by Isaac McCaslin, certainly belong to the order of nature, sharing in the environmental dependencies common to all animals, but they are also differentiated from the other members of the zoological order in their capacity for self-alienation. Isaac's tragedy, his denial of the frontiers of philosophy, stands in sharp contrast to Faulkner's enlightenment. The ideality of human nature in Yoknapatawpha is rooted in the hematological history of a soil soaked incarnadine by the Civil War. According to the ethos attendant on this chronicle, extant vestiges of pure blood require protection and procreation. Cass recognized that no such purity exists; Isaac read as much in the Book of Ham, but he remained determined to prevent the deracination of nature. The Delta was the bulwark to his hallucination concerning the stability of life on earth.

"Nature," writes Soper, "is precisely not a necessary order, but an extraordinary contingency that might either not have existed at all or happened in some entirely other kind of way" (64). Cognitively reflecting upon our "authentic" relations with nature, she argues, alienates us from the world in a self-defeating quest for a universal truth "which is itself a piece of cultural 'imperialism.'" Darwinism is subject to this very sense of self-defeat. However, as Soper acknowledges from Derrida, discourse is "A problem of economy and strategy" (Derrida, *Writing* 282). In other words, because Western sciences have "been guilty of bringing many culture-bound assumptions to their studies," these conjectures must be countered, "explicitly and systematically posing the problem of the status of a discourse which borrows from a heritage the resources necessary for the deconstruction of that heritage itself" (Soper 64). Faulkner's *Go Down, Moses* is one such economic and rigorous problematization of the universal significance of inheritance.

CHAPTER 7

THE ENEMY WITHIN

> One recent summer I myself was having a literary talk at a cocktail party with an obliging Russian. I asked if there were many Snopeses in the Soviet Union. "There are none," he replied sharply. "Under the Soviet system it is impossible to have Snopeses."
>
> Willie Morris, "Faulkner's Mississippi" (327)

THE 1949 NOBEL PRIZE FOR LITERATURE LEFT WILLIAM FAULKNER WITH an increased appreciation of responsible heredity. Receipt of this international legacy raised issues both as to his personal profile and as to the repute of his ongoing literary bequest. Faulkner's response to these concerns, especially his compliance in fulfilling ambassadorial duties, has led to an almost singular interpretation of his subsequent novels: obedience toward governmental summons spells a conservative withdrawal from Modernist principles. This critical tenor, however, is mistaken. At one level, as Kevin Railey argues, "Faulkner's career had really only one motivation right from the beginning—the desire and drive to be a natural aristocrat both in terms of art and life" (44). Faulkner attempted to inhabit this role through an ideology resembling that first articulated in America by Thomas Jefferson. This view constructs society not according to title or wealth, but in a hierarchy "whose most powerful figures are men who are, in theory, naturally better and more superior than others." Hence, rather than altering Faulkner's evolutionary sensibilities, the Nobel Prize actualized them. He "had, in his own eyes, indeed become a natural aristocrat" (43). At another level, Faulkner understood his international recognition as a demand for continued intellectual resilience. Refusing to rest on his laurels, undertaking missions for his government without pandering to sectarianism, the post-1949 Faulkner was at his most sociopolitical.

Excepting *Requiem for a Nun*, publications from this period certainly display a formal conservatism, but this immediate presence is merely the disingenuous vanguard of Faulkner's radicalism. Despite increasing financial surety and lasting health problems, not a single jejune offering would betray his oeuvre. Faulkner would mitigate the New Imperialist zeal attendant on American superpower as a wise artist who was neither a plutocrat nor a capitalist lapdog. His wisdom would be authorial rather than authoritarian. "Faulkner's sensitivity to all aspects of this ideological position," concurs Railey, "allowed him to depict the broadest panorama of America" (46). The Snopes Trilogy, *The Town* (1957) and *The Mansion* (1959) drawing on the evolutionarily endowed *The Hamlet* (1940) in their widening humanitarianism, would become Faulkner's most extensive analysis of this landscape.

Snopeses, as Gail Mortimer suggests, "offer abundant material that reflects Faulkner's pervasive imaginative fascination with evolutionary theory and its implications" (188). That rural tribe, Susan Snell agrees, becoming "so numerous that it would take years to exhaust the vein" (201). Faulkner's evolutionary investment in this trilogy is immediately apparent from the frontispiece to *The Mansion*. "This book," he states, "is the final chapter of, and the summation of, a work conceived and begun in 1925." Tainian seeds from his European tournant had taken almost thirty-five years to mature. Receptiveness to science had helped this development, and Faulkner's interest in this domain never waned. Therefore, when molecular biologists Francis Crick (1916–2004) and James Watson (1928–) discovered the structure of deoxyribonucleic acid (DNA) in 1953, Faulkner appears to have accepted the conclusive discreditation of pangenesis.[1] To marshal his interaction with the world, Faulkner stated during his 1955 tour of Japan, an author relies on his "composition of hormones and genes" (*Lion* 104). Natural selection on a molecular basis is the ineluctable modality of evolution, Faulkner insisting to Russell Warren Howe in 1956 that "there is no such thing as an 'Anglo-Saxon' heritage and an African heritage. There is the heritage of man. Nothing is extinct in any race, only dormant" (*Lion* 264). Is heritage here synonymous with biological heredity? If so, then Faulkner's reference to dormancy probably corresponds to the emergent dominance of genetic *alleles* (any number of alternative forms of particular genes) rather than to the latency of gemmules.[2] Securing this scientific stance on a base of a divinely imbued stoicism, Faulkner reconciled the evolutionary mechanism with the numinous. This approach provided an alternative to archetypal teleology in which species develop because of internal principles alone. Faulkner understood that all species have evolved through adaptive relation to a physical environment within the divine ambit. His later works thereby address the complex relays between personal, social, and ecological relations, that repeated desire "to show man as he is in conflict with his problems, with his nature, with his own heart, with his fellows, and with his environment" (*University* 132). The result is a conception du monde in line with the worldwide development of an increasingly integrated group of epistemological disciplines. Hereon, Faulkner's implicit and prescient mimesis of genetic effects in the Snopes Trilogy and *A Fable* would produce a startling realism almost too acute to bear.

Particularly suited to interpreting this Faulknerian revelation is an evolutionary hermeneutic tailored to Richard Dawkins's notion of the "selfish gene." Dawkins develops this concept from his definition of a gene as a length of chromosome viable as a unit of natural selection. Genes with longevity, fecundity, and reproductive accuracy accrue in the pool constituting the genetic basis of a species. Their constant presence to the detriment of alleles can be interpreted as a genetic selfishness that finds transitive expression at the level of their organismic carriers. The River Thames, a few miles from where this present study originates, provides an environment in which to watch this selfish behavior in action. Many organisms thrive in and about the river, but one species in particular has stimulated scientific interest in recent years, the Chinese mitten crab.[3] This nonindigenous crustacean has proved to be surprisingly resilient in its new surroundings. In Darwinian terms, the crab fits nicely into the temperate environment offered by the Thames. Looking at the southern states of America, one discovers the rampant spread of kudzu, a vine native to Japan, but one that is suited to the Mississippi basin.[4] Alternatively, one recalls Faulkner's commentary on cotton farming in the South. This plant of the genus *Gossypium* seemed a boon, but within the transplanted Mexican seed lay the larvae of a parasitic scourge, the boll weevil. By the early twentieth century, this parasite had "taken over the southern earth" (*Essays* 14). To take an example from Faulkner's literature, consider an invader from the Old World, one brought to America on European ships, one that has colonized the Jefferson of *Requiem for a Nun*. "Migrants too," these English sparrows, birds that had "come all the way from the Atlantic coast as soon as the town became a town" (502). These intruders roost in the courthouse cupola; again members of a foreign species, but they too fit into the environment of Yoknapatawpha. Faulkner's ornithology is adept enough to dispute creationism. Steve Jones sums up the situation: "the common sparrow—the bird that hops around in English gardens—has a bigger body and shorter legs in the north than in the south of the United States. The same is true for sparrows in northern and southern Europe. Creationists see in this a divine arrangement to ensure so [*sic*] that each species fits into the economy of nature; cold places, wherever they are, meriting a subtle change in God's plan" (*Language* 224).

English sparrows have not been in the United States since the time of creation but arrived about a century ago, as Faulkner describes, so how have they come to resemble the native variety? Natural selection provides the answer. Studies of sparrows in Kansas, continues Jones, "show that large individuals with short legs survive better in icy weather. They hence have a greater chance to breed and to pass on their genes when spring comes. Those released a century ago brought from their native land genes for large or small size and stocky or graceful legs. In the north, the big squat birds did better, but in those that spread to the torrid south the opposite was true. In a few generations, American sparrows evolved just the same geographic patterns as those found on the other side of the Atlantic. Natural selection had done its work" (*Language* 225).

The dome of the hall of justice in Jefferson may be dominated by sparrows, but the building itself symbolizes the dominance of another species, *Homo sapiens*; and in the struggle for existence, as Charles Darwin makes clear, although contestation takes place between organisms that are biologically differentiated from one another, evolutionary pressure is greatest between members of a given species. Faulkner recognizes the crucial aspects of this process vis-à-vis humankind. "Man's environment," he argues, "is the only thing that changes. He must change with it. He will cope with it. The problems he faces today are the same ones he faced when he came out of the mud and first stood on two legs" (*Lion* 221). Further quotations from the mid-1950s confirm the importance of ecology to his artistic imagination. "I'm interested primarily in people," Faulkner professes, "in man in conflict with himself, with his fellow man, or with his time and place, his environment" (*University* 19), whereby "I mean his tradition, the air he breaths, his heredity, everything which surrounds him" (*Lion* 203). The South formed Faulkner's familiar topology, a territory in which he identified the persistence of an indestructible union between man and his environment. For Faulkner, Mississippi remained a country undergoing the turmoil of human development and civilization, and he linked this impulse to establish communal stability to the aesthetic sense, a proclivity that keeps humankind "trying to paint the pictures, to make the music, to write the books" (*University* 34). This Darwinian circumambience therefore includes the written word and the recipients of that text. "The writer," Faulkner insists, "has got to write in terms of his environment, and his environment consists not only in the immediate scene, but his readers are part of that environment too" (*University* 41). The Snopes Trilogy emerges from this Faulknerian paradigm with this account of man's initial relationship to the local terrain in *The Hamlet*:

> Frenchman's Bend was a section of rich river-bottom country lying twenty miles southeast of Jefferson. Hillcradled and remote, definite yet without boundaries, straddling into two counties and owning allegiance to neither, it had been the original grant and site of a tremendous pre–Civil War plantation, the ruins of which—the gutted shell of an enormous house with its fallen stables and slave quarters and overgrown gardens and brick terraces and promenades—were still known as the Old Frenchman place, although the original boundaries now existed only on old faded records in the Chancery Clerk's office in the county court house in Jefferson, and even some of the once-fertile fields had long since reverted to the cane-and-cypress jungle from which their first master had hewed them. (731)

This description makes clear the disregard of nature for human ordinance while the definite topology of Frenchman's Bend—hill-cradled as it is—ensures ecological isolation. Darwin describes the evolutionary consequences for such areas in *The Origin of Species*. Of Farnham in Surrey he writes:

> Here there are extensive heaths, with a few clumps of old Scotch firs on the distant hill-tops: within the last ten years large spaces have been enclosed, and self-sown firs are now springing up in multitudes, so close together that all cannot live. When I ascertained that these young trees had not been sown or planted, I was so much surprised at their numbers that I went to several points of view, whence I could examine hundreds of acres of the unenclosed heath, and literally I could not see a single Scotch fir, except the old planted clumps. But on looking closely between the stems of the heath, I found a multitude of seedlings and little trees which had been perpetually browsed down by the cattle. In one square yard . . . I counted thirty-two little trees; and one of them, with twenty-six rings of

growth, had, during many years tried to raise its head above the stems of the heath, and had failed. (56)

No wonder then, concludes Darwin, that "as soon as the land was enclosed, it became thickly clothed with vigorously growing young firs. Yet the heath was so extremely barren and so extensive that no one would ever have imagined that cattle would have so closely and effectually searched it for food" (56).

Protected from the outside by its terrain, Frenchman's Bend is a form of Darwinian enclosure, one that has attained an ESS. The local populace is settled. Even so, with the ever-presence of evolution, such a balance remains liable to invasion from without. At a human level, the burgeoning global population of the twentieth century makes this vulnerability to outsiders especially pronounced and, as migratory pressure builds, foreignness becomes a source of anxiety to indigenous populations. In *The Hamlet*, the spread of tensions related to immigration is evident in the irony of obfuscation that pervades the history of the region. The first master of the wilderness, the eponymous Frenchman of the Bend, is now almost forgotten. Although a foreign national had established the hamlet, this descent provides inveterates with little comfort in the face of outlandishness.

Who Constitutes This Danger?

A Darwinian hermeneutic can apply three broad divisions to an analysis of immigration and ESSs: the *foreigner*, the *outlander*, and the *extrinsic stranger*. Racial terms divide the category of foreigner into the African, the European, the Semite, and the Asian. A stable state of one subcategory tolerates the three others as long as (un)written laws of racial segregation are observed. The outlander category describes those pertaining to a given race, but who hail from beyond state boundaries, while the term extrinsic stranger denotes individuals of a particular race and state who originate from outside the parochial ambit.

In Jeffersonian terms, the Chinese laundryman and the two Jews singled out by Charles Mallison (Gavin Stevens's nephew) in *The Town* exemplify the *benign foreigner*. Physiological difference enables locals to identify these men, a foreign presence that poses no threat to communal stability. Segregated and alone, these outsiders are "not just kinless but even kindless" (269).[5] In the southern states of America, the European subcategory consists of two main types: the Anglo-Saxon and the Mediterranean. Both of these classes are acceptable in Yoknapatawpha because they constitute the Old World antecedents of the majority of residents.

In terms of Faulkner studies, the second category, the outlander, describes those European Americans who hail from beyond Mississippi. Homer Barron in "A Rose for Emily" (1930) is one such immigrant; "a Northerner, a day laborer," his origin and standing arouse local concerns about his intentions toward Miss Grierson (*Collected Stories* 124).[6] The dramatic irony of this anxiety only appears after her demise—Barron was the one in danger. The carpetbaggers shot by John Sartoris for inciting African Americans to vote, as recalled twice in *Flags in the Dust*, also fit this category (6, 263). Faulkner's mystery stories, especially the collection in *Knight's Gambit* (1949), provide other examples. "Smoke," originally published in 1932, concerns the death of Anselm Holland. With a surname that intimates European antecedence, Holland had come

> to Jefferson many years ago. Where from, no one knew. But he was young then and a man of parts, or of presence at least, because within three years he had married the only daughter of a man who owned two thousand acres of some of the best land in the county, and he went to live in his father-in-law's house, where two years later his wife bore him twin sons and where a few years later still the father-in-law died and left Holland in full possession of the property, which was now in his wife's name. But even before that event, we in Jefferson had already listened to him talking a trifle more than loudly of "my land, my crops"; and those of us whose fathers and grandfathers had been bred here looked upon him a little coldly and a little askance for a ruthless man. (3)

Holland remained an outsider, a figure of ruthlessness, so that when his wife "died while the twin sons were still children, we believed that he was responsible, that her life had been worn out by the crass violence of an underbred outlander" (3). In "Tomorrow," which first appeared in 1940, the gambler, hooch distiller, and thief, Buck Thorpe "had appeared overnight from nowhere" (86) while the backwoods Yoknapatawphians of "An Error in Chemistry" (1946) still regard the onetime carnival worker Joel Flint as "the foreigner, the outlander, the Yankee" (109). Each of this outlandish collection suffers an unenviable end: Holland and Thorpe are murdered; Flint is executed for the homicide of his wife and father-in-law.

The third category, the extrinsic stranger, comprises those Americans of European ancestry who live within Mississippi but outside the district in question. Of these characters, most of those who live close to the inner boundary have personal histories and genealogies known throughout the interior and are often kin-related to indigenes. Yet, even local extrinsic strangers can cause consternation as the courtship of Eula Varner affirms.

The teenage Eula is not naïve, fast, or loose. Daughter of the local patrician Will Varner, Eula practices a courtship strategy of domestic bliss in accordance with her social status. Eula's first suitor, a luckless schoolteacher named Labove, experiences this reluctance. Despite his physical attainments at college football, Labove is too much the intellectual. Fending off his most audacious advances, Eula cries, "Stop pawing me . . . You old headless horseman Ichabod Crane" (*Hamlet* 843). Eula, discrediting Labove with this insinuation of impotency, asserts her need for a male (phallic) head rather than a man with brains. Over the next few years, Eula involuntarily attracts numerous admirers, but none court her successfully. Her patient wait for a sexual partner who matches her procreative standard continues. Eula is determined to bear a child fitted to the modern world, a need that shuns inbreeding, necessity that rejects all parochial suitors. Local men are unsuitable but, as Labove's failure demonstrates, this does not mean that any outlander will do. Eula exudes a singular aura; she is one of "the unchaste and perhaps even anonymously pregnant immortals eating bread of Paradise on a sunwise slope of Olympus" (844). Her lover must have remarkable qualities. Faulkner, possibly aware of his inability to render such a courtship at this stage in his career, and in a parallel to his procrastination over his dénouement to the Temple Drake affair, would not reengage with Eula's narrative until *The Town*.

The publication of Faulkner's developing characterization in this novel further substantiates the remarkable extent to which the mature author appreciated the complexity of sexual politics. Eula now has a daughter (named Linda) by a previous liaison and is the wife of her father's erstwhile storekeeper Flem Snopes. As a husband, Flem has provided Eula and her child with material comfort, but his all-consuming desire is money. As the ultimate capitalist, Flem has no carnal urges, a lack of appetite to which the imputation of impotency testifies. In Dawkinsian terms, Flem "does not take risks in order to reproduce" since a celibate marriage actualizes his capitalist potential (*Selfish* 157). His wife's sexuality, however, remains unfulfilled. Eula turns elsewhere to service this need and extramarital courtship follows involving the philandering banker Maj. Manfred de Spain and the dogged county attorney Gavin Stevens. Each of these suitors corresponds to one of the alternative mating strategies in an ESS containing a bipartite divide.[7] In need of sex rather than procreativity, in a sign of desperation rather than looseness, Eula bestows her sexual favors on the philanderer of the two. Manfred has won the initial skirmishes, becomes Eula's lover, and mocks his rival in the process. Owner of the only sports car in Yoknapatawpha, the major persists in opening the throttle every time he passes the lawyer's house. This car equates to Eula, Manfred blatantly opening her up in front of Stevens. Charles Mallison attempts to deflate the major's arrogance by setting the head of a rake, forks upward, in the dirt surface of the road— Faulkner reworking Gowan Stevens's intrasexual assessment incident with his Oxford rivals in *Sanctuary*. Eventually successful in puncturing one of the tires, Manfred turns Charles's minor victory to his advantage. Before the Jefferson annual dance, he sends a mock invitation to Stevens accompanied by a bouquet of flowers tied with a condom. Symbolically, in relation to boasting and bursting, this is the only type of rubber that interests the major.

The Jefferson Ball provides Eula's contenders with an opportunity to square up to one another. Manfred's mastery prevails on the dance floor. Inferior with respect to his opponent, this parallel assessment should prompt Stevens to back down. He does not, but comes to blows with the major. Stevens loses yet again. Crestfallen, the lawyer tends his blooded face in the sanctuary of his law office. Appreciative of Gavin's faithful strategy, Eula soon appears, offering herself sexually. Stevens's idealism, his lust being a mental not a physical emanation, forestalls any passionate intent. Eula's advance rejected, her choice of "major" lover has proven to be correct.

The matter of secondary selection seems settled, but Faulkner's interrogation of Darwinian theory as realized in practice does not end here. For, in *The Mansion*, he painstakingly recapitulates Eula's sexual history, detailing the events leading up to her loss of virginity. After the failure of local suitors, Eula finally meets her match in Hoake McCarron. He is also a Mississippian, he is even from Yoknapatawpha, but according to the parochialism of Frenchman's Bend, he is "some foreigner from four or five or six miles away." Eula, as if according to Darwinian principles, identifies Hoake as a suitable mate, the only suitor "wild and strong enough to deserve and match her" (437). In comparison, as sewing-machine agent and local gossip V. K. Ratliff surmises, "it would a taken that whole generation of young concentrated [local] men to seeded them, as the feller says, splendid—no: he would a said magnificent—loins" (434). McCarron's intentions, however, violate "them outside boundary limits" of the Bend's "range and reservation," which were the locals, the Bookwrights, the Tulls, and the Quicks, home ground (437). These insiders, as if following sociobiological theory, had already made "two years' investment" in Eula before that "single unique big buck jumped that tame garden fence" and finally got through "among the sheep" (439). To stop an outsider sullying one of their women, driven on as they are by hereditary expediency, the young locals attack the intruder. McCarron, fighting as "a wild stag surrounded by a gang of goats," beats off their ambush (440). Faulkner clearly presents this animalistic violence in terms of sexual selection: "the strongest, and with some species the best armed of the males, drive[s] away the weaker" (Darwin, *Descent* 214). Being a man is dangerous—accidents, infectious diseases, and intrasexual conflicts are more regular for them than for women. Hoake McCarron actively partakes in this perilous economy. Yet, despite his broken arm, he manages to bed Eula.

Durable and potent, the extrinsic stranger is certainly disconcerting, but this category provides an even more worrying variant: the *extrinsic alien*, the nonparochial local whose personal history and genealogy remain apocryphal. Paradoxical, the extrinsic alien can be that most dangerous of intruders, the mutinous mutation, the enemy within. Such an alien appears to be at one with his community yet remains unallied to communal interests. These mutineers simply benefit from their new surroundings, an ingenuous environment that presents fewer restrictions on their expansion than apply to indigenes. "Many cases are on record," states *The Origin of Species*, "showing how complex and unexpected are the checks and relations between organic beings, which have to struggle together in the same country" (55). When another species breaches an enclosure, these internal constraints may prove to be ineffective. This is especially true of efficacious extrinsic aliens whose likeness to indigenes initially masks any difference. The presence of extrinsic aliens only materializes when their extensive infiltration appears as a contraindication to the robustness of that community with residents beginning to recognize their alien quality and the threat they pose.

As previously documented, the Chinese mitten crab manifests this danger. First detected in the Thames in 1935, only recently have ecologists identified the damage it causes. Upstream progress of this sand extracting species ensures the destruction of many river islets.[8] Conservationists can do little to halt its advance. Alternatively, take kudzu as an illustration, a plant that has been present in Mississippi since 1937, but one that goes unmentioned in Faulkner's work; it is not, as one might expect, the bitterweed recalled by Malcolm Franklin. The invasion by kudzu remained unremarkable until incursion became infestation. Today, this vine has overrun more than seven million acres of the South. These species provide noted examples of the sustained infiltration of an enclosed ecosystem. Moreover, tangible references such as these exemplify the prescience of Faulkner's creation of the Snopes.

Practically all the residents in the region prosecute a single approach to human interaction, one that can be termed an *exclusivity of doves*, ethical behavior succinctly recalled in *Requiem for a Nun*. These are pioneering people for whom a responsible sense of liberty and freedom "were almost a physical condition like fire or flood" (477). In terms of Dawkinsian biology, *dovelike* conduct is an unconscious behavior pattern fostered by genes in which a community consists of altruistic individuals who rarely, if ever, practice deception. Unfortunately, this form of stability is vulnerable to breaches of trust—and the abusive self-interest inherent in the Snopeses, their *hawkishness*, is an ideal fit to such an environment. So why, one may ask, are this family allowed to remain in Frenchman's Bend? Are the indigenes incorrigibly naïve?

Faulkner's brilliance in presenting this invasion rests on the Snopeses' character as extrinsic stranger*s* of the alien variety. The Snopes family is intrinsic to Mississippi, yet extrinsic to the hamlet. At first, they appear to be another set of dovelike individuals who will practice altruism; any intimations of their hawkish nature go unnoticed by an essentially ingenuous community. Thus, Ratliff may have foreseen the trouble intimated by the arrival of the Snopes family, but "nobody else in Jefferson seemed to recognise the danger" (*Town* 94). This naïveté even recommends the Snopeses as another set of peasants of whom the primary landowners and most overt hawks in the district, the Varners, can take advantage. Will's son Jody complacently rents dirt farms for this very purpose. The distinction between land-rentier and capitalist may tenuously remain, but in accepting Ab Snopes as a tenant, Jody unwittingly brings about his own displacement from the upper echelons of society and the unequivocal closure of that economic distinction. Indeed, most of the residents in the Bend are ignorant of Ab's reputation until Ratliff reminisces about the barn-burning Ab of his childhood. Unfortunately, this disclosure comes too late for the Varners—they have already allowed Ab onto their land. In consequence, Jody employs Ab's son in the family store, hoping to forestall the destruction of Varner property. This dubious insurance policy merely enables a far more efficient enemy to capitalize on the environment offered by Frenchman's Bend, an individual extremely fitted to that ecology: Flem Snopes.

Faulkner makes plain that Flem and his kin are germane to the socioeconomic times because of their biological inheritance. This essential foundation enables the emergent clan to pervade and undermine the evolutionary stability of the Bend. Genes are the Faulknerian basis for the Snopes family. Joseph R. Urgo reasons along the same lines when he argues that all Snopeses are males and biology accounts for their *Snopesishness* (172). This conclusion, however, is not rigorously correct in terms of genetics. The Snopes could be figured in terms of dominant genes where the determining sex is male, that is, Snopesishness is carried on the Y-chromosome so that, although females can bear the Snopes name, they do not carry the Snopes genes. Alternatively, as Jones makes plain, "Many inherited diseases are carried on the X chromosome. In most girls, an abnormal X is masked by a normal copy. Boys do not have this option, as they have but a single X. For this reason, sex-linked abnormalities, as they are known, are much more common in boys than girls" (*Language* 15).

Either option applies to the mutation that causes Snopesishness. Women may marry into the clan, they may bear female children, but females are rarely genuine Snopeses. A supreme adaptation to the twentieth-century environment of socioeconomics exhibits the bodily manifestation, or phenotypic, characteristics of carrying Snopes genes. Individual Snopeses fit into ecological niches from which they practice self-interest to an unprecedented extent. Male Snopeses are Faulkner's figuration of an incipient species descending from *Homo sapiens*. These men, rapacious by nature, are a parasitic affliction on their chosen community. Expanding the earlier Faulknerian quote emphasizes this conclusion. "With the boll-weevil already in it since, like the Snopes, he too has taken over the southern earth" (*Essays* 14); cotton farming is analogous to communal benignancy with the South suffering a parasitic blight.

The Hamlet establishes that Snopeses are a mutant form of extrinsic alien with whom *Homo sapiens* will have to struggle in order to survive. Observers often describe these mutants, individuals who employ deception, lies, and manipulation, as if they were members of another species.

Flem has "the quality of a spider of that bulbous blond omnivorous though non-poisonous species" (784), Lump is a "chipmunk" (878), while Mink is "a different kind of Snopes like a cotton-mouth is a different kind of snake" (815). To Ratliff, this difference has a hybrid essence. He ponders, trying to remember Mink's first name, "*Fox? cat? oh yes, mink*" (814). Similar thoughts emanate from the Snopeses themselves. Mink imagines himself as "a child of another race and species" (953) and Montgomery Ward later sums up the Snopes genealogy as "a family, a clan, a race, maybe even a species, of pure sons of bitches" (*Mansion* 409).[9]

Flem Snopes epitomizes the Snopes mutation. With his singular appetite for capital, he is the selfish gene as the basis for capitalism. Rarely seen eating or drinking, he nonetheless constantly chews. Tasting the local air, Flem is concerned with figuring out the predominant disposition of Frenchman's Bend. He literally manducates, chewing over his surroundings, concocting strategies for drawing the "suption" out of money and extracting all that is valuable from his environment (*Hamlet* 751).

As these calculations become more finely tuned, Flem starts to figure out more local businessmen. As previously noted, the only presence in the hamlet to have foreseen this pervasion is Ratliff. In his eyes, Flem is a Snopes vengeance weapon unleashed by Ab at the time to which it is most adapted. Faulkner's development of the Snopes history in *The Town* makes such a conclusion explicit. Col. Sartoris hanged Old Ab for illegal horse trading during the Civil War, but the Snopeses, even after numerous generations, retain a grudge. In effect, they have immolated Old Ab. Their revenge, believes Gavin Stevens, was to put a "monkey on the back of Ab's commander's descendant as soon as the lineage produced a back profitable to the monkey" (37). The Sartorises may reestablish their communal status during Reconstruction, a primacy symbolic of the ESS to which Jefferson has returned, but this postbellum equilibrium is precarious. The Snopeses exploit this vulnerability in what *The Hamlet* promises to be a Marxist revolution that will level the local hierarchy.

The Sartoris and Snopes genealogies testify to this assurance with Christian names a telling difference. Sartoris forenames are derived from their esteemed antecedents, while the Snopeses garner theirs from contemporary life, with mail-order catalogs, patent medicines, politicians, and even the economic catastrophe of 1893 proving suitable. The Snopes genealogy may lack depth, but the unwavering attitude of its members to the struggle for existence ensures the expansion of their dynasty. In comparison, as *Flags in the Dust* evinces, the wanton risk-taking predisposition of the Sartorises ensures their genealogical demise. A consequence of this genetic difference appears to be the extinction of the old order by the modernity of the new.

The Snopeses' most powerful response to southern degeneration, Flem's insurgency, surfaces at Varner's store. Before this appointment, Flem had labored alongside his itinerant father on a succession of rented farms. Now, ensconced as retail clerk, Flem promptly introduces his relatives, I. O. and Eck, into the local economy. These cousins take over the smithy, the previous incumbent leaving Frenchman's Bend never to return. The next development comes at harvest time, when the locals are surprised to find Flem, not Jody Varner, supervising the weighing of crops. By this time, Flem has moved into the Varner house, going to work on Jody's mare. Soon touring the Varner estate in a horse-drawn buggy, Flem subsequently appears at the Old Frenchman place sitting in the barrel seat so readily associated with Will Varner. He seems to be usurping the position of the landowner, and Flem's influence spreads even further when he becomes a moneylender. Earning interest from European and African Americans alike, Flem exploits both ends of the market simultaneously and then consolidates his social standing by marrying into the modern landowning class. Although his marriage to Eula, pregnant and abandoned by McCarron, appears to be an error, one which solves the Varners' social dilemma and one that is settled with the deeds to a valueless property, Flem's strategy actually guarantees his prosperous presence in Yoknapatawpha. With the Old Frenchman place as his wedding gift, Will believes he has swindled his son-in-law. Flem will prove otherwise.

"The Spotted Horses," as incorporated into *The Hamlet*, signals the newlyweds' return from honeymoon. Faulkner's evolutionary awareness, emergent in that seminal year of 1925, had found cruel grist to the mill with the death of his first daughter, Alabama, within two weeks of her birth in January 1931. In an interview with Louis Daniel Brodsky from the 1980s, Estelle Faulkner's eldest grandchild, Victoria Fielden Johnson (née Franklin) (1919–), insisted, "there was a strain of weakness in Grandmama genetically" (155). Alabama Faulkner, whose grave was left unnamed because her father held that "she had not been in this world long enough to have acquired an identity," was a second tournant for Faulknerian thought. This rethink concerned heredity. Her death was a terrible shock. After her burial, Faulkner "began drinking and went from here to Chapel Hill to New York to Jacksonville and back to New York. Estelle finally had to go get him" (Wolff and Watkins 74). "The Spotted Horses" was the first work he completed after this trauma. With a title suggestive of tainted heredity, this cautionary tale of unfit equine reproduction, attests to Faulkner's evolutionary self-awareness.[10] These wild mustangs, ostensibly the property of a Texan rancher, symbolize the spot or taint from abroad that is now to be found within the enclosure of Frenchman's Bend. These "jackrabbit[s]" (*Hamlet* 1000) are of another species and constitute a "contagion" (986). Their "mismatched eyes" imply a doubtful lineage (983). Sold to gullible locals, these crossbreeds, another example of extrinsic aliens, break out of their holding pen to spread mayhem throughout the county and beyond. Faulkner confirms the correlation adumbrated between mustangs and Snopeses by positing the Texan horse trader as Flem's agent.

Ratliff is one inveterate wise enough not to get cheated in this incident, but even he, one of the most immune of locals, gets infected by Flem when he falls for the Salted Gold Mine scam. Will Varner had thought the Old Frenchman place worthless, but Flem now sells the property to Ratliff, Bookwright, and Armstid. He has tricked them into believing that the grounds to this property are salted with Civil War gold. In this, the closing episode of the novel, with the three men digging up nothing but dirt, Flem finally extracts his revenge on Ratliff for offloading Mink's promissory notes onto him. And so, over the course of *The Hamlet*, Flem Snopes defeats all comers as he rises from blue-collar farm worker to white-collar usurer—the spread of Flem's ambit beyond Frenchman's Bend being compounded by the continued arrival of new Snopeses to Yoknapatawpha.

These developments are narrated in the remainder of the trilogy as Flem evolves into a capitalist per se, a businessman characterized by two words, the Snopes "No" or nope, and the "Foreclose" of the moneylender (*Mansion* 524). Nor can Charles Mallison imagine Flem's "hand writing anything except adding a percent. symbol or an expiration date" (*Mansion* 530). Flem's human interactions are an exemplar of that nexus of naked self-interest identified by Karl Marx in *The Communist Manifesto* (1848) as an inevitable product of capitalism. Coterminously, in terms of an evolutionary hermeneutic, Flem approaches the status of an individual taken over by a cultural construct to such an extent that his own survival becomes inconsequential.[11] Flem's blind faith concerns money, money as an end in itself, money as autotelism, and *The Town* corroborates the opinion of the few discerning peasants in Frenchman's Bend that Flem would cheat his own kin as readily as he would swindle anyone else. This interfamilial willingness becomes apparent whenever a relation threatens, however unintentionally, Flem's rise in Yoknapatawphian society. As the epitome of the selfish gene, Flem both eradicates his unrelated kin and expels unsuitable relations from his suzerainty: the death of that non-Snopes Snopes, Eckrum, is realized; Mink is left to rot in the state penitentiary; Montgomery Ward is ousted from his dubious photographic shop when a substantial quantity of moonshine is found on the premises.

That Flem spent thirty dollars on this latter scheme bemuses Montgomery Ward. He concludes that his cousin's objective was "a little harder than Flem had expected or figured" (*The Mansion* 386). Montgomery Ward's attempt to understand his relative's difficulty even leads to "the horrid aspersion that Flem had let Lawyer Stevens and [the sheriff] Hub Hampton outfigger him," or that Flem "was subject to bad luck too, jest like a human being" (384). Of course, Flem has not been out-thought or become the subject of anthropoidal misfortune. For a moment, however, Montgomery Ward believes that Flem is not "immune neither to the strong and simple call of blood kinship" (386), pleading with his cousin, "aint blood thicker than just water" (393). Flem does not answer this question. Montgomery Ward may figure in terms of pangenesis, but Flem never does: his autotelic capitalism evinces the phenotypic effects of what is certainly hard, rather than soft, inheritance. When Montgomery Ward attempts to tilt the odds in his favor a second time by threatening to reopen his pornographic business on his release from jail, Flem responds, "Yep, that's what I figgered" (393). Anticipating this move, Flem has already collected enough evidence to have Montgomery Ward imprisoned for a much longer period if necessary. While protecting his ascendancy in banishing the pornographer from Jefferson, Flem also intends to lengthen Mink's custodial sentence. If Montgomery Ward plays his part well, Flem will secure his early release. The mechanics of this parole have already been "figgered" along with an open railroad ticket. Flem has both relatives completely figured out and even employs a third, Senator Clarence Snopes, to ensure that Montgomery Ward sticks to the deal.[12] He could have trusted me, insists Montgomery Ward, but being hawkish by nature, Flem did not dare discover at his age "that all you need to handle nine people out of ten is just to trust them" (395). Faulkner dispels aspersions of Flem being outfigured, the subject of misfortune, being soft with respect to his own relatives, or trusting in others, by constructing this episode in the terminology of economics. Flem, of all the Snopeses, is *the* figure of figuration, the master of capitalism, a man with a "pure and simple nose for money" (56). Capitalism is the "pure and simple principle" by which he lives (381). No wonder Montgomery Ward, finally recognizing this obsession, chooses to spend his days on bail in prison. Only behind bars does he feel "safe from the free world, safe and secure for a little while yet from the free Snopes world" (406).

Flem is selfish, undoubtedly, but he also understands the notion of altruism, a concept he has been abusing ever since his entry into Frenchman's Bend. His cuckoldry is a prime example. Major de Spain seems to have triumphed decisively with Flem's wife, but such an assumption is dangerous in Snopes territory. Sitting on the periphery of the dance floor at the Jefferson Ball, not interfering between Eula, Manfred, and Gavin, Flem is an impotent bystander where her sex life is concerned. Nevertheless, aware of the limits to a strict interpretation of secondary selection, Faulkner again demonstrates his command of sexual politics when he reveals the cuckolded passivity of the Eula-Manfred affair to be an essential part of Flem's devastating master plan. Capitalizing on the indignity around town to the revelation of his wife's infidelity, Flem prompts Eula's suicide, ensures his inheritance of her Varner assets, and secures himself the Sartoris Bank presidency following the major's resultant exile. Cynically foresighted concerning altruism, Flem is also mightily aware of that small percentage of locals who are not doves: the Varners constituting one instance and the miscegenate offspring of Byron Snopes being another. Ratliff has previously expressed the common belief that hybrids combine the worst traits from both lineal sides. Will Varner's grandchildren are "already darkening back but carrying intact still the worst of the new white Varner traits grafted onto the worst of their fatherless or two-fathered grandmothers' combined original ones" (*Town* 242). Miscegenation, which by the early 1950s elicits almost no interest from Faulkner, suddenly protests this indifference. What explains the return of this revenant?

The answer lies in Faulkner's encounter with the pioneering Brazilian sociology of Gilberto Freyre (1900–1987). In 1954, under the auspices of the State Department, Faulkner attended an International Writers' Conference to mark the "quadricentennial of the city of São Paolo" (Blotner, *Biography* 2: 1503). Standard biographical sources for Faulkner make no mention of Freyre, but the sociologist could have been present at this gathering. Freyre had received his formal university education in America, gaining a BA from Baylor University and an MA from Columbia University, where (like Earnest Albert Hooton) he had studied under Franz Boas. In 1926, Freyre had organized the first regionalist congress in Recife, he had been prominent at the first Congress of Afro-Brazilian Studies in 1934, and fifteen years later he had represented Brazil at the United Nations General Assembly. His presence at São Paolo in 1954 is quite possible. Faulkner's mission at this event was to restore American prestige and "strike a blow of some sort for hemispheric solidarity" (Blotner, *Biography* 2: 1503). Although incapacitated for two days during his visit, Faulkner's reaction to the project was "positive" ("To Harold E. Howland" 369). A gift of Freyre's *The Masters and the Slaves: A Study in the Development of Brazilian Civilization* (1933) may have contributed to this feeling.[13]

A number of parallels posited by this volume must have struck a chord with Faulkner. Environmental conditions, writes Freyre, form one close alliance between North Brazil and Mississippi, Virginia, and the Carolinas. "The so-called 'deep South,'" he continues, is "a region where a patriarchal economy created almost the same type of aristocrat and of Big House, almost the same type of slave and of slave quarters, as in the North of Brazil . . . a region that has suffered and preserved the scars (when they are not open and still bleeding wounds) of the same devastating regime of agrarian exploitation: fire and ax, the felling of the forests and the burning over of the land, the 'parasitic husbandry of nature,' as Monteiro Baena puts it" (xxv–xxvi).[14] This terminology is telling. For, in discussing his own home, the Chandler House (the model for the Compson Place), and that belonging to his uncle, Rowan Oak, Jimmy Faulkner describes each as "the big house" (Wolff and Watkins 47). Another resonance would have been Freyre's chronicle of incest and miscegenation. On the one hand, states Freyre, "if consanguineous marriages were common in Brazil, this was due not merely to economic motives, readily understandable under a system of individual enterprise, but to social motives as well, based upon aristocratic exclusiveness" (267).

If incest mixes blood of a quality strain, then the resulting children will be healthy. On the other hand, he continues, "those who lament our lack of racial purity and the fact that Brazil is not a temperate climate at once see in this wretchedness and inertia the result of intercourse, forever damned, between white men and black women, between Portuguese males and Indian women" (48).

Miscegenation, necessarily the mixture of bloods of different strain, produces blighted progeny. Having recorded this standard reasoning, Freyre offers his preferred explanation for the degeneracy of these *Caboclos*: their subjugation to insalubrious socioeconomic conditions. The discursive status of Caboclos among the indigenous population emphasizes Freyre's point. This nomenclature not only designates a copper-colored individual, but also bestows praise. Applied to a Brazilian Indian or to a mestizo (the child of external miscegenation between an Indian and a European), the term can mean hillbilly, but Caboclos is usually a tribute to physical and moral endurance against tremendous odds. Miscegenation, in Freyre's estimation, is a positive force. "Hybrid from the beginning, Brazilian society is, of all those in the Americas, the one most harmoniously constituted so far as racial relations are concerned" (201). Freyre draws on European history to explain the congruity between the indigenous population of Brazil and the conquering Lusitanians. The prehistoric anthropology of "the Portuguese people has been a mixed one" (201–2) so that social relations between the conquering and indigenous races has never reached "that point of sharp antipathy or hatred the grating sound of which reached our ears from all the countries that have been colonized by Anglo-Saxon Protestants. The friction here was smoothed by the lubricating oil of a deep-going miscegenation, whether in the form of a free union damned by the clergy or that of regular Christian marriage with the blessing of the padres and at the instigation of Church and State" (182).

Freyre does not openly consider sexual congress between women of European lineage and African men. One must assume this is his "forever damned" form of miscegenation (48). Freyre, then, is progressive until he deals with African Americans. Cited often as an unequivocal advocacy of miscegenation, *The Masters and the Slaves* is rather more circumspect. Freyre's most important conclusion being that while interracial relations work as an agency for smoothing the interaction between different peoples, the miscegene nevertheless continues to suffer in this dynamic.

The relays between Freyre and Faulkner's work demonstrate that the northern region of Brazil and the southern latitudes of the southern states of America were more closely linked in terms of ecological conditions and sociopolitical thinking than people in their anterior homelands realized. Faulkner retained positive feelings about Brazil, but witnessing firsthand the social fluidity of South American life, a state of affairs reiterated by Freyre, may have been enough to trigger his comment to the State Department that he understood "something of the problems the United States has to cope with in Latin America" ("To Harold E. Howland" 369). The full implications of a nation without races remained a troubling concept for Faulkner. Despite his enhanced biological knowledge—his belief in hormones and genes—the notion of the pangenetic miscegene still required exorcism. Southern thought concerning miscegenation, he wrote in the Memphis *Commercial Appeal* within months of his Brazilian mission, continues to "becloud the issue with the purity of white blood" (*Essays* 150). The following summer, he emended this text for publication as "On Fear: Deep South in Labor: Mississippi" (1956). To justify the predominant stance on interracial sex, Faulkner notes, "We must becloud the issue with the bugaboo of miscegenation; what a commentary that the one remaining place on earth where the white man can flee and have his uncorrupted blood protected and defended by law, is in Africa—Africa: source and origin of the threat whose present presence in America will have driven the white man to flee it" (*Essays* 105).

Bugaboo, the *Oxford English Dictionary* of 1933 explains, is "possibly a Celtic compound: Cornwall bucca-bow—a fancied object of terror; a bogy; a bugbear." Haunting and human hybridity, as Faulkner's explicitness attests, still defined southern fears about external miscegenation. The specter of miscegenate offspring remained impossible for a socially vigilant Mississippian author to ignore. *The Town* evinces this conclusion.

Eula's death may offer the chance of formal closure, but Faulkner eschews this opportunity, one associated with the traditional construction of nineteenth-century novels, in favor of "The Waifs."[15] These abandoned children, miscegenate offspring of Byron Snopes and a "Jicarilla Apache squaw in Old Mexico," seem to creep in from behind the back cover of *The Town* (317). With a father who is an extrinsic stranger and a mother who is a benign foreigner, the waifs signify an uneasy mixture to Yoknapatawphians. They are *malevolent aliens*, whose presence immediately undermines Flem's primacy. His maneuvering into and up the hierarchy of the Baptist Church, his search for respectability, is at stake. Religion, as far as Flem is concerned, is a sincere worship of the dollar. Money is his source of social strength, an originary power that he works hard to camouflage with a veil of Christian cant, but his chances of communal respectability are dealt a serious blow when one of

Byron's children—and the identity of the attacker is never known, anyone of the four could have been responsible—literally cuts open Dewit Binford's face. A trail of destruction follows the waifs until the reason for their behavior becomes explicit with their most victimized victim: "a Pekinese with a gold name-plate," an animal that had cost "five hundred dollars," and that sneered through the window of its owner's Cadillac "not just at other dogs but at people too" (318). The pedigree, sneering, capitalist pet of wealthy outlanders, the Pekinese is abducted by the children. A search discovers mere skin and bones. The miscegenes have figured out purity per se by disfiguring the latest object of southern veneration. The all-encompassing environment associated with capitalist "dogs" has produced the waifs as a by-product. Truly fear inducing, these mestizos are definitely to be expulsed not only from Frenchman's Bend, Jefferson, Yoknapatawpha, and Mississippi, but also from America. *The Town* concludes with the "Snopes Indians or Indian Snopeses" being sent back to Byron in Mexico under Flem's orders (319). It is here, at the last gasp, that Faulkner illustrates the positive aspect of Freyre's insight. Ratliff's tenderness to the waifs on the railway station before their departure exposes their biological nature as ordinary children.

Flem is beyond pangenetic thought too, but his rationale counters familial parasitism. Free of Manfred de Spain, his wife, and troublesome relatives, he can again enjoy his reign as bank president. He has reached the capitalist peak to which he aspired when young—Faulkner creating a figure worthy of the provenance deriving from Frank Cowperwood in the Trilogy of Desire (1912, 1914, 1947) by Theodore Dreiser (1871–1945) and from the excoriating biographical sketch of John Pierpont Morgan (1837–1913) by John Dos Passos (1896–1970) in *U.S.A.* (1938). However, this self-interest, Flem's capitalist agenda in which he gives supreme weight to his own desire whatever the cost to others, reveals the initial sense of nascent Marxism in the Snopes Trilogy to be fallacious. Just as Marxism foundered when its proponents took up czarist traditions on moving into the Kremlin, Flem betrays his nonwarrantor inheritance when he moves into the habits of, and a habitation reserved for, the bourgeoisie. This disdain for alterity equally applies to Flem's future selves so that ultimately his self-actualization, his personification of self-interest theory, necessitates his own destruction. Having out-figured all others, he must figure out Flem Snopes. Ratliff's metaphor in the penultimate chapter of *The Town* manifests this inference. The sewing-machine agent sums up the antagonism between lawyer Stevens and bank president Snopes in this way:

> It was liken a contest, like Lawyer had stuck a stick of dynamite in his hind pocket and lit a long fuse to it and was interested now would or wouldn't somebody step in in time and tromple the fire out. Or a race, like would he finally get Linda out of Jefferson and at least get his-self shut forever of the whole tribe of Snopes first, or would he jest blow up his-self beforehand first and take ever body and ever thing in the neighborhood along with him.
> No, not a contest. Not a contest with Flem Snopes anyway because it takes two to make a contest and Flem Snopes wasn't the other one. He was a umpire, if he was anything in it. No, he wasn't even a umpire. It was like he was running a little mild game against his-self, for his own amusement, like solitaire. He had ever thing now that he had come to Jefferson to get. (305)

Ratliff believes that Flem's "game of solitaire was against Jefferson" (306).[16] More accurately adduced, Jefferson is the game or agency by which Flem can unconcernedly test himself.

If capitalism in the form of Flem Snopes's indifference is immoral, then Linda Snopes Kohl's figuration is no less disconcerting. Eula's sexual choice of McCarron had been exceptional. He was not only a strong and vigorous male whose origins abrogated the threat of inbreeding, but also a man of mental prowess as his business acumen avers. Hoake's reappearance many years later at Linda's wedding, a wealthy and healthy man, will vindicate Eula's mating decision. McCarron seems ideal, but if his protracted wooing of Eula indicates a faithful selection strategy, his disappearance after sexual consummation points to a philandering streak. Eula—whose fruitful past with McCarron is imminent—threatens the Varners with considerable embarrassment. They need not have worried. With her marriage to Flem Snopes, she secures a surrogate father for Linda and the material trappings associated with a fully realized strategy of domestic bliss. She has struggled with sexual politics and seemingly safeguarded her daughter's future. The extent of this victory will not be enough for Linda though. Eula had chosen a nonparochial local for a lover, but Linda's adult coyness refuses all Yoknapatawphians. The exception to the rule is Gavin Stevens, whom Linda would marry with the prospect of domestic bliss, but, true to form, Stevens's love remains spiritual rather than carnal. Refused by the one man in Jefferson she deems worthy, Linda's unconscious acumen, fostered by her biological inheritance, comes to the fore. She "evolved the idea," Ratliff believes, of leaving Mississippi (*Mansion* 460). Aware of her stepfather's objection to the idea, the fear of an outsider marrying into Will Varner's money paramount in his mind, she swears out a will in return for her freedom. She signs over "whatever share she might ever have in her grandpaw's or her maw's estate to her father Flem Snopes" (461). In return, Flem concedes a little ground, allowing Linda to attend the University of Mississippi. Her mother's suicide makes this distance too close to home, so she moves to Greenwich Village, encouraged by Stevens.

From Stevens's perspective, one fearful of Snopesish encroachment into Yoknapatawpha, this departure buoys his scheme of turning Linda against Flem. He has been disingenuously schooling Linda as his agent within the Snopes family. A respite from Mississippi should offer her a greater prospect of an outlandish suitor capable of upsetting the Snopes genealogy. Choosing in the Jewish sculptor Barton Kohl a man beyond her race and culture, she does as Stevens hopes. The 1950 census shows that fewer than 20 percent of American Jews married non-Semites. Linda is an exception to common practice and stands on the cusp of a revolution—by 1990 this percentage had risen by over thirty points (Jones, *Blood* 159–60). Stevens acknowledges Linda's choice of a faithful man. Kohl, he muses, must be "the best of whatever he was for her to pick him out" (*Mansion* 473).

Linda and Barton wed. Flem does not attend the ceremony; Stevens gives the bride away. The couple's future is redolent of domestic bliss. Yet, this is a contradictory form of marital happiness, the newlyweds joining the republican cause in the Spanish Civil War. Barton loses his life during the conflict; his wife suffers serious injury. Linda comes home to Yoknapatawpha, but her return is muted. Deafened by a bomb blast in Spain, she requires Stevens's support, especially since her feminism and communism, two ideologies in antithesis with the vestigial codes of the Old South, compound her separation from the white community. Born locally, her neighbors now consider her a foreigner, the extent of Linda's alienation symbolized by the ducklike voice—the voice of another species—that accompanies her wartime injury. Linda invests her social conscience in political and social activities. Living with Flem again, she nevertheless holds communist meetings in his mansion. Only two men ever attend. They are Finns whose foreignness accords with Linda's new status. The antagonism between daughter and father finds expression through this communist presence within the seat of capitalist power. Linda's desire to redress the social divide extends to her voluntary work in African American schools. Although her ventures into teaching often meet polite resignation, her ugly quacking, her obviously different articulation, as Roberts contends, "insists on being heard" ("Eula" 175). This difference finds a new outlet when America enters World War II. Making munitions in a factory, Linda becomes a committed feminist. Returning to Jefferson after the conflict, she revitalizes her interest in the schooling of African Americans. She is the type of woman who, despite growing resistance in the South to the civil rights initiatives of President Harry S. Truman (1884–1972), joined associations such as the Women's Emerging Committee to Open Our Schools (WEC). "These women activists," writes David Goldfield, "represented a minority of white women's views in the South during the tense days of the 1950s" (165). Belonging to political or social movements was dangerous with female members often denounced as communist collaborators and race mixers. Linda is the object of such abuse but is above insults. Moreover, Faulkner contentiously promotes Linda's status through her active passivity concerning Mink Snopes. Flem's relative remains incarcerated for murder in the Mississippi State Penitentiary of Parchman. After almost four decades, Mink's parole is finally mooted. Linda, knowing that Mink blames Flem for complicity in his imprisonment, disingenuously co-opts Stevens to help her vouchsafe the prisoner's release. She says nothing to her stepfather, turning a deaf ear to Mink's arrival at their home, and, showing him safely out of the house after he has murdered Flem, secures her passive involvement in the crime. The *fille de bébé* appears to have matured under male auspices into a *femme fatale*.

Linda Snopes Kohl is both complex and unnerving. She signals Faulkner's return to the perplexing scene of modern women and sexual relations initially considered in *Soldiers' Pay*. Secondary selection, sexual politics, and twentieth-century womanhood had intrigued him for more than thirty years. Eula and Linda, "Helen" and "her inheritrix," as Ratliff describes them, are Faulkner's boasts in this regard: a renowned beauty fatally resistant to the sexual economy of the South whose daughter eventually conquers that system to revenge her mother's suicide (*Mansion* 653). Linda, post–World War II, is adept at sexual politics. Her parting from Gavin at the end of *The Mansion* testifies to this proficiency, Stevens recognizing in Linda's embrace the murderous intent behind her sexual strategy. "*You dont need to tempt them,*" he muses, "*because they have long since already selected you*" (710). Linda has made Stevens an unwitting accomplice in Flem's murder. Under Stevens's duplicitous tuition, Linda has certainly learned; so much so, in fact, that she finally educates him.

Charles Mallison had earlier questioned his uncle's attitude toward women in terms of "virginity or just celibacy?" (505). For Gavin, social conditions had "insisted on his continuing celibacy despite his own efforts to give it up" (681). In addition, like a monk, the intractable bachelor had something to escape into, a monastic translation of "the Old Testament back into the classic Greek of its first translating." On completion of this task, Gavin had planned to "teach himself Hebrew and really attain to purity," but this meditation proved to be the lull before the storm (681). Gavin's dream of "restoring the Old Testament to its virgin's pristinity," a vision that he had projected onto Linda, as if she were the subject of his pet project, has been dispelled (713). Linda's cunning has disillusioned him, a revelation that frees Stevens's stalled sexual maturation and enables him to marry the widowed Melisandre Backus Harriss. Linda has reciprocated Gavin's tuition. Nonetheless, he testifies to the moral fear triggered by her behavior.

For, despite the machinations of the Snopeses, the county attorney had maintained a belief in the predisposition of humankind toward the good of the species. Stevens had interpreted Linda's demand for Mink's early release as altruism, but cognizance of his protégé's motives (elucidation manifest in the shape of a British sports car) disabuses him. Evolutionary selection does not operate beyond an individual level. Linda, compelled to engineer Flem's execution, drives away from Jefferson and out of Gavin's sight, resplendent in a symbol of the economic system that tarnishes her too. Only now, with Linda's departure, does the sobering implication come home to Stevens that "there aren't any morals" (*Mansion* 715).[17] With this, his last appearance in Faulkner's canon, Gavin Stevens, the Harvard and Heidelberg trained lawyer, finally learns the painful answer to his beloved Eula's lament. "We've all bought Snopeses here," she once complained. "I dont know why we bought them. I mean, why we had to: what coin and when and where we so recklessly and improvidently spent that we had to have Snopeses too. But we do" (*Town* 84). With Gavin's enlightenment, Faulkner emphasizes that biological inheritance does not select traits at a group level; concepts of human morality remain forever susceptible to the genetic nature of *Homo sapiens*. Flem's funeral compounds this suggestion with the appearance of three unknown Snopeses, men "not alien at all: simply identical," not alien yet distinguishable, not alien but other (*Mansion* 707).[18] These normal differences disclose the ever-presence of the extrinsic alien, the enemy within the genetic basis that constantly threatens the tranquillity of stable communities. The Snopeses are not mutants; they are representative of humankind. One can see Faulkner's shifting response to this dynamic in his attitude toward Flem Snopes. At times, Faulkner had rather admired Flem, a man who "came from nothing with no equipment" (*University* 119), a character whom he had once mischievously envisaged running for president of the United States (*Lion* 223). By 1959 and *The Mansion*, however, Faulkner was obliged to rub out this figure. Disfiguring Flem with a gunshot to the face, Mink uses a "mud-crusted" (715) gun likened to a "fossilised terrapin" (687). This weapon resurrected from prehistoric depths analogizes Flem's evolutionarily endowed demise. Faulkner's implication is stark. If future generations do not take responsibility for their inherent selfishness, then evolution may account for *Homo sapiens* too.

CHAPTER 8

SELF-INTEREST, COOPERATION, AND BEYOND

> Man is free and he is responsible, terribly responsible.
> William Faulkner, *Lion in the Garden* (70)

FAULKNER BELIEVED THAT FUTURE GENERATIONS COULD TAKE RESPONSIbility for their inheritance. *Homo sapiens*, human but humane, solitary but partaking of solidarity, could prevail. The communal action of common individuals would be vital to ensure this accommodation. Otherwise, evolutionarily engendered self-interest, having been predominant in the Western ethos for over two millennia, would continue to dominate society. Charles Darwin's response to this dilemma had been to posit group selection as an intrinsic impetus toward social sensibility. Primal altruism would have been unusual, explains *The Descent of Man*, but could have arisen from the "low motive" of reciprocation. Proffering aid might have been complemented by the return of help in the future. However, "another and much more powerful stimulus to the development of the social virtues is afforded by the praise and the blame of our fellow-men," which could have stimulated even selfish individuals to act at a tribal level (131). Evolution of human memory has promoted both of these courses. The shadow of the future recommends reciprocal altruism as efficacious behavior. Hence, the Golden Rule is the foundation of morality, "a highly complex sentiment—originating in the social instincts, largely guided by the approbation of our fellow-men, ruled by reason, self-interest, and in later times by deep religious feelings, and confirmed by instruction and habit" (132). Moreover, Darwin counsels, "although a high standard of morality gives but a slight or no advantage to each individual man," an advance in the overall standard of morality "will certainly give an immense advantage to one tribe over another" (132). Altruism must overcome immanent egocentrism; self-interest is a throwback to more primitive times. "Selfish and contentious people will not cohere, and without coherence," Darwin concludes, "nothing can be effected" (130).

Group selection is comforting, but evolution progresses via the longevity, fecundity, and reproductive accuracy of genes. Individual organisms are replicators built by genes for the survival and propagation of genes over countless generations. An organismic group is merely a conglomeration of replicators. If replicators practice altruism, then there is a genetic reason for this behavior. An evolutionary perspective must discard the notion of group selection. Faulkner intimates such a rejection in *The Mansion*. Yes, Flem Snopes is the disquieting epitome of the selfish gene, but Gavin Stevens's collaboration with Linda Snopes Kohl provokes a similar level of anxiety. Self-interest meets altruism in a conundrum.

An evolutionarily endowed philosophy can analyze this enigma by considering conflictual situations where the genetically forwarded actions of an individual depend on the similarly fostered behavior of others. Specifically, these *coordination problems* can be modeled as mathematical games in which, as William Poundstone explains, "one must make a choice knowing that others are making choices too, and the outcome of the conflict will be determined in some prescribed way by all the choices made" (6). The *coordination condition* that impels this dynamic is one's ignorance of the choices decided upon by others until the overall result transpires. These situations often demand extremely intricate modeling, but an evolutionary hermeneutic can use basic gaming tenets to interpret literature without this necessity. A coordination problem relevant to Faulkner studies came to the fore during the American Civil War with the evolution of policies to shoot. Entrenchment was one of the defining characteristics of the hostilities, both armies constructing unprecedented battlefield fortifications. Commanders often instigated the digging of rifle pits to capitalize on the gain of a strategically important site. Spades, shovels, and axes suitable to the tasks of excavation and trench construction became necessary pieces of a soldier's military kit, because if an impasse developed during a battle, then prized temporary refuges could be converted into more permanent structures. Trench stalemates in which small units confronted each other in immobile sectors for extended periods became crucial to the campaign. These situations tended to involve an initial period of interdependent punishment (or tit for tat) in which both sides suffered for little or no relative gain, followed by an extended interval of mutual cooperation.[1] Protagonists even preferred complementary restraint to the random alternation of serious engagement. The sensible behavioral option was one of passivity.

Faulkner must have been aware of this history. For, as his brother, John, maintains, "He was an avid reader of the histories of the War Between the States. He was as well versed in most of them as any professor" (256) and readily understood that during this conflict "there was a great deal of cavalry skirmishing back and forth through Oxford" (54). Lafayette, with troop encampments on either side, became a "No Man's Land and Oxford was the center of it" (55). As John's language infers, and with their brother Jack a survivor of the gas attack at Saint-Mihiel, William must have recognized the historical parallel with sectors of the Western Front during World War I. The opening stages of this conflict had been highly mobile and extremely costly, but as trench demarcations stabilized, nonaggression between opposing troops emerged spontaneously along many segments of the front line. For both sides in such a predicament, explains Robert Axelrod, "the reward for mutual restraint is preferred by the local units to the outcome of mutual punishment, since mutual punishment would imply that both units would suffer for little or no relative gain" (75). Privates of the Allied and Central powers, like their predecessors in the American Civil War, appeared to be disobeying their own leaders by cooperating with their enemy complement.

Even the dominance of tanks over the battlefields of World War II could not prevent the evolution of similar occurrences. The Anzio campaign, a part of the second front that lasted between January and May 1944, became a case in point, when lieutenant general Mark Clark (1896–1984) decided that the Fifth Army must dig in until their beachhead was secured. His desire for consolidation gave field marshal Albert Kesselring (1881–1960) time to mount a counterattack. An impasse ensued. "Anzio," notes war correspondent Wynford Vaughan-Thomas from personal experience, "then became an old fashioned World War I trench system" (Thames Television). The front lines were just a few yards apart, and a cooperative feeling soon evolved across the wire. Troops exchanged goods, confidant in the knowledge that artillery barrages would begin at the same time each day. Trench warfare, incipient in internecine nineteenth-century America, prominent along the Western Front some fifty years later, and present during occasional battles in World War II, inextricably led to the evolution of mutual cooperation. Those in command little understood this symbiosis and often misconstrued such behavior as cowardice.

Only when Hungarian mathematician John von Neumann (1903–1957) and Austrian economist Oskar Morgenstern (1902–1977) presented their *Theory of Games and Economic Behavior* (1944) did enlightenment beckon. The manner in which this volume analyzes genetically fostered behavior soon proved applicable beyond the remit of economics thanks to the intervention of American mathematician John Nash (1928–). Faced with a set of possible outcomes dependent on the choices made by other rational people, reasoned Nash, each individual will adopt a best response to his environment in the form of a decision-making strategy so that an equilibrium is reached in which all players are in accordance with one another. Nash, despite considering both noncooperative and cooperative games, argued that all such strategies are reducible to some noncooperative form. Thus, the need to realize all others as implacably hostile offsets the reassurance gained from a shared sense of prudent stability. Societies are self-adjusting systems built on suspicion and paranoia. Formulated by Nash while working for the RAND Corporation at the outset of the cold war alongside Manhattan Project veteran von Neumann, this conclusion helped to promote the concept of *mutually assured destruction*. During this period, according to Sylvia Nasar, the RAND think tank was "a strange hybrid of which the unique mission was to apply rational analysis and the latest quantitative methods to the problem of how to use the terrifying new nuclear weaponry to forestall war with Russia—or to win a war if deterrence failed" (105). The logical solution to Russian mastery of fission technology for military ends was an equally stocked American arsenal.

Begun in 1944, the year of Clark's stalemate at Anzio and of von Neumann and Morgenstern's groundbreaking publication, Faulkner's *A Fable* (1954) emerged from this extended provenance of paradoxically entrenched and passive conflicts.[2] He intended this work to address the all-encompassing violence of world war with an appeal to the messianic. If Christ, or some spiritual movement in humankind, had effected a mutiny during World War I, believed Faulkner, then the high command must have acted to eradicate that rebellion. If a similar opportunity were to appear during World War II, then this could be the species' last chance of redemption. To reject such beneficence again would be an inane confirmation of humankind's spiritual nihilism. Faulkner wished to depict the qualities necessary to break this Viconian stupidity. He reasoned that at times of global antagonism, the dominant ethos suppresses messianism and only a fable has the requisite qualities to oppose this dominance through literature. At one level, this literary form extricated him from the scrupulous needs of historicism, a problem that he had encountered at Warner Brothers when working on *The De Gaulle Story* in 1942, and at another level, vouchsafed him a particular allegorical power. However, by using a method with which he was unfamiliar, Faulkner was venturing into an untried realm. His struggle to analyze World War I would thereby necessitate the disruption of his own space. The relays between his working environment and that of his aesthetic would be tested to the limit.

A Fable, a rendition of the aftermath of a defining twentieth-century battle, the German's near success—but ultimate failure—in capturing the salient at Verdun, was a shocking translocation for Faulkner. Despite his evident compassion for the combatants, he had not flown in the European skies of World War I, he had not stood on the steps of a dugout, he had not experienced the evolution of trench warfare, nor had he commanded an army from a château behind the lines. How could he apply his consciousness to this unfamiliar landscape? Jack Falkner was undoubtedly one source of information, but in addition Faulkner would carry out research in France during his vacations from Hollywood. Furthermore, he would occasionally return to Rowan Oak to work on the novel. Nonetheless, respites from Warner Brothers were all too brief. Progress on *A Fable* dried up. Eventually, near the end of his tether, a colleague extricated him from his studio contract. His aesthetic imprisonment, so it seemed, was over.

Faulkner retreated to Oxford, where, by the winter of 1947, he completed a short story concerning the adventures of a stable team with a thoroughbred stallion in the American South during 1912. "Notes from a Horse Thief," first published in 1951, although at first sight irrelevant to his major project, seemed to have broken his writer's block. He could concentrate on *A Fable*. However, as the aesthetic demands of fictional transposition again pushed him to the limit, his strategic withdrawal failed too. The World War I power struggle between a disposition for belligerence and emanations of messianism continued to trouble him. Rowan Oak bears witness to this delimitation. When one thinks of writers and wallpaper in American literature, one most readily brings to mind

Charlotte Perkins Gilman (1860–1935) and her "Yellow Wallpaper" (1892), but Faulkner's décor bears comparison. The writing was on the wall for humankind as World War II reached its climax, and at Rowan Oak, the writing remains on the wall, the paper in his study bearing the author's plan for *A Fable*. Faulkner had reached his southern limit, but he had to go on. Drugs now supplemented the alcohol that had been present in large quantities since the 1930s. The Faulknerian demons irritated to their most demonic now required sanatorium confinement and the administration of electroconvulsive therapy. This treatment provided temporary relief, but by 1952, beyond the comforting confines of Yoknapatawpha like never before, Faulkner decamped to the New York offices of his editor, Saxe Commins, at Random House. Writing of France during World War I, writing outside his experience, weighing every word, the strain of the mot juste, required Faulkner's utmost endurance. Forced to write away from Oxford, another two years would laboriously pass before he finished his novel.

A Fable won both the National Book Award and the Pulitzer Prize, but Faulkner's war work garners little esteem today. Gary Lee Stonum sees this reception as the inevitable response to an artistic methodology in which new productions are mere replicas of achievements long gone—Faulkner suffering "from the principal threats to a healthy career: repetition, silence, and dispersion" (152). The blockages that hindered Faulkner from getting his thoughts on paper were a form of silent illness. He stepped into an alien milieu in compensation. *A Fable*, contends Stonum, thereby suffers at birth from two crippling defects. On the one hand, verbiage fails to hide the philosophical and artistic silence, or dead center, of the novel. On the other hand, Faulkner reorients his previous artistic trajectory too drastically via obvious symbolism. "Like most other critics," states Stonum, "I consider the novel a failure"—the symbolic founders on authorial heavy-handedness (160). Ostensibly, a European novel, *A Fable* also suffers critical alienation because the Yoknapatawpha readings of Malcolm Cowley remain so influential. Faulkner, so the argument goes, is a southern rather than an international writer. Inarticulate form is a final cause for concern: entrenched in a tale about European warfare is a relapse to prewar America in "Notes from a Horse Thief."

There is, however, an answer to each of these objections. Firstly, Joseph R. Urgo convincingly argues that Faulkner's novel is not a ham-fisted Christian allegory but a deep meditation on the trinitarian form of human life: "as flesh, a sensual creation destined to oblivion; as mind, capable of defining and ordering the natural world and all of reality; and as spirit, marked by rebellion and forever in a struggle with the doomed flesh and the unquiet mind" (100).

Added to Urgo's interpretation is a related contention. The consequences of the mortal transgressions that arise when individuals are challenged by their human situation were a crucial subject for Faulkner's later fiction. His eschatological stoicism was an elemental participant in this prosecution. A reverence when brooding on his own mortality for the works of the English clergyman Jeremy Taylor (1613–1667) compounds this conclusion. When Faulkner was convalescing, recalls Joseph Blotner, "on the night table lay his standard hospital reading: the Bible, Taylor's *Holy Living and Holy Dying*, and Boccaccio's *Decameron*" (*Biography* 1: 698). Taylor retains devotees today because of the lyrical style of his devotional writings—he was nicknamed the "Shakespeare of Divines"—rather than by his theological importance. Nevertheless, Taylor's conviction that the human intellect was a poor instrument from which to attain metaphysical insight must have appealed to Faulkner, as must his poeticism.[3] Living and sensing the manner of human suffering, Faulkner approached this condition through an oeuvre redolent with an evolutionary and numinous endowment.

Secondly, appreciation of a European context comes more readily to a critic living in Europe.

Thirdly, the inarticulate form of *A Fable* is worthy of reexamination with reference to "Notes from a Horse Thief" and its involvement in the problematic of coordination. This lengthy short story brings about an apposite formal rupture, the shattering of aesthetic form reproducing the global splits opened by World War I. Geographically translocated from the France of Verdun to the American South, Faulkner's break in narrative supports this surmise. Moreover, while traveling across the southern United States by rail, the horse and its stable team—composed of the African American Reverend Sutterfield, his son (the jockey), and Mister Harry (the English groom)—are involved in a serious accident when a bridge undermined by floodwater collapses. In a typical Faulknerian figuration, the train, the stallion, and its handlers come off the rails. The magnificent creature is inoperably crippled. Whether the horse has broken its leg or whether horrific dislocation permanently damages the joint is not clear. What is certain is the end of the animal as a legitimate racehorse. By analogy, suggests Faulkner, the future of humankind is tenuous. As an extended analepsis, the stallion episode also tears at the conventional time frame of the novel. Chronicity, in the wake of Albert Einstein (1879–1955) and Henri Louis Bergson, will never seem the same again. The abrupt return of the narration to the frontline narrative on completion of "Notes from a Horse Thief" reiterates this sense of enforced disorientation. Faulkner's supposed inarticulation is part of his articulate message. Something equally perplexing, demands *A Fable*, must forestall the machinations of war.

Many of the characters in the novel are displaced by the conflict: Stefan Dumont, that corporal, that Christian martyr born in Eastern Europe, arrives in France via Beirut; the battalion runner, that noncommissioned officer who rejects his warrant of authority, joins the vanguard from England; Mister Harry, that mysterious groom, is another Englishman who, like his erstwhile American teammates, the Sutterfields, comes to France via the southern United States. All of these individuals leave home to prosecute a foreign war but in doing so witness the evolution of an unusual belligerence within their own ranks. A similar response, it transpires, evolves among the Germans. Privates across the divide mutually cooperate on two separate occasions. These frontline mutinies, insurrections that evince the live-and-let-live stage of warfare evolution, emanate from the lowest military class. Faulkner's text consistently refers to army personal by military rank rather than by name, attesting to the dehumanizing regime of war; moreover, Faulkner tends to signify the equal status of privates, noncommissioned staff, and officers as human beings by flattening all ranks to a single level with the use of lower-case titles. A generalissimo may command several combined armies, but his textual recognition does not exceed that of a private.[4] Trench stalemate, which baffles the respective high commands, posits a lack of control over their men. The dynamics of this quiescent war within a war must have appealed to Faulkner who models these circumstances intuitively in line with his own baffling artistic situation.

The primary mutiny, which is instigated by Stefan, is an inarticulation of the body. When called to leave their trench, the privates in his division maintain the line but refuse to move. These subordinates not only deny patriarchal authority, but also petition the spirit of man. This empathy between the less-educated and therefore more instinctively inclined combatants is strong enough to span the ontopological gulf of no-man's-land. When the Allied offensive fails, the German infantry reciprocates. Any advantage gained from the inactivity of their opponent is lost. They too are entrenched against their superiors. The bodies constituting each body of men, the respective corps of the Allied and Central powers, rebel through corporeal inarticulation. Corporal Dumont, a character of absolute passivity, is a worthy combatant in this stalemate.

Stefan's quiescence is even more outstanding because of his lineage. He is the illegitimate son of the supreme allied commander, the principal figure of French authority, yet he ably resists patriarchal coercion. His father, in an attempt to win Stefan over to his dominion, offers him a scapegoat and the temptations of Christ.[5] Stefan refuses to renounce his mission. "We," the generalissimo continues undeterred, "are two articulations" (988). He is of the earth, the material, and the mundane while his son is of the heavens, the spiritual, and the esoteric. The generalissimo concedes that even in the circumscribed arena of war these two articulations can coexist—as long as the father's supremacy remains. The symbolic order by which human actions are regimented, "the long heroic roster who were the milestones of the rise of man," a disparate and dubious cast heralded by the generalissimo, which includes William Jennings Bryan, Billy Sunday, Julius Caesar, Alexander the Great, and Genghis Khan, must be continued (833). Biology, so the old man believes, will secure this preeminence. Humankind may be forever "inherent with the same old primordial fault," the selfish articulation of genes, but this biological immanence "will fail to eradicate him from the earth." To his detriment, the generalissimo is "ten times prouder" of his biological inheritance, the heredity that promotes human amorality, than the biological bequest that is his son (994).

Calculating, weighing his investments, the genetic (his son) versus the militaristic (his years in the army), the generalissimo refuses to weaken the coordination condition that maintains the war. He will not renounce his work of a lifetime. To do otherwise would admit the possibility of a higher economy, a reestablishment of the celestial system of inclusive fitness with God as omnipotent and *Homo sapiens* returned to their divinely appointed position within nature and the cosmos. To do otherwise would bring the supposed supremacy of humankind, as personified by the generalissimo, into disrepute. Although his son can see the value in such a resignation, the supreme allied commander cannot. His duty to the army therefore stands face to face with the responsibility of absolute duty, the absolute sacrifice of that which should be dearer to him: absolute love for an only child. But the generalissimo values the economy of man, military laws, politics, and the sacrifice of lives on the ground, above all other considerations, including his biological legacy. He loves to go unquestioned in his quest to dominate and conquer. He has the self-conceit of a *Homo superbus*, a specific kind of man who sets his personal pride above the claims of all other species, including *Homo sapiens*. To renounce manmade rules—and these are male codes—would be the generalissimo's absolute sacrifice. He cannot make that gesture; his decision in dealing with the rebellion is final. "We can hardly imagine a father," writes Jacques Derrida, "taking his son to be sacrificed on the top of the hill at Montmartre" (*Gift* 85). Faulkner's aesthetic offers this unimaginable act. The father must sacrifice his only son. He has Stefan executed. Father abandons son to the role of scapegoat in order to retain control over the people.

The corporal's execution, with his father as a modern aberration of Abraham, is an unforgivable abomination. Nonetheless, as Faulkner's text asserts, moral discourse often sanctions the sacrifice of millions of humans. "The smooth functioning of its [the developed world's] economic, political and legal affairs, the smooth functioning of its moral discourse and good conscience," Derrida corroborates, "presupposes the permanent operation of this sacrifice" (*Gift* 85). The corporal's initiative may force the leaders from both sides to meet, but they agree to an armistice only on condition of maintaining face. To this end, they camouflage their conference with the instigation of a phony artillery barrage. To ensure their position of authority in the interim before peace, the high commands agree to cooperate in mercilessly suppressing further rebellions. The generalissimo sacrifices his genetic future toward this aim, but Stefan, as martyr master, has set an example. Others will reaffirm this ideal. For, unbeknown to the teacher, he has a pupil in the battalion runner, a messianic avatar who is willing to induce a second mutiny.

This secondary rebellion evolves from the conditions of the first stalemate. Called upon to prosecute an attack across no-man's land, the squaddies in the battalion runner's unit refuse, actively restraining the intervention of their officers. Force intended to prevent the misuse of greater force, the battalion runner's use of his gun as a cudgel to incapacitate a number of reactionaries may even necessitate murder. As in the previous mutiny, privates flout the hierarchy, but in this case, their emergence into no-man's land breaches topographical demarcations too. The benefits of mutual cooperation again ensure reciprocation as the unarmed German infantry enter the interstitial zone to greet them.

Live ammunition from their respective artilleries counters this meeting.[6] This measure presents not the obvious separation between "us" and "them," but the more subtle difference between "we" and "us." The pronoun counters its objective form. Activity reacts against passivity within a supposedly unified structure. "We did it," the quartermaster general declares almost incredulously to the generalissimo when they next confer.

> We. Not British and American and French we against German them nor German they against American and British and French us, but We against all because we no longer belong to us. A subterfuge not of ours to confuse and mislead the enemy nor of the enemy to mislead and confuse us, but of We to betray all since all has had to repudiate us in simple defensive horror; no barrage by us or vice versa to prevent an enemy running over us with bayonets and hand grenades or vice versa, but a barrage of both of We to prevent naked and weaponless hand touching opposite naked and weaponless hand. We, you and I and our whole unregenerate and unregenerable kind; not only you and I and our tight close jealous unchallengeable hierarchy behind this wire and our opposite German one behind that one, but more, worse: our small repudiated and homeless species about the earth who not only no longer belong to man but even to earth itself since we have had to make this last base desperate cast in order to hold our last desperate and precarious place on it. (969)

There are, then, two axes in the cooperation dynamic portrayed in *A Fable* with each army exhibiting a hierarchy of noncooperation that is stratified by planes of reciprocation across no-man's-land. The barrage overseen by *Homo superbus* kills Mister Harry and the Reverend Sutterfield, while incurably searing the battalion runner. In this condition, the body of the latter becomes a living symbol of humankind's permanently scarred conscience. His survival and his postwar outburst at the consecration of the generalissimo's tomb are his redress to the hyperbolic eulogies in memory of war. "The biped successful enough to become a general," he rails about the live-and-let-live deniers, "had ceased to be a German or British or American or Italian or French one almost as soon as it never was a human one" (958).

That the military commanders of World War I had to confederate against their own cooperatively inclined men, perversely bridging the coordination condition of no-man's-land to maintain communal separation, is a disturbing conception du monde; yet, Nash's equilibrium ratchets this worldview to a further degree of bleakness in which genetic selfishness dressed up as mutual agreement explains the cooperative battlefield axis. The alogical Faulkner, though, posits something humane that is beyond the inimical cast of genetics. Stefan implies this otherness.

Obviously, the corporal's inarticulation was corporeal; nevertheless, *gradu mutato*, this "effect arises not only from the mutiny itself," as Karl Zender explains, "but also from the Corporal's disinclination to talk about it afterwards. By first refusing to fight and then failing to explain his reasons for doing so, the Corporal creates a rhetoric of silence, one powerful enough to make all Europe his mute and attentive audience" (*Crossing* 33).

Stefan's illiteracy is an adjunct to his reticence. This silence is his other form of inarticulateness. Yet, possibly because of this lack, he powerfully connects with his comrades. The Allied high command had identified Dumont as the ringleader, but observation of the mutineers belies this conclusion. At times during their detention, the men turn to Stefan, but he gives no orders. Rather, he is an embodiment beyond language, a sympathetic communicator of communion and solidarity. Stefan casts this metaphysical shadow not only over his comrades, but also over the Western Front. This ethereal skein negates the coordination condition imposed by the leaders of the war. The Faulknerian implication is that a lack of internal communication lies at the root of intercommunal conflict.

Without percipience attaining to telepathy, however, how can one react toward the no-man's-land between articulations? Faulkner addresses this question on two planes. At one level, his novel demonstrates how to resist the inarticulateness of being face to face with alterity when language is the barrier, how to cope with being dumbfounded through translocation. The generalissimo and his son speak different native tongues. In the fateful secret meeting that seals Stefan's demise, that which passes from the elder to the younger remains a secret of the father's tongue. Such symbolism ensures that this secret passage echoes that between God and his son, and a God and his people, with Faulkner advancing his thesis on the debasement of Christianity. "I believe in God," he would say to the Japanese press in 1955, before qualifying his remark by adding, "that man has a soul that aspires towards what we call God, what we mean by God." Another term is often preferable, he explained, as if reiterating one of the messages in *A Fable*, because Christianity is not the proper manifestation of Christian sentiment but "a nice glib tongue" (*Lion* 100). This secret language is a shibboleth, in Derrida's definition of this familiarly Faulknerian word, "a secret formula such as can be uttered only in a certain way in a certain language," a secret within one's native language—a natural untranslatability in which one either takes pride, like the generalissimo, or in which one recognizes a limitation, as do the corporal and his apostles (*Gift* 88). Any such formal economy of language is a presence linked to one's hearth, one's home, and one's nation. The corporal's act of renunciation therefore attempts to confirm a secular asymmetry: it is, in Derridean terms, "a matter of suspending the strict economy of exchange . . . of that hateful form of circulation that involves reprisal, vengeance, returning blow for blow, settling scores" (*Gift* 102). The formal Christian sense of the Book of Matthew, specifically 5.38–39, echoes this asymmetry in its interruption of vengeful parity with a refusal to pay the other back. The principle of unilateral restraint—rather than that of mutually assured destruction—maintains this economy of exchange. Nevertheless, this benignancy as offered by a Christian God, or the generalissimo as in Faulkner's figuration, is contradictory. The play of the native tongue, the play of translation, means that the *inimicus* is a personal, private antagonist, while the *hostis* is a determinate, political enemy. "No Christian politics," chides Derrida, "ever advised the West to love the Muslims who invaded Christian Europe" (*Gift* 102).[7] Citing Leviticus 19.15–18, Derrida exposes a hypocrisy in which God forbids revenge only if one's neighbor is of the same blood. If one's neighbor is consanguineous, from the same stock, of the same nation or nationality, then the non-neighbor is the enemy, not as personal, private adversary but as a member of a different nation, someone who is foreign by blood. Despite global mobility in the twenty-first century, a lack of population viscosity of which Franz Boas and Gilberto Freyre would have approved, pangenetic discourse survives. Hence, blood fallacy racism can breed not only between nation states, but also between the different peoples of a single nation.

At another level, *A Fable* addresses how to cope with one's own language when abstractions become barriers between individuals. Faulkner's novel, set outside the confines of his own comforting "postage stamp of native soil," holds out for something beyond language: an adumbration that the gap, the no-man's-land of language now called the *aporia*, can be bridged (*Lion* 255). The condition that achieves this span is thereby an inclination toward deconstruction with Stefan and his successor, the battalion runner, opposing the structuralist tendency personified by the generalissimo. Both inclinations originate in biological inheritance. Thus, Stefan is "not another frail and mortal dissident to his politics or his notions of national boundaries," acknowledges the old general, "but the very monster itself which he inhabits" (*Fable* 993)—the rebels in *A Fable*, Faulkner's successive avatars of fraternity, beclouding the boundaries of individual identity. "He has created," concludes Minako Ohba, "a world that has the power to captivate even though it lies beyond our understanding. It is a world in which uncanny and indefatigable forces of life reverberate and respond to the mysteries of the cosmos" (191). A spectral conception, the avatar allows Faulkner to narrow the strait between ontology and the negation of being-present. Self-identity demands less importance than the need to promote solidarity. Human beings, Faulkner acknowledges, are the cause and the solution of the human dilemma. For beyond the genetically fostered tendencies evident in the insurrections of *A Fable* comes Faulkner's appeal to spirituality. That Stefan Dumont travels to France after years in Beirut (where a devout local community made his maternal family welcome) ratifies this conclusion. Significantly, although little is know about Stefan biographically, Faulkner locates the land of his birth as the Balkans, the region associated with the outbreak of the war.[8] Through topographical signification, therefore, Faulkner reinforces his belief in humankind's responsibility for the human condition.

Faulkner had promised that completion of his war work would consummate his literary rebellion. He could then "break the pencil" (*Lion* 255). He failed. None of his fiction appeared saturated to Faulkner; each text was capable of accepting amendment. Rebellion against articulation to that extent was out of the question. He continued to evolve considerations of the human dilemma, but *A Fable* remains his greatest work of retrospective anticipation, his trace without vainglory that is his significant epitaph for two world wars. Lessons, Faulkner avers, should have been learned from the impasse of trench warfare during the "Great War." If this enlightenment had occurred, then German antipathy may not have greeted the resulting armistice.

For in the aftermath of the conflict, the long-term situation for Germany remained uncertain. The Treaty of Versailles, far from securing the creation of a beloved European community, ensured the emergence of future problems by exploiting the German nation to near exhaustion. Faulkner analogizes this unpalatable situation with the thoroughbred stallion in *A Fable*. Nation or racehorse, "the long careful breeding and selecting which finally produced it" is prone to abuse (806). The owner of the animal remains desperate for prospective stud fees. He wants to milk the stallion dry. "To save that horse that never wanted nothing and never knowed nothing but just to run out in front of all the other horses in a race, from being sent back to Kentucky to be just another stud-horse for the rest of its life" becomes the stable team's mission (849). They hide, care, and eventually race the stallion. Despite being crippled, the horse continues to win. Gossipmongers disseminate a rumor that the men are making a fortune from their lame charge (814). Notably, Faulkner is careful to provide evidence to the contrary, because this sedition is an anticapitalist, anticlass, anticaste statement that adumbrates the rebelliousness to come from its members. Forced to shoot the horse to prevent its exploitation, the team breaks up, but each of them eventually enters the war. Arriving in France, the Reverend Sutterfield assumes the name Tooleymon. He is, as his oneness with the world (*tout le monde*) connotes, the figure of a beneficent conception du monde: an African American with "some bond between or from man to his brother man stronger than even the golden shackles which coopered precariously his ramshackle earth" (818). Tooleymon becomes a symbol of deliverance in the role of everyman's savior. The world is still worth saving. Ultimately, the reverend's human ministrations, like those short-lived coordination deadlocks across the no-man's-land of inarticulation, fail as did his earlier equine mission, but *A Fable* pities the arrogance of victors and their impositions on the defeated. The postbellum South and Germany after World War I shared this sense of imposition. Crippling conditions should not restrict animals, humans, states, or nations. Victors too often wear out the vanquished economically and ontopologically. This form of human disfigurement, attests *A Fable*, vitalizes nascent strife. Faulkner's novel, and the dislocation of his fable by "Notes from a Horse Thief," thereby elucidates Germany's active denial of the Treaty of Versailles. With the Allied's insufficient magnanimity in victory, their lack of imagination, their self-protective cunning, and their deliberate breaches of trust, the German people would choose their own battalion runner and corporal: one who would instill in them a belief in their own superiority because of breeding, one who would promote ultraviolence to cure violation, one whose coordination of Europeans would dislocate the continent like never before.

That man was Adolf Hitler (1889–1945).[9]

Faulkner's response to the totalitarian paradigm is to suggest that reasons and persons without blind faith, bad conscience, or proactive tit for tat should be the human eschaton. A disavowal of the Christian economy is crucial to this aim. Christianity, by attributing the immolation of God to the debt of man, establishes a distorted economics. The belief that His grace can grant justice compounds this deformation. Christian tenets ensure that believers feel contrition oblivious to the privileges with which they invest Him. This bad conscience of guilt suspends belief between the self-accredited creditor and the credulous believer.

Faulkner desires a morality beyond any such economy. *A Fable*, his supreme presentation of a divinely imbued stoicism, offers an alternative that eschews the grace of God. Stefan Dumont advances an ethics, or discourse of the Rights of Man, that extends neighborly good will to all human beings. Commitment to this belief forces the church to admit its complicity in the war. His last rites effect this confession. The priest of the sacraments recognizes the divine in Stefan rather than a sullied version of spirituality. Such morality, a revelation that he has spent a lifetime dedicated to Caesarism rather than to Divinity, completely disillusions this man of God.[10] The priest expresses his enlightenment by taking his own life. This death prefigures Stefan's passive suicide before the firing squad. RAF pilot David Levine follows the same course. Suicide is a passionate means for denying the wartime environment, an irreversible possibility for reuniting the spirit of man with the numinous. A condensed concatenation of the name David Levine signifies this desired ascent toward divinity. Such ascendance, dispossession in which responsibility is anterior to any freedom, goes further than altruism.

A Fable makes this beyond evident. Following Stefan's crucifixion, and Faulkner explicitly constructs this symbolism, he is interred in no-man's-land on the family farm. Paradoxically, the pacifist seems to have returned to the front line, but this aporic space must be judged resolutely apt when a shell during the next German offensive atomizes both Stefan's coffin and any sense of irony. This is a crucifixion followed not so much by a resurrection as an insurrection. Stefan's conscience has transmigrated to the battalion runner. Biological inheritance plays an important role in this metempsychosis. Biology may predispose *Homo sapiens* to live and let live in a situation of entrenched hostilities, but the extent to which this immanence surfaces varies. *A Fable* illustrates that innate behavior is more prominent in the ranks than in the ruling classes. Education has cultural benefits for the élite but concurrently suppresses inherence. Privates in World War I were the ones who came face to face with the enemy most often. The persistence of the destructive other penetrated their human quiddity. Living with this harmful presence, combined with the less etiolated predisposition of privates, meant that initial hatred for their enemy counterparts started to dwindle. Internal friction now emerged as a mediating factor in a war purportedly between nation states.

Not about the primacy of the community over the individual as territorial outsider, this was a conflict between the upper ranks of society and the supposedly lower-class members of that community. These subordinate insiders were potential agents for the deformation of the social hierarchy. Under their guidance, World War I would not only level class structures, but also abolish the concept of patriarchal fatherlands. Faulkner's numinously endowed Darwinism links alterity to singularity toward this end. The peoples of the Earth descend from a common origin of unknown divinity. Faulkner secures the covenant between the universal and the singular with the intimation that everyone must be open to every other. This contract is the gift of secret love, love without reserve, love that goes beyond genetics, indices of relatedness, and considerations of nation states. One must give without reserve. Even those whom you believe to be unappreciative must receive this bequest. Such should be the gift of death. In his reassessment of Christian mythology, Faulkner posits the corporal as a man with no alternative but to prosecute his own death. Faulkner's aesthetic of suicide is, then, an act of sublation. The conflict between natural science and theology is resolved into a higher unity. Evolution and metaphysics resound in a mature contemplation of the position of humankind in a universal environment.

Does not proposing a singularity without organized religion signal impersonal lives in which no values are shared other than the selfishness prompted by our genetic constitution? Without a sense of community, will not anxiety return individually and en masse? Post-Faulknerian philosophy helps to answers these questions.

Utilitarian philosopher Derek Parfit argues that to counteract the impersonal strain to metropolitan life one must behave in an impersonal manner (444). One's critical concern must not be oneself, nor must one give the boundaries between lives supreme importance. The fundamental ratiocinative unit must no longer be the agent throughout that individual's life but must become the agent at the time of acting. An impersonal approach to life denies self-interest, gives more importance to each person's particular beliefs, and distinguishes between individuals according to ideation. The fear that such a move engenders is not a surprise. The effect of evolution, the selfishness inherent in the differential survival of replicating entities, promotes self-interest not only at the biological level, but also at the level of cultural inheritance. Does not this immanence excuse egoism? No, to reiterate, an evolutionary explanation neither supports nor undermines an inherited propensity. "The fact that we have this attitude," Parfit insists, "cannot be a reason for thinking it justified" (308).

Postmodernity, the sense of competing accounts rather than a single version of the real, paradoxically engenders an overriding dependence on determinate identity. This reliance predetermines a deep further fact, one that is distinct from physical and psychological continuity. Most people believe in such an entity. The Cartesian ego is one example. However, just as this model begs the question, so the continual existence of any such entity fails. An explanation of the unity of an individual's life must not claim that that person has all the experiences in that life. Personal identity, as far as Parfit concedes to the concept, must be described as the various relations "that hold between those different experiences, and their relations to a particular brain" (445). This is an appeal to psychological connectedness within psychological continuity. In this approach, a description of an individual's life does not claim that that person's existence is some profound further truth. This descriptive process champions the importance of fictional delineation. Persons exist, but persons are not fundamental. This is the impersonal philosophy of Reductionism.

Faulkner had taken initial steps toward the concept of impersonality in "Ad Astra" (1931).[11] This short story is set in the red light district of a French town. The narrative concerns a "subadar," a group of Allied airmen, and their German prisoner at the end of World War I (407). Innate turpitude runs riot. Only the Indian major and the captured officer seem capable of controlling themselves. Each is a Faulknerian sage, and although ostensibly enemies, these two combatants have become wise brothers. They contend that the Great War will not end warfare because nationalism perpetuates barbarism. The patriarchal notion of a fatherland perverts the two-sided genealogy of *Homo sapiens* in favor of the male line. Faulkner's wise men have disowned this privileged descent and formed a bond of brotherhood. In fact, the German has long renounced his birthright by allowing his baronage to pass to a younger brother. "He talks of Germany, the fatherland," explains the captive recalling an argument with his father, "I, brotherland, I say, the word *father* iss that barbarism which will be first swept away; it iss the symbol of that hierarchy which hass stained the history of man with injustice of arbitrary instead of moral; force instead of love" (*Collected Stories* 417).

First born he may be, but ultimately he is a son as genealogical apostate. "Ad Astra" thereby denies a stereotypical bellicose streak in the German people insisting, rather, that there is a belligerent streak in the spear side of the human species, which only wisdom can disarm. The wise men further realize that they can stay the evil of cultural inheritance only with respect to themselves. They can enlighten few others. Irony endorses the stupidity of those around them. Faulkner leaves out *per Ardua* from the RAF motto in the title "Ad Astra." The arduousness of the struggle to reach the stars, the four years of strain for a better world order that was World War I, appears forgotten. Faulkner adumbrates the fate of humankind with this omission. Our species will not transcend the confines of the Earth. Humans remain rooted to the biosphere and haunted by the phantasmagoric environment of the mind. No wonder that the aviators in "Ad Astra" are last glimpsed weighed down to terra firma in a Faulknerian "Nighttown" of drunkenness, brothels, vomiting, and violence.

Faulkner understood evolution to be the universal process. He also sensed that this biological base has spawned a cultural superstructure. Richard Dawkins would later term the cultural strand of this mechanism, the aspect that presented to Faulkner the ready means for social as well as artistic progress, *memetic*. For the Faulknerian paradigm, as for present-day genetics, biological building blocks have their equivalent in the cultural environment. Natural selection works by the rejection of unstable genes; survivors replicate and tend toward stability. Cultural transmission has similarly given rise to a form of evolution, but a movement that outpaces its biological counterpart by orders of magnitude. Language is the basis of this environment. If a single word, name, or phrase is sufficiently distinctive and memorable to be abstractable from its particular context, then it is one *meme*. Dawkins's neologism, resonating with its counterpart of *gene*, ideates a unit of cultural transmission; having a root from the word mimesis, meme concurrently indicates a sense of imitation.

Darwin had understood the importance of imitation to societal evolution. For, "as soon as the progenitors of man became social (and this probably occurred at a very early period), the principle of imitation, and reason, and experience would have increased, and much modified the intellectual powers in a way, of which we see only traces in the lower animals" (*Descent* 129).

Dawkins's list of memes includes "tunes, ideas, catch-phrases, clothes fashions, ways of making pots or of building arches." Moreover, "just as genes propagate themselves in the gene pool by leaping from body to body via sperms or eggs," continues Dawkins, "so memes propagate themselves in the meme pool by leaping from brain to brain via a process which, in the broad sense, can be called imitation. If a scientist hears, or reads about, a good idea, he passes it on to his colleagues and students. He mentions it in his articles and his lectures. If the idea catches on, it can be said to propagate itself, spreading from brain to brain" (*Selfish* 192).

Social geneticists consider the meme a technical and metaphorical living structure, a fertile replicating entity that parasitizes the brain of a new host, as Faulkner demonstrates with capitalism and Flem Snopes, turning that mind "into a vehicle for the meme's propagation in just the way that a virus may parasitize the genetic mechanism of a host cell. And," continues N. K. Humphrey, "this isn't just a way of talking—the meme for, say, 'belief in life after death' is actually realized physically, millions of times over, as a structure in the nervous systems of individual men the world over" (Dawkins, *Selfish* 192). If biological evolution selects genes with longevity, fecundity, and accuracy of replication, then memes similarly experience differential survival in cultural terms with language as the crucial medium. The major advantage of memes over genes is their ability to survive in nonsomatic forms: an environment autonomous of the human brain, an environment of books, magnetic tapes, compact discs, and so forth. As a corollary, human understanding does not merely change, but can improve.

A Fable reiterates the importance to the high command of retaining the meme singled out by the sages of "Ad Astra" for disapprobation. The group commander describes this particular concept for his divisional superior:

> We can permit even our own rank and file to let us down on occasion; that's one of the prerequisites of their doom and fate as rank and file forever. They may even stop the wars, as they have done before and will again; ours merely to guard them from the knowledge that it was actually they who accomplished that act. Let the whole vast moil and seethe of man confederate in stopping wars if they wish, so long as we can prevent them learning that they have done so. A moment ago you said that we must enforce our rules, or die. It's no abrogation of a rule that will destroy us. It's less. The simple effacement from man's memory of a single word will be enough. But we are safe. (715–16)

"Do you know what that word is?" he asks his colleague, meeting a hesitant reply with the rejoinder, "Fatherland" (716). The wise men in this instance are the corporal, the battalion runner, the RAF pilot, and the quartermaster general. Each rebuffs the concept of nation states and each from an impersonal perspective. Nations and persons are analogous. The individuality of nation states and citizens are empty questions, that is, queries in which any solution remains equivocal despite thorough understanding. That one can always make a decision over the empty question of identity leads to a continual wrangling over boundaries, both national and personal. Paul Gilroy's twenty-first-century philosophy in *Against Race* (2000) has recently developed the concept of *planetary humanism*. This approach holds human consciousness responsible for the problems facing the planet, encourages a globally embracing perspective that values all peoples equally, and welcomes the considered contributions from humankind to a more benign future. Gilroy's concept intends a bringing together of organizations—governmental, corporational, civil, and nongovernmental—to further this end. Faulkner seems more radical in comparison. His war work rejects discursive and representational conventions concerning that bounded entity of the father and his land that is nationality. Furthermore, in deconstructing national boundaries, Faulkner puts personal identity at stake too.

The figuration of messianic avatars in *A Fable* hint at the need to promote an impersonal vigilance of consciousness stripped of the subjectivity of that consciousness, a diminution of personal identity as a manner of advancing human solidarity. Faulkner's aesthetic evolves toward Reductionism rather than the return to human paramountcy suggested by Malcolm Cowley, the universal humanism by which Cleanth Brooks categorized him (6), the planetary humanism of Gilroy, or the humanist Marxism promoted by Frantz Fanon. Faulknerian art therefore recognizes but diverges from the reorientation of empiricism advocated by William James. James's pragmatic approach, his insistence that the making of reality takes place in the connections between moments of experience, appealed to Faulkner, for whom stream-of-consciousness techniques were so propitious. "Things," writes James, "are *with* one another in many ways, but nothing includes everything, or dominates over everything." This form of social pluralism collapses the distinction between the individual entity and entities en masse. In political terms, then, social pluralism promotes a "'federal republic' rather than an 'empire' or a 'kingdom'" (776). A federalistic philosophy is evident in Faulkner's evolving ideas of the proper and rightful relation of the South to, and responsibility toward, the United States of America. However, whereas James was, in David Kadlec's estimation, "poised between a liberal 'exceptionalist' vision of an 'organic democracy' and a less nationalistic anarchist vision of a society free from the very political impediments that blocked free transactions between producers and consumers," Faulkner's developing ideas, a philosophy grounded in Darwinism and akin to Reductionism, championed the relationships between moments of experience as a benignant future for humankind (27).

Reductionists do not believe that personal identity involves a deep further fact. Beyond racial politics, living through a fragmented era in which he witnessed the social evolution evident in the expansion of the hamlet into the metropolis, Faulkner's mature aesthetic discloses a coming to terms with impersonal existence. Barriers—those between individuals and those between oneself and one's future selves—must be broken down. *A Fable* demonstrates this deconstruction with the corporal as a messianic avatar, and the battalion runner as an avatar of the corporal. Faulkner's figuration implies that the corporal is vital not in his corporeality, not as a genetic replicator, but in his success as a replicator of memes. The endurance of these memes, those of a deconstructive agency, is required for a benignancy to come. For although proven cultures experience only adaptations and survive across generations, large mutations can produce cultural traumas: regressive regimes forcing the abandonment of large sections of cultural heritage to institute renewed ignorance. In addition, one must accept that cultural inheritance enables *Homo sapiens* to deny cosmological dependence. This resistance spawns new myths—the conquering of space or an exemption from biological evolution—with narcissism making a return. Darwin's lack of hubris in this regard is refreshing. Consider, for example, this quotation from *The Origin of Species*: "Looking to the future, we can predict that the groups of organic beings which are now large and triumphant, and which are least broken up, that is, which have as yet suffered least extinction, will, for a long period, continue to increase. But which groups will ultimately prevail, no man can predict; for we know that many groups, formerly most extensively developed, have now become extinct" (*Origin* 96).[12]

Faulkner's respect for evolution in the year of his death echoes this Darwinian caution. "We don't know what man might evolve into," he said, "just how low he is, what flea he is on, something that we can't even see, it is so great, so vast" (*West Point* 110). Alongside these intimations of beyond, however, there can, and must, be a modern morality that actively sublimates religion. In an environment that circumscribes humans within the world of nature, Faulkner's art intimates a continuous anonymous commune, one without continents, without nations, a solidarity that is not a nameless mass, as pangenesis purports, but a collection of individuals as assured by genetics. This solidarity does not promote deconstruction commensurate with a complete lack of difference. An incongruously anodyne vision of an impelling world—like that decried by Faulkner (again in 1962) in which there is "more and more pressure on the individual to relinquish into one faceless serration like a mouthful of teeth, simply in order to find room to breathe"—is not the aim (Brodsky 200).[13] Indeed, he wished to promote, as Louis Daniel Brodsky confirms, "an individuality of excellence compounded of resourcefulness and independence and uniqueness" (200). Conversely, he did not wish America to be one of the great problem children of societal evolution. Individuals must maintain their active reality but remain capable of feeling the situation of others. He recognized that the construct of solidarity requires freedom practiced with responsibility.

Taking responsibility for oneself is a move toward democratization, but making this move, one that threatens the authority and orientation of a current state, elicits a backlash. Throughout history, the outcast has brought about this reaction from individuals opposed to a less delimited society. Explicit questioning about the social fabric put Socrates to death. In Faulkner's distant Socratic echoes, Joe Christmas is murderously mutilated for his very presence as a possible miscegene, Nancy Mannigoe is hanged for discrediting the patriarchal concept of purity, and Stefan Dumont is shot for his passivity. Their executioners desired a societal stasis: in Faulkner's synonymity, a community of "death" (*University* 271).[14] Faulkner witnessed the response of civilization to the horrors of the American Civil War, World War I, and World War II. These reactions brought the realities of increased freedom and greater tolerance to the fore. Manumission, the Roaring Twenties, and the baby boom of the 1950s are notable examples of the resultant liberalism. Concurrently, however, a feeling of vulnerability brought reactionary demands for a closed society. Redemption, Prohibition, and the House Un-American Activities Committee emanated from this insecurity.

Evolutionary philosopher Karl Popper, in works including *The Open Society and its Enemies* (1945), *Conjectures and Refutations: The Growth of Scientific Knowledge* (1963), and *Objective Knowledge: An Evolutionary Approach* (1972), offers a twofold response to the fears associated with societal loosening. Firstly, rectify abuses and anomalies within the existing paradigm of power to minimize avoidable suffering. Secondly, continue to extend the range of choices open to the individual. To effect a revolution from a closed to an open society, one must maximize the responsible freedom of the individual. Popper's aim is an association of free individuals under the aegis of a benevolent state. Responsible decision making and respect for each other's rights can ensure the prospect of humane democracies to come. Historically significant developments to society arise from human interaction with the physical environment, interaction between humans, and human interaction with the environmental elements that humankind has constructed and continues to construct. Human purpose, asserts Popper, propels historic purpose, and humans endow any meaning attributed to history.

The process of evolution preordains that few people can make any significant difference to life on earth. Realization of this predetermination should produce a double response: one, an antidote to dissolution, such as the Faulknerian writer's trace; two, a determination to effect this cure however difficult that remedy appears. Faulkner argues against political attempts to actualize a blueprint. For Faulkner, as for Popper, the eschaton of any political rationale must accept the current sociopolitical situation as its origin. Authentic alteration, as distinct from unrealistic visions, can only work with existing circumstances. However, as Faulkner's chronicles of the Old South and World War I attest, the reaction from the rulers of society is seldom benign. That many oppose such measures is less surprising when one considers the deep psychological, as well as material, effects of agendas that augur disorientation. Southerners, for example, felt the fear of dissolution and deracination stemming from social transformation. Faulkner understood that despite dreams of perfection, political development requires progress rather than an attempted clean sweep. Evolution in biology and in human sociology, genes and memes, predetermines change as ever present (excluding, that is, complete annihilation). An ideal civilization is unattainable because corresponding to a blueprint petrifies society. *Stasis*, for Faulkner, as for Popper and Parfit, denotes death, while *dynamis* denotes the vitality of "evolution" and "improvement" ("To Albert Erskine" 429). None of them sees humankind as a jaded species devoid of recuperative power. Maturation of the individual mind and the political body will enable the species to endure and to improve.

Faulkner's aesthetic follows such a course. Through a process of constant feedback, his artistic imagination incorporated and slowly sublimated new ideas into his fiction. The resultant critical aestheticism necessarily advanced his art: "So if what I write in 1958 ain't better than what I wrote in 1938, I should have stopped writing twenty years ago, or, since 'being alive' equals 'motion,' I should be 20 years in the grave" ("To Albert Erskine" 429). His ideological course proposes the globalization of secular morality rather than the worldwide expansion of organized religions that is happening today via Christianity or Islam. A model as radical as Faulkner's suggests the deconstruction of this bulwark of individual identity along with concepts of race and nationhood. This approach fits with Parfit's assertion that personal identity is not what matters. One must have a sense, a common sense of morality based on the recognition of alterity, alterity with others and alterity with one's other selves as time elapses. Such a paradigm is ahead of its time, a state to come, a struggle without solution. Faulknerian ideology admits such an irresolvable effort.

In Popperian terms, an endless and gradual modification of the traditional contentions of form and figuration made under the pressure of singular demands accounts for the history of literature. Popper's formula for the pattern underlying this continuous development is P1→TS→EE→P2. P1 is the initial problem; TS is the trial solution; EE is the elimination of error; P2 is the result. This outcome is a new problematic because feedback always modifies the initial situation. If P1 equals P2 then TS does not attempt a solution, or error elimination remains to be processed. Any genuine attempt at TS and EE precludes complete failure. A better understanding of the minimum conditions for a solution is the very least achievement. P2 is always an advance on P1. Popper's formulation disregards Hegelian dialectics because personal identity would become a matter of pure contradiction and prejudice is a judgment that does not admit to being a problem. A task does not begin with the attempt to solve a dilemma but with the delineation of that problem and the reasons for that quandary. The formulation of problems should be the first priority, only then can one search for answers. Successful solutions often arise because the stage of problematization has been thorough.[15]

The preservation of memes enables the process of critical retrospection to continue between different organisms and over consecutive generations. In such a manner, continual adjustments can improve complex abstractions, and histories can be traced as continuous arguments rather than confined to Viconian circularity. Guided by the aesthetic, ideological, and philosophical development of its subject, the present study has attempted to practice this recursive progression. To defy the restrictive borders of race, but to think in these terms, is a necessity.

Starting within this domain, following the consequences on racial thinking of Darwinian pangenesis, and supplementing those repercussions with more accurate findings from genetic science enables an evolutionary hermeneutic to be racially self-effacing. When everyone comes to practice such thinking, rationality will no longer harbor racism. Faulkner's approach to racial politics, and in the larger scheme, to a twentieth-century politics, exhibits this approach in his desire to solve problems productive of committed art. His works combine an intellectual exercise with an emotional involvement in their ecological situation. They improve human understanding of the human condition. If Faulkner the man seems less important in the opening years of the twenty-first century than he did on receiving the Nobel Prize for Literature, then this loss testifies to the success of his self-effacing philosophy concerning "Man in his dilemma—facing his environment" (*Lion* 277).

NOTES

CHAPTER 1

1. One should note, though, that Darwin had made an impact on literate Americans before the Civil War with *A Naturalist's Voyage* (1839). Henry David Thoreau (1817–1862) turns to this account to support his own economy, or philosophy of living, as set out in *Walden; or Life in the Woods* (1854).
2. Henceforth, unless stated otherwise, citations from *The Origin of Species* pertain to this edition.
3. James Allen Cabaniss and David G. Sansing provide the most informative historical sources concerning the University of Mississippi.
4. Little means the Irish scientist and natural philosopher John Tyndall (1820–1893).
5. Isaac Newton (1643–1727) was an English mathematician and scientist. John Dalton (1766–1844) was an English chemist and physicist.
6. More than circumspection reigned in English academia. Writing of his parents, H. G. Wells (1866–1946) rails in *The Fate of Homo Sapiens* (1939) against the prevention of scientific dissemination in the second half of the nineteenth century, especially the lack of desire to impart Darwinian discoveries. "To this day," he fumes, "I will confess I dislike this restriction and distortion of knowledge, as I dislike nothing else on earth. In the modern world, it is, I hold, second only to murder to starve and cripple the mind of a child" (9).
7. Whitman worked for both institutes concurrently in 1888.
8. The Leopold and Loeb case is immortalized today by *Rope* (1948), the Alfred Hitchcock (1899–1980) film based on the 1929 play by Patrick Hamilton (1904–1962).
9. Refer to *The Creation/Evolutionary Controversy: A Battle for Cultural Power* by Kary Doyle Smout for more on Bryan's early skepticism (48–49).
10. Hume made his changes to campus regulations during his initial tenure as chancellor, which lasted between 1924 and 1930. His second period in office covered 1932 to 1935.
11. The worldwide coverage that accompanied Bryan's death in the wake of the Scopes Trial found a comic literary rendering two years later in *Fiesta: The Sun Also Rises* (1927) by Ernest Hemingway (1899–1961). During a day of fishing at Burguete in the Basque region of Spain, Jacob Barnes and Bill Gorton settle down to lunch. "We unwrapped the little parcels of lunch," notes Barnes:

"Chicken."
"There's hard-boiled eggs."
"Find any salt?"
"First the egg," said Bill. "Then the chicken. Even Bryan could see that."
"He's dead. I read it in the paper yesterday."
"No. Not really?"
"Yes. Bryan's dead."

Bill laid down the egg he was peeling.
"Gentlemen," he said, and unwrapped a drumstick from a piece of newspaper. "I reverse the order. For Bryan's sake. As a tribute to the Great Commoner. First the chicken; then the egg."
Burguete, as Hemingway's travelogue from France to Spain suggests, is remote. Barnes must have read of Bryan's demise in the Spanish press. Gorton caps the interchange with the advice that, on reflection, they should "not pry into the holy mysteries of the hen-coop with simian fingers" (106).

CHAPTER 2

1. This list of faiths is in descending order of followers (Brooks 57). The Scopes Trial offered evidence of the religious volatility of these groups. Baptists, Methodists, and Presbyterians were the most outspoken declaimers of Darwinism during the proceedings (Synan 187). Faulkner's fiction would later describe Baptists and Methodists as "incorrigible and unreconstructible" (*Town* 269).
2. Unfortunately, as Susan Snell notes, a fire in the 1940s destroyed Stone's house and there is no catalogue of his library (361).
3. Even so, the Nashville circle was on record from an early date about "Faulkner's promise and his genius" (Brooks 4).
4. In his letters from Europe, Faulkner attests to his interest at the Louvre in the "more-or-less moderns, like Degas and Manet and Chavannes" as well as the excitement with which he viewed "a very very modernist exhibition the other day—futurist and vorticist." In the same letter, however, he also acknowledges the classical tradition: "the Winged Victory and the Venus de Milo, the real ones, and the Mona Lisa" ("To Mrs. M. C. Falkner" 13).
5. Billy Sunday, although in Oregon at the time of the Dayton trial, openly supported the prosecution, proffered the Christian scriptures as consolation for the teachings of evolution, and became, on Bryan's death, a major proponent of fundamentalism. The present study encounters Sunday again when considering Faulkner's *A Fable* (1954).
6. Faulkner, as Helen McNeil notes, would always retain his Francophilia (704).
7. Please note, as a caveat to this statement, that Chapter 3 does tackle *Soldiers' Pay*, but from the specific Darwinian perspective of sexual selection.
8. See Anderson's *Memoirs* for more information about this interlude (198).

NOTES 213

9. Synonyms for the devil include Abbadon, the Arch-fiend, Auld Thief, Beelzebub, Belial, Deuce, the Evil One, Foul Fiend, His Satanic Majesty, Lord of the Flies, Lucifer, Mephisto, Mephistopheles, Moloch, Old Clootie, Old Gentleman, Old Gentleman in Black, Old Harry, Old Hornie, Old Nick, Old One, Old Scratchy, Prince of Darkness, Satan, the Tempter, and the Wicked One.
10. Andrew Jackson (1767–1845), born in the backwoods of South Carolina, became the seventh American president (1829–1837).
11. *Generelle Morphologie der Organismen* translates as *The General Morphology of Organisms*, *Natürliche Schöpfungsgeschichte* as *A Natural History of Creation*.
12. *Anthropogenie oder Entwickelungsgeschichte des Menschen* translates as *The Production of Humans or the Developmental History of Humans*.
13. "We self-protectively interpret as providence," confirms British scholar Gillian Beer, "that which is chance" (178).
14. For another view in agreement with Hunt's thesis, see Cleanth Brooks (123–35).
15. This is an appropriate book, because the Old Testament is one of the first genealogical texts.
16. Read anagrammatically, the name C(olonel) Sartoris approximates to the word aristocrat. Faulkner, of course, was fond of crosswords, anagrams, and the like.
17. Faulkner drew on the history of his own family in this respect. According to his brother, Jack, their paternal grandfather, the Young Colonel, John Wesley Thompson Falkner (1848–1922), "saw his beloved country devastated even more by the carpetbaggers in peace than it had been by the enemy soldiers in war" (7).
18. "In Memoriam" (1850) by Alfred Lord Tennyson (1809–1892) describes the law of nature as "red in tooth and claw" (1105).
19. When the monument to the Confederate soldier in Oxford was to be erected on the north of the town square, notes Jack Falkner, the boys' paternal grandmother insisted "that a southern soldier, even in granite, should be on the south side of anything . . . and should face the south" (30).
20. *A Fable* would offer an evolutionary summation and extrapolation of Ford's influence as one of "the hero-giant precentors" of humankind: "in Detroit today an old-time bicycle-racer destined to be one of the world's giants, his very surname an adjectival noun in the world's mouth, who had already put half a continent on wheels by families, and in twenty-five more would have half a hemisphere on wheels individually, and in a thousand would have already effaced the legs from a species just as that long-age and doubtless at the time not-even-noticed twitch of Cosmos drained the seas into continents and effaced the gills from their fish (839)."
21. "Red Leaves" was first published in *The Saturday Evening Post* (1930) before appearing in Faulkner's compendium *These Thirteen* (1931).

Chapter 3

1. Erasmus Darwin (1731–1802), the grandfather of Charles Darwin and Francis Galton, was an English physician, scientist, and poet. He met Anna Seward

(1747–1809) while living in Lichfield. Although a poet, she published a biography of him in 1803.
2. In archaic terms, a drake is an ensign or standard depicting a dragon.
3. Diane Roberts also decries the identification of Temple as a "calculating slut" (*Faulkner* 135).
4. Indeed, the general argument in this paragraph develops that proposed by Dawkins via Smith in chapter 9 of *The Selfish Gene* (1976).
5. A female could ensure constant attention from her mate by concealing when she is fertile. "Women," notes geneticist Steve Jones, "are the only female primates who do not make it obvious when they are most fertile" (*Language* 155).
6. Popeye the Sailor, created by the cartoonist Elzie Crisler Segar (1894–1938), first appeared in January 1929.
7. Russian-born French surgeon Serge Voronoff (1866–1951) promoted the implantation of monkey gland material into human testes. This procedure was a 1920s prosthetic equivalent to the present-day drug sildenafil citrate (trademark Viagra).
8. One intends the English pun of "tool" for "penis."
9. However, one pertinent example that demands attention here is "A Courtship" (1948). First published in the *Sewanee Review* and then reprinted in *Collected Stories of William Faulkner* (1950), this tale delineates the sexual selection played out between a Chickasaw Everywoman, designated only as Herman Basket's sister, and her three male admirers: David Hogganbeck, a Caucasian adventurer; the Chickasaw leader Ikkemotubbe; and an apparently inconsequential Native American named Log-in-the-Creek. The two main suitors strive in masculine competition for the right to her hand in marriage, but Herman Basket's sister remains indifferent to their antics. Peeved, Ikkemotubbe symbolically shows off his plumage. "Standing on the top of the little house," the chief is seen, "wearing the used general's coat which General Jackson gave [his ancestor] Issetibbeha" (370). This display does little to dispel the woman's disdain for Ikkemotubbe's lineage. Indeed, some members of her clan look upon his "whole family and line as mushrooms" (365). Having proven equally "masculine," both "men" agree to a decisive bout. The first combatant to enter an infamous cave— "a black hole in the hill which the spoor of wild creatures merely approached and then turned away"—and fire his gun into the gloom will be the winner (374). They do not deign to consult Herman Basket's sister who, while they are away contesting this tournament, chooses her spouse, accepting a man with a markedly different approach to courtship, a man who has not competed at all.

This unconventional competitor "raced no horses and fought no cocks and cast no dice, and even when forced to, he would not even dance fast enough to keep out of the other dancers' way, and disgraced both himself and the others each time by becoming sick after only five or six horns of what was never even his whisky" (363–64).

Despite Hogganbeck and Ikkemotubbe's physical overexertion, Herman Basket's sister marries Log-in-the-Creek, this marginal suitor who spends most of his time lying on his back playing the harmonica. Many males "fight together and arduously display their charms before the females," cautions *The Descent of Man*, but others do not so much pursue their intended as "pour forth their song in her presence" (221). Moreover, females often prefer "the best songsters" (214). Making this type of choice is a counterbalance to unrestrained secondary selection in which hypertrophied manifestations of male sexual attractiveness emerge despite attendant disadvantages. Natural selection ought to curb such extravagancies but if not, then females capable of seeing through sexual dissembling offer the only possible evolutionary control. In the absence of such discernment, extinction of the species is a distinct possibility. Herman Basket's sister provides such a restraint. She identifies Hogganbeck and Ikkemotubbe as potentially flawed philanderers. Faulkner's childhood courtship of Estelle Oldham had traversed a similarly disappointed course. "Bill tried to attract her attention," recalls his brother John, "by being the loudest one, the daringest. But the more he tried the more mussed he got, and sweaty, and dirtier, and Estelle simply wasn't interested" (85). No wonder, then, that the conclusive irony of "A Courtship" beautifully undercuts the stereotypical overemphasis on the captivation of demure femininity by aggressive masculinity so often encountered in Darwinian renditions of sexual relations. The logjam of courtship has been broken via a defiance of male bravado from both sides of the male-female divide, the potentially faithful Log-in-the-Creek gaining the right to discharge his weapon inside the dark cave of womanhood.

10. Another possible transcendentalist source in this regard is "Fate" (1860) by Ralph Waldo Emerson (1803–1882).

CHAPTER 4

1. Pythagoras postulated the dominant role of hematology in reproduction; Empedocles (c. 492–432 BC) proposed the notion of blending; historian Herodotus (c. 484–430 BC) used blood amalgamation to explain racial difference; Aristotle (384–322 BC) formulated that both parents contribute blood-extracts to the embryo. Aristotle's epistemological authority ensured the dominance of this concept until the time of Darwin.
2. "Hybrid," "hybridity," "hybridization," and so forth are terms for which, in the sense understood by French historian and social philosopher Michel Foucault, the quotation marks will be assumed, but the enduring importance of these marks remains as a problematization with regard to interracial congress.
3. Madison Grant (1865–1937) is discussed later in this chapter.
4. Alexander Hamilton (1755–1804) was an American politician, financier, and intellectual. Adam Smith (1723–1890) was a Scottish economist and moral philosopher. Matthew Fontaine Maury (1806–1873) was an American meteorologist, oceanographer, and astronomer. Alexander von Humboldt (1769–1859) was a Prussian naturalist, geologist, and explorer. Thomas Alva Edison (1847–1931) was an American inventor, businessman, and industrial pioneer.
5. "As for the poor whites," relates Margaret Mitchell's *Gone with the Wind*, "they considered themselves well off if they owned one mule" (21). "These were the

dirt farmers," relates Bayard Sartoris in *The Unvanquished* (1938), "the people whom the niggers called 'white trash'—men who had owned no slaves and some of whom even lived worse than the slaves on big plantations" (352).

6. Timothy Abbott Conrad (1803–1877) was a paleontologist and natural historian. John Eatton LeConte (1784–1860) was an explorer and zoologist. Joseph Leidy (1823–1891) was an anatomist. Robert Gibbes was an early-eighteenth-century paleontologist, so one assumes this is a mistaken reference to his descendent Lewis Reeves Gibbes (1810–1894), who was a professor of astronomy, mathematics, and physics at the College of Charleston in South Carolina. Francis S. Holmes (1815–1882) was a geologist and natural historian. John Edwards Holbrook (1794–1871) was a physician and naturalist. Henry William Ravenel (1814–1887) was a botanist. Appointed professor of mineralogy, geology, and agriculture at the University of Alabama in 1847, Michael Tuomey (1808–1857) conducted the Alabama Geological Survey the following year.

7. "States' Rights" are, for example, a clarion call in *Gone with the Wind* (209).

8. "A trace of albumin, of sugar, of cardiac arrhythmia, does not prevent life from continuing normally for the man who is not even aware of it," notes *In Search of Lost Time* (1913–1927) by Marcel Proust (1871–1922), "while the physician alone sees in it a prophecy of catastrophes in store." Peabody is one such Proustian physician (4: 610).

9. Oscar Wilde engages with notions of the throwback as an intensely disorientating presence in *The Picture of Dorian Gray* (1891). Lord Henry Wotton is a mentor to the young Gray. From this dubious source comes the gift of a novel portraying sexual and aesthetic hedonism: "For years, Dorian Gray could not free himself from the influence of this book . . . The hero, the wonderful young Parisian, in whom the romantic and the scientific temperaments were so strangely blended, became to him a kind of prefiguring type of himself" (123).

Characteristically a Jekyll and Hyde, not just a romancer and scientist, but an angel in appearance and a scoundrel beneath the skin, Gray contemplates his biological inheritance as a cause for this divide. "He loved to stroll through the gaunt cold picture-gallery of his country house and look at the various portraits of those whose blood flowed in his veins. Here was Philip Herbert, described by Francis Osborne, in his 'Memoires on the Reigns of Queen Elizabeth and King James,' as one who was 'caressed by the Court for his handsome face, which kept him not long company.' Was it young Herbert's life that he sometimes led? Had some strange poisonous germ crept from body to body till it had reached his own?" (137). Amalgamation abounds in this extract. The pangenetic concept of Darwin and Weismann's theory of the germ plasm seemingly intermingle in Gray's thoughts.

One of Faulkner's favored thriller writers and a friend of Wilde's in the early 1890s, Arthur Conan Doyle (1859–1930), would also exploit the idea of reversion in *The Hound of the Baskervilles* (1901–1902). Holmes uses Stapleton's instance as a throwback to unmask him as a distant ancestor of Sir Hugo and the criminal intent on murder to attain the Baskerville Estate. Holmes's evidence

rests on the resemblance between Sir Hugo's eyes, as captured in a family oil painting, and those of Stapleton (422–23).
10. Faulkner's Charles Mallison will later describe this tendency as "a double indemnity" (*Mansion* 502).
11. The *Canidae* comprises coyotes, dogs, foxes, jackals, and wolves. Most dogs belong to the genus *Canis*, most foxes to the genus *Vulpes*.

CHAPTER 5

1. One of the books Adolf Hitler (1889–1945) read while serving nine months in the military prison at Landsberg during 1924 was *Menschliche Erblichkeitslehre und Rassenhygiene* (or *Human Heredity Teaching and Racial Hygiene*) by Erwin Baur (1875–1933), Eugen Fischer (1874–1967), and Fritz Lenz (1887–1976). The views in this volume underpinned the eugenic and sterilization programs of his dictatorship.
2. In noting this controversy for African Americans, the present volume restates the concerns voiced by Houston A. Baker in his plenary address to the Faulkner and Yoknapatawpha Conference in 2002. Baker, who studied *Light in August* under the tutelage of Toni Morrison, was a coeval of Stokely Carmichael (1941–1998). The latter student's hatred of this novel was intense.
3. Faulkner was astute in this regard. With little support, even from their own region, the Fugitive-Agrarian movement would lose several of its ardent practitioners during the 1930s.
4. Faulkner's contemporary, H. G. Wells, understood the uselessness of such criteria. "And I lack exactitude—conspicuously," says Arnold Blettsworthy unconsciously confirming his avoidance of racial stereotyping in *Mr. Blettsworthy on Rampole Island* (1928). "For instance, I do not now to this day whether the Rampole islanders are dolichocephalic or brachycephalic; my impression is that their skulls are just medium assorted" (108). The ostensibly savage Rampole islanders turn out to be Blettsworthy's allegorical impression of Western Europeans.
5. Franklin H. Giddings (1855–1931) was an American sociologist. He used aspects of Spencer's work to elucidate his theory that a consciousness of kind leads to a homogeneous society.
6. Friedrich Rätzel (1844–1904) was a German geographer and ethnographer. He is notable for coining the term Lebensraum ("living space") and for his anthropological-geographical thoughts concerning cultural variation. Johann Friedrich Blumenbach (1752–1840) was German naturalist and anthropologist.
7. *Das Werden der Organismen, eine Widerlegung der Darwinschen Zufallslehre* translates as *The Origin of Organisms, a Refutation of Darwin's Theory of Probability*.
8. Modern science teaches us "that the average genetic difference between blacks and whites is smaller than that between individuals, whatever race they come from" (Jones, *Blood* 183). "The inheritance of acquired characteristics," Dawkins writes, "is not the aspect of his theory that Lamarck himself emphasised." In fact, as Dawkins makes plain, Lamarck "simply took over the conventional wisdom of

his time and grafted to it other principles like 'striving' and 'use' and 'disuse'" (*Extended* 167).
9. Ontopology, according to the definition of French philosopher Jacques Derrida, is "an axiomatics linking indissociably the ontological value of present-being [*on*] to its *situation*" (*Specters* 82).
10. No doubt, Butch's grave was oriented north to south rather than the standard east to west. "The disgrace in being buried north and south," explains Watkins, "is that since the sun rises in the east and sets in the west, on Resurrection Day, the sun will come up in the east; you'll rise up, face the Lord, and, if you're north and south, you're going to be looking the wrong way" (Wolff and Watkins 81).
11. French sociologist August Comte (1798–1857) coined the term altruism in *Catéchisme positiviste* (1852). For the purposes of the present study, altruism connotes individual acts to increase another's welfare at the expense of one's own interests.
12. It was in the late 1920s, as his brother John recalls, that Faulkner "took up hunting again" (156). The invitations "to go on General Stone's deer-and-bear hunt, at his lodge below Batesville in the virgin bottom lands of the Mississippi Delta," would serve Faulkner admirably for *Go Down, Moses* (156–57).

Chapter 6

1. Eight years before the events recounted in "Was," Louisiana physician Dr. Samuel A. Cartwright (1793–1863) had classified absconding from slavery as the main symptom of *drapetomania*. This desire to avoid servitude, explains his "Report on the Diseases and Physical Peculiarities of the Negro Race"(1851), is a biologically endowed mental aberration. His paper maintains that the best precaution against the onset of drapetomania is physical beating with metatarsal amputations reserved for severe sufferers. Diluted versions of this diagnosis continued into the 1920s. Jones notes that some scientists assumed "that there were genes for going to sea or for 'drapetomania'" (*Language* 46).
2. The confluence of the Tallahatchie and the Yalobusha form a tributary of the Mississippi called the Yazoo.
3. This figuration had particular resonance for Faulkner because of his great-grandfather William Clark Falkner. The Old Colonel had exchanged his slave Emeline Lacy (1837–1898) in part payment for a loan advanced by Benjamin E. W. Harris. Subsequently, Emeline bore a daughter she named Fannie. Their descendants, the Faulkner Hugheses, maintain that Falkner rather than Harris was Fannie's father (Williamson, *William Faulkner* 65). The grave of Emeline, lying as it does within fifty yards of the Old Colonel's Oxford interment, aptly shadows his patriarchal plot. Did the suspicion of miscegenation hover over William Cuthbert's estimation of his forebear?
4. Godden and Polk persuasively argue that this bequest is another misreading by Isaac. "*Fathers will*" could equally be L. Q. C. McCaslin's father rather than L. Q. C. himself (*Go Down, Moses* 199).

5. Six years after *Go Down, Moses* Faulkner reexamines this figuration in *Intruder in the Dust*. This novel closes with another demand from Lucas for official recognition. "Now what?" Gavin Stevens asks on receiving Lucas's unsolicited payment for legal services rendered. "What are you waiting for now?" Lucas's reply: "My receipt" (470).
6. That Faulkner intends such a parallel in Section IV of "The Bear" is not an overly ambitious claim. Mick Gidley makes a similar comparison in his reading of *Requiem for a Nun* (303–4). Faulkner's library also evinces his interest in classical literature. There are two copies of *The Complete Works of Homer* and separate copies of *The Iliad* and *The Odyssey* (Blotner, *Faulkner's Library* 25).
7. "If the next book goes [well]," Faulkner confided in a 1940 interview, "I'll buy some more land" (*Lion* 50). The next book happened to be *Go Down, Moses*! Faulkner was aware about the contradictions raised herein. "Brother Will," explains his nephew Jimmy, "felt a conflict about owning land. He owned land, but didn't like to see it exploited. He didn't like anybody or anything exploited" (Wolff and Watkins 172). Zender believes that Faulkner needed to be "a paterfamilias" after his father's death (*Crossing* 69). The possession of real estate helped to establish him in this role.

CHAPTER 7

1. DNA carries the genetic information within the soma. Faulkner's self-confidence in scientific matters was boosted in November 1953 when he met Albert Einstein (1879–1955) at Princeton.
2. Genetics explains dormancy as the result of dominant alleles: the effects of subordinate genes may only become apparent in later generations.
3. The Chinese mitten crab (*Eriocheir sinensis*) is native to the coastal rivers and estuaries of the Yellow Sea in Korea and China.
4. Kudzu, or *Pueraria lobata*, is a climbing, semiwoody, perennial vine of the pea family that the Centennial Exposition in Philadelphia, Pennsylvania, introduced to the United States from Japan in 1876. During the 1930s, agriculturists deemed the extensive root structure of kudzu an ideal solution to the problem of soil erosion in the South.
5. The Chinaman in Yoknapatawpha, continues Charles Mallison, is "sundered from his like and therefore as threatless as a mule" (*Town* 269).
6. *Forum* initially published "A Rose for Emily" before a revised version appeared in *These Thirteen* (1931).
7. John Maynard Smith's evolutionary game theory admonishes these characterizations, because Faulkner's figuration of the suitors is both predictable and unlikely.
8. There are further ecological implications from the explosion of the Thames mitten crab population. An omnivorous predator, the crab devours many organisms, including the rare, native, freshwater crayfish. The sudden increase in mitten crab numbers was considered such a serious threat in the United States

that imports of the species were banned in the 1990s—a law enforced with tough penalties.
9. His wife confirms Mink's speculation when she describes his semen as "rank poison" (*Hamlet* 954).
10. Faulkner's tragic enlightenment echoes the circumstances surrounding Darwin's eldest daughter, Annie. Her death, in 1851 at the age of ten, provided the English naturalist with a practical insight into his theory of natural selection. That Annie's illness was protracted and painful left Darwin convinced of his culpability as perpetuator of a blighted stock. He remained unenlightened, however, as to the larger homology. His own family had become a microcosm for the travail of Victorian life: a society in which physical discomfort, sickness, bereavement, pain, and death were the norm.
11. Dawkins recognizes "lots of these people on the evening news from such places as Belfast or Beirut" (*Selfish* 330). Unfortunately, while one can remove the capital of Northern Ireland from this list, one must now add Kabul and Baghdad.
12. Faulkner continues to supplement the description of Snopeses as other species in *The Mansion* with Clarence and his youngest brother Doris having "the moral principles of a wolverine" (597).
13. Blotner's catalogue entry for this item reads, "Freyre, Gilberto. *The Masters and the Slaves: A Study in the Development of Brazilian Civilization*. Translated from the Portuguese by Samuel Putnam. New York: Alfred A. Knopf, 1946. Autograph (with inscription): São Paulo, 9/8/1954 [indecipherable signature]" (*Faulkner's Library* 103).
14. Antônio Ladislau Monteiro Baena (1782–1850) was a Portuguese soldier, geographer, and historian. Freyre quotes from Baena's *Ensaio corográfico sobre a província do Pará* (or *Chorographic Essay on the Province of Pará*) from 1839.
15. Faulkner first published "The Waifs" as a short story in *The Saturday Evening Post* on 4 May 1957.
16. Flem's solitaire again recalls the figure of John Pierpont Morgan from Dos Passos's *U.S.A.*: "writing at his desk, smoking great black cigars, or, if important issues were involved, playing solitaire in his inner office. . . . Morgan sat in his suite at the Arlington smoking cigars and quietly playing solitaire until at last the President sent for him" (615).
17. Gavin Stevens, of course, had already compromised his high ideals by cooperating with Flem in the framing of Montgomery Ward.
18. Could Faulkner intend these others to be descendants of Flem's unnamed brother in "Barn Burning" (1939), the anonymous Snopes whom the adult Flem never mentions?

Chapter 8

1. Mutual cooperation, a seeming tautology, designates the simultaneous choice of nonaggression across a divide.
2. Davis's games of strategy apropos of *Go Down, Moses* are a different issue. The trickster, gambling, and related social empowerment are her focus.

3. For a detailed analysis of Faulkner and Taylor, see Yayoi Okada, "Faulkner's Christ in Reference to Jeremy Taylor," diss., Kwansei Gakuin University, 2004.
4. This chapter follows Faulkner's precedent.
5. The generalissimo offers the Judas figure for sacrifice. "You could," he cajoles Stefan, "call Polchek a lamb" (292).
6. *A Fable* does not document the months after the evolution of live-and-let-live tactics on the Western Front. During this period, officers tried to remedy what they often deemed to be subordinate lethargy. Their measures included the use of élite corps, the esteemed role of the sniper, and the instigation of raiding parties.
7. One need only think of those highly Christian figures in current global politics, Tony Blair (1953–) and George W. Bush (1946–), and their interventions in Afghanistan, Iraq, and possibly Iran.
8. The assassination of Archduke Franz Ferdinand (1863–1914), heir to the imperial throne of the Austro-Hungarian Empire, was one of the events that triggered the war.
9. Hitler was not directly involved at Verdun, but three other figures later notable in World War II experienced the battle firsthand: Charles De Gaulle (1890–1970), Henri Pétain (1856–1951), and Friedrich Paulus (1890–1957).
10. Caesarism is the tacit approval of autocracy and imperialism.
11. "Ad Astra" was published initially in *American Caravan* (1931) before appearing in *These Thirteen* (1931).
12. Alfred Russel Wallace (1823–1913), though, was guilty of such vanity in his paper on "The Origin of Human Races Deduced from the Theory of 'Natural Selection'" (1864). He believed that man could retain an "unchanged body in harmony with a changing universe" through the mental and moral faculties "which distinguish him from the lower animals" (clviii).
13. Faulkner voiced this fear of nondifferentiation in his final public acceptance speech when he received the Gold Medal for Fiction from the American and National Academies of Arts and Letters on 24 May 1962. His fiction, however, had carried this sentiment for years. "*You are born submerged in anonymous lockstep with the teeming anonymous myriads of your time and generation,*" thinks Harry Wilbourne in *If I Forget Thee, Jerusalem* (1939), "*you get out of step once, falter once, and you are trampled to death*" (531).
14. Richard P. Adams, who looks at Faulkner's novels as examples of arrested motion, thereby fails to appreciate the kind of reader-response theory espoused by Faulkner. When read, Faulkner hoped, his fiction would come startlingly to life. Only in getting his novels onto the page and into print were the forces within life that impel individual animation and generational continuation suspended.
15. For an extended analysis of Popperian philosophy in this vein, see Bryan Magee, *Popper* (London: Fontana, 1985).

WORKS CITED

Aaron, Daniel. "The South in American History." *The South and Faulkner's Yoknapatawpha: The Actual and the Apocryphal.* Ed. Evans Harrington and Ann J. Abadie. Jackson: University Press of Mississippi, 1977. 3–21.

Adams, Richard P. *Faulkner: Myth and Motion.* Princeton, NJ: Princeton University Press, 1968.

Agassiz, Louis. *Structure of Animal Life: Six Lectures Delivered at the Brooklyn Academy of Music in January and February 1866.* New York: Scribner, 1866.

Allen, Leslie H. *Bryan and Darrow at Dayton.* New York: Russell & Russell, 1967.

Althusser, Louis. *Lenin and Philosophy, and Other Essays.* Trans. Ben Brewster. New York: Monthly Review, 1971.

Ambrose, Douglas. *Henry Hughes and Proslavery Thought in the Old South.* Baton Rouge: Louisiana State University Press, 1997.

Anderson, Sherwood. "A Meeting South." *Dial* 78 (1925): 269–79.

———. *Sherwood Anderson's Memoirs. A Critical Edition.* Ed. Ray Lewis White. Chapel Hill: University of North Carolina Press, 1969.

Axelrod, Robert. *The Evolution of Cooperation.* New York: Basic, 1984.

Bachman, John. *The Doctrine of the Unity of the Human Race Examined on the Principles of Science.* Charleston, SC: Canning, 1850.

Baker, Houston A. "Traveling with Faulkner." Faulkner and his Contemporaries. Faulkner and Yoknapatawpha Conference. University of Mississippi, Oxford. 21 July 2002.

Bassett, John Earl, ed. *William Faulkner: The Critical Heritage.* London: Methuen, 1975.

Beer, Gillian. *Darwin's Plots: Evolutionary Narrative in Darwin, George Eliot and Nineteenth-Century Fiction.* Cambridge, UK: Cambridge University Press, 2000.

Beidler, Peter G. "A Darwinian Source for Faulkner's Indians in 'Red Leaves.'" *Studies in Short Fiction.* Newberry, SC: Newberry College, 1973. 421–23.

Bercovitch, Sacvan. *Rites of Ascent: Transformations in the Symbolic Construction of America.* New York: Routledge, 1993.

Billington, Monroe Lee. *The American South: A Brief History.* New York: Charles Scribner's Sons, 1971.

Blotner, Joseph. *Faulkner: A Biography.* 2 vols. London: Chatto & Windus, 1974.

———. *William Faulkner's Library: A Catalogue.* Charlottesville: University Press of Virginia, 1964.

Boas, Franz. "To Professor J. W. Jenks." 31 December 1909. *A Franz Boas Reader: The Shaping of American Anthropology: 1883–1911.* George W. Stocking. Chicago: University of Chicago Press, 1974. 213.

Bowler, Peter J. *The Mendelian Revolution: The Emergence of Hereditarian Concepts in Modern Science and Society.* London: Athlone, 1989.

Brodsky, Louis Daniel. *Life Glimpses.* Austin: University of Texas Press, 1990.

Brodsky, Louis Daniel, and Robert W. Hamblin, eds. *Faulkner: A Comprehensive Guide to the Brodsky Collection, Volume V: Manuscripts and Documents.* Jackson: University Press of Mississippi, 1985.

Brooks, Cleanth. *On the Prejudices, Predilections, and Firm Beliefs of William Faulkner.* Louisiana: Louisiana State University Press, 1987.

Buell, Lawrence. "Faulkner and the Claims of the Natural World." *Faulkner and the Natural World.* Ed. Donald M. Kartiganer and Ann J. Abadie, 1–18. Jackson: University Press of Mississippi, 1996.

Cabaniss, James Allen. *The University of Mississippi: Its First One Hundred Years.* Hattiesburg: University Collections Press of Mississippi, 1971.

Campbell, Modean, and Ruel E. Foster. *William Faulkner: A Critical Appraisal.* Norman, OK: University of Oklahoma Press, 1951.

Campbell, Neil. *Landscapes of Americanisation.* Derby: University of Derby, 2003.

Carothers, James B. "The Myriad Heart: The Evolution of the Faulkner Hero." *A Cosmos of My Own.* Ed. Doreen Fowler and Ann J. Abadie, 252–83. Jackson: University Press of Mississippi, 1981.

Carroll, Joseph. *Evolution and Literary Theory.* Columbia: University of Missouri Press, 1995.

Cartwright, Samuel. "Report on the Diseases and Physical Peculiarities of the Negro Race." *New Orleans Medical and Surgical Journal* 7 (May 1851): 691–715.

Cash, W. J. *The Mind of the South.* New York: Knopf, 1941.

Chambers, Robert. *Vestiges of the Natural History of Creation.* London: John Churchill, 1844.

Cohen, Philip. "Faulkner by the Light of a Pale Fire: Postmodern Textual Scholarship and Faulkner Studies at the End of the Twentieth Century." *Faulkner and Postmodernism.* Ed. John N. Duvall and Ann J. Abadie, 167–91. Jackson: University Press of Mississippi, 2002.

———. "The Last Sartoris: Benbow Sartoris' Birth in *Flags in the Dust.*" *Southern Literary Journal* 18, no. 1 (1985): 30–39.

Colatrella, Carol. *Evolution, Sacrifice and Narrative: Balzac, Zola, and Faulkner.* New York: Garland, 1990.

Collins, Carvel. "Afterword." *Faulkner Studies in Japan.* Ed. Thomas L. McHaney, 199–202. Athens: University of Georgia Press, 1985.

———. "Faulkner at the University of Mississippi." Introduction. *William Faulkner: Early Prose and Poetry.* William Faulkner. Boston: Little & Brown, 1962. 1–16.

Coody, A. S. *Biographical Sketches of James Kimble Vardaman.* Jackson, MS: A. S. Coody, 1922.

Coughlan, Robert. *The Private World of William Faulkner.* New York: Harper & Brothers, 1954.

Crews, Frederick C. *The Critics Bear It Away: American Fiction and the Academy.* New York: Random House, 1992.

Croly, David Goodman, and George Wakeman. *Miscegenation: The Theory of the Blending of the Races Applied to the American White Man and Negro.* London: Trübner, 1864.

Darwin, Charles. *The Descent of Man and Selection in Relation to Sex.* 2nd ed. London: John Murray, 1896.

———. *The Life and Letters of Charles Darwin, Including an Autobiographical Chapter.* Ed. Francis Darwin. 3 vols. London: John Murray, 1888.

———. *A Naturalist's Voyage. Journal of Researches into the Natural History and Geology of the Countries Visited during the Voyage of H. M. S. 'Beagle' Round the World under the Command of Captain Fitzroy, R. A.* 2nd ed. London: John Murray, 1888.

———. *The Origin of Species by Means of Natural Selection, or the Preservation of Favoured Races in the Struggle for Life.* 1st ed. 1859. Ed. J. W. Burrows and John Wyon. London: Penguin, 1968.

———. *The Origin of Species by Means of Natural Selection, or the Preservation of Favoured Races in the Struggle for Life.* 6th ed. London: John Murray, 1888.

———. "To J. D. Hooker." c. 1844. *The Life and Letters of Charles Darwin, Including an Autobiographical Chapter.* Ed. Francis Darwin. Vol. 1. London: John Murray, 1888. 179.

———. *The Variation of Animals and Plants under Domestication.* 2nd ed. London: John Murray, 1888.

Davis, Thadious M. *Games of Property: Law, Race, Gender, and Faulkner's Go Down, Moses.* London: Duke University Press, 2003.

Dawkins, Richard. *The Extended Phenotype: The Long Reach of the Gene.* Oxford, UK: Oxford University Press, 1999.

———. *The Selfish Gene.* Oxford, UK: Oxford University Press, 1989.

Derrida, Jacques. *The Gift of Death.* Trans. David Wills. Chicago: University of Chicago Press, 1995.

———. *Specters of Marx: The State of the Debt, the Work of Mourning, and the New International.* Trans. Peggy Kamuf. London: Routledge, 1994.

———. *Writing and Difference.* London: Routledge, 1978.

Dewey, John. "Darwin's Influence upon Philosophy." *Popular Science Monthly* 75 (1909): 90–98.

———. "Evolution and Ethics." *The Early Works of John Dewey, 1882–1898.* Ed. Jo Ann Boydston. Vol. 5. Carbondale: Southern Illinois University Press (1972). 34–54.

———. *The Influence of Darwin on Philosophy and Other Essays on Contemporary Thought.* New York: Henry Holt, 1910.

Dos Passos, John. *U.S.A.* London: Penguin, 2001.

Doyle, Arthur Conan. *The Hound of the Baskervilles. Sherlock Holmes: The Long Stories.* Leicester: Galley, 1987. 273–454.

Doyle, Don Harrison. *Faulkner's County: The Historical Roots of Yoknapatawpha, 1540–1962.* Chapel Hill: University of North Carolina Press, 2001.

Du Bois, W. E. B. *W. E. B. Du Bois Speaks: Speeches and Addresses, 1890–1919.* Ed. Philip S. Foner. London: Pathfinder, 1970.

Durant, John R. "The Ascent of Nature in Darwin's Descent." *The Darwinian Heritage.* Ed. David Kohn. Princeton, NJ: Princeton University Press, 1985. 283–306.

Emerson, Ralph Waldo. "Fate." *The Norton Anthology of American Literature.* 6th ed. Ed. Nina Baym, et al. Vol. B. New York: Norton, 2003. 1216–35.

———. "The Poet." *The Works of Ralph Waldo Emerson, Volume II.* London: Macmillan, 1893. 305–38.

———. "The Young American." *Essays and Lectures.* New York: Library of America, 1983. 214–37.

Evans, David Howell. "Communities of Confidence: William Faulkner, William James, and the American Pragmatic Tradition." Diss., Rutgers University of New Jersey, 1998. *DAI* 58, no. 7 (1998): 2651.

———. "Taking the Place of Nature: 'The Bear' and the Incarnation of America." *Faulkner and the Natural World.* Ed. Donald M. Kartiganer and Ann J. Abadie, 179–97. Jackson: University Press of Mississippi, 1996.

Evrie, John H. Van. *Negroes and Negro Slavery: The First an Inferior Race; the Latter Its Normal Condition.* New York: Orton, 1861.

Falkner, Murry C. *The Falkners of Mississippi: A Memoir.* Baton Rouge: Louisiana State University Press, 1967.

Faulkner, John. *My Brother Bill: An Affectionate Reminiscence.* New York: Trident, 1963.

Faulkner, William. *Collected Stories of William Faulkner.* New York: Vintage, 1995.

———. *Early Prose and Poetry.* Ed. Carvel Collins. Boston: Little & Brown, 1962.

———. *Essays, Speeches and Public Letters by William Faulkner.* Ed. James B. Meriwether. London: Chatto & Windus, 1967.

———. *Faulkner at West Point.* Ed. Joseph L. Fant and Robert Ashley. Jackson: University Press of Mississippi, 2000.

———. *Faulkner in the University.* Ed. Frederick Gwynn and Joseph Blotner. Charlottesville: University Press of Virginia, 1959.

———. *Flags in the Dust.* New York: Vintage, 1974.

———. *Knight's Gambit.* New York: Vintage, 1978.

———. *Lion in the Garden: Interviews with William Faulkner 1926–1962.* Ed. James B. Meriwether and Michael Millgate. New York: Random House, 1968.

———. *Mississippi Poems*. Oxford: Yoknapatawpha Press, 1979.
———. *New Orleans Sketches*. Ed. Carvel Collins. London: Chatto & Windus, 1958.
———. *The Portable Faulkner*. Ed. Malcolm Cowley. New York: Viking, 1946.
———. *Selected Letters of William Faulkner*. Ed. Joseph Blotner. London: Scolar, 1977.
———. "To Albert Erskine." 7 May 1959. *Selected Letters of William Faulkner*. Ed. Joseph Blotner, 429. London: Scolar, 1977.
———. "To Harold E. Howland." 15 August 1954. *Selected Letters*. 369.
———. "To Malcolm A. Franklin." 5 December 1942. *Selected Letters*. 165.
———. "To Mrs. M. C. Falkner." 18 Aug 1925. *Selected Letters*. 13.
———. *Uncollected Stories of William Faulkner*. Ed. Joseph Blotner. London: Chatto & Windus, 1980.
———. *William Faulkner Novels 1926–1929: Soldiers' Pay, Mosquitoes, Sartoris, The Sound and the Fury*. Ed. Joseph Blotner and Noel Polk. New York: Library of America, 2006.
———. *William Faulkner Novels 1930–1935: As I Lay Dying, Sanctuary, Light in August, Pylon*. Ed. Joseph Blotner and Noel Polk. New York: Library of America, 1985.
———. *William Faulkner Novels 1936–1940: Absalom, Absalom!, The Unvanquished, If I Forget Thee, Jerusalem, The Hamlet*. Ed. Joseph Blotner and Noel Polk. New York: Library of America, 1990.
———. *William Faulkner Novels 1942–1954: Go Down, Moses, Intruder in the Dust, Requiem for a Nun, A Fable*. Ed. Joseph Blotner and Noel Polk. New York: Library of America, 1994.
———. *William Faulkner Novels 1957–1962: The Town, The Mansion, The Reivers*. Ed. Joseph Blotner and Noel Polk. New York: Library of America, 1999.
Flinn, J. William. "Evolution and Theology, Part II." *The Southern Presbyterian Review* 36, no. 3 (1885): 507–89.
Franklin, Malcolm. *Bitterweeds*. Irving, TX: The Society for the Study of Traditional Culture, 1977.
Frazer, James George. *The Golden Bough: A Study in Magic and Religion*. London: Macmillan, 1976.
Freyre, Gilberto. *The Masters and the Slaves: A Study in the Development of Brazilian Civilization*. Trans. Samuel Putnam. New York: Knopf, 1970.
Gidley, Mick. "One Continuous Force: Notes on Faulkner's Extra-Literary Reading." *Mississippi Quarterly* 23, no. 3 (1970): 299–314.
Gilroy, Paul. *Against Race: Imagining Political Culture beyond the Color Line*. Cambridge, MA: Belknap of Harvard University Press, 2000.
Ginger, Ray. *Six Days or Forever? Tennessee v. John Thomas Scopes*. London: Oxford University Press, 1958.
Godden, Richard. *Fictions of Labor: William Faulkner and the South's Long Revolution*. Cambridge, UK: Cambridge University Press, 1997.

Godden, Richard, and Noel Polk. "Reading the Ledgers." *Mississippi Quarterly* 55, no. 3 (2002): 301–59.

Goldfield, David. *Still Fighting the Civil War: The American South and Southern History*. Baton Rouge: Louisiana State University Press, 2000.

Gould, Stephen J. *Leonardo's Mountain of Clams and the Diet of Worms: Essays on Natural World History*. New York: Harmony, 1998.

Gray, Richard. *The Life of William Faulkner: A Critical Biography*. Oxford, UK: Blackwell, 1994.

Hamilton, Walter. Introduction. *The Symposium*. Plato. London: Penguin, 1951. 9–30.

Hartman, Geoffrey. *Beyond Formalism: Literary Essays 1958–1970*. London: Yale University Press, 1970.

Hassan, Ihab. "The Privations of Postmodernism: Faulkner as Exemplar (A Meditation in Ten Parts)." *Faulkner and Postmodernism*. Ed. John N. Duvall and Ann J. Abadie. Jackson: University Press of Mississippi, 2002. 1–18.

Hemingway, Ernest. *Fiesta: The Sun Also Rises*. London: Arrow, 2004.

Higham, John. *Strangers in the Land: Patterns of American Nativism*. New Brunswick, NJ: Rutgers University Press, 1988.

Hitler, Adolf. *Mein Kampf*. Trans. Ralph Manheim. London: Hutchinson, 1973.

Hobson, Fred C. *Serpent in Eden: H. L. Mencken and the South*. Chapel Hill: University of North Carolina Press, 1974.

Hooton, Earnest Albert. *Apes, Men and Morons*. London: Allen & Unwin, 1938.

———. *Up from the Ape*. New York: Macmillan, 1931.

Hughes, Henry. "Reopening of the Slave Trade: A Series by 'St. Henry.'" *Selected Writings of Henry Hughes: Antebellum Southerner, Slavocrat, Sociologist*. Ed. Stanford M. Lyman. Jackson: University Press of Mississippi, 1985. 73–101.

———. *Treatise on Sociology: Theoretical and Practical*. Philadelphia: Lippincott, 1854.

Hunt, John. *William Faulkner: Art in Theology Tension*. Syracuse, NY: Syracuse University Press, 1965.

Hunter, George William. *A Civic Biology. Presented in Problems*. New York: American Book, 1914.

Huxley, Aldous. *Crome Yellow*. London: Chatto & Windus, 1974.

Huxley, Thomas Henry. *Collected Essays*. 9 vols. London: n.p., 1893–94.

———. *Darwiniana Collected Essays*. 2 vols. London: Macmillan, 1893.

———. *Man's Place in Nature and Other Anthropological Essays*. London: Appleton, 1929.

———. "Vestiges of the Natural History of Creation, Tenth Edition. London 1853." *The British and Foreign Medico-Chirurgical Review* 5 (1854): 1.

James, Henry. *Literary Criticism: French Writers, Other European Writers, the Prefaces to the New York Edition*. New York: Press Syndicate of the University of Cambridge, 1984.

James, William. *William James: Writings 1902–1910*. Ed. Bruce Kuklick. New York: Library of America, 1987.

Jann, Rosemary. "Darwin and the Anthropologists: Sexual Selection and Its Discontents." *Victorian-Studies: A Journal of the Humanities, Arts and Sciences* 37, no. 2 (1994): 288–96.
Jones, Steve. *In the Blood*. London: Flamingo, 1997.
———. *The Language of the Genes: Biology, History and the Evolutionary Future*. London: Flamingo, 2000.
Jordanova, L. J. *Lamarck*. Oxford, UK: Oxford University Press, 1984.
Kadlec, David. *Mosaic Modernism: Anarchism, Pragmatism, Culture*. Baltimore: Johns Hopkins University Press, 2000.
Kartiganer, Donald M. "Faulkner and the Ecology of the South." *The Southern Register* 2 (Spring/Summer 2003): 1.
Kinney, Arthur F. *Go Down, Moses: The Miscegenation of Time*. New York: Twayne, 1996.
Larson, Edward J. *Summer for the Gods: The Scopes Trial and America's Continuing Debate over Science and Religion*. Cambridge, MA: Harvard University Press, 1997.
———. *Trial and Error. The American Controversy over Creation and Evolution*. New York: Oxford University Press, 2003.
Levine, Lawrence W. *Defender of the Faith: William Jennings Bryan: The Last Decade, 1915–1925*. New York: Oxford University Press, 1965.
Lewisohn, Ludwig, ed. *A Modern Book of Criticism*. New York: Boni & Liveright, 1919.
Lindberg, David C., and Ronald L. Numbers. *When Science and Christianity Meet*. London: University of Chicago Press, 2003.
Lloyd, Francis E., and Maurice A. Bigelow. *The Teaching of Biology in the Secondary School*. New York: Longmans, 1904.
Loewenberg, Bert James. "Darwinism Comes to America, 1859–1900." *The Mississippi Valley Historical Review* 28, no. 3 (1941): 339–68.
Marx, Karl. *Capital: A Critique of Political Economy*. Vol. 1. London: Lawrence & Wishart, 1983.
Maynard Smith, John. *Evolution and the Theory of Games*. Cambridge, UK: Cambridge University Press, 1982.
Mayr, Ernst. *The Growth of Biological Thought: Diversity, Evolution and Inheritance*. Cambridge, MA: Harvard University Press, 1982.
———. "The Ideological Resistance to Darwin's Theory of Natural Selection." *Proceedings of the American Philosophical Society Held at Philadelphia for Promoting Useful Knowledge* 135, no. 2 (1991): 123–39.
McHaney, Thomas L. "Oversexing the Natural World: *Mosquitoes* and *If I Forget Thee, Jerusalem (The Wild Palms)*." *Faulkner and the Natural World*. Ed. Donald M. Kartiganer and Ann J. Abadie. Jackson: University Press of Mississippi, 1996. 19–44.
McNeil, Helen. "Homage to the Inevitable." *Times Literary Supplement*. 27 June 1986: 704.
Michaels, Walter Benn. *Our America: Nativism, Modernism, and Pluralism*. Durham, NC: Duke University Press, 2002.

Mitchell, Margaret. *Gone with the Wind*. London: Macmillan, 1974.
Morris, Willie. "Faulkner's Mississippi." *National Geographic* 175, no. 3 (1989): 318–40.
Mortimer, Gail. "Evolutionary Theory in Faulkner's Snopes Trilogy." *Rocky Mountain Review of Language and Literature* 40, no.4 (1986): 187–202.
Nasar, Sylvia. *A Beautiful Mind*. London: Faber, 1998.
Noble, David W. "Progress v. Tragedy: Veblin and Dreiser." *Intellectual History of America: from Darwin to Niebuhr*. Ed. Cushing Strout. New York: Harper & Row, 1968.
Nott, Josiah C. *Types of Mankind*. Philadelphia: Lippincott & Grambo, 1854.
Numbers, Ronald L. *Darwinism Comes to America*. Cambridge, MA: Harvard University Press, 1998.
Numbers, Ronald L., and John Stenhouse. *Disseminating Darwinism: The Role of Place, Race, Religion, and Gender*. Cambridge, MA: Cambridge University Press, 1999.
Ohba, Minako. "It Is His Reality." *Faulkner Studies in Japan*. Ed. Thomas L. McHaney. Athens: University of Georgia Press, 1985. 191–92.
Page, Sally R. *Faulkner's Women: Characterization and Meaning*. De Land, FL: Everett/Edwards, 1972.
Parfit, Derek. *Reasons and Persons*. Oxford, UK: Oxford University Press, 1987.
Peavy, Charles D. *Go Slow Now: Faulkner and the Race Question*. Eugene, OR: University of Oregon, 1971.
Pitavy, François. "Is Faulkner Green? The Wilderness as Aporia." Faulkner and the Ecology of the South. Faulkner and Yoknapatawpha Conference. University of Mississippi, Oxford. 23 July 2003.
Poliakov, Léon. *The Aryan Myth: A History of Racist and Nationalist Ideas in Europe*. London: Chatto & Windus, 1971.
Polk, Noel. *Faulkner's Requiem for a Nun: A Critical Study*. Bloomington: Indiana University Press, 1981.
Poundstone, William. *Prisoner's Dilemma: John von Neumann, Game Theory, and the Puzzle of the Bomb*. Oxford, UK: Oxford University Press, 1993.
Proust, Marcel. *In Search of Lost Time*. Trans. C. K. Scott Moncrieff and Terence Kilmartin. 6 vols. New York: Modern Library, 2003.
Radin, Paul. "Boas and 'The Mind of Primitive Man.'" *Books That Changed Our Minds*. Ed. Malcolm Cowley and Bernard Smith. New York: Kelmscott, 1939.
Railey, Kevin. *Natural Aristocracy: History, Ideology, and the Production of William Faulkner*. London: University of Alabama Press, 1999.
Roberts, Diane. "Eula, Linda, and the Death of Nature." *Faulkner and the Natural World*. Ed. Donald M. Kartiganer and Ann J. Abadie. Jackson: University Press of Mississippi, 1996. 159–78.
———. *Faulkner and Southern Womanhood*. Athens: University of Georgia Press, 1994.

Rogers, David. "The Irony of Idealism: William Faulkner and the South's Construction of the Mullato." *The Discourse of Slavery: Aphra Benn to Toni Morrison.* Ed. Carl Plasa and Betty J. Ring, 166–90. London: Routledge, 1994.
Sansing, David G. *Making Haste Slowly: The Troubled History of Higher Education in Mississippi.* Jackson: University Press of Mississippi, 1990.
———. *The University of Mississippi: A Sesquicentennial History.* Jackson: University Press of Mississippi, 1999.
Slovic, Scott. "Visceral Faulkner: Fiction and the Tug of the Organic World." Faulkner and the Ecology of the South. Faulkner and Yoknapatawpha Conference. University of Mississippi, Oxford. 20 July 2003.
Smith, Gerald J. "A Note on the Origin of Flem Snopes." *Notes on Mississippi Writers* 6 (1973): 56–57.
Smout, Kary Doyle. *The Creation/Evolutionary Controversy: A Battle for Cultural Power.* Westport, CT: Praeger, 1998.
Snell, Susan. *Phil Stone of Oxford: A Vicarious Life.* Athens: University of Georgia Press, 1991.
Soper, Kate. *What Is Nature? Culture, Politics and the Non-Human.* Oxford, UK: Blackwell, 1995.
Stepan, Nancy. *The Idea of Race in Science: Great Britain 1800–1960.* Oxford, UK: Macmillan, 1982.
Stephen, Leslie. "Taine's History of English Literature." *Men, Books and Mountains: Essays by Leslie Stephen.* London: Hogarth, 1956.
Stephens, Lester D. *Science, Race and Religion in the American South: John Bachman and the Charleston Circle of Naturalists, 1815–1895.* Chapel Hill: University of North Carolina Press, 2000.
Stocking, George W. *A Franz Boas Reader: The Shaping of American Anthropology: 1883–1911.* Chicago: University of Chicago Press, 1974.
Stonum, Gary Lee. *Faulkner's Career: An Internal Literary History.* London: Cornell University Press, 1979.
Synan, Vinsan. *The Old-Time Power.* Franklin Springs, GA: Advocate, 1973.
Taine, Hippolyte. *History of English Literature.* 2 vols. Edinburgh: Edmonston & Douglas, 1873.
Takaki, Ronald. *Iron Cages: Race and Culture in 19th-Century America.* Oxford, UK: Oxford University Press, 1990.
Tennyson, Alfred. "In Memoriam." *The Norton Anthology of English Literature.* Ed. M. H. Abrams, *et al.* Vol. 2, 1085–131. New York: Norton, 1993.
Tindall, George Brown. *The Emergence of the New South 1913–1945.* Baton Rouge: Louisiana State University Press, 1967.
Trilling, Lionel. *The Liberal Imagination: Essays on Literature and Society.* London: Secker & Warburg, 1951.
Urgo, Joseph R. *Faulkner's Apocrypha: A Fable, Snopes and the Spirit of Human Rebellion.* Jackson: University of Mississippi Press, 1989.
Vaughan-Thomas, Wynford. Interview. *The World at War, 13: Tough Old Gut, Italy November 1942–June 1944.* London: Thames Television, 2001.

Walker, Hollis Daniel. *University of South Carolina*. 2 vols. Columbia: University of South Carolina Press, 1956.
Wallace, Alfred Russel. "The Origin of Human Races Deduced from the Theory of 'Natural Selection.'" *Anthropological Review* 2, no. 2 (1864): clviii.
Watson, Jay. "Writing Blood: The Art of the Literal in *Light in August*." *Faulkner and the Natural World*. Ed. Donald M. Kartiganer and Ann J. Abadie, 66–97. Jackson: University Press of Mississippi, 1996.
Wells, H. G. *Experiment in Autobiography: Discoveries and Conclusions of a Very Ordinary Brain (since 1866)*. Vol. 2. London: Victor Gollancz, 1934.
———. *The Fate of Homo Sapiens*. London: Secker & Warburg, 1939.
———. *Mr. Blettsworthy on Rampole Island*. London: n.p., 1933.
Westrum, Dexter. "Faulkner's Sense of Twins and the Code: Why Young Bayard Died." *Arizona Quarterly* 40, no. 4 (1984): 365–76.
Whitman, Walt. "Song of Myself." *The Norton Anthology of American Literature*. 6th ed. Nina Baym, et al. Vol. B. New York: Norton, 2003. 2147–89.
Wilde, Oscar. *The Picture of Dorian Gray*. London: Penguin, 2003.
Williamson, Joel. *After Slavery: The Negro in South Carolina during Reconstruction, 1861–1877*. Chapel Hill: University of North Carolina Press, 1965.
———. *The Crucible of Race: Black-White Relations in the American South since Emancipation*. New York: Oxford University Press, 1984.
———. *New People: Miscegenation and Mulattoes in the United States*. New York: Free, 1980.
———. *William Faulkner and Southern History*. New York: Oxford University Press, 1993.
Wolff, Sally, and Floyd C. Watkins. *Talking about William Faulkner: Interviews with Jimmy Faulkner and Others*. Baton Rouge: Louisiana State University Press, 1996.
Wollstonecraft, Mary. *A Vindication of the Rights of Woman*. London: Everyman, 1987.
Woodrow, James. *Evolution: An Address Delivered May 7th, 1884, before the Alumni Association of the Columbia Theological Seminary*. Columbia, SC: Presbyterian Publishing House, 1884.
Wright, Willard Huntington. *The Creative Will: Studies in the Philosophy and the Syntax of Aesthetics*. New York: John Lane, 1916.
———. *The Future of Painting*. London: John Lane, 1923.
Young, Stark. *The Pavilion: Of People and Times Remembered, of Stories and Places*. New York: Scribner, 1951.
Zamir, Shamoon. *Dark Voice: W. E. B. Du Bois and American Thought, 1888–1903*. Chicago: University of Chicago Press, 1995.
Zender, Karl F. *The Crossing of the Ways: William Faulkner, the South, and the Modern World*. New Brunswick, NJ: Rutgers University Press, 1989.
———. *Faulkner and the Politics of Reading*. Baton Rouge: Louisiana State University Press, 2002.

Works Cited

Secondary Sources

Aiken, Conrad. "William Faulkner: The Novel as Form." *Atlantic Monthly* November 1939: 650–54.

Althusser, Louis. "Philosophy as a Revolutionary Weapon." *Lenin and his Philosophy and Other Essays*. Trans. Ben Brewster. New York: Monthly Review, 1971. 11–22.

Arendt, Hannah. *On Revolution*. New York: Viking, 1965.

Argyros, Alexander J. *A Blessed Rage for Order: Deconstruction, Evolution, and Chaos*. Ann Arbor: University of Michigan Press, 1994.

Armstrong, George D. *A Defence of the 'Deliverance' on Evolution, Adopted by the General Assembly of the Presbyterian Church in the United States, May 26th, 1886*. Norfolk, VA: John D. Ghiselin, 1886.

Barthes, Roland. "The Death of the Author." *Image, Music, Text*. Ed. S. Heath, 142–48. London: Fontana, 1977.

Bergson, Henri. *L'Évolution créatrice*. Paris: Alcan, 1907.

Bettersworth, John K. *People's University: The Centennial History of Mississippi State*. Jackson: University Press of Mississippi, 1980.

Bhabha, Homi. "Of Mimicry and Man: The Ambivalence of Colonial Discourse." *October* 28 (1984): 125–33.

Blanchot, Maurice, and Jacques Derrida. *Demeure: Fiction and Testimony*. Trans. Elizabeth Rottenberg. Stanford: Stanford University Press, 2000.

Bradley, David. *Six Experiments that Changed the World*. London: Channel 4 Television, 2000.

Brodsky, Louis Daniel, and Robert W. Hamblin, eds. *Faulkner: A Comprehensive Guide to the Brodsky Collection, Volume III: The De Gaulle Story*. Jackson: University Press of Mississippi, 1984.

Brooks, Cleanth. "The Formalist Critics," *Literary Theory: An Anthology*. Ed. Julie Rivkin and Michael Ryan. Malden, MA: Blackwell, 2004.

Brumm, Ursula. "Wilderness and Civilization: A Note on William Faulkner." *William Faulkner: Three Decades of Criticism*. Ed. Frederick Hoffman and Olga Vickery, 125–34. East Lansing: Michigan State University Press, 1960.

Bryan, William Jennings, and Mary Baird Bryan. *The Memoirs of William Jennings Bryan*. Philadelphia: United Books, 1925.

Burke, Edmund. *A Philosophical Enquiry into the Origin of Our Ideas of the Sublime and Beautiful*. Ed. J. T. Boulton. London: Routledge, 1958.

Callebaut, Werner. *Taking the Naturalistic Turn, or, How Real Philosophy of Science Is Done*. Chicago: University of Chicago Press, 1993.

Carter, Everett. *Documents of American Realism and Naturalism*. Ed. Donald Pizer. Carbondale: Southern Illinois University Press, 1998.

Dana, James Dwight. *A Text-Book of Geology. Designed for Schools and Academies*. Philadelphia: Theodore Bliss, 1863.

Derrida, Jacques. "Circumfession." *Jacques Derrida*. Trans. Geoffrey Bennington. Chicago: University of Chicago Press, 1993.

———. *Dissemination*. Trans. Barbara Johnson. London: Athlone, 2000.

———. *The Work of Mourning*. Ed. Pascale-Anne Brault and Michael Naas. Chicago: University of Chicago Press, 2001.
Douglas, Ellen. "Faulkner in Time." *A Cosmos of My Own*. Ed. Doreen Fowler and Ann J. Abadie, 284–301. Jackson: University Press of Mississippi, 1981.
Dupree, Anderson Hunter. *Asa Gray*. Cambridge, MA: Harvard University Press, 1959.
Faulkner, William. *These Thirteen*. London: Chatto & Windus, 1933.
———. *Uncle Willy and Other Stories*. London: Chatto & Windus, 1967.
Fish, Stanley E. "Interpreting the *Variorum*." *Reader-Response Criticism: From Formalism to Post-Structuralism*. Ed. Jane P. Tompkins. Baltimore: Johns Hopkins University Press, 1980.
Foucault, Michel. "The Order of Discourse." *Untying the Text*. Ed. R. Young, 47–78. Boston: Routledge, 1981.
Fowler, Douglas. *A Reader's Guide To Gravity's Rainbow*. Ann Arbor: Ardis, 1980.
Gayon, Jean. *Darwinism's Struggle for Survival*. Cambridge, UK: Cambridge University Press, 1998.
Gidley, Mick. "Some Notes on Faulkner's Reading." *Journal of American Studies* 4 (July 1970): 91–102.
Gould, Stephen J. *Hen's Teeth and Horse's Toes*. New York: Norton, 1983.
Griffin, Larry J. *The South as an American Problem*. Ed. Larry J. Griffin and Don H. Doyle. Athens: University of Georgia Press, 1995.
Haeckel, Ernst Heinrich. *Generelle Morphologie der Organismen*. Berlin: Reimer, 1866.
———. *Natürliche Schöpfungsgeschichte*. Berlin: Reimer, 1868.
Hamblin, Robert W. "'Saying No to Death': Toward William Faulkner's Theory of Fiction." *A Cosmos of My Own*. Ed. Doreen Fowler and Ann J. Abadie, 3–35. Jackson: University Press of Mississippi, 1981.
Hegel, Georg Wilhelm Friedrich. *Phenomenology of Spirit*. Trans. A. V. Miller. Oxford, UK: Oxford University Press, 1977.
Henig, Robin Marantz. *The Monk in the Garden: The Lost and Found Genius of Gregor Mendel, The Father of Genetics*. Boston: Houghton Mifflin, 2000.
Herodotus. *The Histories*. London: Penguin 1996.
Hoffman, Frederick, and Olga Vickery, eds. *William Faulkner: Three Decades of Criticism*. New York: Harcourt, Brace & World, 1963.
Hofstadter, Richard. *Social Darwinism in American Thought*. Boston: Beacon, 1955.
Holifield, E. Brooks. *The Gentlemen Theologians: American Theology in Southern Culture, 1795–1860*. Durham: Duke University Press, 1978.
Hunter, George William. *Teacher's Manual to Accompany New Civic Biology*. New York: American Book, 1927.
Hurston, Zora Neale. *Mules and Men*. New York: Harper Perennial, 1990.
Hutton, Holly. "Consciously Adapted to French Taste: What the Existentialists Learned from Faulkner." Faulkner and his Contemporaries. Faulkner and Yoknapatawpha Conference. University of Mississippi, Oxford. 21 July 2002.

Huxley, Thomas Henry. *Evolution and Ethics and Other Essays.* New York: Appleton, 1894.
James, William. *The Will to Believe and Other Essays in Popular Philosophy.* Cambridge, MA: Harvard University Press, 1979.
Kant, Immanuel. *Critique of Judgement.* Trans. Werner S. Pluhar. Indianapolis, IN: Hackett, 1987.
Kolakowski, Leszek. *Bergson.* Oxford, UK: Oxford University Press, 1985.
Lloyd, Henry Demarest. *Wealth against Commonwealth.* New York: Harper & Brothers, 1894.
Lloyd, James B. *The University of Mississippi: The Formative Years, 1848–1906.* Oxford: University Collections Press of Mississippi, 1979.
Lorenz, Konrad. *Behind the Mirror: A Search for a Natural History of Human Knowledge.* Trans. Ronald Taylor. New York: Harcourt Brace Jovanovich, 1978.
Lowe, E. N. *Plants of Mississippi: A List of Flowering Plants and Fern.* Jackson: Hedermann, 1921.
Lyell, Charles. *Principles of Geology, Being an Attempt to Explain the Former Changes of the Earth's Surface, by Reference to Causes now in Operation.* London: John Murray, 1830-1833.
Magee, Bryan. *Popper.* London: Fontana, 1985.
Magny, Claude-Edmonde. *The Age of the American Novel: The Film Aesthetic of Fiction between the Two Wars.* Trans. Eleanor Hochman. New York: Frederick Ungar, 1972.
Nilon, Charles H. "Blacks in Motion." *A Cosmos of My Own.* Ed. Doreen Fowler and Ann J. Abadie, 227–51. Jackson: University Press of Mississippi, 1981.
Nordau, Max. *Entartung.* Berlin: Duncker & Humblot, 1892.
Okada, Yayoi. "Faulkner's Christ in Reference to Jeremy Taylor." Diss. Kwansei Gakuin University, 2004.
Onoe, Masaji. "Some T. S. Eliot Echoes in Faulkner." *Faulkner Studies in Japan.* Ed. Thomas L. McHaney, 45–61. Athens: University of Georgia Press, 1985.
Pitt-Rivers, Fox, and George Henry Lane. *The Clash of Cultures and the Contact of Races: An Anthropological and Psychological Study of the Laws of Racial Adaptability, with Special Reference to the Depopulation of the Pacific and the Government of Subject Races.* London: Routledge, 1927.
Popper, Karl. *Conjectures and Refutations: The Growth of Scientific Knowledge.* London: Routledge & Kegan Paul, 1963.
———. *Objective Knowledge: An Evolutionary Approach.* Oxford: Clarendon Press, 1972.
———. *The Open Society and its Enemies.* 2 vols. London: Routledge & Sons, 1945.
Rogers, David. "Maternalizing the Epicene: Faulkner's Paradox of Form and Gender." *Faulkner and Gender.* Ed. Donald Kartiganer and Ann Abadie, 97–119. Oxford: University of Mississippi Press, 1996.
Russett, Cynthia Eagle. *Darwin in America: The Intellectual Response (1865–1912).* San Francisco: W. H. Freeman, 1976.

Sartre, Jean-Paul. "William Faulkner's *Sartoris*." *Yale French Studies* 10 (1953): 75–99.

Smith, Sherwin D. "The Great 'Monkey Trial.'" *New York Times*, 4 July 1965: 13.

Stoddard, Lothrop. *The Rising Tide of Color against White World-Supremacy.* New York: Chapman & Hall, 1920.

Stone, Emily Whitehurst. "How a Writer Finds His Material." *Harper's* 231 (November 1965): 58–60.

Thompson, Ernest Trice. *Presbyterians in the South.* 2 vols. Richmond: John Knox, 1973.

Thoreau, Henry David. *Walden; or Life in the Woods.* Boston: Ticknor & Fields, 1854.

Tompkins, Daniel Augustus. *Cotton Mill, Commercial Features. A Text-Book for the Use of Textile Schools and Investors. With Tables Showing Cost of Machinery and Equipments for Mills Making Cotton Yarns and Plain Cotton Cloths.* Charlotte, NC: Published by the Author, 1899.

Tuck, Dorothy. *A Handbook of Faulkner.* London: Chatto & Windus, 1964.

Williams, David. *Faulkner's Women: The Myth and the Muse.* Montreal, Canada: McGill-Queen's University Press, 1977.

Winchell, Alexander. *Adamites and Pre-Adamites: Or, a Popular Discussion Concerning the Remote Representatives of the Human Species and their Relation to the Biblical Adam.* Syracuse, NY: John T. Roberts, 1878.

Index

Agassiz, Louis, 2, 8, 68
Allis Lake Laboratory in Milwaukee, Wisconsin, 11
Alpher, Ralph, 68
Anderson, Sherwood, 24, 29–31, 42, 91, 212n8
Aristotle, 215n1
Armstrong, George D., 5
Arnold, Matthew, 34–36

Babbitt, Irving, 26
Bachman, John, 85, 86
Bacon, Francis, 9
Baena, Antônio Ladislau Monteiro, 220n14
Bagg, Halsey Joseph, 118
Baker, Houston A., 217n2
Balzac, Honoré de, 28, 29
Barnard, Frederick Augustus Porter, 6
Bateson, William, 79, 117
Baur, Erwin, 217n1
Beer, Gillian, ix, 213n13
Beidler, Peter G., ix, 42, 43
Beneden, Edouard van, 77, 78
Bennett, Arnold, 16, 26, 27
Bergson, Henri Louis, xi, 121–23, 192
Bethe, Hans, 68
Bilbo, Theodore G., 82
Billings, John Shaw, 11
biometry, 9, 119, 125
Blair, Tony, 221n7
Blotner, Joseph
    Faulkner's convalescence, 191
    Faulkner's racial attitude when young, 91, 92
    Snopes name, 38

Blumenbach, Johann Friedrich, 115, 217n6
Boas, Franz, xi, 15, 113–16, 136, 156, 176, 197
Bourne, Randolph, 26
Brooks, Cleanth, 22, 36, 124, 205, 212n1, 212n3, 213n14
Brooks, William Keith, 11
Brown, Calvin S., 23
Bryan, William Jennings, 14–19, 22, 80, 193, 211n9, 211n11, 212n5
Bush, George W., 221n7
Butler, John Washington, 13, 18
Butler Act, 13, 54
Butler, Lelia Dean Swift ("Damuddy"), 21, 51, 74

Caldwell, Charles, 86
capitalism, 120, 128, 129, 171, 173–75, 180, 204
Carmichael, Stokely, 217n2
Carroll, Joseph, ix, 25, 26
Cartwright, Samuel A., 218n1
Castle, William E., 79, 80, 117
Chambers, Robert, 1
Clark, Mark, 187, 188
Colatrella, Carol, ix, 96
communism, 181, 182
Comte, August, 218n11
Conrad, Timothy Abbott, 85, 216n6
coordination condition, 186, 193, 195, 196
coordination problems, 186
Correns, Carl Erich, 79
courtship strategies
    domestic bliss, 55, 56, 61, 166, 180

fidelity, 55, 61
he-man strategy, 55, 56, 61
impersonal gratification, 60–62
selfish expoilitation, 55, 61
Cowley, Malcolm, 129
Portable Faulkner, The, 129
Crick, Francis, 146, 160
Croly, David Goodman, 88

Dalton, John, 211n5
Dana, James Dwight, 3
Darrow, Clarence, 14–16, 19
Darwin, Charles, ix, 1–3, 7, 9–12, 14, 17, 19, 29–31, 34, 37, 42, 45, 47, 49, 53, 77, 78, 81, 90, 116, 120, 213n1, 215n1, 220n10
  Annie (daughter), 220n10
  Darwinism, x, xi, 4, 5, 8, 9–12, 19, 33, 34, 44, 68, 87
  works:
    Descent of Man, The, 34, 45, 46, 69, 70, 77, 78, 87, 95, 146, 185, 203, 215n9
    Life and Letters of Charles Darwin, The, 78
    Naturalist's Voyage, A, 42–44, 68, 211n1
    Origin of Species, The, ix, 2, 3, 10, 25, 35, 36, 45, 46, 49, 68, 69, 87, 96, 121, 146, 163, 168, 206, 211n2
    Variation of Animals, The, 10, 77, 94, 95
Darwin, Erasmus (grandfather), 49, 213n1
Davenport, Charles, 90
Davidson, Donald, 24
Dawkins, Richard, 161, 203
  Extended Phenotype, The, 56, 217n8
  Selfish Gene, The, 19, 55, 166, 204, 214n4, 220n11
Dayton, Ohio, 41
Dayton, Tennessee, 13–17, 19, 28, 38, 212n5

De Gaulle, Charles, 221n9
de Vries, Hugo, 10, 79
Derrida, Jacques, 134, 140, 154, 157, 194, 196, 197, 218n9
Descartes, René, 9
Devine, James, 33
Dewey, John, 33–36, 48
  "Darwin's Influence upon Philosophy," 138
  "Evolution and Ethics," 48
  Influence of Darwin on Philosophy, The, 34
Dobson, Austin, 27
Dos Passos, John
  U.S.A., 179, 220n16
Doyle, Arthur Conan
  Hound of the Baskervilles, The, 216n9
Dreiser, Theodore, 179
Du Bois, William Edward Burghardt, 115, 116
durée, 121, 122
Dwight, Thomas, 5

Edison, Thomas Alva, 81, 215n4
Einstein, Albert, 191, 192, 219n1
Eliot, T. S., 16, 147
Ellett, A. H., 81
Emerson, Ralph Waldo
  "Fate," 215n10
  "The Poet," 128, 137, 140
  "The Young American," 128
Empedocles, 215n1
Epperson v. Arkansas ("Scopes II"), 18
ESS. *See* evolutionarily stable strategy
essentialism, 8, 119, 138
evolutionarily stable strategy (ESS), 56, 164, 167, 171
  benign foreigner, 164
  extrinisic alien, 168
  extrinisic stranger, 164
  foreigner, 164
  malevolent alien, 178
  outlander, 164

Falkner, Dean (brother), 21
Falkner, Jack (Murry C., brother), 21, 22, 51, 189, 213n19
  gas attack at Saint-Mihiel, 187
Falkner, John Wesley Thompson (Young Colonel, paternal grandfather), 82, 92, 213n17
Falkner, Maud (née Butler, mother), 21, 51, 74
Falkner, Murry (father), 17, 21, 23, 92, 93
Falkner, William Clark (Old Colonel, paternal great-grandfather), 92, 218n3
Farlow, William Gilson, 11
Faulkner, Alabama, 172
Faulkner, John (brother), 17, 21, 23, 24, 51, 112, 126
Faulkner, William
  birth, 21
  Bryan, William Jennings, 22
  Einstein, meets, 219n1
  electroconvulsive therapy, 190
  Franklin, Malcolm (stepson), 113
  Freyre, Gilberto, 175
  Mencken, 16, 17
  moves to New York, 33
  Nobel Prize, 159, 210
  Rowan Oak, 113, 120, 176, 189, 190
  Snopes name, 38, 39
  University of Mississippi:
    enters as undergraduate, 23
    resigns as postmaster, 15
    withdraws from studies, 24
  Warner Brothers, 189
  West Ivis, 15, 16
  works:
    Absalom, Absalom!, xi, 86
    "Barn Burning," 220n18
    Collected Stories, 165, 202, 214n9
    "A Courtship," 214n9
    De Gaulle Story, The, 189
    Early Prose and Poetry, 29

Essays, Speeches and Public Letters, 24, 31, 44, 161, 170, 178
A Fable, xi, 120, 161, 188–200, 204–6, 212n5, 213n20, 221n5
Faulkner at West Point, 207
Faulkner in the University, 36, 43, 44, 161–63, 184, 207
Flags in the Dust, xi, 33, 36, 38, 40–42, 93–100, 110, 112, 135, 142, 165, 172
Go Down, Moses, xi, 33, 120, 122–25, 130–37, 140–57, 218n4, 218n12, 219n5, 219n7, 220n2
Hamlet, The, xi, 160, 163, 164, 170–73
If I Forget Thee, Jerusalem, 221n13
Intruder in the Dust, 33, 219n5
Knight's Gambit: "An Error in Chemistry," 165; "Smoke," 165; "Tomorrow," 165
Light in August, xi, 33, 104, 106, 109, 112, 124, 137, 217n2
Lion in the Garden, 92, 129, 143, 160, 162, 184, 185, 196–98, 210, 219n7
Mansion, The, xi, 160, 167, 174, 182, 184, 186, 220n12
Marble Faun, The, 24
Mosquitoes, xi, 29–33, 45, 52, 53, 66, 67
New Orleans Sketches, 21, 24, 91
Portable Faulkner, The, 129
"Red Leaves," xi, 42, 43, 136, 213n21
Reivers, The, 33
Requiem for a Nun, xi, 67, 70, 72, 76, 160, 161, 169, 219n6
"A Rose for Emily," 165, 219n6
Sanctuary, xi, 33, 53–61, 67, 72, 76, 167
Sartoris, 36, 95
Soldiers' Pay, 29, 33, 51, 52, 182, 212n7

Sound and the Fury, The, xi, 100, 101
These Thirteen, 213n21, 219n6, 221n11
Town, The, xi, 160, 164, 166, 169, 171, 173, 175, 178, 179, 183, 212n1, 219n5
Uncollected Stories, 91
Unvanquished, The, 216n5
Ferdinand, Archduke Franz, 221n8
Fischer, Eugen, 217n1
Fisher, R. A., 125, 126
Fitzroy, Captain Robert, 42
Flemming, Walther, 78
Flinn, Reverend J. William, 7
Ford, Henry, 40, 213n20
Foucault, Michel, 215n2
Franklin, Malcolm (stepson), 1, 23, 53, 112, 120, 169
Frazer, James George
  Golden Bough, The, 140
Freyre, Gilberto, 118, 175–77, 179, 197, 220n14
  Masters and the Slaves, The, 176, 177, 220n13
Fugitive-Agrarians, 24, 112, 129, 212n3

Galilei, Galileo, 9
Galton, Francis, 9, 78, 79, 116, 213n1
Gamov, George, 68
gemmules, 77, 92, 94, 96, 160
Gibbes, Lewis Reeves, 216n6
Gibbes, Robert, 85, 216n6
Giddings, Franklin H., 115, 217n5
Gidley, Mick, 28, 219n6
Gilbert, Grove Karl, 11
Gilman, Charlotte Perkins, 190
Girardeau, John Lafayette, 4
Gliddon, George R., 85
Godden, Richard, 136
Godden, Richard and Noel Polk, 134, 145, 155, 218n4
Gourmont, Remy de, 27

Grant, Madison, 80, 89, 90, 215n3
Guyot, Arnold, 3
Guyton, Arthur, 112

Haeckel, Ernst Heinrich, 34
Haldane, J. B. S., 116, 118, 125, 126
Hall, Prescott, 90
Hamilton, Alexander, 81, 215n4
Hamilton, Patrick, 211n8
hard inheritance, 79, 80, 100, 117, 118, 120
Harrison, Ross Granville, 118
Hartman, Geoffrey H., x
  Genius, x
  genius loci, x
Harvard, 2, 5, 73, 80, 90, 112, 116, 118, 119, 183
  Museum of Comparative Zoology, 11
Hays, Arthur Garfield, 16
Hemingway, Ernest
  Fiesta: The Sun Also Rises, 211n11
Herodotus, 215n1
Herschel, John, 9
Hertwig, Oskar, 118
Hilgard, Eugene Woldemar, 11
Hitchcock, Alfred
  Rope, 211n8
Hitler, Adolf, 103, 199, 217n1, 221n9
Hodge, Archibald Alexander, 5
Holbrook, John Edwards, 85, 216n6
Holmes, Francis S., 85, 216n6
Hooker, Joseph Dalton, 1
Hooton, Earnest Albert, xi, 113, 116–20, 151, 176
Howells, William Dean, 26
Hughes, Henry, 83, 86, 87
Hume, Alfred, 12, 13, 17, 54, 82, 211n10
Hunter, George William, 13
  Civic Biology, A, 13, 22, 80, 127
Huxley, Aldous, 49, 53
  Crome Yellow, 49, 50, 67, 72

INDEX

Huxley, Julian
   Evolution: The Modern Synthesis, 126
Huxley, Thomas Henry, 1, 2, 7, 34, 47–49, 53, 81, 115, 120

Illinois v. Leopold and Loeb, 14
   Franks, Robert, 14
   Leopold, Nathan, 14, 211n8
   Loeb, Richard, 14, 211n8
   Rope, 211n8
incest, 78, 95, 101, 105, 135, 146, 155, 176
Irigarayan hom(m)o-sexual, 66

Jackson, Andrew, 31, 97, 213n10
Jacquinot, Honoré, 86
James, Henry, 26
James, William, 138
Jefferies, Richard, 38
Johannsen, Wilhelm, 79
Johnson, Victoria Fielden (née Franklin, granddaughter), 172
Jones, Steve
   In the Blood, 101, 181, 217n8
   Language of the Genes, The, 113, 114, 162, 170, 214n5, 218n1
Joyce, James, 16

Kammerer, Paul, 118
Kant, Immanuel, 9, 34, 35
Kartiganer, Donald M., 129
Kennedy, John Pendleton, 50
Kesselring, Albert, 187
King, Clarence Rivers, 10

Lacy, Emeline, 218n3
Lamarck, Jean Baptiste, 9, 90, 217n8
Laws, Curtis Lee, 12
LeConte, John Eatton, 85, 216n6
Lee, General Robert E., 8, 97
Leidy, Joseph, 85, 216n6
Lemaître, Jules, 27

Lenz, Fritz, 217n1
Lesley, J. Peter, 11
Lessing, Gotthold Ephraim, 34
Lewisohn, Ludwig, 26, 27
Lincoln, Abraham, 87, 88
Linder, Felix, 112
Little, Clarence Cook, 118
Little, George, 7, 211n4
Loving v. Virginia, 132
Lubbock, Sir John
   Origin of Civilisation and the Primitive Condition of Man, The, 47
Lyell, Charles, 68
   Principles of Geology, 8

Martin, Thomas Theodore, 17
Marx, Karl, 128
   Capital, 128, 129
   Communist Manifesto, The, 173
Marxism, 10, 171, 179, 205
Massachusetts Laboratory of Marine Biology, 11
Maury, Matthew Fontaine, 81, 215n4
Mayes, Edward, 7
Maynard Smith, John, 55–57, 214n4, 219n7
McDaniel, Benjamin, 112
McLennan, John Ferguson
   Primitive Marriage, 47
Mencken, Henry Louis, 16, 17
Mendel, Gregor, 15, 79
Meredith, James, 18
Miescher, Johann, 77, 78
miscegenation, xi, 88–90, 93, 100, 103, 106, 108, 113, 114, 120, 122–25, 132, 135, 137, 143, 145–48, 150, 151, 153, 155–57, 176–78, 218n3
Missouri Compromise, 86
Mitchell, Margaret
   Gone with the Wind, 54, 215n5
More, Paul Elmer, 26
Morgan, John Pierpont, 179, 220n16
Morgan, Louis Henry, 113
Morgan, Thomas Hunt, 80, 100, 117

Morgenstern, Oskar, 188
Morse, Edward Sylvester, 11
Morton, Samuel George, 85, 86, 113, 114
mutually assured destruction, 188, 197

Nash, John, 188, 195
Newton, Isaac, 7, 9, 81, 211n5
Nietzsche, Friedrich, 34, 37
Nordau, Max, 27
Nott, Josiah Clark, 84–87

O'Neill, Eugene, 29
Oglethorpe College, Atlanta, Georgia, 2
Oldham, Estelle (Lida), 23, 173, 215n9
Orr, James, 6
orthogenesis, 11, 113
Osborn, Henry Fairfield, 80
Oxford, Mississippi, 6–8, 12, 21–24, 38, 53, 82, 187, 189, 190, 213n19, 218n3

Pace v. Alabama, 131
pangenesis, xi, 77–82, 90, 93, 94, 100–116, 125, 148, 160, 174, 207, 210, 216
pangenetic chokepoint (bottleneck), 104
parallel walk, 57, 60
Patton, Francis, 5
Paulus, Friedrich, 221n9
Pearson, Karl, 79, 119
Pétain, Henri, 221n9
Plato, 8, 24, 137, 138
Polk, Noel, 71, 76
population viscosity, 103
Pound, Ezra, 16
Powers, Joseph Neely, 12, 82
Presbytery of Augusta, 4
Presbytery of South Carolina, 2, 4
Princeton Presbytery, 5
Proust, Marcel
    In Search of Lost Time, 216n8

Pythagoras, 8, 78, 215n1

RAND Corporation, 188
Ransom, John Crowe, 24, 36
rape, 53, 62, 63
Rappelyea, George W., 13, 14
Rätzel, Friedrich, 115, 217n6
Ravenel, Henry William, 85, 216n6
reversion (throwback), 78, 90, 92, 94, 95, 104, 105, 216n9
Riley, William Bell, 12
Ripley, William Z., 21, 89, 90
Rowan Oak, 113, 120, 176, 189, 190
Rowland, Whit, 112
Russell, Lee M., 82

saltations, 9
Sauer, Carl O., 25
Scales, Leon, 33
Schopenhauer, Arthur, 34
Scopes, John T., xi, 13–19, 25, 28, 29, 38, 39, 41, 82, 211n11, 212n1
Scudder, Samuel Hubbard, 11
Segar, Elzie Crisler, 214n6
selfish gene, 161, 171, 174, 186
Seward, Anna, 49, 213n1
Shakespeare, William, 8, 24, 26, 30, 191
Smith, Adam, 81, 215n4
Smith, Sidney Irving, 11
Smith, William Benjamin, 81
soft inheritance, 78, 96, 115, 117
Spencer, Herbert, 7, 10, 40, 42, 48, 81, 89, 115, 217n5
Spratling, Bill, 16
Stephen, Leslie, 26
Stewart, Alexander Peter, 7
Stoddard, Lothrop, 40
Stone, Phil, 16, 113
    claims of influence, 28, 39
    Faulkner's mentor, 23
    personal library, 24, 212n2
Stonum, Gary Lee, x, 190

Sunday, Billy, 28, 193, 212n5
Sweet, Ossian, 19
Swinburne, Algernon Charles, 24
syphilis, 58

Taine, Hippolyte, xi, 25–30, 148, 160
Tate, Allen, 24
Taylor, Jeremy, 191, 221n3
Tennyson, Alfred Lord, 213n18
theistic evolution, 3, 7, 11, 34
Thoreau, Henry David, 144
  Walden, 211n1
Tombeckbee Presbytery of Mississippi, 2
Townsend, Charlie, 112
Trilling, Lionel, 67, 122
Truman, Harry S., 182
Tuomey, Michael, 85, 216n6
Tylor, Edward Burnett, 113
Tyndall, John, 81, 211n4

University of Alabama, 216n6
University of Chicago, 11, 19
University of Georgia, 7
University of Heidelberg, 2
University of Japan, 11
University of Kiel, 113
University of Leipzig, 11
University of Mississippi, 6–8, 12, 15, 17, 18, 23, 28, 82, 127, 211n3
University of South Carolina, 5, 7

Van Evrie, John H., 86
Vardaman, James Kimble, 40, 51, 81, 82
Vaughan-Thomas, Wynford, 187
von Herder, Johann Gottfried, 34
von Humboldt, Alexander, 81, 215n4
von Leibniz, Gottfried Wilhelm, 34
von Nägeli, Karl Wilhelm, 77, 78
von Neumann, John, 188

von Tschermak-Seysenegg, Erich, 79
von Waldeyer, Heinrich, 79
Voronoff, Serge, 214n7

Waddel, John Newton, 6, 7
Wakeman, George, 88
Walcott, Charles Doolittle, 11
Wallace, Alfred Russel, 221n12
Walton, Robert, 33
Ward, Robert De C., 90
warranteeism, 83, 86–88, 105, 179
Warren, Robert Penn, 24
Watson, James, 160
Weismann, August, 15, 79, 90, 116, 117, 216n9
Weldon, W. F. R., 79
Wells, H. G.
  Fate of Homo Sapiens, The, 211n6
  Mr. Blettsworthy on Rampole Island, 217n4
White, Charles Abiathar, 10
Whitfield, Henry Lewis, 17
Whitman, Charles Otis, 11, 211n7
Whitman, Walt
  "Song of Myself," 69
Wilde, Oscar, 27, 216n9
  Picture of Dorian Gray, The, 216n9
Winchell, Alexander, 3
Wood, Spencer, 112
Woodrow, James, 2, 4–6
Wright, Richard
  Native Son, 124
Wright, Sewall, 125, 126
Wright, Wilbur and Orville, 41
Wright, Willard Huntington, xi, 28

Young, Stark, 7, 24

Zola, Émile, 27